Shadow of
the Alchemist

BOOKS BY JERI WESTERSON

Crispin Guest Medieval Noir Mystery Series

*Veil of Lies**

*Serpent in the Thorns**

*The Demon's Parchment**

*Troubled Bones**

*Blood Lance**

*Shadow of the Alchemist**

The Silence of Stones

A Maiden Weeping

Season of Blood

The Deepest Grave

Cup of Blood, a prequel to *Veil of Lies*

Booke of the Hidden Series

Booke of the Hidden

Deadly Rising

Historical Fiction

Though Heaven Fall

Roses in the Tempest

Native Spirit, writing as Anne Castell

*available as a JABberwocky ebook

Shadow of the Alchemist

A CRISPIN GUEST MEDIEVAL NOIR MYSTERY

JERI WESTERSON

Published by JABberwocky Literary Agency, Inc.

To Craig, who sends all my shadows away

one

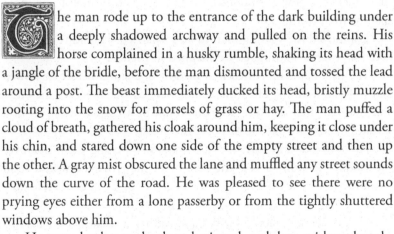he man rode up to the entrance of the dark building under a deeply shadowed archway and pulled on the reins. His horse complained in a husky rumble, shaking its head with a jangle of the bridle, before the man dismounted and tossed the lead around a post. The beast immediately ducked its head, bristly muzzle rooting into the snow for morsels of grass or hay. The man puffed a cloud of breath, gathered his cloak around him, keeping it close under his chin, and stared down one side of the empty street and then up the other. A gray mist obscured the lane and muffled any street sounds down the curve of the road. He was pleased to see there were no prying eyes either from a lone passerby or from the tightly shuttered windows above him.

He turned at last to the door, hesitated, and then, without knocking, opened it and ducked under the low lintel.

The place smelled unwholesome, of strange odors of unknown substances. He wanted to cover his mouth but felt it might appear as a sign of weakness. Instead, he threw back his cloak over one shoulder, displaying the finery of his cotehardie and bejeweled necklace.

He saw no one yet, though the glow of a fire flitted over the wall through an archway. Moving carefully through the dimly lit parlor, he made his way around shadowy chairs and tables with strange beakers and jars sitting on their surfaces. He passed under the archway and finally reached the hearth. Moving to stand before it, he tucked down the kid leather gloves between the joints of his fingers as casually as he could. It served to calm him, calm the ravaging thoughts galloping through his mind.

He was momentarily startled when he noticed the other man waiting for him off in the shadows outside the fire's glow. Perhaps he had been standing there all along, watching him enter, studying him. He had not liked the pale man the moment he had met him weeks ago, but there was little he could do about it now. His sources had told him that the man could do the job and he hadn't time to search anymore.

The pale man in the shadows hadn't moved. One side of his face was barely lit by the flickering light, while the other side fell to blackness. His inky hair flowed over the black gown hanging from his shoulders. The gown's smooth lines and fur trim seemed to be more shadow than cloth.

It annoyed the visiting man to be so startled. He didn't like to be taken unaware. "I am here," he snapped in French.

The pale man's lip curled in a shadow of a smirk before he bowed and still said nothing. His white hands were crossed one over the other and the first man couldn't help but think of a corpse, wrapped in a shroud, hands carefully crossed over the breast.

He glowered and turned to the flames, watching them lick over the wood. He wondered if the pale man knew that he would soon become a loose end, and loose ends needed to be discarded. Preferably in the Thames, where they couldn't be found again.

He opened and closed his fist, kid leather squeaking over his fingers. This was an ill-conceived meeting. He should never have agreed to it. "I don't care how you do it," he continued. "Just get it done."

"What you ask," the pale man said suddenly. His voice had a hint of amusement to it. As if he were laughing at the other. "It will not be easy."

"I'm not paying for easy." He glared at him squarely. "If you couldn't do it, you should have said so in your letters. I've gone to great expense to bring you here. You came highly recommended."

"I am aware of that, my lord. Never fear. It shall be as you wish."

"It had better be. Can you... can you find your way..."

2

"I spent many years in London as a lad, my lord. I know my way around quite well."

"I see. Good."

"When?"

"As soon as possible. There is no time to waste."

A sound in the next room drew his attention away from the pale man. He looked to his left, where the door was ajar. In the dim light, he could just make out a figure, seated. The person was squirming. He could not tell if it was a man or a woman before the figure gave another muffled whimper, as if its mouth were covered by a gag. He narrowed his eyes, peering. Was the figure *tied* to the chair?

He turned away. Not his business.

He reached into his scrip and pulled out the money pouch. After walking to the rectangular table sitting in the center of the room, he dropped the considerable pouch there. The coins clinked together and the leather pouch pooled.

"Don't contact me again," he said. He did not look about the room, did not look back at the pale man or the struggling person through the doorway. He merely adjusted his cloak and strode out the door into the mist.

two

rispin growled. Something poked him in the side and he swatted at it, laying his head again on the sticky table. Table? Not at home, then? He would most certainly have been in bed. And cold. His room was often too cold. But now there was a pleasant warmth to his back, and in the jumble of his mind he reasoned that it probably meant he was at the Boar's Tusk. Yes, if he pricked his ears, he could detect the low murmur of many voices, many men slowly getting as drunk as he supposed he was. He blew out a breath and settled.

It poked again. *What the devil?* "Begone," he muttered, turning his face the other way, letting that cheek get a bit of the table's stickiness.

Another poke. He crushed his lids tighter. "Do that again and you'll find my dagger in your eye."

"Mon Dieu," said a voice above him with a soft French accent. *"Maître* Guest? You *are* Crispin Guest, are you not?"

"I said go away," he grumbled to the table's surface. His thoughts were hazy. Why had he fallen asleep at the Boar's Tusk again? That's right. He'd been caught by Jack staring morosely at that little painting of Philippa Walcote. Stuffing it in his scrip had not relieved the feeling of abandonment that came upon contemplating what was and could never be. He seemed to think of her often these days, even though the task that had caused them to cross paths happened years ago.

With coins in his pouch, he had retreated to his favorite tavern

4

and had made his way easily through two jugs of wine. Well, one and a half. He had just laid his head down to rest a moment…

That damned poking again!

He reached for his dagger and snapped upright, swaying on the bench. Squinting, he stared at a man holding up his hands protectively.

"*What* do you *want?*"

"You are *Maître* Crispin Guest, no?"

"I am. Speak or leave me be."

Crispin watched amazed as the man, unfazed, slid onto the bench beside him. "I need your help."

"Do you? I don't think I am fit to help anyone today. Try me tomorrow." Puzzled, he looked at the dagger in his hand. *Don't remember unsheathing that.* He shoved it unsteadily into its scabbard and leaned on the table, fingers reaching for his wine bowl.

"But you must," said the strange man. He wore a dark cap with long flaps over his ears, and just peeking below that was wheat-colored hair shot with gray. He had a long face and a long brown beard, one that suited the flaps of his cap, which seemed an extension of his expression and clouded his eyes to a blurry blue, like dirty ice. "You *must,*" he said again, leaning toward Crispin.

Even with his senses dulled with wine, Crispin sized him up as a man of means. His clothes bespoke of coin, at any rate. They were clean, fairly new. That particular cloth did not come cheap.

Crispin tried to straighten himself, even smoothed down the stained front of his own cotehardie. He cleared his throat and tried to focus. "Very well. I work for sixpence a day—"

"That does not matter. I will pay whatever you ask. I beg of you… help me—" His voice broke on the last.

Crispin nodded. "What is your difficulty, then?"

But even as the man passed a quaking hand over his face, his sharp gaze darted about the room. "Not here. Is there a place we can talk?"

"Of course." Crispin rose, braced himself on the table, and pushed away from it. Staggering a bit, he straightened, one vertebra at a time. Hazily, he knew he wasn't presenting the best front to this client, but he also hadn't seen any coin yet. He shouldered the door open and stepped out to the bitter cold of November. An icy wind with dots of wet flakes sobered him enough to walk without staggering down

5

Gutter Lane, where he turned right at the Shambles. He glanced back, and the man, head down with his hands buried in his cloak, trudged after.

When he reached the tinker's shop, Alice Kemp, the tinker's wife, was dusting snow from their wares with a broom. She stopped long enough to glare at Crispin and he barely had the presence of mind not to sneer back. It didn't do to show animosity to his landlord's wife when she disliked him so strongly anyway. Instead, he gave her a cursory bow, which caused him to stumble. She snorted. "Drunk again," she grumbled, but took it out on the broom and swept briskly, upturning the cooking pots she had carefully arranged on display.

He shoved a foot on the bottom stair and stopped, turning back to his client. "Mind the stairs. They're icy." He led the way, slipped once, but with his hand firmly on the rail he made it to the landing. He had managed to wrestle his key from his scrip, but the lock kept skirting his attempts to engage it.

The door swung open on its own, and he looked up into his apprentice's amber eyes. "Jack," he said, and cocked his head, indicating the man behind him. "Client."

Jack took in Crispin's state and the fact of a paying client in one glance. The boy grabbed Crispin's arm and yanked him in. *What does the knave think he's doing?* The table stopped Crispin's further progress as he slammed against it. "Jack! What the devil—!"

"Sit, Master. Let me welcome your client." He scowled at Jack, who had seemed to become a tall, lanky lad overnight. He was now somewhere in his fifteenth year, with wild curls of ginger hair falling over his eyes. Crispin sat on the stool and held on to the table as Jack bowed to the as yet unknown man and offered him the other chair. "May I fetch you wine, sir?" the lad asked politely.

Crispin raised his hand, but the boy said out of the side of his mouth, *"Not you!"*

"Insubordinate," he grumbled. "A fine apprentice you are."

The man looked from servant to master and then back to servant. "This *is* the home of the Tracker, no?"

"Yes, my lord. It is just that Master Crispin is sometimes under the weather... as he is now. But he is attentive, I assure you." Crispin sagged and Jack elbowed him hard. He snapped upright again and blinked.

"Er… yes." He ran a hand down his face, wiping away the melted snowflakes and feeling the rough grit of a day-old beard. He was just cognizant enough to realize he probably looked a mess. And here was a man willing to pay for his services. *Snap to, Crispin.* Clearing his throat, he leaned forward. "I do apologize, sir. I am… out of sorts, as my apprentice says." He considered before gesturing toward Jack. "Er… this is Jack Tucker." The man nodded to the boy. "How can we serve you?"

The man laid stained fingers gingerly to the wine bowl Jack set before him. "It is urgent business I have with you. I understand that you are a man who finds things and can be discreet."

"Correct on both counts."

"The matter is… personal."

God's blood. He hated *personal* matters. He sighed and sagged. Jack elbowed him again and he scowled up at the boy. Jack gave him an equally scowling glare in return. *Outrageous, that knave's audacity.*

"Personal matter?" he said weakly.

"Yes. My wife…"

Crispin scrambled to his feet and stumbled toward the fire. Dammit! He didn't want these sorts of jobs! Nothing good ever came from them. Nothing but heartache for all concerned, including him. It was Philippa Walcote all over again, for had he not also met her because of "personal matters"? He leaned heavily over the hearth, feeling the heat scorch up his chest. "I cannot help you, sir," he muttered. "I… do not deal in these troubles."

"But *Maître* Guest!" He was instantly on his feet behind Crispin. "I fear she has run away with my apprentice. I must find her!"

"These are matters for your confessor, sir, not for me. I cannot help you."

"Master Crispin is out of sorts, sir. We *can* and *will* accommodate you," said the voice at Crispin's shoulder. He whipped around to glare at Jack. Did the knave dare to gainsay him?

Jack sidled up to Crispin and, eye to eye, whispered harshly, "What's gotten your humor so sour? We *need* the funds. Let's hear him out, at least."

7

Motioning for the man to sit again, Jack pushed the wine bowl toward him. "What is your name, good Master?"

The man fumbled sitting and stared at the table, shaking his head. "I am Nicholas Flamel. My wife and I came to London to get away from… from prying eyes. There was much work we needed to do, and in Paris there were too many… well. Spies."

Crispin swiveled shakily. He spared Jack a sneer before he turned to the man. "Master Flamel. What do you mean by spies? You are French?"

The man looked up at that and his eyes widened. "Oh no! I did not mean that *I* was a spy. Bless me, no. I do not care for politics. I am no spy, sir."

"One can't be too careful in these grave days. So you and your wife came to London. And this apprentice of yours. Did he come with you as well?"

He shook his head and dropped his gaze again. "No. We hired him here, in London. He came highly recommended. He was ever loyal, always trustworthy. I cannot believe it of him."

"And yet, such things are known to happen. Does your wife have money in her own right?"

"Yes. She was married before I met her. Widowed. And she knows much of my art."

"Your art?"

"That of alchemy. In Paris I am well-known for the alchemical sciences. We were working on a most important venture. But my apprentice is young and fine-looking." He dropped his head on his hand and fisted the stray strands of hair that escaped from his cap. "I never should have left them alone."

Crispin slowly turned away from the hearth and Jack helped him into his seat. The boy was right, of course. He had to set his feelings aside. He couldn't afford to let them get in the way of a fee. It was better to be immersed in another assignment, for the winter did not bring much to the table.

"Had you any indication of this before?"

"No, none." His eyes were glossy and his hands moved restlessly from his hair to the table.

Crispin nodded. The spouse was always the last to know. And yet, what did the man expect Crispin to do? "Am I to find her and bring her back? Take you to her?"

Flamel slid from his chair and paced the small room. "I do not know," he said wearily, rubbing his hands. "I am unfamiliar with the protocol. What must I do, *Maître* Guest?"

Forget her and live on. It was his only true advice, but men seldom wished to take it. It was a point of honor and a slap in the face for one's wife to walk away, or so he imagined.

The conversation was sobering him by the moment. He glanced at the man's untouched wine bowl with a bit of longing.

Jack leaned forward. "Should we not go looking for her first, Master Crispin?"

Crispin rested an elbow on the table, twisted his head, and glared at his impetuous assistant. Jack gazed mildly back at him, clenching his hands and holding his own at first. But as Crispin continued to meet his gaze, the youth seemed to back down and he soon looked quickly away.

"Yes, yes," Flamel insisted, oblivious to the silent war going on before him. "We must find her. I… I will gladly take her back."

"Are you certain?" said Crispin with a glance back at Jack, daring him to interfere. "Once she is—" *Tainted goods,* he was going to say, but even his sluggish mind thought better of it. "Once she has been gone from you for an amount of time, might it be best to simply… er…"

"No! No, our work, you understand? We are very close. Close to a breakthrough. I need her. Not simply because she is my wife and belongs to me. But because our work is so important. She is more than my wife. She has been my work assistant for many years. I believed we worked in tandem, heart, soul, and mind. But perhaps—" His voice cracked at last. "Perhaps I have been mistaken."

Crispin pushed himself upright again. "And perhaps you are making more of this than there is. How long has she been gone?"

"Since this morning—"

"What?" Damn these timid men! "It is midafternoon. You waste my time for the absence of a few hours? Perhaps she has a lengthy shopping list, nothing more than that."

"But my assistant is gone as well—"

"And he's carrying the baggage. Good God, man. You're making a fool of yourself."

"I tell you it is more than that. I know it is!"

"Was there a note, anything telltale, like a sum of funds missing?"

"No, nothing as that."

"No? If she intended to run away, then surely she would need the funds to do so. Master Flamel, I believe you are worrying needlessly." He rose and lurched around the table. He lifted the man by the elbow and steered him toward the door. "Go home. I'm certain they are both there waiting for you."

With sudden vehemence, he shook Crispin off. "No! I know what I know, *Maître*. The alchemical sciences breach the world that *we* know with that of another far from our imaginings. It is not Heaven nor is it Hell but somewhere in between in the ether. I have crossed the paths between, *Maître,* and it has given me an insight that I cannot easily explain."

Crispin recoiled. "What you speak of, sir, is sorcery."

"No, I assure you. I work within God's good grace. Come with me and I will show you. I'll prove it to you."

Crispin sighed again and caught Jack's glance. The knave was making motions that seemed to express "It couldn't hurt to try."

"Very well," he huffed. He moved toward the peg on the wall to retrieve his cloak but noticed that he was still wearing it. Jack pulled his own from the peg and buttoned it up.

"Shall we go, then?" Crispin gestured to the door. Flamel went first and Crispin went after, followed by Jack, whom he trusted to lock the door. At least the boy could *act* like an apprentice.

They trudged over the mud and stomped through icy puddles toward the Fleet Ditch. Skirting down a narrow alley beside a dung cart, Crispin held his nose, recalling the days when he was first cast from court—years ago now, thankfully—and was forced into pushing one of those carts and mucking out the privies along the Thames, one of many disagreeable positions that forced him to come up with something better.

The mud was churned so badly at the "T" of the road that it nearly sucked in Crispin's boots. He grasped Jack's shoulder before he fell over, and Jack's strong arm pulled him free. The lad continued to grasp his upper arm and helped Crispin along, as he was still a bit unsteady on his feet.

Flamel led them down darker and dimmer streets, streets of less repute than even the Shambles. Were they mistaken about the alchemist? Were his clothes not fine? Did the man have money or not? Or was it some sort of ruse to get Crispin into a situation he could not get out of?

He pulled back on Jack's steadying arm and the boy looked him in the eye questioningly. "Where are you taking us?" he asked, directing his scowl to the alchemist.

The man stopped and turned to Crispin, eyeing first him and then Jack. "It is just this way," he said, gesturing.

"What is this? Some French trap?"

His look of shock seemed genuine. "*Sainte Mère!* Of course not!"

Crispin stepped forward and glared nose to nose. "I'm warning you. If this *is* a trap, you will find yourself extremely repentant."

"On my honor, *Maître* Guest. I swear by the Virgin's heart. It is simply that I must live in these humble surroundings so as not to bring spies upon me. In this way I stay hidden and so do my secrets."

"What is so secret in an alchemist's lair that he must hide in such filthy surrounds?"

He tilted his head, staring off to the side. "I... I cannot say, *Maître* Guest. My livelihood depends on these secrets. I am sure you are a man who understands."

Crispin stepped back with a huff and straightened his coat. "Very well. Is it much farther?"

"No. Only this way."

At last, Flamel led them to a mud-spattered door under an overhanging eave that sagged in the middle. The man took a ring of keys from his belt and unlocked the door. Crispin noted that the lock was new.

The man pushed through and let out a gasp.

Instinct propelled Crispin forward and he pushed Flamel aside to enter under the low lintel and into the dim surrounds.

The first thing that caught Crispin's attention was the gleam of brass above his head. He sucked in a breath as he beheld the huge spheres slowly encircling one another, all balancing on metal arms. Around and around they went, revolving, spinning. One sphere had rays emanating from it, and Crispin suddenly realized that this was the sun and the rest must be the planets orbiting the central globe, the Earth, in a monstrous display of brass and wire. It was indiscernible what made it move. Possibly the wind. He blinked in amazement.

An elbow to his gut made him turn to Tucker. The boy cocked his head toward the room, and Crispin tore his attention away from the astronomical display long enough to realize that this was not what he was supposed to be paying attention to. The room itself was in utter chaos. Glass flasks were shattered upon the floor. Clay jars, oozing strange substances, had been tossed about. Furniture overturned and broken. Parchment flung everywhere and fragments were stuck to the plank floor on puddles of some spilled sludge from a pot or canister.

He turned back to look at Flamel. "Was this how you left it?"

The man shook his head. It was plain that he was holding himself together by a thread. Something clearly was not right.

A sound.

Crispin pulled his dagger. All his attention directed to the far corner behind a disrupted pile of books and stools. A shadow, and then a figure emerged.

She looked like a waif, thin arms and a long, slim neck on which perched a faery face of wide blue eyes and a long cascade of silvery blond hair caught in a long braid snaking down her back. She stared at Crispin with incomprehension, until those eyes settled on Flamel.

"Oh, *ma chère!*" he said, and rushed to her.

Crispin lowered his knife. "Well. That's settled, then."

"Do not be a fool," said Flamel, drawing the woman into the light from the doorway. "She is not my wife. This is my servant, Avelyn."

Once he was able to look more clearly under the falling light from the open door, Crispin noted the smudge of dirt on her cheek, the ragged hem of her skirt, and the filthy apron her bony hands clutched.

It was then that Flamel began the strange motions of his hands and fingers before her face, as if he were playing the strings of an unseen harp. But when she replied silently with the same sorts of motions, Crispin's skin tingled with unease.

"Here! What are you doing?"

Flamel patted the girl on the shoulder wearily. He seemed satisfied. "She can neither hear nor speak. I was asking her what happened."

Crispin looked her over again. A deaf-mute, eh? "Well? What did she say?"

"Alas. All of this," he said, taking in the surrounds with the expanse of his gesture. "She does not know."

three

eaf, mute, and no doubt simple, thought Crispin. "She does not know or does not know how to say?"

Flamel clutched at the lapels of his gown, spotted hands tensing over the dark material. "She can express herself very well, *Maître*. She simply does not know what has transpired."

Crispin frowned. "Ask her if she saw anyone or anything. Are your wife's clothes gone? Jewelry? And ask her where she was during this mayhem."

Crispin watched as Flamel began his finger dance, but she didn't seem to be paying attention to him. Her eyes lingered on Crispin and she even moved Flamel aside to walk forward, striding right up to him. She stood almost toe to toe with Crispin and looked up at his face searchingly. She was the height of a child, the top of her head coming only up to his chest. And though not a child, she was perhaps little older than Jack. She studied his face and even raised a tentative finger to touch it. He shied away and glared at the alchemist. "What is she doing?"

"Learning. About you, I suspect. She has a way about her unlike any other."

"Tell her to stop." His hand captured her wrist before her fingers could reach his face and squeezed it once, hard, before pushing her hand away and letting it go.

She raised a silken brow at him but didn't seem at all perturbed, blinking white-tipped lashes. At last, she turned back to Flamel. He

14

spoke in the finger language and she responded in kind. When she was finished, she crossed her arms over her chest and fixed her unnerving gaze on Crispin.

"Well?" he asked.

Flamel shook his head. "She had only just returned and found it this way. There is nothing missing. Our money is still here. Now do you see that something is amiss?"

"Why would your wife ransack your rooms and then take nothing? It makes no sense."

"I… I do not know." He grasped his hair again and shook his head. Avelyn swooped forward, picked up an upended stool, and shoved it nearly beneath him. He slumped into it without looking behind him. It looked to be a well-practiced gesture. "I do not know what to make of it."

"Mind if I look around?" asked Crispin, already moving toward the far wall.

Flamel waved his hand and Crispin examined the disorder. Jack was suddenly at his shoulder.

"It's a mess, right enough," he murmured. He kept glancing up nervously at the slowly turning brass planets.

"Yes. But why?"

"Aye," Jack said quietly, so only Crispin could hear. He looked back at Flamel and sent a long gaze raking over the silent assistant. "If the apprentice ran off with his master's wife—and no man deserves a whipping more if he done it—then why did they leave their goods behind?"

Crispin cast his gaze about the room. And though it was in complete disarray, he couldn't help noticing the finery. The carved tables and benches; the dark walnut ambry; bolts of fine cloth unwound and snaking across the floor. Above beside the brass planetary display perched a loft open to the floor below. He made out the shape of a bed in the gloom. Bedding lay over the railing, dipping into the space below like a frozen waterfall.

Clearly Flamel wasn't lying about his status. But the missing wife was another matter.

He swiveled a little too sharply and nearly lost his footing, forgetting that he was still in his cups. "Just when was it again that you felt your wife was gone too long?"

"It must have been about midafternoon, around None. I was

15

working all morning and had sent Avelyn out on an errand. When I heard the church bells, I remember being startled that it was so late. And that Perenelle hadn't returned. And my apprentice, Thomas Cornhill, was not here at all. It was Avelyn who stoked the fire and prepared my flasks and jars early this morning."

"Cornhill? Is he English?"

"Yes. He came highly recommended and has a head for alchemy."

"So this servant—" He waved a hand at Avelyn. "She stoked the fire and did the apprentice's tasks. And you thought nothing of this inconsistency?"

"Well, sometimes Thomas is… away."

"Away?"

Flamel passed a hand over his face. His hair was wild, sticking up out of his cap. "The lad is—how you say—*beau*. Comely. He catches the eye of many a maid." Pointedly, he looked at Avelyn, but she was unaware of what he was saying and was busy sweeping the broken crockery into a corner with the noisy upstroke of her broom.

Crispin followed his gaze, but Flamel shook his head. "Oh no, *Maître*. Avelyn is very particular. She does not allow liberties. I think she has cuffed Thomas rather well a time or two. But…" He sank again. "My wife… she might not be above his charms. She is… older than I, but handsome."

"Any idea where they might have gone? Does your apprentice, this Thomas Cornhill, does he have other lodgings, family?"

"Family, yes."

"Then we must go there first."

"Avelyn will take you. I cannot leave my shop. I mustn't. I have much work to do."

Crispin turned to the girl again and watched as Flamel gestured to her. Before he was halfway done, she looked up at Crispin with a smile. He sneered back. He didn't like the idea of her, this deaf-mute leading him about.

She made quickly for the door and waited under the lintel, staring at him.

"She's a right comely lass, Master," said Jack at his elbow. The boy was grinning. "Wouldn't mind too much following her about, if you know my meaning."

16

"All too well. Might I suggest you keep your cod laced and your eyes open?"

Looking back at Flamel, he could see the man was already busily sweeping parchments into his arms. He bent and retrieved a small folded piece under a jar and his eyes widened in shock.

"Master Flamel?" Crispin approached. The alchemist straightened and hid it behind his back. Rocking on his heels, Crispin waited. "Did you find something?"

"Oh, no. No, I—"

Though his reflexes were slowed by drink, Crispin was still able to feint in one direction and lean in the other, plucking the parchment from the man's hand. He raised it to the cloudy sunlight from a narrow casement window. It fell across its buff surface. The inked lines were a string of several letters, nothing more.

"What is this?" asked Crispin.

"I—it is nothing," Flamel insisted, and tried to grasp the parchment from Crispin's hand. Crispin pulled it away.

"Nothing? Then why does it vex you so?"

"It is possibly part of one of my important papers."

"It is merely a fragment."

Suddenly the parchment was yanked from his fingers and Avelyn was there beside him, examining it, turning it this way and that. Damn the woman!

"Give that back," he snarled, and grabbed it, but she wrestled with him and managed to tear it away, holding it close to her body as one holds a candle to protect its flame.

Frustrated, he turned to Flamel. "Did she write that?"

"No." Flamel tried to peer over her shoulder, even dancing on the balls of his feet. "She cannot read or write. More's the pity, for we have never quite understood each other."

"Then what the hell is she—"

She stopped examining it and waved it frantically at Flamel, who tried to snatch it back from her fingers.

Crispin plucked it from her at last, and she didn't seem disposed to grab it back. She merely watched him and waited. "She doesn't appear to think this is yours."

"Nonsense!" And he tried unsuccessfully to snatch it again.

"Do you know the meaning of this?"

Flamel sucked in his lips, his mustache drawing down over them both. "I— No."

"Then it is a cypher of some kind. I will examine it later. It might help. You are certain this means nothing to you?" Flamel seemed to school his face into bland regard and shrugged. Crispin didn't believe it. He stuffed the parchment fragment into his scrip, measuring Flamel's eyes as he watched its progress. "In the meantime," he went on, "I suppose I'd best allow your assistant to lead me to the Cornhill house." He strode to the door. When Avelyn noticed, she scrambled forward and edged him out of the way. She put her hood up as she stepped into the street and motioned for him to follow.

He and Jack threw their hoods up over their heads. Snow had begun to fall in thick, lacy sheets. Her footsteps nearly disappeared the moment she made them. Crispin shivered. He could scarce recall a November so cold, and the month had barely begun. He drew his hood low over his face and tried to hide his chin in the folds of the leather cape at his throat, but it didn't help. Neither did his drunkenness help. It lingered just at the edges of his senses. The cold to his cheeks served to sober him, but the snow was making it difficult to even see the street.

Avelyn hurried ahead, heedless of them. In fact, she was moving too fast for Crispin's slower gait. "Wait," he called, and then remembered she couldn't hear him. He trotted ahead and grabbed her shoulder.

Instantly, she whirled around, a dagger in her hand. "Hold, damosel!" He took several steps back, bumping into Jack.

"Not a good idea to startle her," said the boy.

"I can see that." He placated with a gesture, and she gave him a smirk and sheathed her weapon before she turned and hurried up the avenue just as fast as before.

Crispin shrugged. "Best keep up," he said to Tucker.

She turned down lane after lane, until she finally stopped. She pointed to a house in front of her.

"I think she means this is it," said Jack.

Crispin gave his apprentice a withering look. "Yes, Jack. I've made that out for myself."

He approached the door and knocked. A man with a red chaperon hood framing his round face opened the door. "Who is it?" he said.

Crispin bowed. "Forgive the intrusion, good Master. My name is Crispin Guest, and I am looking for your son, Thomas Cornhill. Is he at home?"

The man glanced at Avelyn, who curtseyed to him. He smiled. "Ah. Have you come from Master Flamel?"

"Yes. He was wondering if your son, Thomas, was here."

The man scratched his head over his hood. "Master Flamel knows well that Thomas wouldn't be here. He is apprenticing with Master Flamel. He lives there now. One less mouth to feed here, I daresay."

"And you have not seen him?"

"Eh? Is he missing?"

"Well… er… Master Flamel merely needed his assistance forthwith. Perhaps he is attending to Madam Flamel. Shopping."

"Cold day for it, isn't it?" He peered out the door past Crispin. The snow filled the lane, and none of the broken cobblestones were visible. Other passersby hurried into doorways and there were few on the road. "He's a good boy, is Thomas. That's it, no doubt. Shopping. He gets sent for the oddest ingredients, or so he tells me. Alchemy. It's mysterious, isn't it? Beyond my ken, I can tell you. Thomas has the knack, so they say. Master Flamel is good to him, but he is a strange one. French, you know."

"Yes." Crispin assessed the man, his red nose and open face, and bowed. "Sorry to have disturbed you, sir."

"God's blessings on you, Master Guest. Give my good opinion to Master Flamel." He gestured to Avelyn and enunciated loudly, "AND GOOD DAY TO YOU!"

Avelyn laughed and bowed to him. Her laughter was strange, like a braying mule. She gazed at Crispin expectantly. Dark hood peppered with snowflakes, it kept her face in shadow.

He watched the door close again and frowned. "He is not here," he said to her. She cocked her head at him like a dog, and very like a dog she could understand only little. He cast up his arms in exasperation. "Go home," he said, gesturing.

Affronted, or so she looked, she folded her arms over her chest and raised her chin insolently at him. But she did not move.

"Here now," tried Jack. "Go on. WE HAVE NO FURTHER NEED FOR YOU!"

"She isn't hard of hearing, Jack. She can't hear you at all. There's little use in shouting."

"Oh." He sagged and stared at the stubborn servant. He gestured again. "Shoo! Begone!" He beseeched helplessly to Crispin, but Crispin merely turned on his heel and began walking back toward the Shambles.

Side by side, he and Jack proceeded through the streets. After a few paces, Jack looked over his shoulder. "She's following us," he whispered.

Crispin rolled his eyes and nearly stumbled into Jack. "You don't have to whisper. She'll understand in a moment. Just keep walking."

But even as they trudged through the deepening snow in street after street, Avelyn continued to track them a few paces behind.

"She's still following, Master."

"Ignore her."

Several streets later, they turned the corner at the Shambles and made their way up the avenue toward the tinker shop ahead, and when they finally stopped at the bottom of the staircase leading up to their lodgings, she stopped as well.

Crispin turned to glare at her.

"What does she want, Master?" asked Jack, still whispering. "Maybe if we give her a coin?"

Crispin reached into his scrip and pulled out his money pouch. He plucked a precious farthing from the bag and stretched out his hand, offering it. Her face, speckled and damp from snowflakes, glowed with a sudden bright smile. She snatched the coin from his hand, turned it over and over in her fingers, and finally closed it in her reddened fist. Turning her face up toward Crispin, she continued her enigmatic smile but didn't move.

Jack sighed. "Now what?"

"Now we leave her to her own devices." He spun toward the stairs, steadied himself by clutching the railing, and started up. Jack followed... but so did the woman.

"Master!"

"I know, Jack. Just ignore her."

They reached the landing and Crispin fitted his key in the lock. He gave her a glance and a nod, and she seemed to finally take note. She bowed to him once and bounded down the treacherously icy steps like a nimble-footed goat.

Crispin blew a cloud of breath. He hadn't realized how uncomfortable she had made him until her departure. Why Flamel kept a simple-minded servant was beyond his ken.

Concentrating on the key in the lock, he discovered that the door was *not* locked. He shot an accusatory glance at the oblivious Tucker before pushing the door open... and stopped in his tracks.

Leaning back on Crispin's chair before the fire—a fire burning unusually bright and hot with oak logs—sat Henry of Derby, the son of the duke of Lancaster.

four

Startled, Crispin nearly fell over the threshold. "Your grace!" Henry turned and smiled. His auburn beard had fleshed out from last year, curling across the line of his jaw, and his hair framed his face with just a hint of a curl under his chin. He wore a white-leopard fur cloak over his blue velvet houppelande as he sat before the fire. Crispin noted a bundle of fuel—sticks and real logs—sitting on the hearth. The sight was almost more joyful than his seeing Henry again. But he sobered quickly when he realized that Henry—his former charge—was seeing for himself his poor lodgings and meager existence. Heat crept up his collar.

"My lord." He bowed awkwardly.

But Henry continued to smile. His gaze fell on the surprised Jack peering over Crispin's shoulder. "Well, don't leave the door open. It's damnably cold in here."

Jack pushed Crispin the rest of the way through and barred the door after him. He unbuttoned Crispin's cloak—since Crispin felt incapable of moving—shook it out, and hung it on one of the pegs beside the door.

Henry turned again to the fire and rocked back on his chair. "Have you wine?"

Crispin, terrified that there was none, stared at Jack. The boy hurried to the sill to fetch the jug and turned to the pantry to grab two bowls. After a pause, he put one of the bowls back and poured the cheap red wine within, and, with a shaky hand, he offered it to Henry.

The young lord took it with a nod and sipped, pausing at the sharp taste.

Crispin fretted at his wet sleeve, toying with a loosened button. "I beg your pardon, my lord. I know the wine is not what you are used to...."

"It doesn't matter, Crispin. I am just glad to see you. Sit."

Slowly, Crispin lowered to the vacant stool and leaned heavily against the table between them.

Henry continued to stare into the fire. "My lord father the duke must have come here many a time."

Crispin licked his lips. He would have been grateful for a little wine—fie on his apprentice!—but did see the sense in Jack's hesitation. He steadied himself against the table. "Only once, your grace."

"Henry, Crispin. You used to call me Henry."

"Your *grace*," he answered stubbornly.

Henry sighed. "My father came here only once?"

"It is not meet that he should be here, my lord."

"Meaning I shouldn't be either, eh, Crispin?"

Crispin lumbered to his feet. "No, you should not. Henry, I thought you would have more sense than this. You know what the king thinks of me!"

His mild gaze sought out Crispin. A smirk stole across his face. "Indeed. Does not all England know what my lord cousin thinks of you? Convicted of treason, you were cast from his court. Was it ten years ago now? Eleven? Since my father urged him to spare your life, he thought you would die on the streets without your title and wealth. Proved him wrong, did you not?"

"Not easily, my lord."

"And yet you did. So I do not worry overmuch what his grace the king thinks."

"Henry," he warned.

"Oh, very well." He rose and turned his chair around, sliding it up to the table. "No more dangerous talk. I'm here for a reason."

"And that reason is?"

"Crispin, sit. It sounds as if you would be rid of me. Surely that is not the case! You practically raised me."

Crispin lowered himself to the stool again. "The Lady Katherine was your governess, not I."

"But you and I spent many an hour riding and practicing with arms. And jesting, too. And laughing."

"Ha!" Jack threw his hand over his mouth. Clearly he had not meant to vocalize his astonishment. Though little wonder. How often had Jack seen him laugh over the last few years? Yet he used to laugh. Often. With the good company of young Henry and his siblings and with Lancaster and even with Geoffrey Chaucer, they were as a big family, laughing, dancing, hunting, dining. All the things families did. Until he was wrenched away from it all because of his own stupidity.

Henry smiled at Jack's gaffe. His eyes sparkled. "And so he did, my young apprentice. Your master played tricks and laughed quite a bit before he grew so dark and gloomy."

Crispin cleared his throat. "Well, that's enough about me," he grumbled, face red. "You were telling me why you felt it appropriate to visit me in person at my lodgings, a forbidden place for those at court."

"What did I tell you?" he said to Jack, raising his brows.

"Henry!"

Even as exasperated as he was, Crispin couldn't help but gaze at his former charge. Henry was a man now. Broad of shoulder, thick arms, auburn hair that tended toward ginger when the firelight caught it. His beard and mustache were perfectly coiffed. At almost two and twenty, he was nearing the height of his power. And, Crispin remembered, he was also a new father, only since September.

"I must offer my congratulations to you, Henry. You're the father of a fine son, I hear."

Henry's smile split his face with laugh lines. "Indeed! A very fine son. He is hale and hearty, God be praised. Another Henry. My wife insisted."

"I'm very pleased," said Crispin. His heart ached to see the child, but he knew he never would. "And your lady wife? Well, I pray?"

"Oh, yes. A strong lass. There will be many sons, I am certain of it." He took up the bowl and slurped the wine, his gloved finger wiping the remnants from his mustache. "And you, Crispin? Still no wife?"

24

He looked away. "I cannot bring a wife to this."

"But surely other men do as much."

"I am not like other men."

"Hmm. So you are not. The things you used to teach me. The things you could have taught my son. If only..." Derby sat back, appraising Crispin across the table. "Well." He had the decency to look contrite, and Crispin's heart ached all the more for the futility of the thought.

Crispin stared at the flames dancing up from the chunks of wood Henry had brought. The fire should have cheered him, but he knew the rumors circulating all over London. Nothing had died down from the disquiet at court of last year. In fact, the only reason Henry was in London and not in Spain in his father's army was that he'd been appointed to command an army made up of a group of noblemen and bishops gathered by Parliament to look into the excesses of Richard's household, to investigate his favorites, to restore order, and to force Richard to fulfill his obligations as king.

Trouble was definitely brewing. Trouble of the kind where good men took up arms and bad men gathered their own armies. Crispin smelled treason on the wind, but he wasn't sure from which direction it blew.

It made him all the more anxious to find Henry in his home. "Your grace, why are you here?"

He seemed unaware of Crispin's misgivings. "I'm interested in your vocation. This tracking you do. I'd like to help."

Out of the corner of his eye, Crispin noted Jack stiffen at his place by the door.

Henry noticed, too, and tilted his head. Crispin wasn't being as subtle as he thought. "Shall I supplant your apprentice, Crispin? After all, I can be of valuable service to you, going where you cannot."

Jack pressed forward, his feet faltering across the plank floor. "My lord? Y-you don't mean it? I mean, I've served Master Crispin for nigh on four years now."

"By the saints, the boy is troubled."

"No one is supplanting you, Jack. Lord Henry is jesting."

"Not a bit of it. I came to help. Consider me your new apprentice!"

Jack's face flushed and his hands curled into impotent fists held

25

tight at his sides. He said nothing. What could he say against such a nobleman? Crispin didn't find it funny. This was his livelihood, dammit. He'd be damned if it was made a point of ridicule.

He leaned forward. "God's blood, Henry! Stop it. Even if your generous offer was sincere, I would never give up my apprentice. I trust him. He is ever loyal to me, and I know he will continue to be so to my dying breath. I will not—*we* will not—be made sport of."

The young lord's expression softened. "Ah, Crispin. You have shamed me. I did not mean to make sport of you. But I do find these things you do extremely intriguing. Who would ever have thought, eh? This private sheriffing you do. When I first heard of it, I thought it was something best left to the coroner's jury. But you do prove to be successful time and again. And an asset to the sheriffs."

"They are not as enamored of me as you seem to be. Very often they get in my way."

"Do they? Well, it is a pity you are not an alderman, for you would make a very fine sheriff."

"Perish the thought. They do little to keep the peace and have nothing whatsoever to do with bringing miscreants to justice."

"Such savage criticism of the king's sheriffs, Crispin. Were they not duly appointed?"

Crispin clamped his lips shut. Never should he have an argument on such topics when he had been drinking. He shoved away from the table and stood unsteadily. "My lord, forgive me for speaking out of turn. But as you see, I am not entirely... myself."

The smirk was back as Henry rose. "Yes, I can see that," he said into his shirt. "But I shall not be put off, Crispin. This tracking you do. How do you go about it?"

"My lord?"

"I mean, a weaver cards the wool and spins it into thread and then his thread is eased into the loom and he weaves. But *you* find, say, a dead man. How would you proceed? Further, from what I hear, many of your assignments seem to exclude anyone who has seen or heard anything of the crime. It is impossible, what you do. How is it done?"

He couldn't help but be flattered by Henry's interest, and he felt his cheeks heat up. No one had ever asked him before. Even Jack seemed to learn it by example. "I... I observe. The area around the corpse. How long ago he was killed and by what means. I ask questions and listen carefully to the answers. I am an interpreter of lies."

"Just like the old days, eh, Crispin?"

He chuckled in spite of himself. "Yes. I find that court politics was good practice for my current vocation. And just as deadly."

"But these questions you ask. How do you know whom to ask?"

"Sometimes the answer to that presents itself. Sometimes I stumble upon it. And sometimes I ferret it out for myself after much digging. That is what makes it rewarding, after a fashion. The work that must be done is primarily in the mind."

Henry smiled. "I can see how that suits you. And how much…" He looked away. "How much righting wrongs suits you as well."

Crispin nodded. He caught only a glimpse of Jack's fond gaze. "But surely there is another motive for your being here," he said to Henry. "After all, you are a busy man and I am not deaf to the rumors circulating throughout London. These are troubled times. And your father—"

"My father is not here," he said, losing something of his cheer.

"And the king has said that those who oppose his… his decisions, are traitors. I know you have been appointed by these commissioners, Henry, to raise an army. If you oppose Richard, force him to do the will of Parliament, impede in any way his royal rights, then it shall be called treason. Indeed, he threatened that he was anointed by God and, as such, may dissolve Parliament."

Derby gritted his teeth. "Just so. And even invoking the name of his sovereign ancestor Edward II in these terms was construed to be an act of treason."

Little wonder, Crispin snorted, when Edward II was deposed for insisting on similar rights… and with fewer favorites than had Richard.

"So you will forgive me," he said, bowing to Derby, "if I seem skeptical at your personal interest in my welfare. If there is something you want of me, you should simply ask. I think it particularly imprudent of you to come to my lodgings at this time." He leaned forward. "You do know you might be in danger," he said quietly. "And you are most certainly being followed."

"Am I?" He turned toward the fire, but Crispin caught the edge of his smile. "Well, while it is true that I am occupied with curtailing the treasury and my cousin the king from imprudence, there is always time for leisure, to visit friends." The sparkle in his eyes dimmed and he spoke confidentially, for Crispin's ears. "But a word of caution is in order. Do take care, Crispin. Keep a sharp eye in the direction of Westminster. There's a storm on the horizon. I do not trust Richard's advisers. Especially those who were once loyal to my father."

"Suffolk," Crispin breathed.

Henry barely nodded. "Stay awake, Crispin."

He strode to the door, stopping in front of Jack. He tapped his knuckles none too gently to the boy's chest, making him take a step back. His smile and sparkle had returned. "Take care, young apprentice, or you shall find your shoes filled by a better man." He laughed and opened the door. "It is good to see you, Crispin. God keep you." His laughter echoed all the way down the stairs.

Jack went to the door and slammed it hard before he threw the bolt. He swung to face Crispin, glared at him once, before stomping to the fire. He picked up the iron and jabbed the wood with it, watching the logs crumble into glowing blocks of coal.

Crispin dragged himself wearily to the bed and sat. With a long sigh he fell back, throwing an arm over his eyes. The room felt unnaturally warm and comfortable. Enough wood in the hearth, for once, kept the small room snug while the snow fell relentlessly outside. After a long pause wherein Tucker said nothing but could be heard clanging the iron against the stone hearth, Crispin finally said, "He brought fuel, at least. We are warm, for once."

"He'd be better than me, there's no mistaking that." Jack's tone was sour and he spoke low to the fire. "He's rich. He's handsome. He's better than me in every way I can think of."

God's blood. Jealous again? Every new person in their life lately had caused Jack to lose his nerve, to grow insecure of his place. Was it his age? Did Crispin act this way when *he* was fifteen? Possibly. Fifteen was a time for stretching one's legs, for doing battle and riding furiously. Crispin had been a blur at fifteen. Why shouldn't Jack feel anxious? "Give it a rest, Tucker. He will not replace you. For one, he is a lord and heir. Why would he content himself with doing our business? He has far more important work to do." He winced at that. Those sentiments could have been better expressed.

Jack snorted and Crispin heard the chair creak as he leaned it back. "He shall rule the duke's lands someday," Jack muttered. "He is leading an army now, isn't he? But *we* find murderers and stop them. Murder is a great sin. What's more important than that?"

You are seeking a knot in a bulrush. "Be still, Jack, and stop being a fool. No one's replacing you. Now give me a little peace so I may recover myself."

Jack fell silent again and Crispin let his worries fall away. He let thoughts of Henry and Lancaster and treason disperse. It wasn't long till he dozed.

He awoke with a start and saw that it was early morning. Jack was already up, casting his wash water out the back garden window. Crispin squinted at the rosy sky. Clear, at least. No snow today if God smiled on them. But he shivered at the cold draft, and Jack snapped the shutter closed.

"Good morning, Master. Should we not go in search of Madam Flamel today?"

Oh God. That hadn't been a dream, then? He rubbed his head, shaking loose the cobwebs. "Remind me, Jack. What is it we are doing… exactly?"

With his fists at his hips, Jack glared at him. "Don't you recall anything?"

"Well… I seem to recall… a French alchemist?" Jack nodded. "And a strange female servant?"

"Aye."

"And then…?"

"God blind me, Master Crispin! You give a man gray whiskers. Here's a client—a *paying* client—and you don't remember?"

He cradled his head from Jack's loud admonishment. "Give me a moment."

"Well, I was there, too, so I can tell you all about it, I suppose."

Jack moved about the room, fetching Crispin's wash water and explaining about the missing wife and apprentice; how they had gone to the apprentice's family, but the man wasn't there. And then, as he handed Crispin a bowl of watery broth, he mentioned curtly about the unexpected visitation of Henry of Derby.

Oh, yes. Crispin seemed to remember that! He made a secret glance at Jack as he stoked the fire and noted the red tips of his ears. Crispin smiled into his bowl. A jealous Jack was an amusing one.

But none of it was amusing once they got outside. It might have been a clear day with only a wintry haze along the horizon, but it was starkly cold. His feet were already numb even under two layers of stockings.

"Tell me, Jack," he said, climbing carefully down the stairs. "Had we any idea where to start this search?"

He still wore a hurt expression, one he seemed to hold dear from last night when Henry taunted him. "*I'm* not the Tracker, *you* are."

Crispin would have rolled his eyes, but his head still hurt. "Very well. We could— God's blood!"

A cluster of women chattered close together in front of the poulterer's, vying for the plumpest hen hanging by its feet from a hook in the front of the stall, and the poulterer smiled broadly at his good fortune. But just beside them, not part of the group, stood Avelyn.

Her sparkling eyes followed Crispin as he descended the stairs, but she made no move to approach.

"What's she doing here?" said Jack, voicing Crispin's thoughts.

"I don't know." They both stood on their own patches of dirty snow, regarding each other across the lane. But the longer they stood at this silent battle, the more foolish Crispin felt. "She doesn't seem to have anything to offer. Let us go, Jack."

As he threw his hood up over his head, his foot hit the street and sank into the cart-rutted snow. Slyly, he looked back over his shoulder. Avelyn hadn't moved. Very well, then.

Of course, he had no idea where he was going. It seemed foolish to simply wander all over London looking for a lost wife. Though more likely, she had returned. If the servant Avelyn were only able to talk, he might have asked her. He stopped and whipped around, looking for her tiny frame, but she was no longer standing in the drift by the poulterer's.

He supposed it might be best to see this Nicholas Flamel again to find out what had transpired.

He turned and headed toward the Fleet. Shopkeepers set out their wares. A baker's apprentice wandered the streets with a heavy canvas bag slung across his shoulder. Inside were warm meat pies and small loaves of maslin. Whenever he was stopped to sell his wares, the apprentice opened the flap of the bag and steam arose, sending the tantalizing whiff of fresh bread and meat spices into the air.

The broth seemed a mere memory in Crispin's belly, and his mouth watered to smell the aromas.

Along the way, Crispin let the familiar scenes of an awakening London trickle past him. A master here and an apprentice there, plying their trade in open doorways. Braziers burned with sticks and dung along the avenues, and travelers warmed their hands and faces over the smoky fires.

He passed a familiar shop with its heavy posts in each corner. Crispin had passed it hundreds of times, perhaps a thousand times, without giving it thought. But this time, he came to an abrupt halt. Walking backward, he returned to stare at the dark wood of the corner post. It rose to the second story with white lime plaster swathed in between window and corner. He'd never had reason to take note of it before, but today, carved crudely into the wood, was a set of strange symbols.

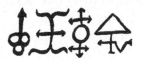

He approached and raised his hand. Cold fingertips slid over the crudely carved shapes. "Jack," he said softly, "am I imagining this, or…" He had been about to ask if the symbols had always been there only he had never noticed. But the truth was under his fingers, for the carving was new and even left a splinter in his skin.

He rubbed it free and studied the wall. Jack came up beside him. "What is that, Master?"

"I don't know. It is writing of some sort. Reminds me of something." Try as he might, he could not recall the memory.

Dismissing it, he turned and suddenly came face-to-face with Avelyn. Her unexpected appearance disconcerted him.

"What do you want, wench?" He realized even as he said it that she could not hear him.

But her face was drawn in consternation and she grabbed his arm, yanking him forward.

Reflexively, he pulled away from her, but she was not put off. She leapt up and grabbed him again, jerking his arm hard.

"What the devil—"

Jack grabbed her shoulders and pulled her back, but she spun in his arms and elbowed him in the gut with surprising strength. Jack doubled with the blow, and she seized Crispin's arm again, pulling him into the middle of the lane.

"I'm going to go with her, Jack. Are you all right?"

The boy sputtered and staggered after him. "Aye… Master. God's teeth but she's got a sharp jab."

Crispin let himself be dragged along. It was useless trying to slide her grip from him. She'd only grasp on again like a limpet.

They were steadily making their way to the alchemist's shop. Passersby stared at them with amusement, but Crispin was far from amused. He'd give the man a piece of his mind for his servant's actions!

They turned the corner and she let Crispin go to run to the shop. She stood at the door, looking back at Crispin and beckoning with urgency. Crispin felt compelled to trot forward, his heart thumping faster, a strange feeling stirring in his gut.

When she opened the door, he stopped dead.

The alchemist sat on the floor on his knees, weeping. Above him, swinging gently back and forth, hung a young man.

Upside down he hung, his left leg bent and tied behind his right to form a triangle. He'd been hung by his left foot, which was wrapped with a heavy rope leading up to the rafter beam.

And on his chest a dagger was thrust through, holding in place a piece of parchment with dark writing and a blotch of blood.

five

ack had gone to fetch the sheriffs while Crispin carefully removed the dagger and the bloodied parchment.

"How long, Master Flamel? How long were you absent from your shop? This had to have been a difficult thing to hang him thus without anyone seeing."

"I was gone all morning," he said between wiping his eyes. "Doing *your* job, *Maître*! Looking for my Perenelle. Oh, my saints. Oh God, keep his soul, the poor, dear boy. For I had accused him most foully of great sin. The greater sin is mine."

Guilt twinged Crispin's gut. Had he not been in his cups... "This is your apprentice, then? Thomas Cornhill."

"Yes," he said, sobbing.

Crispin directed his attention to the spidery script of the parchment. In Latin, he read:

You will deliver up the Stone or the fair Perenelle will die.

Crispin read it twice. "Do you recognize this hand, Master Flamel?"

The man did not look at Crispin and shook his head.

"What does he mean by 'the Stone'? Some gem you possess?"

Flamel wiped his eyes and moved quickly to the other side of the room. "Can we not cut him down?"

"We must await the sheriffs." Crispin looked up at the dead man, one leg extended, one leg crooked. "The gem, Master Flamel. It must be worth a great deal to kill for it."

"It… I do not know of what stone he speaks."

Crispin glared at him. "Do you not? You are aware that I am here to help you. And the person who has captured your wife has already killed once. I suggest you confide in me."

His hands closed over his robe, clenching tightly. "I tell you I do not know!"

"He thinks you do. What could he mean, then?"

"I… I do not know," he said in defeat.

Of course he was lying. But Crispin couldn't make the man confess. Well, one couldn't if the man was a client. Exasperated, Crispin cast his glance at the servant girl, who was watching the proceedings with a keen eye. She caught Crispin's glance and held it, gazing at him steadily as if trying to impart her knowledge with just a look. What did she know of it? How could he ask? How could she answer?

"I need to ask your servant girl questions." Flamel crushed his head in his hands, rocking back and forth. Annoyed, Crispin bent down and grabbed the man under his arms and hauled him to his feet. "Master Flamel, gird yourself. Obviously… I was wrong. So, I need your assistance now. If you still want my help."

Flamel's eyes were red when he raised them. "Of course I want your help. Do you think I trust these English sheriffs?"

"Forgive me, Master, but do not forget that I am English."

He waved his hand distractedly. "Yes, yes. But you are more French in your rational thinking." He winced when his eye caught the slowly swinging man again, a counterpoint to the brass planets and stars moving distractedly overhead. He turned away and spoke over his shoulder. "What help do you need from me?"

"I need you to communicate with your servant. Ask her what she might know of this. Was she with you?"

"Yes, she was with me. We discovered him together."

"Please, Master Flamel. Ask her."

Flamel waved at Avelyn, and the girl gave him her attention. His fingers danced again and she replied in kind. But an argument seemed to have ensued, and they went back and forth, Flamel growing increasingly flustered.

"What is it?" asked Crispin, looking from one to the other.

"She says she knows nothing, only… well. It is ridiculous."

"I'll be the judge of that. Come now."

"Well, she says that Thomas—his position—is familiar to her."

Crispin turned again, eyes scanning the dead man in his macabre condition, purposely hanging upside down. "In what way?"

"She... cannot say." Flamel suddenly jumped up. He bustled about the place, turning over books and parchments, opening small coffers, and collecting things in his hands. "I must pay you your fee, before the sheriffs come. Here, *Maître* Guest." He offered his cupped hands to Crispin.

Expecting coins, Crispin cupped his own hands to receive them, but instead, a collection of strange objects fell into his palms. A nail, a spoon, a key. Crispin was about to object until he noticed they were all made of gold. He scratched the spoon with the key. They appeared to be solid gold.

"What... what is this?"

"Your payment, *Maître*. I hope that will be enough."

Crispin gauged the heavy weight in his hands. "Far more than sufficient," he said distractedly before dropping them into his scrip.

A commotion at the door told him the sheriffs had arrived. He prepared himself. It was Simon Wynchecombe all over again, only doubled. Both sheriffs, appointed as was the custom on Michaelmas, had no liking for the Tracker they had inherited. Already, with each assignment, they had proved they did not appreciate Crispin's help or interference.

Sheriff William Venour, alderman and grocer, stepped through the open door, followed by Sheriff Hugh Fastolf, alderman and pepperer. They were both momentarily diverted by the huge moving display of planets before they turned their attention to the strange swinging dead man. Fastolf gripped the hilt of his dagger and crossed himself, twice. "Holy Virgin!" he said. His bald pate was covered with a chaperon hat with a dagged coxcomb trailing down over his right shoulder.

Sheriff William nervously stroked his ginger beard. "God's teeth, Hugh. What do you make of that?"

Eyes wide, Fastolf walked a turn completely around the hanging man, his gloved hand firmly over his mouth as if he might be sick. "For the love of the Rood, can we not cut him down?"

Jack scrambled in just as the sheriffs' serjeants entered, drawing their knives. One held the man while the other sawed through the rope.

Crispin was about to offer the sheriffs the note and the dagger, but Flamel stayed his hand and gently took the things from him, laying them aside. Keeping silent on it, Crispin observed the scene before him instead, examining the discarded frayed end of the rope until Sheriff Venour snatched it out of his hand.

"And what are *you* doing here, Guest?"

He bowed. "As always, Lord Sheriff, I am only nigh when called."

"Oh?" He glanced at Jack, standing anxiously behind Crispin. "And how came you so quickly? You sent your boy in all haste. But this corpse is still warm. How is it you were hired before there was a body?"

Crispin dared not look at Flamel, but the man stepped forward and bowed formally. *"Mes seigneurs,"* said Flamel, "I hired *Maître* Crispin a day ago to… to… find something dear to me. We could not have known that *this* would be the result!"

Fastolf tried for an air of indifference as the body was lowered to the floor by his underlings. He pushed his long-toed shoe forward and rested a fist at his waist. "The result of what? Just what is it you were sent to look for, Guest?"

Again, Crispin deferred to Flamel. The man reached into his pouch and pulled out a golden arrowhead. "This, *Shérif de Seigneur*. As you can see, it is quite valuable and it was lost. Stolen. By… by this man. He was my apprentice."

"Eh?" said Venour. "Your apprentice? And who did this to him?"

Flamel shrugged. "I do not know. The shop was empty all this morning. Someone perhaps played a poor jest that went terribly wrong."

"And how did he die?" Fastolf nodded toward the dead man now lying on the floor. One of the serjeants had knelt beside him and untied his crooked leg from his other, then tossed the rope aside.

Both serjeants looked up, thinking perhaps that they were being addressed. Crispin moved forward, and the serjeants seemed only too happy to get out of his way.

"Here, Guest!" cried Fastolf. "What are you doing?"

But just as quickly as Fastolf moved forward to stop him, Venour stepped in and took his companion by the arm. He slowly shook his head. *Of course,* thought Crispin. *Don't do any of the work yourselves.*

He knelt by the body and examined it. He looked at the tear in the fabric on the breast where the dagger had stabbed. There was very little blood. So the dramatic placement of the parchment note was done postmortem. He pushed the high collar aside and saw the bruising around his throat. "Strangled," he said aloud. A bruise on his chin seemed to indicate he had not come quietly. He picked up the limp arms, pushing back the sleeves. Red weals about the wrists. He was tied up.

"Well?" asked the strained voice of Sheriff Hugh. "What else?"

Crispin turned back toward them. "My lords, did you wish to hire me to investigate the matter for you?"

Hugh rapped him sharply against the side of his head. "Insolent dog! Do you think you are the only man in this city with a brain?"

Prevented from answering truthfully when Sheriff William shoved him out of the way, he slowly rose.

"There's something to that," said Sheriff William. He cast his glare upon Flamel. "You, then. You're French, are you not? And the French bring trouble with them wherever they go."

Instead of speaking up to defend himself, Flamel stayed quiet but tense.

"I think you should hire Guest here. He favors toiling with the dead, discovering… things." He said the last with a sneer.

Flamel bowed. "I should be only too happy to."

Crispin studied his shoes. Well then. Only more coin for him. And he'd planned on investigating anyway.

A glove slapped his face and he raised his head sharply to Venour. The man's twisted scowl was aimed at him. "Look at me when I'm speaking to you, knave. You heard the man. Er… who is this Frenchman?"

Flamel bowed again. "I am Nicholas Flamel, alchemist."

The curl to Venour's lip indicated he was not impressed. "Find the murderer, Guest. And report to me. And don't dally. There is enough trouble in the city without your adding to it."

"My lord?"

His scowl grew darker. "Don't you know anything? Noblemen are stirring up anxiety at court. No one is spared from these events. The world has gone insane," he lamented. "It's now in the hands of Parliament."

Crispin tried for nonchalance. "And what of... what of the king's commissioners? What of Lord Derby?"

The sheriff jutted his chin. "What of him? Oh, that's right. He was your pet once. Or were you his?"

Crispin ground his teeth. *Just tell me, you jackdaw!*

The sheriff seemed to take pleasure in saying, "Lord Derby and Nottingham stand against the king, or so the rumor holds. How do you *think* he is faring? At any rate, no one knows where he is, and if *you* know anything, Guest, you had better come to us forthwith. The king wishes to see his cousin at court."

Henry's visit of the night before ran through Crispin's mind. He desperately tried to remember what he had been telling Crispin besides the silly jesting. Damn the wine that punched holes through his memory!

"But Lord Sheriff—"

He turned on his heel and signaled to Fastolf. "I'm not your herald, Guest. Go to an alehouse if you wish to get more news." He talked to his serjeants about taking the body away to the apprentice's family before he turned a last time to Crispin. "In any case, Guest, we expect results from you."

Crispin bowed. "As always, Lord Sheriff." He caught Venour rolling his eyes before the man pushed his way out the front door, followed quickly by Fastolf.

The serjeants carried the man away, and all was quiet again. Yet a rope still hung from the rafters, swinging from the draft of the ever-moving planets.

Crispin picked up the discarded bit of rope cut from the man's leg and turned it over in his hands. Good-quality rope. Not a fisherman's rope. New. Bought for this purpose? He placed it on the table beside the bloodied knife and parchment. The sheriffs had been so anxious to allow someone else to do their job that they had not noticed these items among the clutter, for which Crispin was grateful. He did not like to have to explain to the sheriffs the intricacies of what was truly happening. Nor did he care to lie… too much.

Just as he reached for the parchment, Avelyn swooped in and snatched it up.

"Damnable woman! Give it here!"

She pulled it away from him, holding it up to the window and studying it.

"What is she doing, Master Flamel? Make her give it to me. I—"

But he saw it. She held it up to the oiled hide covering the window opening. It allowed golden light to filter through, but it cast enough light that he saw faint lines etched on the parchment. He stepped up and took it from her, and this time she let him, nodding. He held it up for himself, finger tracing the careful invisible writing evident only with the backlighting from the window.

"Master Crispin?" Jack was at his side. "What is it? God blind me! There's more writing there!"

Crispin brought the parchment to the hearth and took up the poker. He pulled some ashes from the cooling fire and scraped them into a pile on the hearthstone. He crouched and took some of the ashes in his hand and sprinkled them on the parchment, gently rubbing them in with his fingertips, taking special care to embed them into the words etched with an empty quill. When he'd filled in the lines, he tipped the parchment and blew away the remaining ashes.

He squinted. The lines were only just legible. He read aloud:

"'Leave the Stone at the niche at Saint Paul's feet in his cathedral by Sext today. Do this or she dies.'"

Jack took it from his hands and read the lines carefully, mouth moving silently.

Crispin turned to Flamel. "You knew this secret message was here."

He shook his head frantically. "No."

"You know far more than what you are saying. Do you realize your wife's life is at stake? If you know the man who abducted your wife, you had best tell me."

"Of course I don't!"

"Then why did your servant know of this secret message?" He turned to Avelyn. She scrutinized Crispin with narrowed eyes.

"She… she is familiar with my own ways. I do many of my notes in codes and with such methods because the work I do is secret and dangerous. Of course she would naturally look for it."

Crispin was unconvinced. "This Stone he speaks of," he said. "And don't waste my time lying that you don't know what it is."

Flamel wrestled with himself and finally nodded. "Yes. Yes. It is a very valuable broach. The most valuable thing I own, save my wife."

Satisfied, Crispin fit his thumbs in his belt. "Well then. I suggest you fetch it. We will place it at the feet of Saint Paul as instructed and await this abductor. We'll trap this rat with the proper cheese."

And yet, Flamel still hesitated. Was any object worth the life of a loved one? Crispin watched the contortions of the man's mind written clearly on his face. And then he looked to Avelyn. She was also watching Flamel. Her body tensed, as if waiting to run or jump to his bidding. Then suddenly she turned to Crispin. Her eyes seemed to bore through him, searching his soul. She was a changeling, he was certain of it. No human could have such pale hair and eyes. No human could see so clearly inside of him. He wasn't entirely certain that she liked all she saw, but it seemed to satisfy her enough. Without being asked, she pivoted and dove into the clutter of the alchemist's things, shoving papers aside, moving coffers out of her way to get to the doors of an ambry. She opened it and hesitated, then looked over her shoulder at Crispin. An elfin smile drew up her mouth as she touched a carving around the edge of the ambry's opening. An audible click sounded, and a drawer that had not been there before slid forward. She reached inside, still looking at Crispin with that strange, enigmatic smile, and blindly retrieved a velvet pouch.

She pushed the secret drawer closed and it vanished as mysteriously as it had appeared. She handed the bag to Flamel with an absent curtsy. Those slanted faery eyes moved with Crispin as he walked over to the man and looked down into his hand.

He pulled forth a sapphire broach. It was nearly the size of a robin's egg, deep and pure, surrounded by clear faceted crystals. Three teardrop pearls hung from the bottom of the oval of stone. "Magnificent," Crispin whispered. Jack whistled. Crispin knew little of jewelry, but he knew enough that he reckoned the sale of a stone like this might buy him a very decent wardrobe… for everyone he knew.

"This was a gift from King Charles," Flamel said softly. "We—Perenelle and I—did him a great service."

"A great service indeed," said Crispin in the same quiet tone. "I understand your hesitation, but your wife…"

"Yes, *Maître*, of course you are right."

"You will take this and place it as he specified. But I will be following you and waiting nearby to capture the knave."

"Is… is that all there is to that?" asked Flamel, wringing his hands. "You capture him and he tells you where my wife is? For I have never been involved in such matters before."

"I assure you, sir, that the matter will be over quickly."

Flamel readied himself, told Avelyn to stay, and ventured forth. Crispin allowed him a lead and then made his way out the alchemist's door.

He had not gotten far when he encountered a crowd gathered around a man with coarse ruddy hair, waving his arms about. He had a thick Southwark accent with just the hint of somewhere else.

"… Then Satan, the enemy of the Father," the man was saying in a loud voice, hoarse from speaking, "wishing to trouble the peace and Kingdom of the Holy Father, knocked upon the door of Man. And Man, because he is not vigilant and is weak of heart and soul, did not set guardians on his door and allowed him in. And, hidden amongst them, Satan began to solicit them with false promises. Time and again, Satan, the Great Deceiver, the one true enemy of God the Father, slew the soul of Man because he would not take the narrow gate! Look! Look here! Signs of sorcery and witchcraft." He flung his hand toward the stone foundation of a weaver's shop. Etched upon the surface was another odd set of symbols, something that Crispin did not recognize.

"See!" the man went on. "See the devilry at work. Have we forgotten so soon the punishment sent down upon us by our generous Lord to cleanse us of our sins? Do we not recall the terrible plague that swept our midst a mere generation ago, taking the high and the lowly, for Death does not aim his scythe at only the one or the other? All men must die, all men must suffer for to be worthy of the presence of our Father in the sky in His heavenly chamber."

The man swept the crowd with his gaze and it landed upon Crispin, where it stayed. That pointing finger swept toward Crispin. "Lo! See the evildoer emerging from the alchemist's lair! Foul Sorcerer, Tempter! Dabbling where angels have forbidden. Your fate is sealed, as are the fates of others so inclined to follow the path of Satan."

Crispin straightened his coat. "Rubbish."

Some in the crowd gasped. It stopped the mouth of the preacher, but only for a moment. He narrowed his eyes and his thin lips spread into a feral smile, revealing one gray tooth. "He does not repent. And so his sin spreads to the good people of London like a disease. To you, dear friends. His sin compounds and leaves open the unguarded door. For a traitor to God shall suffer the fate of traitors and hang by his heel to be devoured by dogs. Plague shall return unless we repent of our sins and make the sinner pay!"

Laying a hand on his dagger hilt, Crispin took a cautious step back. But the crowd seemed disinclined to make good on the preacher's admonitions.

"For God's sake," said Jack, stepping protectively before Crispin. The lad was just as tall and blocked Crispin's view of the crowd. "This man is not a sinner nor an alchemist. He's—"

Crispin jabbed Jack in the ribs with his elbow, and the boy winced. What did this preaching man know of men hanging by their feet? Just at that moment and from the look on the man's face, Crispin did not wish to identify himself.

"Come, Jack." He yanked his apprentice along but kept an eye on the ruddy-haired man.

They turned a corner and Crispin ushered them quickly away until they had made a circuitous route toward Pater Noster Row above St. Paul's.

"Master," Jack said, flustered, "what was that all about? Why did you stop me from putting that man aright?"

"Did you not listen to him? He spoke of a man *hanging upside down.*"

Jack stopped. "Blind me. Do you think…"

"I do not know what to think. I like guessing even less. Go back and keep an eye on him, Jack. Tell me where he goes."

"You will go on to St. Paul's?"

"Yes. Meet me later back at our lodgings."

"Aye, Master."

"I need not tell you that the man must not know you are there."

Jack gave him a crooked smile, not dissimilar to Crispin's own. "I know that, Master Crispin. I'll not let him see me. Of that you can be certain. God keep you, sir."

"And you. Go on, you knave."

Jack saluted and took off back down the lane, snow flying from his boots.

Crispin gathered his cloak tighter across his chest and proceeded down the street. He turned the corner at St. Paul's and stood in the slush at the bottom of the hill, looking up toward the cathedral. Its spires, tipped with frost, sparkled in the frail sunshine. He raised his hood to keep the cold at bay and to disguise himself. At this distance, he had a clear view of the courtyard and arched entry. Men were coming and going through the church's doors. It was a place for clerks and lawyers to solicit business, milling as they did in the cold nave, out of the weather. The nave was known as Paul's Walk, and merchants, too, wandered, selling trinkets and sometimes food. Boys played rough games as well, until they were chased out by the bishop's servants. Crispin often thought of the Scripture where Jesus drove the merchants from the temple and just as often wondered why the bishop did not do the same.

Crispin headed toward the church and trotted up the steps, walking in under the arch into the dim interior. He dipped his fingers into the icy holy water from the font and sketched a cross over his brow.

Just as he imagined, men were moving within the open nave under the vaulted ceiling and around the columns. They congregated in groups or stood stoically alone, trying for an air of something between eagerness and indifference. He made his way through, meeting the hopeful eyes of the men looking for employment but giving them only a slight bow in return. Ahead stood the statue of Saint Paul, and Crispin stood opposite, leaning against a pillar, pretending to do his prayers while keeping an eye trained on the statue.

Flamel appeared out of the shadows of the cathedral's archway and walked through the nave. He found the statue and fumbled his way, depositing the ransom between the feet of the effigy. He stepped back and moved jerkily across the nave again, looking over his shoulder, until he disappeared out the door again beyond Crispin's sight.

Men moved near the effigy, but none went directly to it. Crispin settled in, watching his breath fog around his face. The noon bell for Sext startled him. It reverberated above his head from the aerie reaches of the bell tower. The sounds resonated along Paul's Walk and gamboled up into the vaulted ceiling high overhead. Crispin didn't move, waiting anxiously now, eyes darting throughout the gloomy nave for anyone who showed an interest in the effigy of Saint Paul.

Could he have missed him? He hoped he had not been so foolish as to let the opportunity slip through his fingers.

The last stroke of the bell echoed throughout the cavernous nave, pinging from column to column and settling into a muted tone that disappeared into the dim, arched ceiling. A lone figure approached the statue, heading directly for it. His spurs clinked with each step on the square tiles, and even in the low light Crispin could see the fine material of his long cloak that hid his frame while his face was shadowed under a chaperon hood.

Crispin moved. Cautiously he drew nearer, eyes now riveted to the back of the man who stopped before the statue of Saint Paul in its tall niche, looking up at it. The man checked slyly over his shoulder, first to his left and then his right, before stepping up to the very foot of the statue.

Softly, Crispin drew his dagger. He made certain his steps were quiet.

The man reached forward to the effigy and stuck his hand deep between the stone feet.

In an instant, Crispin's dagger was at the man's neck and he stuck his face near his hooded ear. "Do not move. Do not cry out."

The man stiffened, his hand still poised beneath the statue.

"Slowly," said Crispin. "Take your hand out, but keep them both where I can see them."

The man did as told, his gloved hand empty and his other hovering waist high, surely itching to grab his own dagger.

With his knife still at the man's neck, Crispin spun him to get a look at the knave who had killed, had abducted the innocent wife of the alchemist.

His dagger fell to the floor in a shock of metal on tile. Heads turned toward them, but Crispin never noticed. His gaze was fixed on the man before him, who was looking back at him with an air of annoyance.

"What game are you playing now, Crispin?" asked Henry, Lord Derby.

six

hat… what are you doing here, your grace?" Crispin looked toward the niche and the velvet pouch he could just see under the statue's shadow. But then his gaze traveled back to the man before him.

Henry gazed at him mildly, his eyes flicking to the dagger on the floor. "Pick up your weapon, Crispin. And for God's sake, sheathe it."

Stiffly, Crispin crouched and retrieved his blade, absently shoving it in its scabbard. Mouth dry, heart pounding, he faced Henry again. "What are you doing here?" All other questions seemed to have been chased from his mind. This was the only question he wanted, *needed,* to know the answer to.

Henry smiled, but it didn't make it to his eyes. "Why, I am merely paying my respects to Saint Paul. What else would I be doing?"

Crispin peered over his shoulder at the many men in the nave, some still regarding them with curious or alarmed expressions. His mind snapped back to the problem. Henry had clearly been reaching for the ransom. He had known it was there. And the only reason for knowing it was there was that he had told Flamel to put it there.

His voice was hoarse when he finally said, "My lord, what were you doing at this particular statue… at this particular time of day?"

Henry's expression had been placid, but as Crispin observed, it slowly darkened. His eyes shuttered, became unreadable. "My time is my own, Crispin. I need not detail my itinerary to anyone. Even you."

"It is just that... just that... God's blood, Henry. I know why you are here. You must tell me the truth!"

"I *must?*" His voice took on the quality of his father's. With a simple lowering of a brow and the stern pronouncement of one word, he could make it plain that he was the son of a duke and Crispin was far lower. "Master Guest, I do not think that I *must* do anything of the kind."

"M-my lord," he tried again. Instinct made him lower his eyes, but his own pride made him raise them again and his chin as well. "My lord, a man was brutally murdered and another man's innocent wife is in the hands of a foul abductor, awaiting a ransom left here at the foot of this statue. What can you tell me of these monstrous events?"

Henry's expression never wavered. "Indeed? Interesting tidings, Crispin. What makes you think I would have any knowledge of such doings?"

"Because you are here!" he hissed, losing patience, heart aching at the same time. "And you knew where the ransom was kept."

"Did I?"

"Yes! Why are you toying with me? I caught you in the act of seizing it. For the love of all the saints, Henry, tell me."

"I do not know your meaning, Master Guest." The formality drew thick around him, like a cloak of ermine. It reminded Crispin that Henry was no longer the boy he had known, with flushed cheeks and ready hugs for his household companion. He was a man of duty now, a man with great responsibilities and the power to back it up.

"And know this," he went on in a cool, emotionless tone. "Remember to whom you are speaking." He stepped closer, his face so close to Crispin's that Crispin could count the freckles on his nose. He spoke with a steady whisper. "Do not get in my way or you shall regret it." He dealt one last look of finality, turned on his heel, and stalked away.

Crispin let out his breath in one long cloud. With his heart breaking, he watched Henry retreat. Surely not. Surely Henry was not involved in murder and abduction. But Henry was a powerful lord. He was the head of these commissioners, above even that of his own uncle, the duke of Gloucester. Did it have to do with this commission? What if he should need an army of his own, as the sheriffs hinted at? He would need money for such a venture. And to extort such funds from a French citizen seemed rich indeed. Yes, soldiers were not above taking noblemen for ransom, even killing their retainers to do it. But to abduct Madam Flamel seemed outrageous. Yet Henry must have known of the stone broach, else why choose this secretive man, this alchemist? The stone came from King Charles of France. Was it because of the broach's provenance?

Feeling sick in his gut and in his heart, Crispin turned to leave but stopped and noticed with some small relief that the velvet bag was still there. For all Henry's posturing, he had not bothered to take it. Had he been embarrassed to do so in front of Crispin? Crispin took it and placed it into his scrip.

He trudged through the dirty snow back to Fleet Ditch, looking at no one, mind a whirl. The alchemist's shop came into view and he knocked hesitantly on the door. It flung open and Avelyn was there. She grabbed his arm and dragged him in.

The room had been straightened, debris removed and furniture put back to what it once was. Flamel sat at his worktable, but it didn't look as if he was working. He raised his head, an anxious expression parting his dry lips.

Crispin bowed his head. "He… failed to arrive." From inside his pouch, he brought up the velvet bag and laid it gently on the table. Flamel stared at it. "But we must not give up, Master Flamel. There is more to learn. I will discover her whereabouts and return her unharmed to you. That, I vow."

Flamel shot to his feet. "*Mon Dieu! Vierge Marie,* what shall I do? *Ma chère* Perenelle! *Maître* Guest! I fear greatly for her life. What must I do? Help me, please!"

"Master Flamel, you must gird yourself, sir. All is not lost." He hoped. He did not yet know Henry's game, but he would soon learn it. And he hadn't forgotten the preacher's words. That man knew something, too. Were they working together? It seemed an absurd notion, but Crispin had encountered far stranger things in the past. He'd find out more when next he spoke to Jack Tucker.

Out of the corner of his eye, he saw Avelyn take the discarded velvet bag and slip the stone from it, but it was not the sapphire broach Crispin had seen before. Like a flash of lightning, his hand shot out and closed over her wrist. He squeezed tight, forcing her hand open, and a plain piece of river stone lay there. "Master Flamel!" He snatched the stone from her hand and held it up to him. "What is this deception?"

The alchemist's eyes widened like bezants. "Oh. I... I hoped to buy us time."

"Buy you time? By giving your extortionist a false ransom?"

He looked toward Avelyn as if she could help him. She answered by kicking Crispin in the shin.

"Ow! You bitch!" He grabbed her before she could escape and slapped her across the face. She was momentarily off balance but soon righted herself and turned her face obstinately back at him... before stomping on his foot.

He stumbled backward. "Dammit! Stop that!"

Wrestling her arm free of him, she glared. His handprint on her cheek changed from pink to red.

"Call off your mastiff," he growled.

Flamel moved like a much older man around the table and rested his hands on her shoulders. His mere touch seemed to calm her, and her tensed shoulders dropped back to their normal posture. But she still glared at Crispin.

"She seems to know what we are saying," he said, watching her warily. His foot and shin both throbbed.

Flamel sighed. "She reads the movement of our lips. She can understand both French and English, possibly other languages as well, though she cannot hear them. Very accomplished is my Avelyn. I do not know how or when she learned it."

"But you speak to her with your hands."

"Yes. It was *she* who taught *me* that."

He looked at her anew and she offered a smug smile. It seemed she *did* know what they were saying. He gave her a sneer in return.

"Be that as it may," said Crispin, moving out of range of Avelyn's feet, "I do not understand why you would risk the life of your wife with a false ransom. How did you hope to buy time with a simple stone instead of the valuable jewel he wanted? This might have angered him, forced his hand."

"You don't understand, *Maître* Guest."

"No, I don't. And I like all this even less. You are keeping information from me, and that might cost Madam Flamel her life. If you do not wish to aid me, then there is little I can do for you."

The alchemist wrung his hands. "If only I could explain it all, *Maître*. But I cannot. There are ancient secrets that must be kept. Alchemists swear oaths to keep these secrets sacred. Even for the life of my dear Perenelle, I may not divulge all. She would surely understand that. If only you could believe me. And trust me. Please. You must help me."

Crispin raked his fingers through his hair. "I don't know how to help you if you will not tell me the truth." Though he, too, was keeping secrets from Flamel. For could Henry of Bolingbroke be both a murderer and an abductor?

No. He refused to believe it. Though he had often allowed the people he trusted to deceive him, he was also a good judge of character, and this did not fit in with Henry's character at all. He was as wealthy as they came. He wouldn't need to extort an expensive broach from some unknown alchemist. Even if that broach did come from the King of France. Henry *was* in charge of an army. And even if he needed an additional one, one for himself for selfish purposes, he still wouldn't need another man's money to do it. No, something else was afoot here. Something more. If Flamel would not tell him, he would find it out for himself.

He breathed, calming down. "Very well. Since the exchange did not go as planned, we must await a message from the abductor. I believe it will be soon." Avelyn had moved closer to Flamel and was petting his arm soothingly. Crispin tapped the table in front of her and she looked up at him. "Take care of your master," he said. He was amazed when she nodded.

"Master Flamel, I must go. Alert me when you receive another message. Do nothing until you talk to me."

"Yes, *Maître*. I swear I will."

Crispin nodded, bowed, and left.

He stood in the street, inhaling deeply of the heavy cold. Now that he thought on it, Henry's visit to the Shambles seemed even stranger. Had he been trying to warn Crispin? Or trying to see what he knew? But this was before the dead man was discovered or the note about the ransom. The uncertainty gave him a headache.

50

He walked on, and when he finally turned the corner of the Shambles, he halted. Both sheriffs sat in their saddles. Their horses bowed their heads, snuffling for dead grass through the snow. The sheriffs' gazes fell on Crispin, but they did not beckon him. What else would they be doing in the Shambles except to watch him? Did they not trust he would do his best to find the killer? They'd seen him accomplish as much before and were as ungrateful each time.

He bowed slightly to them and they pointedly turned away, refusing to acknowledge him. "Whoresons," Crispin muttered, and continued on to his lodgings.

He made a quick stop at a meat pie seller, handing over his coins and taking the greasy pastry in exchange. The pie warmed his fingers and he was grateful for that as he trudged up the stairs, hoping Jack would be there. But when he opened the door, he found Avelyn stoking his fire instead. "God's blood!" How had she gotten here so fast? He stomped toward her and she turned, perhaps sensing his steps through the floor. The fire lit a halo of her already fair hair. Her eyes took him in and a small smile graced her face. She still looked elfin, like a changeling, yet he could appreciate her more feminine charms. And she was using them, either consciously or as part of her nature. Much softer than he intended, he asked, "Why are you here? You should be by your master, easing his anxiety."

She smiled and simply knelt by the fire. He noticed she had a pot of wine steaming there and grabbed the pot's handle with the rolled-up hem of her apron and poured its contents into a bowl. How had she accomplished so much in so little time? She must have raced here when Crispin left the alchemist.

With a smile, she offered the bowl to him. Disconcerted, he took it reluctantly. "Yes… thank you." He sipped the hot wine. It felt good as it warmed. He set it aside and sat on his chair, leaning toward her. "You must not stay." She turned to the fire again and he tapped her shoulder. "I say, you must not stay. You must return to your master. He needs you."

She shook her head and got up on her knees, touching his to keep herself steady. Her fingers fluttered as she tried to speak her hand language, but he closed his larger hands over her petite ones. "No. I don't understand you."

She sighed and clasped her delicate fingers together. After merely looking at him for a long moment, she rose again and made more motions, seemed to act out something, but it still made no sense to Crispin.

"I'm sorry. But I do not understand you. I thank you for the wine, but it might be best to return to—" She laid her fingers to his lips. When he stopped speaking, the fingers slowly withdrew. She touched the bowl, made a motion with her fingers, and then waited. She repeated and waited again expectantly.

"Are you... trying to teach me?" She made the motion a third time and, tentatively, he imitated it.

A broad smile broke out on her face and she repeated the motion. He did a better job of imitating her and she clapped her hands. She jumped to her feet and pointed to the hearth, making a motion with her fingers. And then she pointed to the candle flame. Her fingers meant "fire," he supposed, and, feeling slightly foolish, he made the motion back. She smiled again and treated many objects in the room in the same way, going to the next only when he made the correct motion.

The strange language intrigued him. He'd always enjoyed learning languages, and this was no different. He marveled at the simplicity of the movements, which reminded him of some of the dancing movements he'd seen in miracle plays. She cupped her hand for the bowl, she wiggled her fingers to represent fire or flames, the same movement only downward represented water. Over and over she'd teach him simple words, the movements a poetic accompaniment to each object she'd encounter.

She laughed her braying laugh again and settled with a flourish of skirts at his feet, hands resting on his knees.

"Where do you come from?" he said to her when she looked up at him with laughing eyes. "Did you come from France?"

She nodded, hands still on his knees. He looked down at her tapered fingers curled around his joints. She tapped his knee and made a motion. He repeated, for if he didn't, she would repeat it endlessly as if he were a dim child.

She sat up and slid her hands from his knees over his thighs. Her smile was softer and her eyes shadowed by her lashes. She tapped his leg and made a sign. He repeated it.

She scooted closer, touched his chest, and made the sign. She did not wait for him to repeat it when she reached up and touched his lips. She quickly made the sign with her other hand but did not take her fingers away. The fingers began a slow caress. He gave her a small smile and gently took her wrist, removing her hand. But as soon as he released her, her fingers were back, touching his lips and then his chin, the pads of her fingers catching on the stubble.

She withdrew a moment to touch her chest and made the sign of her name.

His voice was roughened when he pointed to himself. "I am Crispin."

She made a sign for it and he repeated it.

She touched her lips and then touched his and made a sign.

"I don't understand."

She repeated the sign, repeated touching her lips and then his. He could not help but lean forward. "I'm sorry. I don't think… I don't understand."

Her hand closed on his coat and dragged him forward. He nearly fell out of his chair when she pulled him farther until his lips touched hers. Startled, he tried to pull away, but her grip on his coat was surprisingly strong. She was gentle as their mouths slid together and then, teasingly, barely touched.

"Avelyn," he murmured, lips tingling against her nibbling mouth. He took her upper arms in a gentle grasp, trying to push her back. "Avelyn, you shouldn't be here." She should be with her master. This was foolish. But the softness of her mouth, moving gently, patiently, over his, as patient as the motions and signs she taught him, grew captivating. Their noses prodded each other. He held his breath when she angled her head and pressed more firmly, hot breath searing his mouth. His lids drifted closed. Slowly, she opened her lips with maddening tenderness. Her tongue caressed. He resisted, but she swiped her tongue over his mouth again before snaking it forward, breaching the seam of his lips. She barely touched the tip of her tongue to his, but all at once, it seemed to be the invitation

Crispin was waiting for. His arms enveloped her and he opened his mouth to cover hers.

He inhaled her warm scent and clenched his eyes, feeling little but their wet brush of tongues and the warmth of her breath on his cheek.

Her fingers unwound from his coat and slid up his chest, arms moving around his neck. Her body was suddenly pressed tight to the length of his. Small breasts crushed against his chest, and her spindly arms embraced. He pulled her up until he was sitting back against the chair and she was standing between his spread legs.

They kissed deeply with a mutual need that sent Crispin's senses spiraling upward. Lips and mouths slid together and they knew nothing but each other's breath and taste, felt their two bodies react to each other. His hands eased over her shoulders, back, buttocks.

He stood and held fast to her lithe frame, holding her so that her feet lifted from the floor. She was so small, like a child, and her kisses, too, were like a child's in their sweetness while at the same time like a woman's in their bold exploration.

He swung her around to the table and laid her down, pushing up her skirts, but she shook her head, rolling it from side to side, nearly toppling the candle. He drew back, perplexed, and she sat up, hopping off. Her wicked smile was back and she curled her fingers over Crispin's belt and dragged him toward the bed.

He followed without complaint and stood over her as she sat on the straw-stuffed mattress. She busily unbuckled his belt and let it fall to the floor, then began on the buttons of his cotehardie from the bottom up, determined, it seemed, to unbutton each and every one slowly but efficiently.

She stood and peeled the coat off his shoulders and let that, too, fall. Digging into the laces of his linen chemise, she spread open the neckline and used both hands to push the fabric up his chest until Crispin took the hint and lifted it over his head himself, letting it join the cotehardie.

Standing in only his braies, stockings, and boots, he reached for her, but she stretched her open hands over his chest, sliding her fingers through his dark chest hair before they found the many scars puckering his flesh. Her fingers, touching light as a butterfly's wings, skimmed over the knife wounds, the sword cuts, the burn marks of torture.

They told the story of his life, and her fingers moved over them as if reading their tales. He stiffened and didn't move as her hands and fingers paused over each one. Her gaze was intent on his skin with parted mouth, until those large, luminous eyes flicked up to his face.

Her brow furrowed and she gestured as if to ask, "Why?"

He closed his hand over hers and breathed again, holding her small hand against his chest, which was rising and falling vigorously. "I was once a man of great property and responsibility. I was a knight. But I chose an ill-considered path and lost it all."

She pulled her fingers loose from his hand and sketched the scars from the torture of ten years ago. "Yes," he said quietly. "Those were inflicted upon me. They were deserved. I committed treason, after all. But I live, as you can see."

Her face expressed her disbelief, but he offered a grim smile. "It's quite true, I assure you." He sat on the bed beside her. Her head came only to his shoulder. She wore no veil, and he looked down upon the shiny crown of her hair. It was gathered in one large plait at the back of her neck. He lifted it, feeling the heavy, silky braid. He wrapped it around his wrist, toying with it.

She reached around, grabbed the end of the braid, and slowly began to unwind it.

He watched her for some moments. Each strand of hair that was freed kinked and lay raggedly on her shoulder. His fingers found them and he ran the silken strands over the calluses on his palms and fingertips. "I know nothing about you," he said, though she wasn't watching his lips as he said it, so he knew she could not "hear" him. "You are from France, but that is all I know. I don't know your age or your family or… anything else."

She pulled her fingers through her hair, loosening it all, and shook it out. White hair, fine like spun silk, drifted over his hands, a waterfall of elfin silver. He twisted it in his fist and bent her head back, leaned in, and kissed her again. Her fingernails ran hard over his bare skin, raising gooseflesh.

He drew back. His fingers caressed her face where the red mark from his hand was fading. "I'm sorry for this."

She blinked slowly and looked up at him with drowsy lids, breath slipping over her parted lips. Her tongue poked out and licked them to dampness, and he decided to speak no more.

He unbuttoned her cotehardie, laying open the rough-spun material and pushing it down her shoulders. She shifted to slip it farther. He didn't wait. He attacked the laces of her chemise and opened it wide, reaching in with his hands and closing them on her small white breasts.

His face fell to her neck, nuzzling the musky scent of her. The fine strands of her hair fell over his nose and cheeks. She was silent, except for her ragged breathing and small sighs.

seven

The captive looked up as the pale man returned, stomping through the dark room. His hands scrambled over the shelf, making noises of wood against stone, until a spark struck and he moved back within her vision and lit the cold hearth.

"Well," he said. His tone conveyed anger, and anger was the one thing she did not wish to cause. "So. We are delayed." He stood up from his ministering to the fire and turned, looking down at her. "Shall we see about food?"

"Please," she said softly. "You must let me go. There is no profit in this, you know it."

"Profit? Oh, but you are wrong. There is indeed great profit. More than you realize. Yet there are... forces... in my way. But that is no matter to you. What matters is, you must be hungry."

She hated that jovial tone that masked his ire. It was a false beguilement, and for its strangeness it seemed more terrifying than his anger.

He continued to move about behind her, outside her vision. She tried to turn, to see what he was about, but she could not twist that way in her bindings. He dragged something to the table—a sack—and drew something out. She heard him sawing on it. Bread, she hoped. But water would be better. She was so thirsty, and she had been alone for so long.

"Your soul, then," she said softly, licking her dry lips. "Your soul does not profit from this."

"What do I care of that? God will deal with me one way or

another." The sawing went on. More sounds. Liquid being poured into a wooden cup. She licked her lips again. It smelled like sweet ale.

"Now then." He moved to crouch in front of her. His eyes tracked over her face in so familiar a gesture, it almost made her weep. Weep more than she had. At first she had wept for the sight of him, and then for all that came after. "You must be thirsty," he said. He seemed oblivious to her turmoil. "But just to make this interesting, let us see if you deserve this ale."

"Please. For the love of our Lady…"

"Now, now." He raised one hand in a gesture of silence. In his other hand, he clutched the cup. She could see the glimmer of the foamy liquid within. "This will be amusing." He set the cup behind her again on the table and took a deck of cards from the scrip on his hip. They seemed newly printed, like the finely carved block-printed decks she had seen before in Paris. The reverse design was Moorish, and the deck itself was clean and unmarred. "Tell me what the card is on the top of this deck, and I shall grant you a drink."

She shook her head. "I am no seer."

"It's only a game, *Madame*. Come. Play with me. Look, I'll make it even easier. You just tell me the suit. Coins, cups, swords, or batons? That's a twenty-five percent chance. Much better than most people get. Much better than I got." His eyes gleamed with a malicious glint, with memories that should have been long forgotten but had, instead, festered.

He tapped the deck with his finger. "Tell me."

"I don't want to play this game. Please. Just give me the ale. I thirst."

"But you must play. Play the game with me. Coins, cups, swords, or batons? Come now, beautiful *Madame*. Tell me."

She inhaled a shaky breath, twisting her wrists in the bindings. Already the flesh was raw when she had strained, trying to free herself when he was gone.

"I would not have imagined this of you," she whimpered.

"Did you not? Well. Then you did not know me at all." He rubbed at his clean-shaven chin. His small eyes glimmered, but his smile did not reach them. She could tell by the tense set of his heavy brows, by his teeth digging into his lip, that he was pretending a calm he did not feel. He shoved the cards nearly under her nose. "Choose."

"I don't know." She struggled to look back at the ale on the table, but she couldn't see it. "Please!"

"Tell me!"

"Swords!" she cried, sobbing. The first thing to come into her mind was a weapon to slay him with.

He relaxed and sat back on his heels. The cards lay on his palm, and with his other hand, he slipped the topmost card off the pile. Pinching it between two fingers, he turned it over. Two of cups. "A pity. You lose. No ale for you."

She moaned and more tears spilled from her eyes.

He put the card under the deck and rested his fingers on the top again. "Shall we see if you get any bread now?"

eight

Spent, with a sheen of sweat cooling on his skin, Crispin lay back on the bed with Avelyn tucked into the crook of his neck. She was signing again, giggling as she showed him new words for impolite things.

She must have felt him chuckle against her face, and she raised her head. Her silvery blond hair lay in disarray over her shoulders, framing her petite breasts and small, round belly. Her smile was bright. Pearly teeth caught the firelight. "Who are you?" He felt soft and warm against her, and utterly relaxed. He pointed to her chest and enunciated. "Who... are... *you?*"

She frowned and signed the motion for "Avelyn." He shook his head. "No. Who is..." And he made the sign for her name instead of pointing.

She seemed especially pleased by that and leaned in quickly to kiss his mouth. His hand slid along her flank, down her hip, and over the swell of her bum before she drew beyond his reach when she pulled swiftly back, sitting cross-legged. She did not seem burdened by the cold, sitting naked, clothed only in her long hair. Shadows hid her privities, though irregular wavering hearth light lit in brief flickers the tuft of ash blond curls directly below her belly. He watched her with languid eyes.

Her hands tried to explain, but he was not versed in the intricacies of her alien language. He allowed her frustration for several slow breaths before he grabbed her and pulled her back against him. "No more talking," he said to the top of her head. "With your hands or without." He tilted up her chin and repeated himself to her bright gaze. "No more talking. You must leave soon to return to your master. What if he received a message while you were gone?"

She blew out a sigh and began signing again. He closed a hand over hers. "No more. Sleep a little, eh?"

She tried to continue to sign, but his hand squeezed hers and he pulled her down beside him. His eyes drifted shut.

Crispin awoke sometime in the middle of the night. Avelyn still lay beside him, and in the light of the glowing ashes, he saw the shape of Jack Tucker, snuggled down in his pile of straw in the opposite corner.

He should have sent her on her way instead of selfishly holding her to him. There was little to be done about it now. He wanted to hear Jack's news as well, but that would also have to wait. He lay back and stared up into the gloom of the rafters. Avelyn stirred, mewling like a kitten, and suddenly her bright eyes opened and she moved, propping her chin on his chest.

"You shouldn't be here," he whispered.

She merely smiled under heavy-lidded eyes. Still keeping his gaze, she bent her head and kissed his chest, lips trailing over his flesh until she reached a nipple and took it between her teeth. He hissed at the sensation that shot to his belly and lower. Eyes darting quickly toward Jack, still snoring, he grasped the blanket and threw it over their heads before he nuzzled his face into the warm softness of her body.

Crispin yawned into the rosy light of morning drifting in through the shutters. Jack stood stiffly, pissed into the chamber pot beside his bed of straw, and scratched his backside. Yawning as he finished his business, he shuffled toward the fire and picked up the poker. Sleepily, he jabbed it into the ashes before leaning it against the hearth and grabbing a small square of peat and a few sticks. He placed them on the glowing coals and blew on it until it sparked to a quick flame. More sticks and one of Henry's quartered logs made for cozy warmth and light.

It was then that Avelyn jumped out of bed and stretched her small limbs. She was naked and the firelight flickered over her pale, smooth skin.

Jack's head snapped toward her and his jaw dropped open and remained that way as, unconcerned, she stretched again and languidly bent to pull on her shift.

Crispin shivered at the cold and tugged on his own shirt, forcing himself out of bed. He stood with his backside toward the fire. "Morning, Jack."

"Good morn, M-Master Crispin. Er…"

She offered a lazy smile and a wink to Jack and leaned her head against Crispin's chest as they both stood by the fire, warming themselves.

"Should I… er…"

"You should heat the water," said Crispin with a smile.

"Erm… right." Jack scrambled for the bucket by the door, broke through the thin layer of ice, and poured a splashing dollop into an iron pot. He dragged the cauldron to the fire, kicked the trivet over the flames, and set the pot atop it.

He turned back to them, staring, eyes traveling particularly over Avelyn and her shift, which was not as opaque as Crispin would have liked.

Crispin tapped her shoulder. "Your gown. Are you not cold?"

She smirked and bent to retrieve Crispin's braies and stockings, balled them into a bundle, and shoved them into his hands. Next she retrieved her own cotehardie and shook it out before shrugging into it.

Crispin casually donned his braies and then the stockings, tying each to the linen underwear.

With her undone buttons still gaping her gown, Avelyn handed Crispin his cotehardie and helped him slip an arm in each sleeve. She took her time buttoning it up, from the hem, lingering at his groin, then up his torso, and at last to his throat.

"Thank you," he said, and finger-spoke it at the same time. She kissed him as a reward, and Jack made a squeak.

"What's that, Tucker?"

"I… uh… I…"

"How's that water coming?"

His eyes flicked to the steaming cauldron while Avelyn took up the chamber pot and retreated outside and downstairs, presumably to the privy in the back garden.

"What's she doing here?" he rasped as the door closed. Crispin gave him a lopsided grin and Tucker scowled. "Never mind. I can see for myself."

Crispin chuckled.

"So you can speak her finger language now, eh? Amazing what a night of concentration will do for a man."

He cuffed the boy good-naturedly, and Jack chuckled with him.

"Just a few words," said Crispin. "Not enough to have a proper conversation, as I suspect she was trying to do." He frowned. "But you had your own course yesterday. Tell me, what did you discover?"

With a cloth wrapped around the pot's bail handle, Jack lifted the cauldron from the fire and poured half of the water into the shaving basin. He returned the pot to the fire and shuffled to the back window where the wine jug sat, took it to the fire, and poured some into the remaining hot water.

"Well," he said, swirling the water and wine in the pot. The steam curled around his face. "I returned to that preacher fellow and listened to more wailing and accusations. I don't know if he's right, sir. I don't know if a man will go to Hell if he don't take the path he was talking about. I mean, men like us, we do our best, do we not?"

"That is true, Jack. We do our best, we say our prayers, we ask forgiveness of the Almighty, and we serve the least of our brothers. What more *can* a man do?"

"Just so. But that man didn't have no good words for nobody. According to him, we're all going to Hell, no matter what."

"That may be true for some, Jack. For those who do not repent."

Jack glanced over his shoulder toward the door just as Avelyn returned. "Repent, eh?" He grinned.

Crispin was tempted to snap his belt at the boy but buckled

it around his waist instead. He unbuttoned the sleeves of his coat, pushed up his shirtsleeves, and dipped his cupped hands into the basin of hot water, sluicing his face. He reached for the soap cake and the razor, but Avelyn was faster and urged him to sit.

Jack looked on amused as he poured the hot watered wine into two bowls. He sipped his and slid the other near Crispin. Crispin first offered it to Avelyn, who shook her head vigorously while she readied his razor.

Jack gestured with his steaming bowl. "Do you suppose she knows what she's doing?"

Crispin sipped the warmed wine, savoring the heat. "We'll soon see. Either I will be well shaved or no longer burdened of this workaday world."

Jack hovered, suddenly looking worried. Crispin kept his expression neutral as the woman, with fierce concentration, steadily ran the razor over his soaped-up jawline.

"You were telling me of the preaching man, Jack."

"Oh, aye." He sat back, sipped his wine, and then set the bowl down with his hand still wrapped around it. "Robert Pickthorn is the scoundrel's name. He is a lay preacher. New to London. I followed him as he preached. Didn't even stop to take a piss. He talked on and on. And then he just... disappeared."

"What do you mean?"

"The crowd had gathered, he said his piece, and then, even as I watched, he slipped away."

Crispin jerked in his seat. Deftly, Avelyn took the razor away from his skin before he cut himself. He pushed her back and wiped his face with a rag. "He what?"

"I'm sorry, Master, but he got away. I questioned all and sundry, but no one had seen him go and none knew where he lives. I searched and searched."

"And when was it that he disappeared, Jack? What time of day?"

"Well, let me think." He scratched his head. "Round about Sext, by the church bells ringing not long thereafter." He looked up, alert. "What of the ransom drop, sir? What happened? After I searched for the whoreson, I returned to Master Flamel's shop in the hopes that you would be there, but you had gone. He said… he said the man had failed to show. Is that what happened, sir?"

Crispin stood at the table and consumed the rest of his now luke-warm wine. "Not exactly. Someone did come to claim the ransom."

Jack finished and set his bowl aside. "Well? Who was it?"

The sick sensation swooped in his belly again. "It was Henry Bolingbroke," he said, voice rough.

"Oh, Master! It couldn't have been."

With a surge of frustration, he heaved his wooden bowl into a corner. Wine fanned across the table. The bowl clattered against the floor, spun, and finally came to rest. "It *was* him, dammit! Don't you think I know my own—" Family? Charge? Whatever it was he meant to say died in the smoky room.

"But why, sir?"

"I don't know. I… I confronted him. He told me in so many words to back off. That I was not seeing what I thought I was seeing, or some such nonsense. He claimed to know nothing of the ransom, but he was there, Jack, at the statue with his hand there at Saint Paul's feet, as guilty as any rogue. He knew. I know he did."

Jack slumped onto his stool. "Blind me." He shook his head in disbelief and stared at the floor.

He and Crispin both looked over at Avelyn as she noisily mopped up the spilled wine and retrieved the upturned bowl. She turned it in her hands, looking for cracks, he presumed. Satisfied, she returned it to the pantry shelf and waited, looking only at Crispin.

"You must go home now, Avelyn." He made the hand movements for "home." Jack watched, rapt.

She stubbornly shook her head and made a series of signs.

"I don't understand you," he growled. He took her by the shoulders and propelled her roughly toward the door. "You must leave!"

She shook him off and gritted her teeth in frustration. She looked around the room and ran from corner to corner, etching more signs on the walls with her fingers.

"She's gone mad," said Jack in a whisper.

"She is trying to tell me something, but I don't have time to deci-pher it." He ran his hand over his face. He had passed quite a pleasant night with her. It cheered his heart and made some of the pain go away, but now the light of day had arrived and the fancies of the night were best forgotten.

Night. He looked at his apprentice, who kept his eyes on the young woman. "Where were you most of the night, Jack?"

"I was at Master Flamel's, sir. I thought I should await a message from the abductor since the ransom was not taken."

"And was there a message?"

"No, sir. None. And Master Flamel was having a right fit. I spent most of the night calming him down. I thought to spend the night, as Avelyn had not returned.…'Course, now I see why. But I thought you would want me back, so though it was late, I returned. But Master Crispin, if it *was* Lord Henry in St. Paul's to collect the ransom and you caught him at it—"

"I am not convinced he is involved."

"Oh. Well. Perhaps. But if not him, then who?"

"I don't know. They want this precious stone. And yet Flamel exchanged the ransom for one of no value. He told me it was to buy time, but that is a very unsatisfactory answer."

"Wait," said Jack, eyes pinging back and forth between Avelyn's still frantic movements and Crispin's stillness. "Why would Lord Henry have need for a valuable commodity such as that broach? He has his own wealth, almost as rich as the duke."

"I know. I did wonder that, too. Which makes me all the more convinced that Henry had little to do with it."

"A coincidence his being there, then?"

"No, not a coincidence. I don't believe in those."

"What, then?"

"I haven't worked it out yet, Jack. What of this Robert Pickthorn? He left about the time the ransom was to be collected."

"Did you see him at the cathedral, sir?"

He slammed his fist to the table. "I must admit, once I laid eyes upon Henry I did not look anywhere else. He could have been there and I missed it. But once I left, I took the ransom with me. The false ransom, that is."

"'Buy him time.' What could that mean?"

"I don't know. Best to— Will you stop that, you insufferable woman!"

But of course, Avelyn could not hear him as she continued her strange dramatics. Finally, she threw herself at his feet, hiked up her skirts, and lay on the floor.

Jack backed away. "What is she doing now? Is it a fit?"

But Crispin finally looked. She had positioned herself upside down, head at his feet, with one leg crooked behind the other… just as the dead apprentice had looked. "Jack, she's showing us Thomas Cornhill."

"The dead man?"

"Yes."

Once she saw that Crispin understood, she jerked her head in a nod, jumped to her feet, and began to repeat her wall drawing in the corners.

"Wait. Jack, those drawings. She is trying to show us something of those symbols. I have seen them in several spots throughout London." Two strides took him across the room. He grabbed her arms and spun her to face him. To her eyes he said carefully, "Avelyn, what is it you wish to show me?"

She made a huffing noise and nodded, satisfied at last. Grabbing her cloak from the peg, she cast open the door, and headed quickly down the stairs.

Crispin looked at Jack, and as one, they both grabbed their cloaks and bolted after her.

She ran through the gently falling snow, her footsteps disappearing as she fled over the whitened streets. They ran after her, and when she stopped at a corner, pointing at the carvings in the wood, Crispin knew he had been right. It was possible she had tried to get him to understand her last night, tried to make him go out to show him, but she had distracted him, as a pretty face was wont to do. Careless, to be so distracted when a woman's life was at stake.

When the preacher Robert Pickthorn pointed out the sigils as the Devil's work and looked directly at Crispin and described a man hanging by his heel, that's when he had made the tenuous leap that the symbols might be related to the apprentice's death and to Madam Flamel's disappearance. But was it warranted?

Avelyn kept prodding the carvings with her finger until he drew nearer, examining them. They did not look like any writing he understood. How many of these were there? And what did they mean?

Before he had a chance to speculate, she grabbed his hand and ran with him down the lane, with Jack close on their heels.

Down lane after lane they trotted, until finally she pointed ahead to a stone archway and pulled Crispin up to it. His fingers traced the etchings. Different from the ones before. And someone had tried to scratch these out.

She tried to grab him and pull him again, but Crispin stopped her, turned her to him. "Avelyn, do you know what these mean? Do they have to do with Madam Perenelle?"

She didn't seem certain but insisted he follow. "Wait, wait, Avelyn. Please." She stopped and looked at him questioningly, blinking the snow from her pale lashes. "I need a way to decipher these. Can you help me?"

She thought a moment, gnawing on one of her red-chapped knuckles. Her eyes brightened and she grabbed his sleeve again, pulling him along. He took her hand from his sleeve and smiled. "I *can* follow, you know."

She laughed that rough, alien laugh and hurried forward, looking back from time to time to make certain that he was there.

Jack came up beside him, eyes on Avelyn. "She's a ball of fire, isn't she?"

"Indeed," he said with more passion than he meant to reveal.

Tucker laughed. "You do find them, don't you, Master? Or they manage to find you. Ah me. You expend your energies teaching me languages and how to read and write. But surely you can spare the time to tutor me in this, sir."

"You're a knave, Tucker. I have no wish to be your whoremaster."

Jack laughed again. Avelyn frowned when she turned back to look at them. Impatiently, she tapped her foot.

She proceeded on and they grew quiet as they moved through the streets full of citizens at their daily tasks. A man moved his oxcart by tapping the beasts with a stick on the oxen's rumps. Under an ale stake jutting into the street, servants shouted the praises of their master's alehouse. A pelt merchant held aloft his wares hanging from racks on poles and he walked up and down the avenue, carrying it like a banner into battle. The food merchants, the water carriers, the servants hauling fuel upon braces on their backs. Through all of that, Crispin still noticed them. The shadowy figures trailing along the edges, slipping into the alleys, standing in the closes. Shadows that followed them no matter what street they turned down. He elbowed Jack and gave a flick of his head. The boy was quick to get his meaning and take notice. Surreptitiously, they both watched the figures follow. Crispin counted three and opened that number of fingers in his hand at his flank on the side facing Jack, tapping them until the boy saw and barely nodded.

Three, then. Crispin allowed Avelyn to lead him. He hoped it wasn't to a trap.

They wove through the people down a narrow lane, and Avelyn finally stopped before a door. Above the lintel hung a wooden sign covered with snow. A symbol was painted on both sides of its worn surface:

Crispin moved toward the door, but Jack held him back. "Master Crispin," he whispered. He eyed the sign fearfully, almost afraid to take his eyes from it. "You're not going in there, are you? That… that's the Devil's sign."

"Don't be a fool, Tucker. That is the symbol for Mercury, a well-known alchemical sign. She has brought us to another alchemist."

He stepped forward under the creaking wooden sign, feeling a chill as he passed under it, and pushed open the door. A small shop. A curtain covered another doorway. Barring the way stood a sturdy table. More small tables and shelves lined the walls, with canisters and ceramic pots on shelves. A tripod was pushed as far into the hearth as it could go next to the blackened plaster of the wall. On the tripod hung a cauldron on a chain. The contents bubbled with chunks of unidentifiable objects roiling to the surface, only to sink below the shivering liquid. The stench coming from it made him wince. A crucible with dried yellowish matter that smelled of rotten eggs sat on a trivet near a raised hearth that looked more like a forge. Crispin knew it was called an alchemist's athanor, and beside it, a ceramic retort sat on another trivet.

"Is anyone here?" he asked, standing as far from the fire as possible. Jack stood beside him, eyes wide as they scanned the shelves.

Avelyn seemed at home and poked around at the canisters, opening lids or pulling off their canvas drapes to peer inside, sniffing experimentally.

There was a rustle at the curtained doorway. Steps scraped across the floor. The drapes parted and a man, older than Crispin, peered at them. His dark, greasy hair was covered by a felt cap with ear flaps. A dark beard hung from his jaw, and his nose was noticeably uneven and enlarged by carbuncles. His heavy robes were stained and seemed to weigh him down, or perhaps his stooped shoulders and dragging shuffle came from years bent over a workbench, devising his alchemy.

"Yes?" He eyed them with tiny brown eyes set close together under bushy black brows. He never raised his chin fully, perhaps more interested in his compounds than in faces, and clutched the table, which served as a barrier between him and his customers. "What is it you want?" Then his gaze fell on Avelyn. "You! What are *you* doing here?" He cast about for something and found it in a corner: a broom. He took it up and brandished it. "Get out before I chase you out."

Crispin stepped in front of her and frowned down at the crooked man. "There's no call for that. She led me here to you. For information."

He scowled at Crispin and rumbled in his gruff voice, "If you know her, then I can scarce trust you."

"Come, man. If you know her, then you must know her master, Nicholas Flamel."

"Nicholas Flamel? *That* is her master?" He stared at her anew. Admiration bloomed on his features, and the broom lowered.

Alarmed, Avelyn looked from one man to the other and rushed to Crispin, covering his lips with her fingers.

"No, Avelyn. Stop. Yes, you've heard of Master Flamel, then?"

"Of course! What alchemist of any worth will not have heard of Nicholas Flamel! But I did not know he was in England." He almost smiled at Avelyn, though it seemed as if his mouth were unused to such an expression. Avelyn was beside herself, trying to get their attention. She banged on the man's table with the flat of her hand.

Crispin grabbed her and handed her off to Jack. The boy wrapped his large freckled hands around her arms, and though she tried to flail in his grip, he held firm.

"Quit fighting me," he cried. "Or I shall throw you into that foul pot!"

"Foul pot?" said the alchemist.

"Aye, sir," said Jack, motioning to the bubbling cauldron with his head. "That. What manner of alchemy are you making there?"

The alchemist raised his bulbous nose indignantly. "My dinner!"

"Oh. Beg pardon." Jack looked contrite for only a moment… right before Avelyn kicked him in the shin.

He swore and let her loose. Hopping about, he grabbed his leg. "Sarding woman!"

"Yes, I should have warned you," said Crispin. He gave her a stern look and she quieted immediately, crossing her arms over her chest. She turned a glare on Tucker, daring him to approach. He wisely kept his distance.

"Pray, sir," said the alchemist, while frowning at Avelyn, "what brings you here? How can I help you?"

"I am assisting Master Flamel with a… well, a discreet task."

The alchemist's smug smile seemed to indicate that this was expected.

"I am Crispin Guest. And this servant led me here to—"

"Crispin Guest? No! No, no, no. You must leave at once, do you hear? Leave my property!" He raised the broom once more, but this time he looked reluctant to approach.

"But sir!"

"Out with you! Or I shall call in the law."

Irritated, Crispin stiffened. "Very well. There will be no need for that." Though many in London had heard of him and were anxious to assist his course, he knew there were many more that were wary of having anything to do with a traitor to the crown.

He swung toward the door and cast it open, minding not at all as it slammed against the wall. He heard glass breaking behind him with a satisfied smirk.

nine

Crispin heaved a frustrated sigh at the closed door of the alchemist's shop. Avelyn waited beside him, bouncing on her heels. "This was a useless venture," he told her. "He would not talk to me."

She clenched her eyes and shook her head. She kicked the door and bent down, scooped up snow from the porch, and hurled uneven snowballs at it.

He took her arm and pulled her away. "There's no use in doing that. Take us back to your master."

With a lilt to her shoulders, she pointed at yet another set of symbols scrawled on a post, hastily scratched out.

He shook his head. "Take us back to your master."

She kicked the mud with her damp shoe and stomped up the lane, furiously scuffing the dirty snow as she went.

He certainly empathized with her frustration. Perhaps Flamel could translate her petulance. Though he wondered why she had not taken him to Flamel in the first place. Was she trying to hide something from him? And what about Flamel's supposed fame? Even this fellow, this alchemist, seemed to have heard of the Frenchman. Yet when it was mentioned, she had tried to silence him on the matter. Perhaps she had not wished the man to know she was the servant of Nicholas Flamel. If only he could ask her and get an answer.

They reached the Tun and were stopped by a procession. The three of them backed up against a wall out of the way. The procession took up the width of the road, and it was plainly that of a funeral. A young boy in clerical robes, no more than ten or eleven, swung a smoking censer back and forth before him, filling the street with the aroma of musky incense. He was followed by a priest in a dark cassock, reading aloud in Latin from a small Psalter clutched in his gloved hands. Behind him, a man led a horse pulling a cart decorated in black drapery on which lay a shrouded child, dried rose petals sprinkled on her chest. Behind it, people cried softly, and a man comforted a woman wailing openly, stumbling through the snowy lane. The parents.

Children died in London all the time, this he knew. Its streets were treacherous to the young. Women and children drowned in its waterways. A rushing horse might knock over a wayward child with nary a look back.

He couldn't help but glance at Jack. The boy had survived against the odds. Orphaned at eight, so he had said, Jack had been on his own for three years before he'd forced his stubborn way into Crispin's life. He could easily have been just another dead child in the city, another fallen to poverty, to starvation. Crispin shuddered at the thought that such a quick and nimble mind could have been snuffed out, lost to the despair of the streets.

The wail of the mother howled like a wind through the narrow lanes, rising and falling, even as they moved farther on. He supposed this child had succumbed to illness or accident. The occasional eruption of the plague caused panic and fear, though the plague was more likely in the spring, not the dead cold of winter. A terrible waste. A child was always needed to do the work of the household, to learn his father's business, to be married off to cement alliances. But such was the whim of the Almighty. One never knew when He would send His Angel of Death to his task.

Crispin and Jack crossed themselves and lowered their heads, each offering a silent prayer for the soul rising to Heaven. They watched as the procession passed them.

"I hate death," Jack whispered. He sounded more like the uncertain boy Crispin had first encountered nearly four years ago.

"Yes," Crispin agreed. "And yet death is part of our peddler's goods."

"So it would seem. But I never get used to it."

"I pray that you never do."

Avelyn stood at the far crown of the road, clapping at them impatiently.

"Don't she have no respect for the dead?" Jack grumbled.

Crispin set out again, folding his cloak over his chest as the last vestiges of the incense dispersed and the sharp smell of dung and cooking fires returned to fill the lane. "Perhaps she has seen too much of it herself. We all have our pasts."

Jack said nothing more, and they continued on, even as the snow-fall grew heavier. When they arrived at Flamel's shop, Avelyn sprinted ahead and disappeared through the door. Crispin and Jack walked through just as Flamel was admonishing her to "slow down, *fille*. I cannot understand."

"Master Flamel," said Crispin. The man spun. His exasperation with his servant fled and he almost fell into Crispin's arms.

"Where have you been? Have you word of my Perenelle?"

"No. I take it you have not heard from our abductor."

"No. Alas." He sank to a chair. Avelyn was nearly vibrating with the need to speak.

"Your servant seems to wish to convey information to us. I cannot understand her well. Not as well as you. Please. Could you translate?"

He beckoned the girl to him and she knelt at his feet, still a bundle of unspent energy. He signaled his question to her and she began to gesture furiously. Flamel took it all in. Crispin tried to follow with what little knowledge of her language he had acquired. He saw words hurl by: "apprentice," "parchment," "stone," "signs," and many more he could not assimilate.

Once or twice during her fluttering fingers, Flamel turned toward Crispin with a narrowed gaze, especially when she signed the word "kiss." Crispin felt heat rise on his neck, before Avelyn gently touched the alchemist's face to turn him back to her so she could continue with her tale.

At last she seemed to slow. Her movements looked more like questions than explanations, and Flamel waved them off, face turned away from her.

"Master Flamel. What did she say?"

"Mostly nonsense. She is like to say things that are meaningless. You'd best be aware of that, *Maître,* if you intend more congress with her." A whisper of a warning flickered in his eyes. "It is not that she lies, but that the truth is… *quelque peu différente pour elle*… as you would say, not quite the same to her."

"Indeed. Perhaps it is a trait of your vocation, for I do not think *you* value truth quite as I do either."

He chewed his lip. "My English may not be as good as I thought it. Please forgive any errors."

Crispin leaned down, pressing his hands to the chair arms and trapping Flamel in place. "Your English is perfectly serviceable. It is the content that is not. Why do you lie to me? Why do you leave out valuable information that I can use to find your wife? I have learned that you are well-known, Master Flamel, even here in England. Why is that so?"

He wriggled, flustered. "Absurd. I have heard how impetuous you are. It is why you are in your present circumstances, no?"

Crispin straightened. "My history is not important. You hired me to help you. Do you want it or not?"

"Yes," he breathed. "Yes."

"Then tell me what she said."

The old man pressed his fingers to his eyes. "You mean well. But you must forget what you think you know. Beware of what you find."

Crispin snapped his head up and stared at the man. "*What* did you say?" He grabbed him by the collar and hauled him to his feet. "*What did you say?*"

"I… I…"

"Master Crispin!" cried Jack. "What are you doing?"

Flamel's eyes were wide and frightened. There didn't appear to be any deception there, but his words had sent a chill down Crispin's spine. Were those not the exact words, the *last* words, that his old friend Abbot Nicholas uttered to him as he lay dying a year ago? The words that he used, trying to explain why relics and venerated objects came into Crispin's hands?

Crispin spared a glance at Jack, poised between rising and sitting, hands outstretched, a stunned look upon his face.

Crispin looked down at himself, at his hands on Flamel's gown. What was he doing?

Slowly, he unwound his fingers. He released Flamel and stepped back, breath gusting from his heaving chest. The alchemist surely meant no harm. He was fairly certain of that. But those words...

"Forgive me," said Crispin, still breathless. "I... it is just..." He shook his head. "Perhaps... perhaps that is why your servant brought us to another alchemist, for you only wish to speak in riddles where I need facts." He wiped the sweat from his forehead. Was he going mad? Had he heard what he thought he'd heard?

Flamel seemed to have forgotten Crispin's outburst and straightened from this new revelation. "She took you to another alchemist?" He leapt forward and grabbed the girl's arm. "You fool! Why did you do that? You know how dangerous it is!" He backed her against a table. She collided with it, knocking over retorts and horn beakers. "You must never do that again, Avelyn. Promise me! *Ne me décevez pas!*"

Crispin stepped closer and closed his hand over Flamel's. It was foolish getting between a man and his servant, but Crispin was helpless to resist, helpless under the repentant eyes of Avelyn. "Master Flamel, I'm certain she meant well."

"And you!" He turned his anger on Crispin, releasing his servant from his grasp. He pointed at Avelyn. "Why do you defile her? Surely she is beneath your notice. You, who were once a nobleman. Leave her alone!"

But Avelyn, obviously reading the movements of their mouths, pushed forward, hanging on Flamel's arm and gesturing toward Crispin. Flamel shook her off and postured before her. "You are a servant, not a whore. Try to remember that!"

"Why are you afraid of another alchemist, Master Flamel? She obviously wanted to convey something to me that you would not."

Flamel clenched his hands into fists and pulled at the disarrayed hair hanging below his cap. "My business is *secret*. Why do you think I traveled all the way from France to be in England? Do you think I *want* to be in England? It is very dangerous here for a *Français*. You toy with me, *Maître*, when I trusted you. I asked for your help, I paid for it, and so far you have failed me, you have dallied with my servant, and you threaten me when I cannot answer your questions. There is a very good reason I cannot answer as you wish. I am not paying you to wrest this information from me. I am paying you to accomplish your task!"

Opening his mouth to protest, Crispin decided otherwise and closed it again, pressing his lips tight. He bowed. "You are right, of course. I apologize for my rudeness, Master Flamel. My methods may seem unusual, but they get results."

Flamel drew himself up, clutching his gown. "So do mine."

They studied each other for some time before Flamel sighed, resigned. "We must try again, *Maître*. We must leave the ransom again. The false one. Please. Don't ask why. Trust me that it must be done." From the pouch at his side, he pulled out the velvet bag. "I will take it again to Saint Paul's and leave it at the feet of the statue. He will come. He wants it. I can only hope he wants it more than he wants to harm Perenelle."

Flamel seemed to sense Crispin's unease with this tactic, but he raised his hand to silence any arguments. "I cannot be certain of the wisdom of this course, but let us try this little ruse to see, eh? To see if I am not completely mad."

I already think you're completely mad, thought Crispin, but he did not say it aloud.

Flamel shuffled to his feet, took the cloak Avelyn offered him, and, with one backward glance at Crispin, slouched out the door.

Crispin and Jack reluctantly returned to the Shambles and did not hear from Flamel for the remainder of the day.

Pacing restlessly, Crispin went from window to hearth over and over again, peering out the slightly open shutters to the street below. He saw nothing of the French alchemist. No word from Avelyn, nothing from Flamel. He had made himself into the biggest fool. Flamel was right. He had no business forgetting his task to play paramour to the man's servant. It was base, even for him. His loneliness was not an excuse. Perhaps it might be best to practice some humility. Or celibacy, at the very least. Though the thought made him grimace.

Jack lay with his head on his arms, sitting at the table. Crispin thought he heard him snore.

Finally, Crispin could take it no more. He stalked to the door and pulled down his cloak, whipping it over his shoulders.

Jack jerked up, sputtering, "Master Crispin? Where are you going?"

"I'm going to talk to that alchemist."

"What? Flamel?"

"No, the other. Avelyn took us there for a reason."

Jack lumbered up from his chair and shuffled toward his cloak. He shrugged it on and buttoned it up. "But you heard Flamel, Master. He said she was mad."

"There is far more to this than meets the eye, Jack. I will make that man talk to me." He yanked open the door and stalked onto the landing.

"Now, Master Crispin. There's no need to be getting into any trouble. Them sheriffs are none too fond of you."

He trotted down the stairs with Jack behind him. "And I am none too fond of them."

Crispin looked both ways down the lane. At least it had stopped snowing. The sky extended its pale wash of blue down to a blushing horizon. The naked trees in back courtyards stretched their spindly arms into the heavens, looking more like cracks against the dense flatness of the sky.

Crispin walked briskly, satisfied that he was at least doing *something*. He inhaled deeply of the heavy, cold air and warmed himself by swinging his limbs freely.

Jack's long strides kept pace. The boy might argue, but he always complied. He knew in the end that he would at least learn something of value.

"What do you make of this Nicholas Flamel, Jack?"

The boy ran his sleeve under his reddened nose and exhaled a long white cloud. "He's strange, sir. I reckon it's all them compounds he works with. But why is he lying, you mean?"

Crispin nodded, kept moving.

"Why does a man lie?" said Jack, throwing back his head and blinking into the fading sunshine. He ticked it off on his fingers. "Well, he lies because he is dishonest; because he is hiding something he'd rather not anyone else know; he's protecting someone else who is guilty... and... er... he's just a whoreson and likes to lie?"

"Close. He may also lie to misdirect."

"Oh, aye."

"Or it could be a combination of many of those reasons."

"Then what is his game, eh? Don't he want his wife back?"

"By all indications, he does."

"Then why not cooperate with us? We only mean well. Except... that you lied to *him,* too."

"About Henry Bolingbroke."

"Aye. I understand why... mostly. I think you are trying to protect Lord Derby. But from what, I know not."

Crispin said nothing and stared straight ahead. Maybe he had taught the boy too well.

"Master, just because you used to know Lord Henry doesn't mean he is the same man. You have been deceived before by that very family."

"I don't need to be reminded," he bit out, voice low.

"I don't mean naught by it, Master Crispin. I'm only doing what you told me. I'm walking my mind through the facts. *The roots of education are bitter, but the fruit is sweet.* So says Aristotle."

Crispin's ire quickly fled and he tried to hide his gratified smile by looking away toward the icy buildings.

"And so as far as I am concerned, we must not rule out Lord Derby as having something to do with these same crimes," Jack went on. "Even though it is well established that he is not in need of the money himself."

His heart filled with pride at the boy's logic, even if the cause of it still pained him. But his words were also slowly sinking in. He stopped, unmindful of the wet snow dampening his boots. "No, he doesn't need the *money.* But what if he needed that *broach*?"

"Ah!" Jack stomped and patted his arms to keep warm. "A curious thought, Master. That broach. It came from the King of France. What might that mean? Something to do with treaties or other such nobleman's vows? Or *maybe* it didn't belong to Flamel at all. After all, we only have his word that it was *given* to him by King Charles."

"God's blood, Jack, but you might be right. I wonder how he fared with his ransom deposit today."

"Would you like me to go see, sir?"

Out of the corner of his eye, Crispin spotted figures standing under the eaves of the frost-slickened buildings. He might not have noticed them if they were moving as everyone else did on the street, winding down their labors for the end of the day. But these lingered, moving ahead slowly and in step with Crispin and just behind his vision. Their hoods were drawn low over their faces and it was impossible to discern whether they were known to Crispin or not.

Crispin knelt down to pretend to adjust his boot and looked slyly over the leather cape of his chaperon hood bunched on his shoulder. There were four of them now, two on either side of the lane, and they were looking at one another and making vague and unsubtle gestures in communication.

"Jack," he said quietly, "don't look up, but our shadows are back. And one more has been added. Two each side." He rose. "I think you should continue on with me. I'd rather we have two sets of eyes to track them."

"Aye, Master."

They hurried their pace and finally turned the corner to where the other alchemist was. Crispin glanced at the scratched-out signs scrawled on the post of the shop on the corner but kept moving. His shadowing men were still with them, but they hung back. He saw that Jack took note, too, and headed directly to the shop. He pushed open the door under the snow-covered sign of Mercury, and when Jack entered behind him and closed the door, they waited for the alchemist to appear.

No foul cauldron bubbled now, but three coneys hung from the beam near the curtained doorway and Crispin wondered if there was some deeper significance or whether they were merely more of the man's supper.

He leaned toward Tucker. "Jack, you call out."

He cleared his throat. "Oi! Master Alchemist!"

"Patience," said that gruff voice from beyond the curtain. "I shall be there anon."

They waited a moment more before the same man appeared, bulbous nose and small, squinting eyes. "I am Bartholomew of Oxford, at your humble service. How may I—" But when he beheld Crispin, he pointed toward the door. "Get out!"

Crispin didn't hesitate. He darted over the plank separating them, grabbed the man by his tattered fur collar, and dragged him over the table. "Perhaps I didn't make myself clear. I'd like to ask you a few questions."

The man sputtered and fluttered his lids, turning his face away from a possible blow. "P-please. Don't hurt me!"

With a snort of disgust, Crispin let him go, even smoothed down where he'd wrinkled the man's collar and gown. He helped the alchemist to his feet. His Adam's apple bobbed as his widened eyes darted between Crispin and Jack.

"You have seen that woman before, the woman who brought me here earlier."

"Yes. Too many times. I thought she was a beggar… or worse. She came sniffing around my shop and seemed far too familiar with my goods, as if she planned to steal them. Always touching, touching." He wiped his hands down his gown from the memory.

"And yet once you discovered she was the servant of Nicholas Flamel…"

"Oh yes!" He seemed only now to remember that. "Well, then, of course, I… well. I would welcome her to, perhaps, talk. Though she does seem a bit strange, truth to tell."

"She's deaf and dumb."

"Oh." He wrinkled his brow and pulled down on his dark, greasy locks, stroking absently. "Pity. I should have liked to ask her… well."

"Ask her what? Tell me, why is Flamel so well-known to you?"

He studied Crispin this time, looked him over with particular care. And when he was done with him, he turned to Jack with equal scrutiny. "We alchemists… we use ancient secrets to perfect our art. As old as Scripture. Sometimes our methods are judged badly by outsiders. The Church does not always approve of this science, and in truth, some alchemists are more sorcerers than craftsmen. I have known a few. Not myself, of course. I would never dabble to endanger my soul! No, not at all." He touched his collar and adjusted it before he crossed himself. "It is just that there is much we have learned that cannot be understood by the simple laymen. And Nicholas Flamel has gained his own amount of fame through his skill and expertise... And one thing more."

He motioned silence to Crispin before pushing him aside. He crept to the door, opened it a crack, and peered out to the street. Satisfied, he closed it again and threw the bolt. When he gestured for Crispin to draw closer, both Crispin and Jack stepped into the circle of his open arms.

"You see, Master Guest," he said confidentially, "Nicholas Flamel has achieved the ultimate goal of all alchemists. He understands the transmutation of matter. He has worked out the science, he has transcended the planes of knowledge. In short, Master Guest..." He drew Crispin even closer. Stale wine breath gusted over Crispin's cheek. "Master Flamel," whispered the alchemist, "has discovered how to create the Philosopher's Stone."

ten

rispin rolled his eyes, disappointed. "You must be jesting."

"No! No, not at all. He has gained fame far and wide for this remarkable achievement. Why, even pagan scholars from the East are said to travel over great distances merely to consult with him. And now you say he is on these shores! Well!" He rubbed his hands together. "I will beg an audience with him, naturally. Of course I will. Although, I doubt he will share his secrets with anyone other than his own apprentice. More's the pity. But a man can try."

"His apprentice is dead. Murdered."

"Saint Luke!" He wrung his hands and wandered toward his fire, gaze lost in the flickering flames. "W-why did they slay him?"

"I wonder. If many others knew that Flamel made this Stone, then they might wish to have it for themselves."

Jack smacked his forehead with his hand. "*Stone,* sir! The ransom demanded the *Stone,* not the *broach.*"

"So I am beginning to see."

"But begging your pardon, sir…" Jack addressed the both of them. "What *is* this Philosopher's Stone? Why is it valuable?"

The alchemist stared at him. "You ignorant boy! Don't you know about the Philosopher's Stone?" He turned to Crispin. "Does he not know?"

"Clearly," said Crispin.

The alchemist shook his head, disgusted. He grabbed more sticks and tossed them on his fire. They sparked with green and purple flames before billowing a black cloud up the athanor's flue. "Some alchemists have spent their entire lives searching for the answers to its creation. It isn't merely a simple combination of formulas. No! Everything must be perfection. The position of the moon and stars, the time of day, the time of year, the purest ingredients. Salt, sulfur, mercury... It is said that even pulverized unicorn horn *might* be used in the process—extremely rare, you understand. But such ingredients might be mere mythos, to send a lesser Adept off the scent. Hard to say. In order to achieve the Grand Arcanum, the *Lapis Philosophorum,* one must dedicate one's life to this research, to experimentation." He nodded with a greedy look in his eye. "Few Adepts can be found who truly understand the Lesser and Greater Circulations. A clear understanding of roots, herbs, plants... even poisons. And then the metals, so important, so complicated in nature.... Ah, but I have gotten off my course. The Philosopher's Stone, the *Lapis Philosophorum.* Many men wish to possess it for its use in turning simple metals into the most precious of all, into gold. If that were all it did, then perhaps lesser Adepts might be able to accomplish it."

"Isn't that enough?" asked Jack, entranced.

"For *fools,*" spat the alchemist. "But for true Adepts educated in the highest Arcana, that is only the beginning of knowledge. The true, the purest, use of obtaining the *Lapis Philosophorum* is to create the Elixir of Life."

Jack leaned forward. Quietly, he asked, "What does that do?"

"Those who drink of the Elixir of Life are given immortality."

"God blind me!"

"Indeed."

Crispin's hand clenched and unclenched on the hilt of his sheathed dagger. "But such a thing is a myth. A fool's errand. Why would you believe such mad babbling? Unicorns, indeed!"

"Why should I believe? I can see that you are a man with little understanding, Crispin Guest." He pointed an accusatory finger. "You are not an Adept. One would have thought that a man with your education could be more accepting. But I see," he said with haughty pique, "that you are not."

"Never mind me, you fool. What makes you think that Flamel has made this Stone?"

"All of the continent know it. I met some Greek travelers only last year who mentioned having met him in Paris. Oh, they did not mention the Stone, of course, talked around it. But I have a wily mind, you understand?" He tapped his temple. "I could see it behind their eyes and between their words. There are many and many who speak of the Philosopher's Stone and Nicholas Flamel all in the same breath."

"Nonsense. This is utter nonsense."

Jack sucked on his lip. "Aye, Master, but if others believe it, like *this* man, then that makes Master Flamel just as vulnerable as if he did possess it."

He nodded. "That's true enough, Jack. Master Bartholomew, what does such a Stone look like?"

His brows clustered over his forehead. "Well… I have never actually seen it for myself, you understand. Rumor has it that it is a simple stone. Something nondescript. Like a lump of tin or of coal. And yet, I have also heard that it can be a very lovely stone, like a crystal."

"So it would not appear as a fabulous gem?"

"It might. But with the materials used to make it, I should think not. And I would never attempt to facet it. That might render it useless."

"I thank you, Master Bartholomew, for assisting me."

"If you seek the Stone yourself, I should warn you, Master Guest. It is protected, not just by the secret nature of it, or by the spirits that watch over such things. But by the communion of other alchemists. I know nothing about it in other places, but in England the alchemists communicate with one another. We are a… a guild of sorts. We protect what is ours. Our secret knowledge that we have accumulated with toil and sweat is not to be given to just anyone. A man must earn his right to be allowed into the circle. It would be wiser if you left that which you little understand alone."

"I understand murder, sir. And the abduction of an innocent woman. Would you shield these crimes behind your guild's need for secrecy? Loyalty should only take you so far."

"I… I had no idea…"

"If I thought you did, I would haul you before the hangman myself." He smiled unpleasantly. "What do you know of the murder of the apprentice of Nicholas Flamel?"

"Why, nothing! I never even knew Master Flamel was in London until you told me. Neither did I know of the man's murder until you also related that information."

"Why would his servant bring me to you, then?"

"How should I know that! You said yourself that she is deaf and dumb. And mad, most likely."

He could tell Jack was about to agree, but he interrupted. "I do not think her mad. The way about her, perhaps, but I am of a mind that she is cannier than anyone thus far has given her credit for."

Crispin knew that he was allowing his sentiments to get the better of him. "Be that as it may, I believe she drew me here for your help. Not just with telling us of the Philosopher's Stone, of which the old alchemist did *not* tell us, but with the symbols that have been cropping up all over the city."

"Eh? Symbols? What are you talking about?"

"Have you not seen them?"

"I do not leave the confines of my shop very often, Master Guest. I am at my own Great Work, you understand." He tapped a leather-bound volume sitting on his table. A symbol was etched on its cover.

"I will show you if you will come."

The alchemist nodded and followed Crispin out the door.

"It is only this way," said Crispin. "There are many more throughout London. I have no idea how many." They arrived at the house on the corner, and Crispin pointed. The symbols were scratched over hastily but still easily read. The light was fading, but they were clear enough when the sun breached the low swag of clouds. "There. What do you make of it?"

The man's eyes grew fearful and he tugged his cap low over his head. He pushed Crispin aside and marched back to his shop.

"Master Bartholomew!"

He waved his fist over his shoulder. Crispin and Jack exchanged a look before they trotted after. The alchemist met him at the doorway, blocking it. "I cannot help you, Master Guest. I pray that you go else-where for your information from now on. Please. Do not trouble me again. I have my own work to do." He slammed the door and bolted it for good measure, leaving Crispin staring at the worn wood.

"God's blood. What ails the man?"

"It meant something to him," Jack pointed out.

"Indeed it did. But what? Jack, there may be other alchemists in the city. He said as much. They are a guild. Perhaps we can reason with their leaders, come to some mutual agreement."

"What if they are all scared of them markings?"

"I don't know. Perhaps we can persuade Master Flamel—"

A boy dragging a priest through the street was shoving people out of the way and making a ruckus.

"Slow down, boy," said the old cleric.

"But my lord, my sister is dying. She can't die without the sacraments!"

"God will help us, child."

"Can *I* help?" said Crispin, trotting forward.

The cleric looked him up and down. "Oh! Well, perhaps you can clear a path. Where are we off to, boy?"

"Down on Thames Street. Hurry, my lord, by the grace of God!"

Crispin and Jack pushed the passersby out of the way and led them, by the boy's guidance, to the house in mourning.

Crispin didn't know why he followed them in, but he was ushered along with some of the other neighbors and they all found themselves squeezed through the door of the humble dwelling and watching the priest administer the bread of Christ to the dying girl.

She was thin and wan, lying on a pallet bed. She could be lit-tle more than eight or nine. Breathing shallowly, she could barely take the Host between her lips, but a woman Crispin took to be her mother propped the lolling head on her thigh and with great gentle-ness brushed back the lank hair from her perspiring forehead. Her body was convulsing, and foam pooled at the corners of her mouth. When her eyes rolled back and her body gave a great heave, she sud-denly stilled and the woman sitting above the girl, head cradled in her lap, began to weep.

"She went with Christ," the priest declared. "She took the Host and renounced Satan. She squeezed my hand to tell me so." He signed a benediction over her sunken form and then another over the weeping mother and sad-eyed father. The boy who had brought the priest gave the cleric a cup of ale and a coin and thanked him wearily for coming. He did not look well himself, with dark circles around his eyes and a yellow pallor to his skin. His thin fingers clutched at his belly as if it pained him.

The old man drank the proffered ale, bowed to them, and set the beaker aside before he shuffled toward the door, shaking his head.

"Such sadness," he said as he passed under the lintel. Crispin met him outside, allowing more neighbors to crowd in. They offered bread and jugs of ale to the family. "It was only yesterday that I offered the last sacraments for their little boy."

"Two deaths in two days?" asked Crispin.

"It is the way of it sometimes," he said, pocketing his coin. "Tragedy often compounds upon tragedy."

"The boy in there, he does not look well. What illness is it that has taken their children?"

"I do not know. It is not like any illness I have seen before. Usually, there are signs. But these came on suddenly. Much as the others in the parish."

"Others?"

"Yes. Yesterday it was an old woman and an old man. And the day before a young boy and his grandfather in another parish. Little signs of illness in the rest of the family, though some were briefly ill. But by my Lady, I know what a plague is and this looks nothing like it. They died very quickly after feeling weak and unwell. But very painfully."

"Odd. And what of the sick families? Did they succumb?"

"No, they said that they dosed themselves with garlic and thick pottage."

"Only the very young and the old died? Any in swaddling?"

"No, none, thank the Virgin. I have seen plenty in all my years, Master. Many ways that men die."

"But this does strike you strangely."

The priest put up his hood and shivered when a cold wind swept down the lane. "Yes. It has the foul stench of the demon's work about it. Witchcraft, striking the innocent. There is a preacher that has been going about the city proclaiming loudly of the sin and corruption of the soul. He says that witchcraft and the works of Satan are nigh. Those foul symbols. They should be scratched off when they are discovered."

"Symbols? Do you think they have to do with these illnesses? How can that be?"

"It is the way of God's mystery that is beyond our ken, good Master. If I see another of those foul Devil's marks, I shall eradicate them!"

"I wish you would not."

"Eh? What? Preserve the signs of Satan himself? Let him get a foothold in our city, smiting the young and the old?"

"I am investigating something, my lord. Something equally heinous. They might help me. They might be a clue to what I need to discover and who I need to bring to justice."

His eyes scanned Crispin and then fell on Jack. "Are you... are you by any chance that fellow they call the Tracker?"

"Yes, my lord. Crispin Guest."

"Blessed Mother. I have heard strange tales of you. A onetime traitor who purges himself by serving the people of England. A new Robin Hood. Strange tales indeed.... I've also heard that you were the friend of the abbot of Westminster."

"Yes to all of that. Will you help me? Will you tell me the other places you have seen these symbols?"

"What is it you are after, man?"

"A murderer, perhaps. One of flesh and blood."

"I see. Then yes, I will help you, of course."

"Take my apprentice here. His name is Jack Tucker." Jack bowed. "Jack, see that this kind father makes his way home safely."

"Yes, Master Crispin. My lord? Lead me."

Crispin watched them go, thinking. These illnesses did not sound like a plague to him, at least not any plague he had ever heard of. The young and the old had fallen. But no one of middle years. And no infants. And those who fell ill seemed to recover with a quick remedy. As he'd watched that young girl die, his mind had brushed against the notion of poison, but it was a fleeting thought. Foolish. What and who would poison so many different unrelated people? He dismissed it as unreasonable.

A bell chimed from the nearby church, and soon each one sounded in every parish of London, echoing, calling to one another like ravens in the trees. Vespers.

Too many mysteries. His plate was already full with a murdered apprentice and a missing woman. These symbols might have to do with it, but of that he wasn't certain. He needed to seek out that preacher. If only Crispin were two people!

He suddenly thought of Lenny, the nearly toothless beggar and thief he had used many a time to help in his investigations. A farthing would go a long way with Lenny, but Crispin also recalled that they had had a falling-out. Crispin had been fed up with Lenny's thieving ways and threatened him with the law… and more.

He reached back and pulled his leather hood up over his head, securing it in place. Standing in the middle of the emptying street, he wondered what to do, which way to go. Back to Flamel's? To Avelyn? To the Boar's Tusk for a much-needed drink, bite of food, and warmth? Back home, where he might ponder these strange events?

It was late. Home won out, and he made his way back to the Shambles but paused when he turned the corner at Cheap and saw a horse tied up below his stairs. The owner of the horse might be visiting the tinker, his landlord, Martin Kemp, whose shop lay below his lodgings. But it was a fine horse with an even finer tack, and he did not think such men patronized a lowly tinker on the Shambles.

He girded himself and climbed his stairs. The door was open, which meant his landlord had let the person in. Cautiously he pushed on the door with his foot, and it whined, falling back.

Henry Bolingbroke was there with more fuel in and beside Crispin's fireplace. His smile was not as broad as it had been before, but he beckoned Crispin in.

"Crispin. By God, you are seldom here! Come in. We have much to talk about."

eleven

rispin stood at the door, leaning against it. "Have you come to confess?"

Henry did not look as stern as he had a day ago. But his smile did not reach his eyes. "You're an impudent knave. Have you always been so? Is that what my father liked about you?"

"Your father—his grace the duke—was fond of me for my loyalty and perseverance." He pushed away from the door, glanced at the new stack of wood piled by the hearth, at the haunch of what smelled like lamb roasting over his fire, and turned to Henry with his thumbs thrust in his belt. "We also confided in one another... after a fashion. Why are you here?"

Henry had the decency to look abashed, but only slightly. "I treated you badly yesterday, Crispin. I never meant to do that."

"I do tend to bring out the worst in people."

"Nonsense. I was out of sorts and you caught me off guard. A foolish thing to be caught at in these times." He raised his face. Contrition was written all over it. "Please sit with me."

After a moment's pause, Crispin pulled out the stool and settled himself. Resting his clasped hands on the table, he waited. He did not offer wine, for he did not want easy camaraderie just now. He preferred answers.

But Henry wasn't giving any. He studied Crispin instead. If they weren't to sit in silence for the remainder of the evening, then Crispin decided to blink first. "Well, Henry? What were you doing in St. Paul's?"

"Would you believe me if I said it was a coincidence?"

"No."

He chuckled and seemed to mean it this time. "Very well. I told you I wanted to help you in your investigations. And so I set out on my own, investigating… something. I did not know what I was to find."

"Why to St. Paul's?"

"Ah!" He laid a finger alongside his nose and grinned. "*That* I cannot say. But tell me. You seemed to think there was a ransom to be laid. Why? What is the crime?"

"I do not believe *I* can say either."

"Fie on it! We cannot trust each other."

"So it would seem."

Henry closed his lips and tapped his fingers on the table.

Trying another tack, Crispin scooted closer. "What of the news of court? One doesn't hear many details outside of Westminster Palace. And what is heard is surely little better than rumor."

"First, why don't you serve us some meat? And I brought wine. That miserable piss you call wine nearly burned through my gut."

Crispin reddened at his words but saw it, sitting beneath his back windowsill. A shouldered jug of mustard-colored glaze stamped with the arms of Lancaster. He fetched it as well as two bowls and poured a dose in each before setting them on the table and kneeling by the meat. He used his knife to cut off steaming hunks. The juices flowed as his blade sliced, and his stomach growled. He had not eaten fine cuts of meat such as this in a very long time. He dropped the slices in a ceramic pot beside the hearth and brought that, too, to the table.

Henry poked into it with his knife and brought out a slice. He blew on it and nibbled on the crispy end. Crispin did the same, chewing the moist, savory meat, grateful to have it. Henry took a swig from his bowl and smiled. "French wine. Go on. I think it will be to your taste."

Crispin sipped. It reminded him of the old days, of dinners sitting at the head table with Lancaster on one side and young Henry on the other. "It is very good. Thank you, my lord, for the wine and the meat."

He waved his hand and continued to eat. "You asked about court," he went on with his mouth full. He wiped the wet from his mustache with a finger. "And I tell you, Crispin, I wish you were in my retinue."

So do I. But he would not voice it aloud. Instead, he bent his head to his meal, looking up only when Henry seemed to want acknowledgment that he heard.

After a time when they both fell silent, eating and drinking, Crispin suddenly said, "By the way, the sheriffs are looking for you."

Henry chuckled. "Are they? Did you tell them that you saw me?"

"No. Nor shall I. Unless it proves necessary."

Henry looked up from his food. "'Proves necessary'? Why, Crispin. Are you not still loyal to the house of Lancaster?"

"My new fealty is to the law, your grace."

Henry stared at him, clearly surprised. Crispin chewed his food uncomfortably. The lamb stuck to his throat when he tried to swallow. He cleared his palate with a little wine, and then he sawed at his meat again, not looking up at Derby. "Why do you shy from court?"

Henry poured himself more wine. "Because, my dear Crispin, I have no wish to follow in your footsteps and be arrested for treason myself." The blunt delivery was not meant to wound, but the words always made him wince, like rubbing a sore spot. "I am not a traitor. I and my commissioners merely wish for my cousin to see to what detriment he is bringing the realm. He has no heirs, yet he has far too many favorites and bestows on these men honors and titles they do not deserve, honors that are more fitting for his own kin. They are taking advantage of his good graces and he does not see that they spend the treasury as if it were their own strongbox."

"Surely Parliament—"

"Parliament acts as his tool. Five lords stand between the king and despotism: my uncle Gloucester, Richard Fitzalan the earl of Arundel, Thomas Beauchamp the earl of Warwick, Thomas Mowbray the earl of Nottingham... and me."

"Do you truly believe that, Henry?"

"If I didn't, I wouldn't be here. I'd be happily at my estates in Chester or in Spain with Father."

"But... what can be done? Last year you made no friends at court trying to impose your will over Richard."

"Not *our* will, Crispin. He might have been anointed by God, but he is still lawfully bound to do good in the realm. We merely want to remind him that there are limits to his powers by law and that he must protect the privileges of his lords."

"How does your father the duke see this move?"

"My uncle Gloucester has a fire in his belly over it. He has sent messages to the earl of March."

The sweet wine went sour on Crispin's tongue. "Roger Mortimer? The... king's designated heir?"

Henry seemed unusually interested in his meat and would not look up. "It is only a precaution."

"Does Richard know messages have been sent to March?"

"No. It is not advised that he does, though I have little doubt that he has some inkling. Hence the accusation of treason."

Crispin clutched his knife, thinking faraway thoughts.

"And so," said Henry, "you are uneasy at my presence."

Crispin got up from the table, wiped his knife on a rag by the bucket, and washed his hands. "I am now. But you haven't answered my question. What does your father say?"

Henry looked cross for only a moment and then seemed to let it go. "He... is not pleased by it. He begged us to await his return, but we cannot. We cannot let these grievances continue to compound. Who knows when Father will return?"

Crispin made his way to the fire and stood with his back to it, relishing the warmth. "But you can see his point of view, can you not? When Richard first took the throne, Parliament expected that your father would steal it from him. Conspiracies abounded." He shuffled, eyes downcast. "As you well know," he said softly. "He swore again and again to Parliament that he would uphold Richard as king. He will not forswear himself now."

The young lord rose and went to the same bucket to sluice his hands. "My father is not here, Crispin. I am my own man. And times are different."

"If you say so, my lord. It is just that... well."

"Well?" He stomped back to the table, moved around it to face Crispin toe to toe. "What? Speak!"

Crispin rocked before the fire. "Young men are hot to see their way and often move forward without considering the consequences."

More quietly, he said, "When *my* troubles began, I was not too much older than you are now, my lord."

"How dare you! You say that to *me*? *Me*, who has led armies and fought battles?"

"Be still, Henry!" It came out how he used to say it, when Henry was a child and he needed correction, and Henry reacted much as he used to do. He snapped to and stared wide-eyed at his former minder. "I have led armies, too, do not forget," said Crispin. "And I am older and more experienced than you. Why else would you have come to me? To hear me agree with everything you say? I was never that man. I never will be. That much should be obvious, even to you!"

Chastened, Henry took a step back, considered, then swiveled and walked slowly to the front window. He pushed the shutter open to stare down at the snow-covered Shambles.

"I have always valued your advice," Henry said softly. "I sought *you* out more than I did my own father. After all, you were often there when he was not. I came to think of you as..." He inhaled the cold air, hand resting on his hip. The street below still held his attention. "You left me," he said quietly, voice roughened from the cold, or so Crispin hoped.

"I am sorry, my lord. I did not mean to leave you."

"I hated those times, Crispin. No one would say anything. No one would tell me what had happened to you. And when I tried to ask, I was silenced. I had nightmares for years afterwards, thinking that they would come for me, too." He turned then.

With his wide, dark eyes and his fragile mouth, Henry suddenly seemed like the child he had been ten years ago. In the depth of that gaze, the years of hurt and uncertainty rolled forth like words on a scroll. Crispin could only imagine how it must have been for young Henry. His best playmate, his child-minder, suddenly gone, and Crispin's name spoken of only in hesitant whispers. Certainly Henry must have known, must have been told eventually.

"I'm sorry," he said again.

Henry barked a laugh. "You're apologizing to *me*?"

"I would never have hurt you, my lord, or dared put you or the duke at risk."

"I know." He returned to staring out the window again. His hand rested on the squeaky shutter. "I am a father now. I am not at my son's cradle every hour of the day. I well understand that others must take on the duty of advising and teaching my son. I have my own duties. As did my father. As did you, I daresay."

"So why will you not listen to the advice you so crave?"

He faced Crispin once again. "My uncle Gloucester also offered his sage advice. He is in the thick of it with me and understands more clearly. More than I can explain to you. I listen to *his* guidance as well, and he thinks we should press on. It is what is right, Crispin. Richard cannot be allowed to go on as he has. He must be made to see reason, and if he will not do it of his own accord, he will be *made* to do it. King or not."

Crispin nodded. "Very well. Your mind is made up on the matter. So why come to me?"

"To apologize. To show you what I have accomplished. To help you, where I can. And to ask… that you not interfere."

"My lord…"

"I'm only asking, Crispin. No more threats."

Henry strode toward the door, then plucked his cloak from its peg and slipped it over his shoulders. The fur lining looked pleasantly warm. He pulled the door open and stopped when Crispin called out to him.

"Henry. Can you truly tell me nothing of why you were in St. Paul's?"

Henry did not turn as he gritted out a laugh. "Stick to the crimes you can solve, Crispin, and stay away from the rest."

A swirl of snow spiraled in over the threshold, taking Henry with it as he closed the door.

twelve

eeling unsettled, Crispin left his lodgings. He felt unclean, as if he had just been manipulated. Henry was his father's son, true enough. He might not be able to tell Crispin what he was doing at the cathedral, but it didn't mean Crispin wasn't going to damn well find out what it was.

He needed to clear his head, for much of it was stuffed with the wool of Henry and his deceptions, the much-felt absence of Lancaster, the dead apprentice, the stubborn alchemist… and his strangely beautiful servant.

Flamel had not wanted to divulge if he had such a thing as the Philosopher's Stone, or what he believed to be the Stone. But Avelyn had no such reservations. She *had* wanted Crispin to know. Why else would she have brought him to the second alchemist?

And he definitely wanted to talk to this Robert Pickthorn, the preacher. It seemed unbelievable that his fiery speeches and the symbols on London's streets could possibly be related to the dead apprentice, but he had seen the like before. Recent events had molded him into less of a skeptic than he used to be.

When he looked up from walking, he realized he had been going west, following the Thames. Lantern light glittered off the surging water and darkness descended over the city. He skirted a water carrier straining under the yoke of his burden, a last trip from one of many of London's cisterns. He did not envy such men, especially in the winter, for it meant perpetually frozen hands and cold water splashing over one's legs. He hoped they were paid well.

He could have stopped his wandering at Ludgate. He should have, and returned to the Shambles, but he kept going, following the Strand, and then before he knew it, Charing Cross came into view ahead.

He arrived at the crossroads. The stone cross and its rambling structure of arches, covered in snow, served as mean shelter to a young beggar. The boy crouched in its shadow out of the weather, staring at Crispin with large, luminous eyes as he passed. He tossed the boy a silver penny, always thinking of Jack Tucker when he saw such beggars. The boy scrambled out of his shelter, snatched the coin from the snow, and ran off into the gloom.

It wasn't long before Crispin stood outside the spires of Westminster Abbey. Its gray stone stood dark against the pale sky. He stared up at it a long time until he felt foolish, like some country pilgrim, and walked up the long path to the north entrance. It was marginally warmer on the inside. No wind, but the stone arches, columns, and tile held the cold close to it, like a virgin over her virtue, refusing to let it go.

Men gathered in furtive clutches, conferring, seeking employment, just as they did at St. Paul's in London. A frail man in a long dark gown approached Crispin. "Clerk, sir? Have you need of an accomplished clerk to pen your documents before the day is out?"

"No, thank you."

Disappointed, the man bowed and wandered away.

Down the nave was the quire and beyond that the rood. Monks moved silently, lighting candles that had gone out or sweeping the floor with mute brooms. Always, they kept a judicious eye peeled on the men wandering the nave. There were gold candlesticks to protect, after all, gilt stone to keep an eye on. It was not uncommon to catch a man scraping the gilt from a stone runner with his knife blade.

The nave walkers would be ushered out soon enough. The day was over and it was time to think of the morrow and start again.

Crispin walked down the long space, skirted the quire, and came upon the rood screen. Beyond it hung a wooden cross with the figure of Christ, lit by two large candles below it. Crispin gazed at it through the open woodwork of the screen.

He stood a while before he felt the presence of the monk long before the man spoke.

"Master Crispin. It is good to see you. It has almost been a year since last you came."

He turned but hadn't needed to. "Brother Eric. God keep you, sir."

"And you." They stood silently, both in their own thoughts, when the monk spoke aloud what they were both thinking. "He is sorely missed, is Abbot Nicholas."

"Indeed. I do miss him greatly."

"I was told that whenever you returned, I was to take you to Abbot William."

"Oh? So the archdeacon William Colchester was made abbot? I thought the king favored Brother John Lakyngheth."

Eric glanced carefully over his shoulder before he answered. "Our treasurer *was* so favored by his grace the king… but the monks elected our archdeacon instead last year. The pope's commission only arrived a month ago, but our abbot has been serving faithfully even when his appointment was in doubt."

Crispin knew that Colchester had spent much of his years in the monastery on foreign travel, going to and from Rome. He was a man of books, so Abbot Nicholas had said. Crispin had met the man only once, years ago. Now he was abbot, taking the place of a much-beloved man.

"Are you still Abbot William's chaplain, as you so served Abbot Nicholas?"

The monk, a man much the same age as Crispin, though there was gray in the hair at his temples, gave a condoling smile. His hands were tucked warmly in the sleeves of his habit. "Alas. His temperament is different from our former abbot's. His needs are therefore different. I will escort you, but Brother John Sandon and Brother Thomas Merke will attend you."

Crispin girded himself, nodded to the monk, and allowed the man to lead him along the familiar path to the abbot's lodgings.

The early twilit sky bathed the courtyard in tints of blue. The snow-patched grass was brown, but a rabbit in the far corner nibbled tentatively, looking for green shoots that were yet months away from appearing.

Ravens called to one another from the red-tiled rooftops of the abbey precincts, looking like monks themselves in their dark raiment and scowling down at Crispin for trespassing.

Brother Eric suddenly stopped and gestured toward the worn stone path. "You know the rest of the way, I daresay, Master Crispin."

"Thank you, Brother." Crispin continued down the path, stepping up to the doorway. He knocked and waited. At length, the door opened, and a young monk with a pale face and a noticeable shadow of a beard peered at him from out of his cowl.

"Yes? Who are you?"

He bowed. "I am Crispin Guest, Brother. Brother Eric instructed me—"

"Oh!" The young monk's face opened into smiles and he threw back his hood, stepped forward, and grabbed Crispin's arm. "You are the famed Crispin Guest? Come in, come in."

Crispin stepped into the comfortable surroundings he knew so well. The warmth of the abbot's parlor thawed his bones. But amid the familiar was the unaccustomed sound of a harp playing a quiet tune. Abbot Nicholas was not given to the enjoyment of music. Things *were* different in the abbot's lodge these days.

"I have heard much about you from the other brothers," the monk continued. "I am Brother John." He bowed. "I will let Abbot William know you are here." He bowed again and left through an arch into the abbot's private solar.

Crispin waited, listening to the somber notes of the harp, until Brother John returned. "Will you come with me? Can I get you refreshment, sir? Wine?"

"Yes. Thank you."

He turned the corner and spied a monk sitting at a long, rectangular table. The man wore the vestments of his office, a gown of black wool, but they were also trimmed in dark fur and subtle embroidery. It was not overly resplendent, but neither would an observer question his power and wealth. He was older than Crispin, older even than the duke of Lancaster, but he wore his years well. His fleshy face, round nose, and prominent chin looked more like those of a tradesman, but Crispin knew him to be a man of property.

The room itself looked different. Chairs with crimson cushions and an ambry that Nicholas had not possessed were situated about the room. Likewise a tapestry hung on a far wall depicting Adam and Eve. The abbot sat at a table covered with a fine carpet in maroons and gold thread, and on either side of him, large silver candelabras lit his work with tall beeswax candles. A corona of more candles hung in the middle of the room, lighting the vaulted space in cheerful, golden light. Gratifying to Crispin was a shelf against a wall with a good number of books and scrolls ensconced upon it. He itched to peruse the shelf himself, as he often did when Nicholas was at home, sometimes reading the texts in silence next to the older man, while Nicholas schemed with his seneschal, contriving some hunting festivity on his lands he was planning for the nobility of court.

A fire burned warm and bright in the hearth, and beside it sat the harpist on a stool, plucking a song on the strings of the instrument balanced on his thighs.

Crispin searched for the old greyhound, Horatio, that used to sit at Abbot Nicholas's feet, but he surmised that the dog was also gone, not long after its master left this earth.

The abbot pored over his ledgers, quill scratching. He continued to write without looking up. Meanwhile, Brother John proffered a folding chair for Crispin, silently bade him sit, and soon brought him a silver goblet filled with floral-scented wine. Crispin tasted it, and the sweet flavors surged in his mouth. Even better than the Lancaster wine Henry had brought. Having little better to do, he drank and watched the harpist play for a while before he turned his attention toward the abbot. The man's finger slid carefully down the page over notation after notation, before his quill made a sharp check by each one.

"So you are Crispin Guest," he said, startling Crispin, as he had not looked up or stopped what he was doing. His voice was strong, his mouth set in a stern frown.

Crispin rose slightly as he bowed. "Indeed. May I offer my congratulations at your appointment as abbot of Westminster?"

The abbot's pale blue eyes rose to him only briefly before turning back to his pages. "You may," he said in a clipped Essex accent. "Though I was compromissioned *last* December by my own monks. I suppose these tidings are new to London nearly a year late."

Crispin longed to ask how Richard took this news but held his tongue. After all, he did not know William de Colchester. He did not think he was in Richard's pocket since his election went against the royal favor, but after a year, Crispin assumed Richard had made peace with the decision or would very well soon have to.

The abbot laid his quill aside, sprinkled sand on his ledger, blew it off, and closed the books. He rested his hands on the leather cover and studied Crispin from across his table. "You are this Tracker they speak of," he said without preamble. "My predecessor seemed intrigued by this vocation of yours. But I am well acquainted with your tale. I am not as enamored."

Crispin tapped his finger against his goblet. "Abbot Nicholas and I were friends. We were friends before my disseisement and we continued our friendship after. Discreetly. If you fear that my being here has endangered you in any way—"

He waved a hand in dismissal. "Be at ease, Master Guest. I shall not toss you out to save myself."

Crispin raised a brow at that.

"No," the abbot went on, "not that I wish to be a martyr, either. But I am, perhaps, more cautious than our dear late brother. And so I hope that you will not have too many occasions to visit the abbey. Except to use the church, of course, for the enlightenment of your soul."

And don't allow the door to hit you as you make a hasty exit, thought Crispin with a grim smile. He rose and set his goblet aside. "I see. That sounds like a request to leave."

"Not at all," said the abbot, making no move to stop him. "Our dear Abbot Litlyngton advised me on you, Master Guest."

Crispin paused. "Oh?"

"Indeed. He told me to trust you. But also to guide you. I will, of course, do my best. You are, after all, a soul in need of much guidance."

Crispin scuffed his boot against the floor. "A man is never too old for guidance, especially where his soul is concerned. *Educating the mind without educating the heart is no education at all.* But I would not let it trouble you, my Lord Abbot. I doubt I shall return for your good counsel." He bowed and strode toward the door, jaw clenched.

"I would not be so hasty," said the abbot, rising from his chair at last. The harpist continued to play, the soft strains serving as a counterpoint to the tension between the men. The abbot walked around the table. "One never knows when counsel will be needed and in what form it might take."

"True. But I am not often to go at my leisure where I am clearly unwelcomed."

"Did I leave you with that impression?" He looked Crispin up and down. They were of similar height. "Not at all." Crispin itched to leave, but the abbot suddenly seemed reluctant to allow him to do so. "I asked to see you," said the abbot, "because Brother Nicholas bequeathed something to you."

Crispin stiffened. The thought was painful and at the same time warmed a spot in his chest. Abbot William motioned to Brother John, who had entered from a rear door, and whispered something into the monk's ear. Brother John nodded and trotted off. The abbot didn't move. His stoic posture spoke of his years as the abbey's emissary. No doubt there were many such instances where he was forced to wait in the halls of Bruges, Paris, or Rome, and he had learned how to do so with patience and calm.

When Brother John returned, he was carrying a small coffer wrapped in a silky cloth. He handed it to Crispin.

It was heavy. He looked to the abbot, puzzled.

"It is a chess set. Brother Nicholas mentioned spending many a pleasant afternoon with you playing games of strategy. He often spoke of you fondly." His expression took on one of bewilderment, as if he could not fathom the like.

Crispin looked around the room, searching for that familiar chess set, but did not find it. Apparently, it was now under his arm.

"At any rate," continued the abbot, "we did not know how to get it to you, but Brother Eric was certain that you would somehow… appear."

Bollocks. Who was easier to find than Crispin? How would he get clients if they could not find him? *Bah!* It mattered little in the end. Crispin clutched the box tightly. It was a fine remembrance of the man.

"I thank you, my Lord Abbot. I bid you God's grace."

The abbot signed the cross over Crispin, but even as he passed over the threshold, the abbot called out one last time, "Discretion, Master Guest." As if he needed reminding.

He tucked the heavy box under his arm as he made the long walk home in the falling light. He wondered about the man he had just met, wondered how he would receive the news of Henry's lords forcing the king to bend to their will. Would he be an ally to Richard or would he prefer to stay clear of politics? In Crispin's experience, clerics seldom stayed on the fence.

He was back on the Shambles just as the church bells struck Compline. He trudged up the stairs and opened the door, pleased to find Jack there.

"We had another visit from Lord Henry?" asked the boy, gesturing toward the wood and the meat, cooling off to the side of the hearth.

"Yes. I will tell you of that later." He set the box on the table and unwrapped the cloth from it.

Jack approached the table and looked it over. "What's that?"

"A bequest from Abbot Nicholas."

"Oh." It was part sigh, part exclamation.

Crispin opened the coffer and took out the chessboard. The pieces lay snugly in their own velvet-lined niches. He set up the board. "It's a chessboard, Jack."

"It's beautiful, Master Crispin. Is it worth a lot?"

"Probably." He examined one ivory pawn before placing it on its square. "But worth far more in memories."

"I remembered it from the abbot's lodgings, sir. You played often with Abbot Nicholas, didn't you?"

"As often as time permitted. It never seemed like enough time."

The abbot favored the white men, and Crispin automatically set up the board so that black was on his side. He looked up at Jack. "Would you like to learn to play?"

Jack's eyes brightened. "Oh yes, sir! Indeed, sir!" He scrambled for the stool and pulled it up to the table, sitting and waiting.

"First," said Crispin. "What did you learn from the priest about those symbols?"

Jack picked up a knight, examining the intricate detail of the carving. "They was all over, sir. He pointed them out on our way back to his church, but I found a few more when returning home. Most were scratched out. What do they mean?"

He shook his head, toying with the king. "I don't know. We must find that preacher again."

"I hear of him, that is for certain. He should not be difficult to find. I'll begin my search again first thing in the morning. But in the meantime…" He placed the knight back on its square. "Can you not tell me of this game, Master?"

He smiled. "And so, each piece has its own rules. Each moves differently, can achieve different ends. But the object of the game is to capture the king. When the king can move no more, when he has nowhere to go, then he is lost."

Jack gave him a significant look.

"Yes, well. It does have its parallels in our current political circumstances. It is a game of strategy. Of thinking far ahead of the current state of the board. Of being able to adjust your thinking depending on what is presented to you."

"Blind me, sir. It's like what we do all the time."

"Indeed. As I said, it's a fine metaphor for the games of court and politics. But unlike politics, the outcome can sometimes be predicted. Even directed."

Crispin grasped his pawn and moved it two squares forward, but just as he placed it on the square, a knock sounded on the door.

They both straightened, hands on their knife hilts. At a signal from Crispin, Jack went to the door and opened it.

Avelyn stood there, hands behind her back, rocking from side to side. When she spied Crispin, her smile widened impossibly.

She rushed past Jack, nearly toppling him. "Oi! Watch it!"

She stopped right in front of Crispin, looking up at him with her chin high. It bared her throat, *and a long, lovely throat it is,* he mused, though it was slightly marred by his love bites. His eyes could not help but travel downward to the shadow of her bosom, where he remembered proffering a few more gentle nibbles.

They looked at each other for a while before Jack loudly let out a gust of exasperation. "I'll be outside, I reckon," he grumbled, grabbing his cloak, and he slammed the door behind him.

Crispin didn't even wait for the last click of the lock. His hands reached up and grasped her shoulders and slid up to her neck. He ran his fingers over her hair, but it was tightly braided again into one long plait. "I do prefer your hair loose," he said softly.

She moved her face into his hand, nuzzling. She lifted her arms, running her hands up his chest until she reached his neck and tugged him down. He bent obligingly and their lips touched. He opened his mouth over hers, clutched her small frame, and lifted her off the floor. Her feet dangled just below his knees. She weighed nothing at all.

Their tongues tangled slowly, slick and wet, and one hand traveled down her back, lower, until he was able to cup one arsecheek and squeeze it.

They kissed for a long time, until he drew his mouth away mere inches from hers. "Have you come with a message from your master?" he asked breathlessly, thinking that he should at least ask the question. Her mistress was, after all, still in peril.

But he wasn't far enough away for her to see his lips and he quickly forgot the question and molded his mouth to hers again. They kissed another few moments before she tore away and landed on her feet. Swallowing hard, he shook his head to clear it. "Avelyn?" He didn't even realize he was still reaching for her when she pushed him back. With determination she shook her head and then started to gesture.

"You know I can't understand." He slipped his hands around her petite waist and pulled. When she was flush against him, his hands cupped her jaw and he bent over and found her mouth again. She kissed back, but with far less enthusiasm and pushed him away again.

He looked down at her in puzzlement and she continued to sign.

"Clearly you are trying to tell me something." He ran his fingers through his hair in frustration. "You are right, of course. Something must be done about Madam Flamel." What did he know of abductions? For the most part, he knew of instances where knights were captured on the battlefield and they would be kept until a ransom was paid. They lived at ease, for the most part, for courtesy demanded they be treated with care, only they were unable to leave the precincts of whatever castle or manor house kept them. Even Richard Lionheart was kept for years until his brother, Prince John, collected enough ransom in taxes to set him free.

And on the streets of London, a woman might be captured by her rival's family until her own family agreed to marry her off to the abductor's son. Such things were not entirely legal but were well-known.

But an abduction for a ransom alone, and one involving murder, was *not* oft heard of. Would she be safe? Would the abductor exercise patience? God's blood! He had been careless and selfish, getting distracted by the likes of Henry and this seductress, who was even now trying desperately to tell him something. He had dismissed her in favor of asking her *master* the questions he needed to ask, but he had been a fool.

"Avelyn," he said, sobered, "tell me. Try."

She looked around the darkening room when her gaze landed on the chess set. She grabbed a knight and showed it to him. He shrugged, taking it from her hand.

With a breath of vexation, she gestured to the corners of the room. But still he did not know her meaning. She ran to the bucket, dipped in her hand, and wrote with her wet finger on the wall. She made one of those symbols he had seen on the streets of London.

He hurried over to her. "Do you know what they mean?"

She gave a tentative nod. Crispin grabbed his cloak, and when he opened the door, he beckoned a sleepy Jack to come along.

thirteen

The muddied snow was tinged blue in the dark. People had retreated to their homes, as they were obligated to do. The curfew was in place and shutters were closed and locked. Horses were stabled and suppers consumed.

And it was cold. Night crept in like a thief in the house, and Crispin, Jack, and Avelyn made their careful way over the streets, keeping an eye skinned for a slippery patch of ice as well as for the Watch.

With her hand clutched around the hem of his cloak, she pulled Crispin to a corner and showed him the symbol. "Yes, I see it, but I don't know what it means. Master Bartholomew, the other alchemist, seemed afraid of them."

She nodded but kept pointing to it.

He looked at Jack for help. Jack tapped her shoulder, and keeping his voice low, he enunciated, "HE DON'T KNOW WHAT IT MEANS."

Scowling at him, she winced away from Jack's touch.

"We must return to Flamel," said Crispin. It was a long night ahead for all of them, he decided. They needed to decipher once and for all what these symbols might mean.

They hurried as the darkness enveloped them. Only a slice of moon lit their way now. Occasional sparks swirled up from a chimney but quickly died in the cold and gloom. The smell of cooking fires on the wind took them all the way to Fleet Ditch, and Avelyn led the way directly into the alchemist's shop.

Instead of worrying at a rosary or pacing the floor, the alchemist was busy at his crucibles. A leather-bound book lay open to the side, and on its parchment pages were many of the same symbols Crispin had seen all over London. More symbols, written in chalk, decorated the alchemist's table, floor, and walls, connected by long straight lines. Strange smells issued from his bubbling retorts, and the fire beneath each beaker lit the man's determined face with dancing shadows. In fact, more shadows flickered wildly against a far wall in shapes that Crispin dared not look at.

Directly in front of the alchemist was a shallow basin filled with dark water that did not move. He appeared to be staring into it with great concentration, leaning farther and farther toward its unnatural plane.

And above it all came the creak and groan of the metal planets circling endlessly, fire rippling over their brass faces.

Crispin drew back, alarmed. This was sorcery!

"Master Flamel! What are you doing?"

The alchemist startled and jerked up. "*Maître* Guest!" He cast his glance across his work. "I am doing what I can, what I *must*, in order to find my dear wife. Alchemy is much more than using the simple elements of the earth."

"It looks very much like witchcraft to me."

Flamel scowled. "Oh? And you are very much acquainted with witchcraft, are you?" He raised his hand before Crispin could speak. "As acquainted as you are with alchemy, no doubt. I assure you, *Maître*, it is not sorcery or witchcraft! It has been a full day and I have received no more messages and no one has ever approached the statue of Saint Paul."

"We must put our heads together and think on it, Master Flamel. Not delve into these... dubious methods." He interrupted what were to be the alchemist's indignant protests. "No more distractions. No more detours." He sat and settled beside the alchemist. "There are symbols etched on the walls of the city," Crispin explained. He pointed to the chalked sigils on the table. "And they look like these. What do they mean? A preacher called them the work of the Devil, for indeed, they are mysterious and strange." He eyed Flamel's glyphs with suspicion. "But he also seemed to know about your dead apprentice, and he looked directly at me when he said it, thinking that *I* was an alchemist. I have reason to believe they are connected with these crimes, and I want you, Master Flamel, to come with us."

"Now? It is the fall of night and my work—"

"Night is better. We will go unnoticed. Fetch a lantern."

Avelyn fixed a small candle in a conical metal lantern and held it aloft by its ring.

"We must be cautious of the Watch," he told them.

Quietly, they filtered out of the shop. Under the small glow of Avelyn's lantern, they moved quickly through the street. She showed the alchemist the signs and he made a small gasp. "Oh! Alchemical symbols."

"If these are signs an alchemist would recognize, then why would an alchemist fear them?"

"We do not leave our marks for just anyone to see them. They are easily misconstrued as a sorcerer's writings." He narrowed his eyes at Crispin.

"Then is it safe to say that the person who made these marks is an alchemist?"

"That very well may be true," Flamel said reluctantly. "On the other hand, these symbols mean nothing. They are random, as if merely *using* the symbols, like a child who makes letters but cannot read them."

"Then what you are saying is that this miscreant may *not* be an alchemist?"

Flamel shrugged. "They are... very random."

Crispin pointed to the strange glyphs. "There is Hebrew there. Perhaps a Jew wrote this."

Flamel gave Crispin a measuring gaze. "How did *you* know it is Hebrew?"

"Another investigation from some years ago."

He nodded. "As it happens, I do have an acquaintance with the language of the Old Testament. Alchemy has close ties to the Jewish scriptures and to their magical writings, as well as numerology. Are you familiar with the Kabbalah?"

A shiver passed up his spine. "Intimately."

"Well... the Hebrew glyphs are used along with the sigils found in the Kabbalah for our special writings on alchemy. Alchemists have used this language since ancient times, even before Christianity. They are considered suspicious by the Church, and so we must be cautious… but why are they here? What does this have to do with Perenelle?"

"Your servant seems to think they are important."

He looked at Avelyn and she looked back at her master earnestly. "Take us to the next one," he told her.

By lantern light, they moved deeper into London.

The four of them spent hours traipsing through the icy lanes. On two occasions they nearly ran into the Watch, but Crispin carefully directed them down what looked like a dead end but what he knew better to be merely a narrow close.

Crispin watched the old alchemist squint at the symbols, whether scratched out or not, but each time the man shook his head. They were random, he told him. They made no sense and offered no further clues. Crispin was beginning to think that someone was playing an elaborate prank. But why would they take the time?

With Flamel weary and distracted, Crispin called a halt to their investigation and they all returned to the alchemist's shop in the early hours of the morning.

It was still dark when they turned the corner and the little candle in Avelyn's lantern was nearly spent, but she suddenly sprinted for the door without them, leaving them alone in the dense gloom.

"Sarding woman," grunted Jack.

Crispin was about to mouth the same sentiments when he saw it. Her lantern's light glinted off the dagger stuck into the wood, and Crispin ran forward. He heard Jack's steps behind him and they both stopped in front of the door.

The dagger held a parchment fragment in place. Crispin grasped the dagger just as Flamel jogged forward, huffing and wheezing. "What is it? What is it? My Perenelle!"

"Hush, man. Do you wish to wake the whole parish?" As it was,

Crispin spied a shutter across the way open and a curious shadow move across the candlelight within.

Crispin quickly pulled out the dagger, grabbed the note, and ushered the others inside.

He crossed to the fire beside Avelyn, who stoked it roughly with an iron poker. They crowded round him. In Latin again. He translated it aloud:

"'You shall never see her return unless you play fairly. You had best begin at the beginning.'"

Flamel tore the cap from his head and heaved it to the floor. "What are we to do? What is it he is doing to us, to her!"

"Calm yourself, Master Flamel. This is a good sign. It proves he is still interested, still in the game."

"It is *not* a game!" he insisted. Spittle flecked his beard.

"It is to him. What does he mean by 'begin at the beginning'?"

Jack shrugged. "Sunrise? Matins? Should we be at a church?"

"At St. Paul's," offered the alchemist. "Should I leave the ransom there again?"

"He was more straightforward before about placing the ransom where and when. Why not simply pick another place and tell us so? What has changed?"

"He saw us trying to deceive him," said Jack.

Crispin nodded. "He must be watching us as much as we are watching for him." And he suddenly remembered the men in the shadows following him and Jack. Should he see them again, he would leave little left for subtlety.

"So what *does* it mean, sir?"

"Jack, I wish I knew."

Exhausted, Flamel moved to a chair before the hearth. Crispin followed suit, the momentary excitement from the discovery of the new parchment fading, making him feel how tired he was. He edged his chair away from the chalked symbols and settled. No one spoke. Flamel stared into the flames. Crispin clutched the parchment and followed his example, hoping to find enlightenment within the leaping fire, while Avelyn scrambled about, seemingly as energetic as ever, heating wine and serving them hunks of bread and cheese on a wooden platter.

Crispin ate absently, just to fill the hollowness in his belly. The wine warmed him and the fire thawed his cold feet. He picked up the parchment from time to time, just to feel that it was real. After their night of scrambling after these alchemical symbols, Crispin wondered for the hundredth time if the abductor was referring to those signs. With a shake of his head, he realized he was becoming more and more obsessed with the symbols. They couldn't be random, as Flamel suggested. They had to mean something. "It's as if he's playing some sort of game with us," he murmured.

Crispin folded his arms over his chest. But then again, why did they have to mean anything at all? Flamel said as much, said that the symbols meant nothing. Was he relying too much on the ramblings of this preacher, whom neither he nor Jack had been able to confront?

"I still do not see how you think these things have truck with my Perenelle?" The alchemist's sudden words in the relative peace and calm jarred Crispin's senses.

Crispin rubbed his chin. The stubble was as pronounced as when he woke in the morning. But of course, it was nearly morning again. He realized if he wished for truth from Flamel, it was time to share some of his own. "On the day we left the ransom," he said quietly, "the earl of Derby was there. He seemed to know of the exchange. Do you know Henry Bolingbroke?"

Flamel's eyes were haunted, but there was no deception there. Only bewilderment. "No. I do not know this Henry Bolingbroke. Why did you not say anything of this before?"

Crispin did not look at Jack, but he felt the boy stir, sit up taller. "He is the duke of Lancaster's son. And... I am acquainted with him and his family."

Flamel staggered to his feet, his horn beaker falling to the floor in a splash of wine across the hearth. "Lancaster," he breathed.

"Master Flamel?"

"These names," he said. The effort it took to control his outburst was written on his face in strained lines and pronounced veins at his temples. Slowly he sat again, stroking his gown in a futile gesture of calm and looking for his wine. Avelyn fetched the cup from the floor and filled it again. She pressed it into his hand. "I... get them confused sometimes. There are similar lords in the court of France."

Crispin drank a dose of wine while studying the man over the rim of his cup. He set the wine aside and licked his lips. "Can you tell me, then, of the Philosopher's Stone? May I see it?"

The alchemist froze. Only his eyes moved, darting from here to there, terrified. Slowly he recovered, even tried to chuckle. "Silly. You misunderstand. The Stone is not a real object, *Maître* Guest. It is the alchemist's quest to attain purity of the soul."

Crispin cocked a brow. "Is it? And have you found it? Purity of soul, that is?"

"It is an endless search. A lifetime's worth."

Crispin set the parchment down and rose. He sauntered toward him and looked down at the shorter man with his thumbs fitted in his belt. "Harken to me, sir. There is no use in denying it. I know you have it, or think you do. Show it to me. Or I shall walk out that door."

Flamel stammered and tried to look away, but in the end he raised his face to Crispin with a mixture of fear and a good dose of amazement. "How... how did you know?"

Crispin threw back his shoulders with a haughty tilt. "I am the Tracker, sir. I am paid to discover the truth."

The man inhaled a shaky breath and slowly got to his feet. "Very well. You have earned the right to see it."

Jack canted forward, looking at Crispin with wonderment.

Flamel shuffled to that same ambry that held the broach. But as his hand slid along the side, another hidden drawer popped open. Shadows surrounded him and Crispin could not see clearly what he was doing, but he brought forth a small glass phial and held it gingerly, walking with care when he returned to the fire. He held it up. The phial was no more than two fingers wide and was made of crystal or clear glass, like a reliquary. Inside was what looked like another piece of amber glass, but as Crispin drew forward and peered more carefully, he saw that the amber lozenge was rough on one side, like something hewn from a rock, but the rest was like a crystal: clear, smooth, and unblemished. It was only the size of a small parsnip and shaped very like one, too.

"This," said Flamel with a hint of awe in his voice, "is the Philosopher's Stone. I was able to re-create it from my grandfather's notes and from the papers given to me by an old Jew I met once in the Holy

Land." He turned it and the firelight caught its facets, shooting bright pinpricks of light outward to dazzle Crispin's eyes. The man smiled, gazing at it. "From this small stone, I have been able to transmute simple metals into gold. Mere playthings."

Crispin suddenly remembered the odd collection of gold objects with which Flamel had paid his fee, objects that still sat in his scrip.

No, this is not possible. "You... made this?" His hand came near it, whether to touch the phial or to snatch it, he did not know.

But Flamel pulled it away, his fingers covering the small object. "I did. Years ago. And it works. It is the crowning achievement of my life."

"And the Elixir? Have you... have you made that?"

He raised the phial again, unable to look away from it, turning it, letting the firelight play off its surface, first the rough side and then the faceted side. "No. Not yet. My permutations have been unsuccessful. My wife and I were close to achieving it. Very close." His fingers closed over the phial, and he lowered his hand, hiding the Stone from view in the drapery of his gown. "You see, *Maître*," he said quietly, as quietly as the soft crackle of the flames or the caress of the wind against the shutter, "alchemy is more than science, more than the transmuting of one element into another. It is Humanity itself, the spiritual progress that transforms us. I was not far wrong when I spoke of it as a metaphorical quest. For it is that and more. When you create, when you use such *Prima Materia,* you begin to understand the intricacies of Life itself. How can you not?" His face darkened. "But it is not a plaything for the greedy, a toy for the bored nobleman. Instead, it is a sacred duty, a keen responsibility for the initiated, and I take that responsibility very seriously. I would never share this knowledge with just anyone. Oh no. And surely you, *Maître* Guest, covet your knowledge the same. For I cannot imagine that you would share your art with one who was not a worthy apprentice."

Jack squared his shoulders and raised his spotted chin. Crispin gave him a glance and a soft smile. "I may be a skeptic as to the veracity of your claims about the Stone itself, Master Flamel, but I can understand your sentiments as concerns your work." He bowed. "Can you tell me, then, who is it that wants this Stone? Surely you must have an inkling." Crispin's gray eyes met the pale blue of the alchemist's.

"I have many acolytes, *Maître,* as you might have surmised. But many enemies as well. Greedy men, men with no fortitude, no scruples, who would use the power of this Stone for selfish ends. It is not to be trifled with. So many vile men I cannot count them all, have tried to wrest this Stone for themselves. But they will not have it!"

"Is that why you put the false ransom in the bag?"

"Yes, yes. I knew it would buy us time, for he would think it *was* the Philosopher's Stone. You see, no one knows what it truly looks like. No one... but the four of us here... and my wife." His eyes tracked from face to startled face. Only Avelyn showed no signs of amazement at all.

"And if what you say is true concerning these signs and sigils," the alchemist went on, "then my wife's abductor must be an alchemist himself... or he is using an alchemist for his ends. In which case, more than my wife will be in danger. You must solve this, *Maître.* You must get my Perenelle back in all haste. We must not let him get the Stone."

Crispin and Jack made it home before the market bells rang for the start of the business day. Wearily, they stumbled into the room. Jack sank onto the stool. He yawned loudly. "I'm bone weary, Master. I can't think no more."

"You can't think *any*more," Crispin corrected absently. "And neither can I." But thoughts of the Stone played in his mind like a minstrel's song, tumbling over and over again in an endless refrain in his thoughts. He dug into his scrip and pulled out his money pouch. He untied the string and poured its contents onto the table beside the chessboard. Out spun silver coins of various sizes, the image of the king imprinted upon them. But also there were the gold key, spoon, and nail. He picked them up, having forgotten all about them, and examined each of them carefully.

He could understand someone wishing to have a gold key or even a gold spoon, but a golden nail? What would be the purpose?

He turned the nail in his hand, startled when Tucker lit the candle on the table, giving him more light.

Jack tossed the lit straw into the fire and sat back down. "What are these, Master?"

"Payment." He did nothing as Jack took up each one, turned them in his hands, and then set them down again.

"Strange. Who gave them to you?"

"Nicholas Flamel." They exchanged glances.

"You don't mean to say…"

"These could have been made out of gold in the first place, Jack. Who's to say they were not? The man has that broach, after all. It is likely that the King of France or some other eccentric French noble had them made and gave these to him."

"But Master! Who would have cause to make this nail? In gold? It must be that Stone he has. It *does* work! What a man could do with that!"

"And for that he would kill. And steal a man's wife."

Jack's expression suddenly turned hard. "Even if he were already a rich and noble lord?"

Crispin felt sick. How many times could a man be betrayed? How many times could he allow his heart to be so used?

"You're thinking of Henry."

Jack jumped from his stool. "Of *course* I'm thinking of Lord Henry! But you're too stubborn to consider him."

Crispin slammed his hand to the table. "Watch it, Tucker."

"No. It's my task to be your conscience, sir. For if you will not listen to the wisdom inside you, it is up to me to point it out. You must go to Lord Henry and ask him straightaway."

"Don't you think I already have? And do you think for one moment he would tell me the truth?"

He hadn't wanted to say it, to think it. He was too afraid that it was true, that Henry had lied and that Crispin had believed that lie. Because he had wanted to.

Crispin scrubbed his face. "I'm too tired to think. Let us get at least a few hours of sleep before we begin again. You have a preacher to find, after all."

Jack slumped. He nodded. The boy was tired, too. And just as the two of them meandered to their separate corners, there was a knock at the door.

They froze, hands on hilts. Jack went first and opened the door a fraction.

"Is this the home of Crispin Guest? That Tracker fellow?"

The voice was familiar, and Crispin moved Jack aside and opened the door. It was the priest he had met on the street the day before. "My lord?" he said, stepping aside to let him in.

The priest stepped over the threshold and looked around the small room. "I must say, I expected something... more."

"Yes, well. What can I do for you, Father?"

"I should have introduced myself before. I am Father Edmund from St. Aelred's church. We talked of the deaths yesterday...."

"I remember you, Father. Please, sit." The old priest lowered himself to the chair. "Jack, bring wine for this good priest."

The priest didn't argue as Jack scrambled. He grabbed a bowl and wiped its rim with his sleeve and then went to the back window and stopped short, marveling at the jug left by Derby. He shook himself loose and quickly uncorked the wooden stopper and poured.

While Jack brought the wine, Crispin poked the fire and got it going. "It is late, Father Edmund. What brings you to the Shambles?"

"Late? Why, it's early." He sipped the wine and his brows rose in surprise at the fine taste.

Crispin chuckled tiredly. "So it is. It only seems late to me."

Father Edmund set the bowl aside. "My mind has been capering on those deaths, Master Guest. I cannot seem to forget them. I have learned from my fellow priests of many more. Twenty-five so far."

"Oh? Tell me."

"So many more than I could ever have imagined. Blessed Virgin. I prayed on it and the Divine presence seemed to hint to me that this was no mere plague."

"Father..." His brief suspicion suddenly rose up again. "Have you any reason to believe that they might have been... poisoned?"

"Poisoned? To what end? Why should a weaver, a cordwainer, a cobbler, and any number of other craftsmen's children have been poisoned?"

"It is merely a notion I had in passing, my lord. I have no basis for this theory."

"Evil witchcraft, more like, targeting the children for some offense. I would pay you to find the source, Master Guest, but I am but a humble priest."

Crispin eyed his fur-trimmed gown and his rings without comment. "As it happens, I would happily investigate for you on my own. As a concerned citizen."

"Is it witchcraft, then? How can I help our flock?"

"I know nothing of witchcraft, but something of poisons."

"Do you persist in this notion, then, of poison?"

"It is not any stranger a notion than witchcraft, is it, Father?"

He shrugged and crossed himself again.

"Perhaps you could tell me the names and streets that are mourning a loss," said Crispin. He turned to Jack, who looked back at him with puzzlement before he figured out what Crispin wanted and scrambled to the coffer. The boy opened it and pulled out parchment, quill, and ink. He set them on the table, and when he saw that Crispin had no intention of taking them up, he set them up himself by smoothing out the parchment and uncorking the ink from its clay pot. He dipped the quill in, and with tongue set firmly between his lips, he waited.

The old priest recited names and the streets where the families could be found. Crispin listened to the litany and scrubbed at his eyes. God's blood, but was weary. Madam Perenelle's fate was dire, but these random citizens had all been targeted with death. Something had to be done. But he and Jack needed rest.

Once the priest was finished, Jack stoppered the ink and set the quill aside, glancing over the tiny scrawl of his writing.

"Father Edmund," said Crispin, "I thank you for coming and assigning me this task. But you must excuse me and my apprentice. We were up the whole of the night on another grim matter. We need a little sleep."

"Not me, Master. I've got a second wind, as it were. Let me go in search of... er..." He looked at the priest eyeing him suspiciously. "You know who," he said cryptically to Crispin.

Yes, the preacher Robert Pickthorn. The man needed to be found.

"Good Father, have you seen this lay preacher, this Robert Pickthorn, again? We would very much like to speak with him."

"Do you? I daresay he could tell you a kettle full of the sin and vile corruption that permeates the city."

"Do you know where he is staying? With the bishop or some other worthy?"

"Dear me, no. I know nothing of him. But he is a fiery speaker, so they say."

"So I have seen." He turned to the boy. "Go on, Jack. I need at least a few hours' rest. Come fetch me when you've found anything of this Pickthorn."

Jack nodded, bowed to the priest, and fled out the door.

Father Edmund rose. "Then I shall leave you as well. It seems your hands are full at the moment. I pray that you have the strength to do all you must, Master Guest. I shall light a candle for you."

Crispin took a coin from the table and pressed it into the priest's hands, even as he scooped up the others and the golden objects and dropped them again into his pouch. "Do that, my lord. I could use all the help I can get."

He slept for several hours, waking only when the bells tolled for Sext. Groggily, he sat up and rubbed his eyes. He rinsed his mouth with the leftover wine from the priest's bowl, brushed and straightened his cotehardie, and left his lodgings.

With Jack's parchment in his hand, he made his way to Threeneedle Street. He asked some shopkeepers which house it was and was soon led to a weaver's. When he knocked, a maiden let him in.

"Is this the house in mourning?" he asked of the young woman. The walls had been hung with cloth, and shelves were stocked with bolts of varied weaves and colors.

"Aye, sir," she said sadly. "My younger brother. Three days ago."

A baby cried in the next room, a lusty, healthy cry.

She looked in that direction, raising her chin. "My other brother."

"Has anyone else taken sick?" Her wary expression gave him

pause. "My apologies, damosel. I don't ask out of prurient interest. I am Crispin Guest. You may have heard of me. I am called the Tracker."

Her eyes widened. "I shall fetch my father."

She departed through the other door, and he was uncertain as to whether this was a good sign or not. Presently a man emerged. His tunic was covered in bits of varied-colored threads cast off during his time at the loom. "My daughter said you were that Tracker man we hear tell about. Is this true?"

He bowed. "It is, good Master. Can you tell me about your son's illness?"

"Are you investigating *that?* Don't waste your time. It was a sickness that took my boy. If it were anything but God's will, I'd have called in the sheriffs."

"It is merely my own fancy that leads me here. And the priest Father Edmund. And so. Can you tell me of his illness?"

The man shook his head and crossed himself. "It was sudden-like. Over before it began. He felt unwell, too sick to work. A bad stomach. He was a good lad, God preserve him, not like to shirk, even though he had always been a slight lad. He got worse, over a span of two days. And then it was done."

"Did anyone else feel unwell?"

"Well, Mary, here," he said, motioning toward his daughter. "Headache and bellyache. But she felt better after the cure. But no one else."

"Cure?"

"Mother said it would settle my belly," she said. "Drank raw eggs and chewed garlic."

Crispin winced. "I see. A good cure, then." He touched her chin to look at her face. She still looked listless but did not seem worse for wear. He let her go. "I am heartily sorry for your loss. I pray that all will be well."

"God's blessings on you, sir."

He left a coin with them for their loss, looking back at the humble shop as they closed the door. Nothing unusual about it. And as he visited three more homes, he heard much the same. The elderly had died, grandfathers and grandmothers. The youngest ones were also afflicted, especially the weakest. Yet the babes in swaddling or toddlers went unaffected. Nor did anyone else in the household feel ill or aggrieved, except by their great loss.

Something was tapping at the back of his mind, and the notion emerged once again that it sounded to him like a poisoning. But why on earth target those humble people? None of them were important, they did not know one another, and they did no harm. They had nothing in common except as hardworking citizens. What good would it do to kill the children of a weaver, a corn merchant, or a chandler? Or any number of these others on his list that he had not yet talked to?

He walked slowly through the streets, ignoring those around him to immerse himself in his thoughts, or, as he had told Jack, to walk through the facts.

The youngsters or elderly. As long as they were the weakest. But by far, most were children.

He sat on a stone step that led to the cistern near Cornhill. Christ, but he was tired. He ran his hand through his hair under his hood and leaned back against a post. Absently, he watched a boy trying to lift his coneys away from the yapping of a dog at his heels. Two nuns walked side by side, the wet hems of their brown habits rippling over patchy snow. Water carriers hurried up and down the steps, giving Crispin a sneer as they skirted past him, for Crispin sat in their way. Heavy yokes burdened their shoulders, each with a heavy water skin hanging from either end. Boys like these were paid to quickly fill their buckets from the cisterns throughout the city, for the water of the Thames was not fit to drink, with its privies and butchering stalls along its banks.

An old man was moving a hog through the streets and he beat it as the pig stopped near a turnip seller's cart and began rooting through it. An argument ensued between the pig man and the turnip dealer, and Crispin watched dispassionately, wondering idly if it would come to blows.

He had rested enough and was ready to depart until he saw a cluster of small children running up to the cistern. Each took a drink from the ladle that was there and then let it fall again into the font. One of the children, the smallest, wasn't running as fast as the others and had to stop to catch his breath before he hurried to keep up. He did not look well.

A notion struck Crispin. A foul, diabolical notion. He looked back at the water carriers trudging to their duties. Others, maids and housewives, also moved under the burden of heavy buckets or skins swollen with chilled water from the cistern.

No.

Crispin leapt to his feet and ran back the way he had come, knocked on the doors of the grieving houses he had only just visited to ask one question: Which cistern did they use to get their water?

Each section of London had its own cistern. There was the Standard down Cheap, where Crispin got his water, and the Mercery near the hospital of St. Thomas of Acon, and the Tun up Cornhill way, and numerous other smaller cisterns and conduits. Some of the wealthier patrons even had running water through pipes, a rare innovation stolen from the ancient Romans, as Crispin had seen in his younger days in Bath and in Lancaster's castles.

But the three families afflicted used the water from the Tun. Crispin looked down at the parchment in his hand. Unmindful of the stares, he raced down the lane in search of the others.

His suspicions were confirmed. All the families with losses had partaken of the cistern at the Tun. And only those who most frequently drank of the water—the youngsters and a few elderly—took sick and died. Babes in swaddling and toddlers did not, for they suckled at their mother's breasts. And the rest of the family consumed ale.

As diabolical as it seemed, someone had poisoned the cistern.

fourteen

rispin stood in the lane, a sense of helplessness dragging at his limbs. How could he stop such a horrific scheme? To whom could he go?

He thought of Henry but did not know how to find him. The sheriffs, then. His only hope in the matter.

He trotted toward Newgate, weaving in and out among the people along the busy avenue and up and around alleyways. When he arrived at last to the stone gate, he straightened his clothes and dusted the snow from his shoulders. His feet were wet and cold, but there was nothing to be done. He approached the two guards and nodded to them. "Are the sheriffs in?"

One of the serjeants, Tom Merton, cocked back his kettle helm. He looked Crispin insolently up and down. He well knew that the majority of the sheriffs that passed through these doors did not favor Crispin's presence.

"Why do you want to know, Guest?"

"Because I have important information to impart to them. Why else would I ever have cause to be here?"

"Well, you never know," he said, picking his teeth with his dagger. "You are known to be a man to cause mischief."

Crispin let the matter slide. He knew better than to engage the sheriffs' henchmen. They were more brawn than brain.

"Are they in?" he tried again.

"To you? Not likely." He sheathed his dagger and spit on the ground before Crispin's boots. Stubbornly, he leaned on his pike and blocked the entrance. The other, Wendell Smythe, just as blunt-faced as his companion and standing by the brazier, laughed behind Crispin's back.

"Masters, may I *please* pass? It is urgent that I speak with them."

"Urgent, he says, like we are supposed to wait on him," said Tom to the other.

"I am not asking you to wait on me or even announce me. I merely ask for permission to pass."

Wendell joined Tom at the entrance. "But it is our duty to guard the way," he said, elbowing Tom. "We can't let just any knave through, scumming up the place."

Crispin eyed the both of them with a sneer. "Too late."

As soon as he said it, he knew it had been a bad idea. Tom growled and swung his fist. Crispin ducked but jabbed upward into the man's belly. Tom doubled over, but his companion tried to grab Crispin and managed to shove him up against the wall. Wendell tried for a gut punch, but Crispin rolled out of the way in time for the serjeant to deliver his blow to the stone wall. He yowled and spun away, clutching his injured hand.

By then, Tom had recovered and remembered he had a weapon. He grabbed the pike and aimed the point at Crispin's midsection, drawing it back to strike. The spear point jabbed and Crispin jumped out of the way at the last moment. The iron point clanged against a stone column instead. Recovering, he stabbed toward Crispin again, but Crispin sidestepped nimbly out of the way.

Crispin grabbed the pike's staff and swung it wide, while Tom, still clutching it, slammed against the wall. Tom tried to wrestle it from Crispin's grasp… and kept getting smashed into the wall for his trouble.

"By all the saints, what is going on here?"

Tom froze, with Crispin holding tight to the pointed end of the pike. "Crispin Guest," Tom snarled in explanation, as if that were all the reason anyone needed for violence.

Sheriff William Venour made a sound of disgust. "Guest. I should have known. God's wounds! Why do you vex us? What sin have we committed to be so abused by you?"

126

"Call off your serjeant, my lord. I merely come for your help. It is your duty."

The sheriff did not look as if he would comply, but after a moment that went on far too long, he finally motioned for Tom to put away his weapon. Crispin released his hold of it. Venour glared at the other serjeant, who was still nursing his hand. "What happened to you?"

Wendell motioned with a jerk of his head toward Crispin.

"Fools and incompetents. I am surrounded by fools and incompetents. Come, Guest." The sheriff turned up the stairs and didn't look back.

Crispin kept a careful eye on Tom, who had lowered his spear but did not relinquish it. He followed the sheriff upward to the parlor, past a wizened clerk scratching on a parchment by lantern light, and into the warm room.

Sheriff William took a seat behind a large table, with bulky round legs carved and scrolled with leaves and vines. Sheriff Hugh was nowhere in sight.

He did not offer Crispin a chair as he folded his hands over his pouched belly and looked down his long nose, ginger mustache twitching. "Well?"

Crispin took a breath. "My Lord Sheriff, I have discovered a plot that has left twenty-five of London's citizens dead."

He jolted to his feet. *"What?"*

"Twenty-five at last count, my lord. I do not know how many more there might have been or might be in the future if you do not act."

"Me? What can I do?"

"You must close the cistern at the Tun. It is poisoned."

"Poisoned? What utter nonsense is this, Guest?" He passed a hand over his face and sat again. "God's toes, you had me worried for a moment. Poisoned indeed! Is this another ploy to extort a fee from this office? I have heard of your tricks. This is foul, even for you."

Hands on the table, Crispin leaned in toward the man, much closer than he would have liked. "I am not lying. The cistern is poisoned and children have died. More will die unless you shut the cistern."

"Your imagination astounds me. What next, I wonder? French spies

127

creeping into our houses to slit our throats? I suppose it's the French poisoning the wells, then, correct? I receive reports all the time from hysterical fishwives, thinking a Frenchman is hiding in their cellars. They blame the French now for souring their milk or when their horse goes lame. The French are the new boggart. Begone, Guest. I'm sick of you."

"Lord Sheriff, I entreat you. Do not dismiss me. More people will die. I don't know whether it is a French plot or not, but it is there nonetheless."

"Where's your proof, Guest?"

"I have spoken to Father Edmund of St. Aelred's parish, and he had ministered to the families of these children. They died suddenly and hideously. No one else in the house was affected. Don't you see? Only children who regularly drank water were affected. Not babes that suckled, and not older ones who drank ale."

"Children, you say? What of it? Children die with great frequency in London. No one has bothered about it before."

"They have not been murdered and in these numbers before."

He shook his head. "Look at you. You believe your own tales, Guest. A murderer behind every shadow. I haven't time for you. Begone, I say!"

He stood fast, fisting his hands. "If I bring you proof, Lord Sheriff, will you close the cistern?"

The sheriff rubbed his eyes wearily. "Oh, for the love of the Holy Ghost. You are a thorn in my side, do you know that? Yes, damn you. Bring me proof and I will consider it. Only *consider* it, mind."

Tight-lipped, Crispin bowed and turned on his heel. Proof, eh? What could he do to bring the man proof? He'd have to think of something.

Down the steps he went. He paused near the bottom, looking out for Tom and Wendell. He saw them by the brazier. Wendell was still nursing his hand. He probably broke it. Crispin smiled. He trotted the rest of the way down and passed them by through the arch. They jeered at him but did not approach.

Proof, he thought, striding down Newgate Market. Perhaps the waters could be tested. Perhaps Nicholas Flamel, with all his alchemical craft, could detect a poison if it was present. It would help the man take his mind off his troubles. As for Crispin, Perenelle was no nearer to being saved. But if the key to her freedom lay with those symbols, he would have to get to work on deciphering those with all haste.

Crispin arrived at the Tun early in the afternoon and surveyed the round stone structure. Looking like the lower portion of a castle's tower, it captured sweet rainwater and quenched a thirsty city. But now it looked to be a tower of disaster, dealing death to the weakest within its shadow. Who was doing it? Had the sheriff stumbled upon the truth in his flippant remarks? Was it French spies? He suddenly thought of the shadow men who had followed him earlier. If these miscreants could get to the water, what else could they poison? Grain? Livestock? While Lancaster and the chivalry of England were off to Spain, was an insidious plot being concocted by England's enemies in France?

He watched with growing anxiety as maids and young children came to the cistern, filled their buckets and bougets, and trotted away, bringing the befouled water into their homes.

He stopped a boy with a bucket. "Boy, I will give you two pence for your bucket."

The boy's openmouthed shock muted him until he came to his senses and tentatively asked, "For the *whole* bucket?"

Crispin smiled kindly. "Yes, the whole bucket. Along with its water."

"Aye, sir. As you will."

Crispin handed over the coins and the boy presented him with the full bucket. But then his small face furrowed with worry. "Shall I carry it for you, sir? Where are you bound?"

"For another farthing, lad, we're headed to Fleet Ditch."

"I can do that!" said the boy, brightening. He took the bucket back from Crispin and walked, swaying from side to side with the weight of it, sloshing the water onto the snow.

Enough water remained in the bucket when they finally arrived to Flamel's shop. Crispin thanked the boy, gave him a farthing, and, before the boy left, stopped him with the lifting of his hand. "And boy, promise me you will not get water from the Tun for some days."

"Eh? Not the Tun? But it is the closest cistern."

"I know that. But promise me you will not." He handed over yet another coin to seal the bargain, kicking himself for the mawkish fool that he was. He couldn't very well pay all the urchins in London not to take water from the Tun.

The boy whooped as he sprinted away, surely to relate to his family how a strange and foolish man had paid an exorbitant price for their leaky old bucket.

He knocked on the alchemist's door and Avelyn opened it. She looked as fresh as if she had gotten a full night's sleep, but he seemed to expect no less from her. She looked puzzled at the bucket he carried inside but didn't question it when Crispin set it on a table still chalked with sigils.

Flamel, heavy dark bags under his eyes, was slowly climbing down the ladder from his upper loft. He seemed to pay no heed to the whirling planets mere inches from him. "What have you brought, *Maître*. More clues?"

"Something else, sir. Perhaps it will distract you from your troubles while doing this good deed for others."

"Eh? What good deed?" He eyed the bucket. He looked smaller dressed as he was in his long shift with a loose unbuttoned gown thrown over it.

"I have reason to believe that this water has been poisoned."

"Poisoned? But why?"

Crispin shook his head. Avelyn was suddenly there, offering him a chair. A good thing. He was exhausted and fell into it. "I know not why, Master Flamel. But I only hope that you can discover the poison from this sample and tell me what it is and how to counteract it. If poisoned it is."

"But how do you know it is poisoned?"

"Because many have died from consuming it. I have surmised that much."

"Died, have they?" It had indeed served as a distraction, for Flamel was hitching up his sleeves and scooping up some of the water into a beaker. He poured it into a retort and set the glass object over a trivet in his fire.

"Yes," Crispin said wearily. "Young children, mostly. Some old people as well."

"Weaklings?"

"I suppose."

"Ah," he said, and set quietly to work.

Crispin watched him grab different canisters from his shelves, peer inside them, and either use a wooden spoon to remove some of the powdered contents or put the canister back untouched on his shelf, muttering all the while.

After a time, Crispin rose. He could see no sense in spending the day there. He told the man he was leaving, though he doubted he heard. Avelyn's eyes tracked him as he strode out the door, and she followed. He stopped on the step outside and turned to her.

She threw her arms around his neck and pulled him down toward her. Face very close to his, he felt her breath on his lips. It was tempting. She licked her lips, knowing he was looking at them.

"You are a seductress, do you know that?" He reached up to his neck and disengaged her arms, holding them a long time. "I have work to do," he said.

She made the sign for "kiss," but he shook his head. She pouted and made the sign again. "No," he said firmly, and turned away, striding down the lane. But when he looked back, she was stalking right behind him.

He stopped and glared at her. "What do you think you are doing?"

Her lips formed that elfin smile and she licked them yet again, tongue trailing over them slowly. Sighing with just a bit of a quickened heart, he glanced quickly around the street, grabbed her by her cloak, and dragged her forward. "I'm beginning to think that you have bewitched me," he said to her lips before he kissed them, exploring the shape and fullness of her mouth for a long time. When he finally drew back, it was to the whistles and guffaws of the men passing by.

He smirked at her and walked away. And when he looked over his shoulder, he was satisfied that she had retreated back to her master's shop.

It took little time to return to the Shambles. Crispin bade good day to the tinker Martin Kemp, who was rearranging his wares on his display table, before Crispin stumped up the stairs to his lodgings. He closed the door once inside. After stoking the dying fire, he lit the candles in their sconces along the walls and kept his cloak on as he sat at the table, eyes traveling over the discarded chessboard.

He picked up a bishop and turned it in his fingers. The carvings had always intrigued him. The design depicted each piece as its model was in life, only fatter and squatter. Easy to put in one's hand. The abbot had told him it was an old set, possibly had been in his family for a generation. It was an expensive behest. He was certain that Abbot William would have rather sold it or gifted it to some other noble for a favor. But a behest was a behest. Crispin was glad to have it.

With a grunt, he wrapped himself tightly in his cloak. Those were treasured days. He did not realize how much he had relied on the old man for advice and counsel. He wished the old abbot were here now to talk to. He supposed, in a way, the abbot had been a substitute for Lancaster, whom he had started speaking to again only a few years ago.

And now Lancaster's son. He closed his eyes. His mind drifted along, snapping up memories of those long-ago days, when Crispin was a household knight and had been given the privilege of training young Henry, just as Lancaster had trained Crispin. He had taken the lad hawking and riding, had trained him in archery. They had discussed warfare and strategy and, yes, had played many games of chess and tables together. But gone were those carefree days. So much had changed. Richard was a man now and so was Henry. The old abbot was dead, and Lancaster was far away in Spain. And Crispin was left with a dead apprentice, a missing wife, poisoned water, and… what? Strange clues etched on the streets and alleys of London? Shadowy men following him for some unknown reason? It seemed absurd, beyond the realm of reality. And yet over the years, he had encountered far stranger things.

Still, this abduction seemed particularly insidious. Someone was playing games, relishing the confusion it elicited. But did it have to do with Perenelle Flamel or something else? Something worse? Something… like a poisoned cistern?

Crispin turned his head, staring at his own bucket in the corner by the door. Such a simple thing. Water. One needed it for one's stews and pottage. To clean. To drink, when there was no ale or wine about. A necessity of life. It was worse than poisoning bread. What foul demon would do such a thing? To what end?

And what had Henry to do with it? For he could not put out of his head the possibility that Henry was somehow involved. The man had ambition. Impatience. No wonder Lancaster had left him at home. Of course, the public excuse was that he needed him to watch the estates, but if Henry was anything like Crispin at that age, it was because of his impetuosity. If Henry believed he needed this Stone or believed in its power, then he would have no qualms about taking it....

Wait.

Crispin felt like the biggest fool. It couldn't be Henry. Derby would never stoop to this waiting game, not that impatient youth. He would simply go to Flamel himself and force him to give over the Stone. He wouldn't have time to play these games.

That meant Henry was innocent.

Crispin sat back, feeling relieved. He had not wanted his young lord to be the cause of this crime or of any other. Henry might be a dupe, but he was not an instigator.

Which did beg the question as to why he was there in the cathedral. Had he been sent? And if so, by whom? If he could couch it in this way, Henry might be persuaded to answer. Henry was involved in some way whether Crispin liked it or not.

He pushed it all aside. It didn't matter. As long as Crispin stopped the plot, prevented more deaths, *that* was what mattered.

He glanced out the window. The sun had moved and the bells had recently rung for None. He picked up the parchment fragment again. *You shall never see her return unless you play fairly. You had best begin at the beginning.*

Play fairly. Begin at the beginning. There was something he was missing, but his mind wouldn't work on it. For now, he had to know how Flamel fared with testing the water. He had to go back and see what the man had discovered.

fifteen

rsenic," declared the alchemist.

In the back of his mind, Crispin had not wanted to believe it, but to hear confirmation sent a deep shiver down his spine. "How... how bad is it?"

"A very weak concentration. Little wonder only those very feeble succumbed. But already I see that the solution is being diluted. More rain and snow and the problem will resolve itself."

"But how long will that take?"

"It all depends on how much rain and snow is added. Days. Weeks. Hard to say." They both looked toward the window and to the sun shining through.

"Should the cistern be closed?"

"I would advise it. And have a guard set on the others."

"Will you come with me to the sheriffs to explain it? They won't listen to me without proof."

He wrung his hands and cast glances about his shop. "But who will await a message? How shall we 'begin at the beginning'? My Perenelle. What has become of her?"

"When my apprentice returns we will know more. Have patience, Master Flamel. Please. You must come with me."

"Patience is all I have. Very well." He took the cloak offered by Avelyn and shrugged it on. "Quickly, now. We must hurry back."

Crispin grabbed the bucket and Flamel's arm and pushed him out the door. They traveled through the busy streets with all haste, stepping aside for a small contingent of armed soldiers marching down the lane. Crispin did not recognize their captain, but they wore the arms of the king and their presence was enough to remind all and sundry that Richard was still England's ruler.

Crispin and Flamel moved on, the bucket knocking against Crispin's leg as they hurried.

They arrived at Newgate and both serjeants were there. Wendell had a bandage wound tight around his hand and they both stood to attention when Crispin neared them.

"You have your nerve showing your face here again, Guest," said Tom with a deep scowl.

"It is the only face I have, I'm afraid."

Wendell clenched and unclenched his good hand over his spear shaft. "You broke my hand, you churl."

"You broke it yourself. Have a care, Master, or your other will suffer the same fate."

Tom jabbed his spear forward. "Get out, Guest."

"The sheriffs are expecting me." It was a little lie. "How would it go for you if they expected me and you would not allow us to pass? Not well, I should think. Losing one's position in these troubled times? You wouldn't want your families to starve, now, would you?"

Tom's silent scowl said it all. He gestured with a jerk of the pike up the stairs, and Crispin wasted no time. He hauled Flamel after him, taking the steps two at once.

They emerged into the lantern light of the outer alcove. The clerk looked up and squinted at Crispin's face. "Eh? Master Guest? Back so soon?"

"May I?" he asked, gesturing toward the archway into the sheriffs' parlor.

"You might as well." He turned away and wriggled back into his seat, positioning his quills before him.

Crispin entered and bowed to both sheriffs. Venour sat at the heavy table, while Fastolf stood by the arched window, looking down into the street below. They both turned at Crispin's step. "My lords," he said.

"Guest," spat William Venour. "What are you doing here? I thought I told you—"

"You wanted proof, my lord. I brought you proof."

He set the bucket down but pushed Flamel forward.

"Isn't that the alchemist with the dead apprentice?" said Hugh Fastolf.

Flamel bowed. "*Oui, mes seigneurs.* But I come to you now by request of *Maître* Guest. I tested the poisoned water myself."

Fastolf frowned. "What is this? Poisoned water? What's he talking about?"

Venour propped his head on his hand. "Guest came in earlier spouting something about a poisoned cistern. Plainly it is rubbish, as are all his complaints, but now he would bring this Frenchman in on it." Something seemed to fall into place in the sheriff's mind, for his eyes narrowed. "Wait. *Frenchman?*"

Flamel cringed. Clearly he had seen the like before.

"He's an alchemist," Crispin explained. "He knows about poisons. Uses them in his work. There is nothing particularly sinister in that."

"So *you* say," said Venour. "Sounds terribly suspicious to me."

The old alchemist looked at each sheriff, then back at Crispin for confirmation. Crispin urged him on.

"It seems, *mon Shérif de Seigneur,* that arsenic has been given into the water. Enough to kill the feeble and to make others sick."

"Preposterous. Where's your proof?"

"I did the tests. It is unmistakable."

Crispin moved forward. "Will you close the cistern, my lords? Master Flamel here says that it will take only a few days of more rain and snow to dilute the solution so that it will do no further harm."

"No, I will not! Close the cistern at the word of you and this Frenchman? Are you mad?"

"More people will die, Lord Sheriff. Is that what you want on your conscience?"

"Very thin ice, Guest," said Sheriff William with a snarl.

Sheriff Hugh slapped his hand over his sword hilt and stepped forward. "And *I* don't believe you either! What nonsense. Who says anyone has died?"

"I spoke to Father Edmund of St. Aelred's parish and he attests to the strangeness of these deaths. I can bring him forth, if that will appease you. I accompanied him when he administered the last rites to a young girl. Only the day before a boy died in the same household."

"A pestilence, then."

"Only the weakest succumbed. Those that drank the water. The others were fine. Including babes in swaddling."

"It proves nothing, Guest!"

Tight-lipped, Crispin snatched the goblet from the sheriff's table and tossed its contents out across the floor. He grasped the bucket he'd left nearly under the table and dipped the goblet in. He thrust the dripping cup toward Sheriff William. "If you think I am lying, then you will not fear to drink this."

Venour shrank back. Crispin turned to Sheriff Hugh and stepped up to him, offering the cup. "And you, Lord Sheriff. Will you drink and call me a liar?"

Fastolf refused to touch it, to look at it. He skirted Crispin and glared at the alchemist. "I will do no such thing. You probably tampered with it yourself."

"To what end? Blame me for closing the cistern, if you must. But you must close it! Take the credit yourselves when no more die."

"Oh ho!" said Fastolf. "So you *would* have your name involved?"

Crispin lowered his head and shook it. "Do what you will with my name, my lords. But for God's sake *close the cistern*."

For the first time, the sheriffs looked uncomfortable. They exchanged mute glances and then stared at the same time at the goblet Crispin had set down on their table.

Venour scowled. "But if we close it, the people will rage. They will blame the king."

"They will blame him with great cries and lamentation if he allows more innocents to die and could have prevented it. *You* stand for the king and his justice. Do this and be champions."

"Do it and be thrown into the stocks!"

"Now wait, William," said Fastolf. "A few days, did you say?" he said to Flamel.

Flamel shrugged. "When it rains or snows again."

They all looked toward the window. Clouds had moved in and Crispin was never so glad to see their dark undersides, heavy with snow.

"For three days only, then." Fastolf looked to Sheriff William for confirmation, and the man reluctantly nodded. "And a guard will be sent to the others. Will that suffice?"

"It will do very well, Lord Sheriff," said Crispin with a bow.

"Oh, good. I'm so glad you're pleased. Now, take *this* away." Fastolf flapped his hand at the untouched goblet.

Crispin took the goblet and tossed its contents into the fire. The fire hissed and flamed blue for a moment before settling down. He bowed to the sheriffs again without another word, took Flamel's arm, and left.

Escorting Flamel back to his shop, Crispin couldn't be certain if his shadows had returned. There were too many people on the streets, too many horses and carts, but he thought he saw men in the shadows pacing them, until he quickly turned at the last moment before they rounded a corner... No one there.

"Master Flamel," he said quietly into the man's collar, "do you suspect any connection between these poisonings and your missing wife?"

He shot Crispin an astonished look. *"Mon Dieu!* Do you believe that to be so?"

"I don't know. But they coincide, and I have a mistrustful nature. Do *you* believe it? I'll admit that alchemy and its practitioners are strange to me."

Flamel lowered his brows in thought just as they came to the steps in front of his doorway. "I do not see any connection, *Maître*. Would that I could. If it would bring back my Perenelle..." He breathed a quivering sigh.

Crispin scowled. The weight of her disappearance lay heavy on his shoulders. He hated this helpless feeling, these dead ends where he had nowhere to turn, no one to ask. That damnably abstruse parchment! He hoped that Jack was back with some good news.

They passed over the threshold into the warmer lodgings. Avelyn was at the fire, tending it, rocking her head from side to side as if singing some silent song in her mind.

Jack rose from his seat. He looked distinctly uncomfortable beside her. "Jack!" Crispin rushed to the boy. "What have you learned?"

"Precious little, Master Crispin. But I did discover he is staying at an inn at Billingsgate."

"An inn? Not with a local bishop or priest?"

"Seems not, Master."

"Perhaps his preachings do not adhere to the current mood."

Jack shrugged. "All I know is, I sat in that inn, the Cockerel's Tail, all morning and saw naught of him."

"We will return, Jack, and see what a coin or two can do that your diligence did not."

The lad nodded. He sat at the table with the others. Before Crispin could ask if Flamel had ale, Avelyn pushed a metal cup toward him, full of amber wine. He signed "thank you" to her and she beamed, reaching up to kiss him on the cheek. Jack smirked and Flamel looked aghast. Crispin cleared his throat and ducked his head, hiding his face in the cup. After he drank a dose, he leaned toward Flamel. "We must make some sense of these symbols and of the parchment that urges us to start at the beginning. What beginning does he mean?"

Avelyn served the others, and the alchemist scratched his head over his cap. "What does it *all* mean, *Maître*? How can these symbols help?"

"I don't think that someone would have gone to all this trouble simply to leave nonsense about the city. There is a purpose. Can you think of anything? You said that they were alchemical symbols."

"And I also said that they were random, meaning nothing." He laid his forehead in his hand. "I am so weary with anxiety. I cannot think any longer."

"Childish games," Crispin muttered.

Avelyn hovered behind Crispin, running a feather-light hand over his hair. He gave her an admonishing look, but he might as well try to make friends with the sheriffs as stop her from doing anything she was set on doing.

He did his best to ignore the caresses and Tucker's impertinent chuckles.

They all fell silent. There was only the sound of the fire flickering in the hearth and Avelyn's cooing sighs.

They all startled when Jack slammed his empty cup to the table.

"It's no use, sir. There's no sense to any of it. If they were some sort of clue, then we can decipher it. There needs to be reason from disorder."

"Indeed," said Crispin, lulled by the gentle fingers running over his hair, the good wine at his elbow, and the few hours of sleep this morning. "Reason from disorder," he murmured. He closed his eyes, sitting back. Oh, to sleep! To allow the peaceful respite from the chaos around him. At least the sheriffs finally acted to protect the city. The citizens who used that cistern would not like being inconvenienced, but it was surely better than the alternative. He doubted that the sheriffs' guards would be informed as to why they closed the cisterns and guarded the others. No use in fostering panic, but discord, no doubt, there would be.

He sank lower on the chair, relaxing. Avelyn's fingers softly caressed his neck and shoulders. If only he could figure out the meaning behind the symbols. He supposed the best direction would be to decipher them all. Though Flamel had said they meant nothing. A code, then, that the alchemist was unaware of? Crispin had come upon many such codes in his travels when he acted for the old king. Diplomacy was full of such secret messages. He'd just start at the beginning with the first one he found and—

He jerked upright, eyes wide. "God's blood!" His exclamation had startled Jack, who blinked at him with mouth gaping. "We need to 'begin at the beginning.' To be able to find the pattern—if pattern there is—then we must find the *first* symbol."

"But how do we know which the first one is?"

Flamel wiped the wine from his lips. "Might the answer be in the symbols themselves?"

"Yes," said Crispin, scooting closer to the table. "These are alchemical symbols, so you said."

"But from what I have seen," said the alchemist, "nothing suggests a starting point." He sat back, slumping. "What is the key?"

Jack scratched his head, making his messy curls messier. "We're missing something vital. What did that parchment say, Master? *You shall never see her return unless you play fairly. You had best begin at the beginning.* If these symbols have aught to do with that note and they are meant to be clues, then that miscreant would have left us some way to reckon it."

Something ticked in the back of Crispin's mind like an annoyance, a half-remembered thought or dream. He closed his eyes and knocked his head back. Avelyn carded fingers through his hair, now hanging free over the back of the chair. "Stop it, you damnable woman," he muttered. "I'm trying to think." But she either had not read his lips or didn't care to comply. She had been like this from the moment he'd met her, though he recalled very little from that night, as drunk as he was.

He opened his eyes slowly. He had been drunk, yet Avelyn had been playful but determined. She had done something that annoyed him. What was it?

He turned to look at her. She smiled and cast her eyes down to his scrip. Her eyes were bright with amusement.

He grabbed his scrip, still captured by her gaze, and fished around until his fingers lighted on a scrap of parchment. It wasn't a dream, then. They had found a parchment that night that Flamel tried to claim was something of his. But it obviously had not been. It had been left by the abductor. And Flamel knew it.

He pulled it out and compared it with the other note. Yes, they looked to be from the same hand. The smaller fragment held Hebrew letters, Greek letters, Latin.

Flamel grabbed his hand. "What are you doing with that?" But then he stopped himself. He remembered, too.

"You knew this wasn't something of yours. You knew this was from someone else. Why did you lie to me?"

"I was worried what it might be. And then you took it before I could assess. Sometimes, *Maître*," he said, shaking a finger, "you are a very impetuous man!"

"So I've been told," he said absently, studying the fragment. "This is very strange. There are only these letters, the same in succession, over and over."

"Ah! Look here." Flamel pointed with a finger with a broken, yellow nail. "You see, don't you? The Greek letter alpha α and the symbol for the Hebrew letter aleph א. And here. Do you see this symbol? ♈ It is the astrological sign for Aries. It is the first of the signs. What does that suggest to you?"

"Beginnings. 'Begin at the beginning.' Then we must find *these* symbols among all the rest, to begin. *This* is the key."

"Right, then," said Jack, leaping to his feet. "Let's go."

"Wait, Tucker. Where?"

"Eh?"

"Where would you suggest we begin?"

Jack sagged back down to his seat. "Oh."

"Would we find these symbols randomly around London, or would they begin at a specific location? The more I see of this fellow, the more he makes a certain sense to me. I do not believe he would start us just anywhere. Where should we look to find the first clue? Where would anyone begin?"

They sat quietly, thinking, until Jack perked up again. "Birth."

"Too broad an idea. It could be a manger, a church of the Virgin, anything."

"Well," said Jack, scratching his chin and the few sprouting hairs there. "Scriptures?"

"'In the beginning God made of nought heaven and earth. For-sooth, the earth was idle and void, and darknesses were on the face of the depth; and the Spirit of the Lord was borne on the waters. And God said, Light be made, and the light was made.' Should we look for light, then? A sunrise? A candle?"

Jack frowned. "As you said. Too complicated." He screwed his face up in thought. "Master, a *journey* is a beginning. And it begins on a road."

"No," said Crispin, thinking. "It begins at one's front door."

Jack rubbed his nose. "I've not seen any carvings at anyone's front door. It would make the most sense to have it at *this* front door."

"True. But there is none here." He looked at Flamel, who was staring back at him with interest. "A front door. What is the front door of London?"

"The Tower?" said Jack, brow furrowed.

"The Tower is not a door. If anything, it is within doors."

"The gates!" Jack said quickly.

"Better. Which is the right one?"

Jack ticked them off on his fingers. "Ludgate, Newgate, Alders-gate, Cripplegate, Bishop's Gate, Aldgate, Postern Gate. That's too many front doors to choose from, Master."

Crispin sat back, arms folded. "In days gone by, when I rode in and out of London, mostly toward Westminster, I often took Ludgate. Let us start there."

sixteen

velyn could not be persuaded to stay behind at the shop, no matter how many ways Flamel threatened her.

"You need to discipline your servant more thoroughly, Master Flamel," said Crispin, taking the lead. "I suggest a good beating."

"That will not curb her willful tendencies. She is a strong-willed girl. Obstinate. Perenelle fawns on her as if she were her own child. And Avelyn thrives on it. It is no use, she has always been this way. There is no schooling her."

"Put her on bread and water for a week. That might help."

Avelyn trotted up to him with a calculating smirk on her face. Surely she had not read their lips, for she had been behind them. She tried to take Crispin's hand, but he shook her off. "Are you quite certain she's deaf?"

"Quite, *Maître*. And quite mute. She would have a great deal to say if she were not. As it is, her fingers can talk rather quickly."

Again, she tried to take Crispin's hand and he shook her off with a flick of his wrist. He stopped in the middle of the street and wagged his finger in her face. "No! You must stop this at once. I am not some ploughman or stable boy."

She shook her head and smiled. Her humoring him infuriated. But he said nothing more as he stalked ahead. He turned at Jack's snort, only to catch her imitating Crispin's furious stride and posture.

There was nothing to be done. It was best to ignore her.

Since they were already outside the city walls, they headed down the Ditch to Fleet Street, passed over the bridge spanning the pungent Fleet stream, and meandered down toward Ludgate. Upon reaching the stone archway, they separated and each scoured the structure, both on the west side, the inside, and the eastern side in London proper.

It was Jack who found it.

"Oi! Master Crispin! Over here!"

Crispin and Flamel came running. Avelyn looked up and soon followed. On the London side, Jack pointed upward to the arch and to the right. "When did they carve this, I wonder, and escape the guards' wrath?"

It was a good question, thought Crispin, examining the carving of the alpha, the aleph, the sign of Aries. They had not seen this one before. Who knew how many more symbols were carved over the city?

Avelyn was suddenly at his shoulder, staring up at the markings in the stone. He studied her face, proving his desperation by trying to glean something from her furious scrutiny of the gate. Crispin turned from her and laid his hand over the markings. He felt the rough edges where a steel implement had etched deeply. If this was where to begin, then what now?

He slid his hand down the wall from the carvings, the wet stone slick under his hand. It was as solid as the city itself, as solid as its walls. Yet before he dropped his hand away, his fingers slipped into a niche, a mere crevice between two stones... where he felt the edge of a parchment.

"God's blood," he whispered. Reaching farther, he closed his fingers on it and then pulled it forth. A folded scrap of parchment. He unfolded it and examined the writing, which looked like Hebrew sigils. Jews? How could they be involved?

Jack nearly ripped it from his hands. "Master Crispin! What have you found? Blind me! Could they all have parchments hidden somewhere near them?"

He stared at his apprentice in the falling light as his words sank in. Was that the reason for the markings? To hide clues?

Flamel took it from him and studied it.

"More Kabbalah?" asked Crispin, cringing at the thought.

"Perhaps," he said. But then he held it up to the light. More quill scratch writing between the lines. Crispin snatched it back and held it up to the pale yellow sun.

He read aloud, translating as he did, "'A bow o'r reaches, grass, water, grass. Unless one is willing, he shall not pass. From here to there, o'r wavering glass.'" Crispin turned it this way and that in the sun. "Grass, water, grass?"

Jack edged forward. "Grass and water. A river's edge?"

"Not a river. Something *over* a river. A bridge."

"London Bridge?"

Crispin turned the parchment end over end. "If there is a riddle by each of these symbols all over London, then we must follow each one to find... what?"

"The answer," said Flamel.

"The answer to what?"

He looked up. His face seemed more lined than before, his eyes sagging with weariness and worry. "To what to do next."

seventeen

he bells rung for Vespers. She slumped on her chair. She had managed to get a little wine and bread at last later that morning, but now there would be no more. She had lost the toss of the dice and he had ticked his head with regret.

She knew what he wanted. He was a fool if he thought he would get it. But why treat her in this way unless he was mad? Yes, he was most likely mad. Circumstances had made him so, from those long-ago days. From the many things he'd said, all in that falsely cheerful way of his, she had pieced together the simple message that it had been this Lancaster's fault. He blamed him. She tried to reckon it but could not come up with the logic and so kept silent. Better that way. For now, he played these games for her food and relief. But there was no way of knowing if he would become more violent.

"Your husband seems not to care for you."

She stiffened at the sound of his voice in the doorway. His shadow approached, stretching across the floor. She had won herself a fire in yet another game of tables, so at least she was warmer and there was light, for there were no windows deep in this strange room. Was she even in England anymore? Her head was light from lack of food and the bit of wine she had consumed. But at least he had removed the blindfold and hadn't even mentioned putting it back on her again.

She said nothing as he approached. He was trying to goad her.

"Did you hear me, *Madame*? He does not care for you as you had thought. For there is no rescue."

"He will not give it to you."

"Will he not? I think, then, that you are a poor bargaining chit. It might be best, then, to…" Suddenly his lips were against her ear, and she shrank back. "Dispose of you," he whispered.

She tried not to shudder, to show her fear. He wanted that. She was no fool. But it was hard, so hard, when she was so tired and hungry, and her arms and shoulders ached from the position in which they had been tied for so long.

"I disposed of your apprentice when he got in the way, *Madame*. He was useless to me, in the end. Do you know what I did?"

She shook her head, unable to stop herself. She wanted to cover her ears but couldn't. She recited the rosary instead, but it didn't block out his voice, especially as close to her ear as it was.

"I put my hands around his slim white throat and slowly squeezed. Squeezed, until his choking breath began to slow. His eyes bugged. I was curious to see if they would *pop* out of his head."

She sobbed, turning her face as far away from him as she could.

"Alas. They did not. His tongue protruded, though, with my thumb pushing hard on his windpipe. He stopped breathing. His eyes remained open, wide, seeing less and less. His lips became pale. And then… he was quite dead. And finally, I hung him up in your shop by his heel to confuse and confound. I wonder what your precious husband said to that."

He dragged a stool from the table and set it before her. Sitting, he pondered her face, cocking his head one way, then the other. Reaching forward, he ran a finger down her cheek. "Still beautiful after all these years. Will he discard you as he had so many others? You mustn't trust him, you know."

"I trust him. It is you I do not trust."

"Me? But *Madame!* You say this to *me*, of all people. No, never fear. I will not so easily dispose of you. I have a greater plan. A better one." He caressed her cheek once more, a smile teasing his mouth. "Would you like to wash? I'm certain you would. It's been days."

She angled her head away from his touch. "No more games."

"But they are such fun, don't you agree? It's different when so much is assigned to the winning or losing. When so much is at stake.

I learned that lesson years ago. I'm certain that Nicholas never told you that."

"Release me."

"Not yet. Perhaps... not ever."

"Oh, God! O merciful Father! Help your poor child!"

He jerked to his feet, kicking the stool aside. "That's right. Pray! Pray, for all the good it will do you. We won't play any more games tonight... and so you shall *not* wash."

He grabbed his dagger and pulled it from its sheath. Breathing hard, he looked at her.

A strange calm overcame her. Was it to be over, then? "What will you do with that?" she said quietly.

He strode toward her until he was standing directly over her, still breathing hard, still brandishing the knife. The blade gleamed dully in the candlelight. He grabbed her by the hair and pulled back her head with a jerk. She wasn't prepared for it and gave a little shriek before quieting. Her exposed throat rolled with expectation.

"What are you waiting for?" she whispered. She glared at him at first with anger in her eyes, anger at the waste of it all. But her emotions soon changed to regret. Prayers, not anger, were more apropos now. She would not go to her death with the sin of anger on her soul. Her thoughts were full of forgiveness. "Blessed *Jesu* deliver me," she sighed up at him, before the blade swept down.

eighteen

The four of them made their way down to Thames Street, passed the Vintry and the Ropery, and finally arrived to Bridge Street. There was a queue to pay the toll to cross the bridge—which seemed to be held up by a man with an oxcart who had lost his cargo halfway through the gate.

Jack pushed his way through, jumping above the crowd to get a look at the archway. He turned back to Crispin and shook his head.

"Perhaps it isn't on the arch," he muttered to Flamel. Avelyn stayed at Crispin's side like a dog with his master. It annoyed him, but she had proved observant before. After all, she seemed to have led him to the parchment in the niche. Had she seen it… or had she put it there for him to find?

He turned to watch her as she stumbled down the embankment, falling on her bum and sliding a little on the way down. How *had* she known it was there?

He went after her and grabbed her arm when they both slipped and rolled the rest of the way over the rough stones. He cursed and brushed himself off. She got to her feet, rubbing her temple. He grabbed her again and said to her face so she could read his mouth, "How did you know that parchment was there?"

She only smiled softly and shook her head. He tightened his grip and she looked down at his hand in puzzlement. "No, that's not good enough. Did you put it there?"

Her mouth opened in an "O" and she shook her head slowly. Her long braid swayed from side to side like a donkey's tail.

"If I find you are lying to me, you shall regret it."

She shook her head again and signed to him.

"Master Flamel!" he called. "Come translate what this bitch of a servant has to say."

Flamel clutched his gown and hiked it up, making his way slowly down to the shore. Jack came up beside him and anchored him.

They both reached the stony shore together, and Flamel turned the girl to face him. "What are you saying, child?"

Her hands flew and Flamel nodded, saying only occasionally, *"Lentement, lentement."* At last she seemed to have finished, and Flamel turned to Crispin. "She says she is hurt that you should accuse her. She says she trusts you like none other—and insists that she is not a whore or a she-bitch. She says that she is more observant than you, who are more taken by the sounds of the wind and the people and the carts and the birds calling in the sky, and that all these things serve as a distraction to what is truly important. And she says also… that you must apologize to her or… or she will not… er… lay with you again."

Mute, Crispin stared at her and her jutting chin. He saw now the hurt written on her face and deep in her wounded eyes.

"I trust her, *Maître,*" said the alchemist. His voice was as soft as the water of the rushing Thames. "I have known her too long not to."

Crispin swallowed and cleared his throat. Flamel stared at him expectantly, as did Jack. Perhaps it was not a good precedent to apologize to a pretentious servant, but of course, he had already lost that battle long ago with Jack.

He took her hand, ignoring the men beside him. "Avelyn, I do apologize most humbly. I… spoke before thinking. Can you forgive me? And not because… because we lay together. But because I was wrong in accusing you."

She lowered her eyes for a long time before she brought his hand up to her cheek and used it to caress its smoothness. She kissed his scarred knuckles and fingertips before lowering his captured hand, swinging it in her own. When she looked up again, her mouth had spread into a wide smile.

Crispin felt like the biggest fool, especially when he released her hand and looked at Tucker, twisting his lips as if trying to keep from bursting out with a laugh. It was bad enough he indulged his apprentice with an unusual amount of camaraderie, but it was much worse to treat a servant girl like a lover. He didn't know why he did it, except that the hurt on her face ached his heart and her smile gladdened it.

This is what comes of loneliness, Crispin. Abbot Nicholas may have been right; 'tis better to marry than to burn.

Jack placed a neutral expression on his face and cleared his throat. "Er... Master... did you find anything?"

"Hadn't had time to look yet," he muttered, and then moved toward the piers revealed by the low tide.

The smell of wet, sandy riverbed and fish was strong in the air. River plants and reeds lay exposed and pungent on the shore, and the smell of the privies downstream made his eyes water.

They all searched, and it was Tucker who cried out, calling them over.

Crispin trotted toward him, followed by Flamel and Avelyn. She was holding the alchemist's elbow, unmindful of her skirts trailing in the mud.

Crispin arrived and looked where Jack pointed. More symbols. Crispin searched against the wall, hands reaching and feeling. He reached well above his head when he found it. He pulled the parchment out, heart pounding with the thrill of discovery.

He opened the damp kidskin and held it up to the fading light of late afternoon. This time there were no sigils, just carefully penned Latin.

And here you are, having found the second parchment. You are clever to have found it. The game proceeds.

Crispin turned it over and held it to the light, searching for shadow writing, but there was nothing there. "He tells us we are right, but he leaves no clue." He shoved it into Jack's hands. The boy turned it over and over.

"But that's... that's not playing fair!"

Crispin shook his head, thinking. "No, he is playing. And so it will be fair. That is the game he wants to play." He scrambled back to the place they'd found the symbols and searched the stones. There! A tile. The other stones were worn and mossy, but this was new. A tile with the raised image of a lion's head.

"Look here." He ran his fingers over it. The tile was definitely new. The mortar for it was clean and unblemished by the rot from the river. This had been recently set and for no discernible reason.

Jack came up beside him and peered at the tile. Crispin continued to explore it with his fingers. He took out his knife and pried it loose. The mortar was still fresh and hadn't had time to set properly. Crispin fished around behind it but found nothing. With his knife, he scraped the mortar from the back of the tile, but there was nothing there, not even a tiler's mark. He turned it over and over in his hands.

"A lion's head," said Jack. "What could that mean?"

"It must be the message, for there is no place beside it or behind it to hide a parchment." He came out from under the bridge and joined the others as they helped one another up the embankment. When they reached the street again, meeting the curious looks from the others still waiting to pass through the gate, they huddled together out of the wind near an alehouse, looking at the tile.

"A lion's head," said Crispin. "Something in London that has to do with a lion."

Jack threw up his hands. "That could be anything, sir, from the king to… to…"

"Yes. It is ambiguous. Thoughts?"

"The Lion Tower at the Tower of London," said Jack.

"Impossible to get to. He wouldn't make it that difficult."

Jack snapped his fingers. "The Lion's Head Inn!"

"Better. Simple. Let us go there now."

nineteen

rispin and his entourage arrived at Thames Street, where the Lion's Head Inn overlooked the river. Merchants with heavy cloaks milled in the courtyard, watching as young boys stabled their horses. They passed bored glances over Crispin and his fellow travelers before they entered the inn.

Crispin looked up at the sign hanging over the street. A painted lion's head, mouth opened in a silent roar. "Everyone search," he admonished them, and Jack went with Crispin while Avelyn followed Flamel. They searched the walls with their fingers and eyes, by the stone foundation and up into the lime-washed plaster of the walls.

Avelyn clapped her hands for their attention. Crispin trotted over and looked where she pointed. A niche above the lintel had a small carving of an alchemical symbol. "Give me a boost, Jack," said Crispin. The boy steadied his back against the wall and made a step with his interlaced fingers. Up Crispin went, stepping as lightly as he could into his apprentice's hands. He eyed the sigil and then poked his fingers into the niche. They touched parchment and his heart flared with excitement. He pulled it out at the same time he jumped down.

But once he'd unfolded it, his heart, which had so leapt with anticipation, suddenly chilled.

Alas. So close, but wrong. Choose again.

Crispin had been forming a plan before they had reached the inn. If the clues were always by the symbols, why not simply search all of them? But now he saw the futility of that. For not all of them were clues to the next venture; some were warnings and taunts such as this. They had made the wrong decision. He crumpled the parchment in his fist and let it fall to the mud.

"Bastard," he muttered. "It was a good guess, Jack. But it was wrong. Now what?"

"He wants to be clever," said Jack, pacing. "He don't want it that simple."

"No, he doesn't. But it does have to do with a lion. What do we know of lions?"

"I still say the Lion Tower where the king's menagerie is. There are lions kept there, so they say."

"Possibly. But still. We cannot enter there. Does that mean *he* can?" That brought him back to thinking about Henry... no. Suffolk, perhaps. But if the abductor was playing fair, then he would know that Flamel could not enter the Tower precincts. "Lion, lion. Lion... el. Lionel of Antwerp. The duke of Clarence. Richard's uncle."

"But he's dead, sir."

"And buried at Canterbury. Too far. Lion... heart. King Richard I."

Flamel shook his head. "But he is buried at Anjou, at *Abbaye de Fontevraud.*"

"Yes," Crispin agreed. "Much too far."

"I still say it's the Tower," muttered Jack, kicking at the crumpled parchment in the dirty snow.

"The lion is the symbol of the monarchy. It is on the king's arms. A lion passant. What else is it the symbol for?"

Flamel shrugged. "Strength. Courage. Kingship."

Jack toed the parchment. "Daniel in the lion's den."

"Biblical," Crispin said with a nod. "Very well. Lion's den. Lion skin. 'And lo! a swarm of bees was in the lion's mouth, and an honeycomb.' Bees? No, foolish. It is winter now. No bees. Samson, perhaps?" And then he smacked his forehead with his hand. "Saint Mark! His symbol is a lion."

Flamel edged forward, hope in his eyes. "Is there a St. Mark's church in London?"

"No," said Crispin, sagging. But he perked up immediately. "But there is a Mark *Lane*." Without another word, he turned and hurried down the road to Tower Street and headed north until they reached it.

"Jack, you go that way, and I'll go this way." Flamel followed Jack while Avelyn grabbed Crispin's cloak and held on. He took care to scour each post and lintel on every shop and house but found nothing. He looked once or twice at Avelyn's concentrated face as her eyes tracked over plaster and wood.

By the end of the street where it changed names, they had searched all the structures. Crispin turned to survey Jack and Flamel, but they had disappeared beyond the curve of the road. Crossing his arms under his cloak, he'd just begun to wonder if he should look again when a stone post caught his eye. An iron ring hung there to tie off a horse, but there was a raised carved surface where the ring met the stone.

He allowed a heavy cart burdened with winter fuel to lumber by in front of him before he ventured into the street to cross the lane and stand over the granite post. Now that he was upon it, he could clearly see that there was the carving of a lion's face with the iron ring protruding from either side of its mouth. He reached around it, beneath it, where the iron ring pierced the stone… and touched parchment.

After withdrawing the tightly rolled piece, he unfurled it and held it up to the fading light.

> *You are clever and shall be rewarded for your diligence:*
>
> *We're those who reach toward heaven, scale the heights, an assembly which one bond unites. As he who clings to us, through us on high alights.*

Thinking a moment, Crispin read the words again. "An assembly. One bond uniting. Scale the heights. Ah. A flight of steps," he said aloud. "Avelyn, go get your master and my apprentice."

Off she went, moving quickly over the snowy street until she, too, disappeared around the bend.

Crispin worked on the problem of what staircase could be meant by the riddle while he waited, and it wasn't long until she returned with Jack on her heels and Flamel picking up the rear, breathing hard.

"You found something?" The alchemist huffed, swallowed.

"We need to find a staircase."

"A staircase?" He looked around. The light was falling quickly now, and the street lay almost in darkness, mostly because of the tall buildings shadowing the lane. "Where?"

Crispin racked his brain for an idea as to where he could find a prominent staircase in the city. Had to be St. Paul's. Not only did it have the widest, grandest stair, but, as the riddle said, it would *reach toward heaven.*

"I think St. Paul's cathedral," he said. "It sits on a hill and is therefore the highest church with the highest staircase in the city."

No one would gainsay him, whether through weariness or because they thought him right. Together they moved through the darkening streets, as windows became shuttered and storefront doors were bolted. Candle and lamplight from windows and open doorways painted the snowy ground with gold, even as the snow itself tinted blue from the falling darkness.

"We will soon need a lantern," said Jack as they turned up Budge Row.

Avelyn tapped the boy's shoulder and Jack turned to her. She motioned to herself, made a nod to Crispin, before she lifted her skirts and ran like the wind toward the Ditch. She'd have to be fast to get out of the gate and back through before the guards closed it up. He doubted she would make it.

"I suppose she will meet us at the church," said Crispin.

They hurried, not wishing to be stopped and told to go home by soldiers or the Watch. They threaded over Watling Street and then dropped down to Carter Lane before going up Old Dean's Lane to the west door of the cathedral.

Clerks were hurrying down the steps, eager to get home to their meager suppers after an unsuccessful day of soliciting work within Paul's Walk. Crispin bumped a few shoulders, and the men looked back at him with scowls. He tried to bow, to be polite, but his mind was on other things, on finding more symbols and more parchment.

Jack made it to the top step first and waited with an impatient jiggling leg for Crispin and Flamel. When they arrived to the top of the stairs, they all spread out across the porch, searching for symbols.

This is damnable, thought Crispin as his eyes scanned anything and everything. How many more clues would they be required to find? *Flamel must be going mad. But of course, because of the cruelty of it all, this might very well have been the plan all along.*

Yet after many minutes of fruitless searching, Crispin swore under his breath.

"I don't see anything here," said Jack, voicing all their concerns.

"No," Flamel agreed. "Should we look around the rest of the building?"

Crispin gave the church door one more glance. "It makes more sense that he should have led us inside. There are steps up to the quire as well."

In they went, entering through the smaller door cut from the large double doors. Crispin's steps echoed in the quiet church. Long shadows fell diagonally across his path down Paul's Walk, a busy thoroughfare during the day, but dark and ominous once night had fallen.

Crispin could see monks in the arcades beside the nave. Their cowled heads turned warily toward his little group as Crispin led them up to the quire's wide steps. He motioned for Jack and Flamel to search while he went off to do the same.

Each carving and floret suddenly looked different. He had seen them hundreds of times before, but now he doubted his own senses. *Had* he seen them before? Were they new to his eyes? He felt the weight of the lion tile in his scrip. Were any of these recently added?

Flamel made a shout, which echoed throughout the long nave. Whirling, Crispin saw him point and he trotted through the arcade to halt beside him. The carving was not an alchemist's sign, but the rudimentary drawing of a fox.

Crispin frowned. "How do you know this is it?"

"*Renard.* What you call… a fox. This is the protector, the cultivator, of the Elixir of Life."

Nodding, Crispin searched. Yes, it was plainly not of the mason's art, for it was carved on the stone with a metal instrument, quickly and crudely… and recently.

His hands felt along the *pilier cantonné,* higher, higher, around the wide, irregular column. Fingers dipped between the stone shafts flying up the pillar. The mortar was solid nearly all the way up… until his fingers found where it had been scraped away. A fingernail passed over the parchment, but his fingers were too big to grasp it.

He turned to Jack. "You have nimble fingers. Come." The boy complied and stood before Crispin in the darkening nave.

Jack stepped up and balanced against the stone. With two fingers, he reached it and snatched the parchment, waving it to show he had done it. He jumped down and immediately surrendered it to his master.

Crispin opened the parchment as Jack and Flamel crowded around him, peering over his arm. Jack translated and read aloud:

"'I congratulate you. You play the game well. Your reward: I perch in silence on my peak. A tongue have I, but do not speak. Until I'm moved I must be meek.'"

They looked at one another.

"Perched. Does he mean a bird, like a crow?"

"No," said Crispin. "Listen to the words. *A tongue have I, but do not speak. Until I'm moved I must be meek.* Perched on a peak," he muttered. "Has a silent tongue… until moved. What has a tongue but is silent until it is moved?"

"People have tongues," said Jack. "And animals. A donkey? They will not move and then bray when forced."

Crispin shook his head. "Too literal."

"Something with a tongue that speaks when moved," Jack muttered. "But not a true tongue… Ah!" His face brightened. "A bell, of course."

As one, their gaze rose directly above their heads into the darkened tower with its set of bells.

"Do we have to go up *there?*" wailed Jack.

Crispin sighed. "It would seem so."

Jack stared up into the gloom of the tower and whistled. "I hope you haven't seen fit to offend the bishop of London, Master Crispin. We might need his help."

Crispin tried to think. He could not recall ever offending Bishop Braybrooke. At least not lately. In fact, he might even be on the bishop's good side for helping him stop some boys from using bows and arrows to take down the pigeons that had gotten inside and roosted in the vaulted arches above Paul's Walk. But it was just as likely that the bishop would choose not to remember him.

"We must wait, at any rate, for Avelyn's return." Avelyn. Her name slipped so easily off his tongue. His face warmed as he thought of her. She had certainly gotten under his skin.

They decided to wait outside under the shelter of the porch, even as the last of the light dimmed from the pink-streaked sky. The church's arched doorway gleamed gold and then gray as clouds covered the retreating sun. The cathedral loured above the nearby lanes already set in the gloom of their own chasm of shadows. As the night fell, the city drew quiet, as if drawing a blanket over itself, ready for sleep. Candlelight flickered behind shutters and cooking smells fluttered over the rooftops, and there was, perhaps, the gentle murmur from behind closed doors and little else but the occasional barking dog or mewl from a stray cat.

Crispin spied a light jogging along between the houses on Bowyers Row, and soon the figure of Avelyn appeared in the gloom, carrying her dented lantern. She marched up the steps right up to Crispin and smiled her devilish grin before looking to her master, whom she should have greeted first. Crispin was beginning to wonder how he was to tell her that theirs was a brief affair and that nothing whatever would come of it. Surely she did not expect anything. He had told her the truth about himself.

Still, her unbridled cheer and boldness did appeal to him. He wouldn't mind another night in her company.

After exchanging their finger language, she pushed past Flamel and led the way through the arch and inside to Paul's Walk. A few cressets burned within, lighting the path, but the columns threw the long nave into inky gloom. Avelyn's little lantern helped, but it was a small circle of light, and the four of them clung to it like moths around a flame.

They arrived at the crossing and looked up high into the dark bell tower again.

"Maybe it's not up there," Jack said hopefully. "Maybe it's somewhere directly below the bell?" He looked around on the tiled floor, directing Avelyn's arm with the lantern to shine where he searched. She didn't seem happy about it and tried to snatch the lantern away. "Master Crispin, make her help!" he cried.

"Avelyn," he said, voice stern, though surely she could not tell the tenor of his voice. Nonetheless, she seemed chastened, at least as chastened as she ever looked.

Whatever accomplished it, Avelyn assisted Jack, but by the sighing sounds from the lad, Crispin could tell they had no luck.

Avelyn handed over the lantern to Jack without any fuss. "So now you give it to me," he muttered. He looked up once at Crispin. "I'll go up into the tower, sir. Which way?"

Crispin pointed toward a door. "Mind that no one sees you." He directed the others to wait alongside a column. If the monks should come through after Vespers, it might serve as a good hiding place while at the same time offering a position to keep an eye on the bell tower's stairs. And just as he thought it, he spotted the little light slowly climbing within the tower, making its careful way upward. He knew Jack would be checking the walls all along the stairwell, but if Crispin knew this abductor, the message would be situated as close to the bell as possible, for that would be the most out of the way, the most troublesome to get to, and wasn't that what this abductor was hoping for?

But what was this leading to? This hunt was all well and good, but what was its ultimate purpose? Crispin kept his eyes on Jack, or at least on the little light. He feared that Perenelle might be in graver danger than he had originally thought. Murder was not foremost on the mind of most abductors. Their goal was the ransom. In this case, it was the Stone. But what if he wanted something else? For this was more than a simple ransom for a hostage. If that had been the case, he would have instructed Flamel to leave the Stone someplace else. No, instead he sent them on this insane chase all over London. And Crispin feared that they would find Madam Perenelle's lifeless body at the end of it. Maybe he should tell the sheriffs of this crime... but he rejected the notion almost the moment he thought it. They would do nothing. Nothing would be accomplished by bringing them into it, and wisely, Flamel had seen that from the start. Not only would they be useless, but they would most likely get in the way. And if Perenelle was not in danger now—though Crispin was fairly certain that she was—the sheriffs, through their bumbling course, would make certain that she did fall into danger's path.

No, there was no help from the king's anointed. It was up to him and Jack. As usual.

He looked up again and found the little light had climbed higher, almost as high as it could go... and stopped. It seemed to sway for a moment, seemed unsteady, when all at once, it fell. The light streaked downward through the widest part of the tower, never touching the stair. It lit the walls as it went, until it crashed to the floor.

Crispin stifled his cry and ran. His heart beat a triple measure as he arrived at the crossing of the transepts. He raced up the quire steps and slammed into the locked gate. But instead of the lifeless form he expected to see lying on the floor, a crumpled bit of metal lay there. The extinguished candle from the ruined lantern sent up a wisp of smoke.

Crispin looked up.

"Master!" hissed the distant voice of his apprentice from above, and never had he been so relieved to hear it. "I found it. But I dropped the lantern."

"Forget the lantern. Just get down here, you knave."

He heard Jack's hurried steps along the stairwell and waited, his breath and heartbeat returning to normal. The fool and his slippery fingers. The boy could cut a purse as nimble as you pleased, but he could not keep hold of a simple lantern?

Jack jumped through the stairwell door and landed on the tiled floor. He ran up to Crispin and looked up at his face. "What's the matter with you? You're white as a winding sheet," he said.

Crispin straightened. "Never mind me. Where's the parchment?"

"I was reaching up and I slipped. It was almost me going over the side, and no mistaking." Jack looked back at the ruined lantern. "Blind me."

"Where is the parchment?" Crispin asked again. He took Jack by the arm and steered him over to the column where Flamel and Avelyn awaited them.

"What is it, *Maître* Guest? What is the riddle this time?"

"Jack," Crispin said impatiently, "for the last time, where is the damned parchment?"

"There was no parchment," he said, looking from face to face. "It was the bell."

"What was the bell?"

"There was an inscription *on* the bell. In Latin. It said, 'It begins and has no end. It is the ending of all that begins.'"

"This is a foolish waste of time!" cried Flamel.

A noise. Perhaps a step. They all fell silent as they listened.

"Monks," Crispin whispered to them. "Let us go."

They hurried together out of the arch and down the steps. A burning brazier stood in the cathedral's courtyard and the four of them surrounded it, warming their hands over the flames.

Flamel rubbed his eyes. "Where are these riddles taking us? Is he not laughing at our antics? What does it mean, *Maître* Guest?"

"We are set on this course now, Master Flamel. Unfortunately, he holds the reins. We must do as he bids. At some point, he will tell us to leave the ransom, and so we must be accurate as to which riddle we find and in what order. When we are wrong, he tells us."

"And so what is the meaning of this riddle?" Flamel asked again.

"*I* know!" said Jack. His face was bright with the excitement of discovery. But Crispin saw his features change as he realized the gravity of the situation. "I mean… I sorted it out on my way back down the stairs. *It begins and has no end. It is the ending of all that begins.* The answer is… death."

Flamel gasped and Jack immediately saw the lack of grace in his pronouncement. The boy still had far to go in learning when to keep silent.

Crispin touched Flamel's sleeve. "It is merely another riddle, good Master." *I hope.* "The clue is 'death.' And so. What are we to conclude? He means a churchyard, gravestones."

Jack's contrition was evident by the set of his brow. "But Master," he said softly, as if his tone could erase the harshness of his earlier declaration, "there are many graves in the city. How are we to know which one it is? Should we look here at St. Paul's?"

"Two clues we have found here already," Flamel offered anxiously. "And here is where he would have had me leave the ransom."

"True." Crispin pondered. But something about it did not sit well. "Since we are here, we might as well look."

They would have to go back inside, for those of high stature were buried within the cathedral itself. Again they wandered separately. Crispin wished he had the broken lantern, for he could not seem to adjust to the dark as easily as young Jack did or Avelyn.

Crispin found one of the older tombs, erected before the fire in

Norman times. The stone seemed to be crumbling from age, and even though it remained indoors, time had not been kind to its worn effigies. Still aware that a wayward porter or servant might be about, Crispin moved carefully around the tomb, studying the carvings and raised patterns. A skull with crossed bones caught his eye and he knelt, running his fingers over the cold, uneven stone. Another parchment in a niche. Hurriedly, he removed it and read:

> *Close. But not here beneath the vaulted ceilings. Beneath another greater vault you must look.*

"Dammit!" He caught Tucker's attention by waving the parchment. Jack, in turn, tapped Avelyn's arm. They trotted over, collecting Flamel along the way.

"This is not the place." He handed it to Jack, who read it slowly, mouthing the words.

"Where, then, Master Crispin?"

"A 'greater vault' would be the sky. But I do not think it another churchyard or plague pit. Something out of doors, certainly. Something that reeks of death."

"Tower Hill," whispered Jack. His face was in shadow, but his eyes glistened from the distant cressets.

"Yes," Crispin agreed. That sounded right.

"It's late. Surely the Watch is patrolling," said Jack.

He set his jaw. "When has that ever stopped us before?"

They made their way to Candlewick Street and headed for the Postern Gate. Crispin let Flamel fall behind with Avelyn. He got in close to Jack and said to him quietly, "I do not like this game, Jack. He is setting us up for a purpose, and that purpose may very well be a diabolical one."

"Do you mean to say that Madam Flamel might already be… be…"

"It's possible. The cruelness of leading us on this chase without the possibility of renewing his bid for a ransom seems out of proportion."

"He knows Master Flamel."

"I would say so. Knows him well and has a grievance."

"So he don't want the Stone."

"I think he does, but he obviously feels he has time to savor the getting of it."

Jack looked back over his shoulder at the alchemist. "You said that you thought Master Flamel knew the abductor."

"He might. What vexes me is the time it has taken to plant these clues, to invent these riddles. This was thought out very carefully, Jack, over a long period of time. What sort of grievance would he have? How did he know that Flamel was coming to England? It was supposed to be a secret." He lifted his head and listened to the darkening city.

When they turned at Tower Street, they all stopped, listening. Crispin plucked the small noises of night from the chill air: a dog barking down the lane, a sign creaking in the wind, the restless whisper of leafless trees scratching against a garden wall, a rat rustling in the underbrush, the soft voices like a hum coming from the houses. Crispin felt like a thief, creeping through the streets, trying to avoid capture. Especially now that they had lost their lantern. It was difficult to see their way.

Ahead were the high curtain walls of the Tower of London and, above that, Tower Hill, where the gibbet awaited its next victim.

They turned up the rutted lane, climbing toward the lonely hill. Jack fell silent and pale beside him. It wasn't all that long ago when the boy was in danger of ending up there, and well he knew it. Crispin, too, approached with trepidation. Here was the place that the other conspirators in the Plot were dispatched: hanged, drawn, quartered. A particularly nasty and lingering death for daring to venture into treason. And well Crispin knew, too, that he was damned fortunate to have escaped it. His pride often made him wish he had been executed with the others instead of living in his humiliation, but he had grown accustomed to life, and the notion of giving it up had become harder and harder. Not that he particularly relished his existence on the Shambles, but it had its advantages. And with a curt glance to Avelyn, he recognized one of them.

As they neared, they could see that the gibbet stood empty, and for that Crispin was grateful. He had no liking for the idea of searching underneath the body of a dead man, and a man bound for Hell at that.

The wood of the post and jutting beam glistened from damp under the starlight. A well-used rope hung from its beam and swayed with the night wind. It reminded Crispin of the rope back at Flamel's shop hanging from its own beam. Thomas Cornhill met his death swiftly and was hung by his heel on it. But Perenelle Flamel lingered. Who knew what peril she was in at this very moment?

Standing below the gibbet's platform, he heard Jack swallow and breathe, even above the constant wind. The boy was murmuring prayers, and Crispin decided to spare him. "You look here below, Jack. I… I will go up."

He trudged farther up the hill to the gibbet's steps. He hesitated only a heartbeat before he put his foot to the first step and slowly climbed. God's blood, but it felt as if he were going to his doom. What a fearful place, full of ghosts and evil spirits. No matter how many prayers a priest chanted, no blessing ever seemed to permeate its dark wood.

He stood on the platform at last and looked down. Yes, he knew how very lucky he was. Perhaps when next he met the duke, he could be civil again.

Get to work, Crispin, he told himself. It helped to assuage his choking fear of the place.

He began to search. And it didn't take long. The carving was on the post of the hanging tree. A crude drawing of a raven. Crispin didn't need an alchemist to tell him what it meant.

He felt around it and found the parchment in a gouged-out niche.

> *You are a worthy opponent. The game is soon over. Stand and enjoy the view before you continue.*
>
> *Your reward: Eyes bold, skin cold, silver-armored, breath hold. Multiplying, fortifying, never thirsting, shore shying.*

The references to death should not have disconcerted him so, yet he thought of little but Perenelle's jeopardy. Ever mindful that he should not discount anything the abductor said, Crispin stood on the gibbet and looked out over London, trying to discern what he was supposed to see.

London lay before him. Its many slanted roofs, covered in clay tile and lead sheeting, gleamed with damp. Smoke rambled over the rooftops like sheep in a meadow. Small lights from braziers or candles in windows sparkled, jewels on black velvet. In the distance, the dark Thames glittered when a wave caught the starlight. But he saw little else, for the night had closed in, and with it the mist from the Thames laying all under a blanket of gray fleece.

He descended the steps again and adjusted his leather hood over his head.

"It is late," he announced to them. "It grows colder by the minute. We should return you to your shop, Master Flamel, and resume this search on the morrow."

"What… what did you find?" asked the man, his eyes fearful.

"Another riddle, Master Flamel. But… we are close to the end. He has said so."

He looked up at Crispin with a concentrated stare. "The end, *Maître* Guest?"

"Let us talk back at your lodgings."

Weary, the four of them returned to the darkened shop. Flamel used a very ordinary key to unlock the door, but he had taken only a step inside when his foot scuffed upon something that was out of place.

"Avelyn," Flamel muttered. "Foolish girl…" His voice died on his lips. There wasn't much light, except for that thrown out by the banked hearth, but as Crispin's eyes adjusted, he could see, too, what Flamel was seeing: that the place had been ransacked yet again.

"Avelyn!" cried the alchemist. He grabbed her arms when she came up beside him. "Go look!"

Her eyes were wide with concern. She bounded like a doe over the ramshackle debris and minced over an overturned table to the ambry. She released the secret door where the Philosopher's Stone was kept and reached inside. A strange cry, like a dying dove, made Crispin wince. He realized it came from her. She looked up at her master, a sorrowful expression on her grimacing face.

twenty

O!" gasped Flamel. He tried to scramble over the debris, but Crispin held him back.

"I'll go," he told the man, and climbed carefully over the broken chairs and pots. Once he made it over, he stood beside Avelyn and looked into the empty drawer. She opened the other one, just to make certain, and reached for the velvet bag that held the river stone. That remained untouched. She threw it down with such ferocity, it broke a jar. Clutching her head, she shook it from side to side.

Had she not locked the door when she fetched the lantern? No, Flamel had to unlock the door to enter. Worse, had this hunt been all a ruse to get them out of the way so that the malefactor could do his will at his leisure?

"We've been fools."

Flamel sobbed against a broken table, covering his eyes. "My wife! My dear wife! What will become of her?"

Crispin sagged. He felt as forlorn as Flamel looked. And then anger swept over him. "This isn't over, Master Flamel. I *will* get to the bottom of this. And I will make whoever is responsible pay. Jack, come with me."

Without a word, Jack followed Crispin out the door. Suddenly, a hand was pulling on Crispin's coat, and he turned to face Avelyn's wide eyes. "I'm going to end this," he told her.

She pointed back into the shop. He resisted, but she pulled on his coat harshly and pointed again. With an exasperated breath,

Crispin poked his head in and looked where she was pointing: to the bit of rope still tied to the roof beam, the rope that had held the dead apprentice. Then she lifted her skirt and crossed her foot behind her knee, just as the apprentice was positioned. She dragged Crispin farther into the room and showed him the only upright table. After spitting on its surface, she used her spittle to draw a symbol.

♃

It could have been just her gibberish, as Flamel had said she could not read or write, but it looked to him like one of the many symbols they had already seen.

"Master Flamel," he said.

The alchemist wiped his face of tears. He looked older than he had when they had met three days ago.

Crispin pointed to the wet sigil on the table. "What is this sign?"

Wearily, the man rose and lumbered over to them. He looked. "That is the symbol for the planet Jupiter. It is also the sign for the higher, finer work of alchemy."

"And that would be?"

The man leaned against the table, seemingly unable to hold himself up anymore. "The Greater Arcana… that of the creation of the Philosopher's Stone."

Crispin looked at the symbol again and then up to the snippet of rope that remained. Yes, the shape that the hanging man had taken *could* be construed as this sigil. Was it a message, too?

"Your servant seems to think that Thomas Cornhill was placed here in the shape of this sign. Would that indicate the man's intention?"

The alchemist did not even rise to it this time. "Of course. I should have seen it myself. He was making plain what he wanted." He finally looked up. Saw the rope fragment above him and with a small wince lowered his eyes to gaze at Crispin's. "The work. The work is so important. That is why we came here, to get away. How did they find me? How did they know?"

"Master Flamel, this murder and abduction, this hunt all over London, speaks of a grievance that is very deep. It took planning to accomplish all of this. Someone who was intimately acquainted with London. Can you think of someone—anyone—with such a great complaint against you?"

"No. No one alive, at any rate. True, there have been many men jealous of my successes, but I cannot fathom anyone that would hate me as much as this scoundrel surely does."

"And yet, at one time I thought that you might—"

"No. It was only a fleeting thought. But he is dead. Long dead."

Crispin nodded, looking back at Jack waiting patiently in the doorway. "Very well. We will discover him, have no fear. Let's go, Jack."

"Were these signs a waste of time, then, Master Crispin?" asked Jack as they went carefully into the night. "Were they just a ruse, do you think, to send us out of the way?"

"I'm not so certain of that, Jack. A man could have used any number of ways to get Flamel out of his shop and get himself in there. Or he could have done great harm to him or even to Avelyn. But he chose not to. Chose to steal the man's wife and bargain with his most valuable asset. That speaks of something very personal."

Jack shook his head, keeping a sharp eye on the dark lane ahead. "I wouldn't want anybody to hate *me* that much."

"Nor would I."

"Where are we off to, Master Crispin? To find that last clue?" said Jack after a time. He shivered and looked up at the cloudy sky, at the shuttered windows above them, before he turned his pale, freckled face to Crispin.

"We are on our way to the Cockerel's Tail Inn at Billingsgate. Now is as good a time as any to talk to this preacher. If he has anything to do with this, I would know it now."

"He might be abed."

"Then we'll wake him up."

The Cockerel's Tail Inn wasn't the best inn, but neither was it the worst. The innkeeper was a sly man of loose reliability, and though the watered pottage and watered ale made for a quick stay for most of his tenants, it was mostly clean and mostly safe.

Crispin knocked on the oak door and waited. It was well past the hour a patron would arrive, so Crispin remained patient, knowing the innkeeper might be abed.

In time, a shuffling sounded beyond the door and someone called from the other side of it, "Oi, who is there? It's past curfew."

"I know that, good innkeeper, but I seek one of your patrons."

"It is well past the hour," he said behind the wood. "Go away and come back on the morrow."

"I'm afraid I can't do that."

There was a pause before he asked tentatively, "Is this... Crispin Guest?"

"Guilty, Master."

Another pause. "Christ Jesus." With more swearing, the bolt scraped back and the door opened a crack. "So? What poor bastard would you be needing to show your fists to this night, Master Guest?"

"Nothing as violent as all that, I hope. A patron by the name of Robert Pickthorn."

"Oh, him," said the innkeeper with a sneer. "He's a strange one, isn't he? Can't keep his mouth shut even around the evening fire when men would rather talk of their accomplishments and greed. And here he is, mucking up their pleasure with talk of damnation. I'm losing patrons because of him. I tell you, Master Guest, I wouldn't mind a *little* violence put his way to even the score."

Crispin smirked. "Then may I enter?"

"Aye. I can't see my way to barring you, as you would find a way in at any rate. And there's young Jack Tucker with you, I see. Come in, gentlemen. It's a good night for it."

The hearth was banked, but it was still warmer in the room than outside it. Crispin waited for the man to bar the door again. The inn-keeper scratched his backside and with a grunt pointed up the stairs. "Second door. Try not to make too much of a mess."

Up the stairs Crispin went. His hand was on his dagger hilt, but he did not draw it. With Jack behind him, he arrived at the second door. He listened. The inn was quiet except for the creak of the wind in the rafters and the muffled sound of people talking and laughing down the gallery behind their own barred doors. He knocked and leaned in close to the door. "Master Pickthorn!"

They both heard a shuffling within. Through the door a rough-ened voice asked, "Who is it?"

"You don't know me, sir. But I would speak with you."

"In the morning. It is too late tonight."

"It is most urgent."

"It can wait."

"I'm very much afraid it cannot. I beg you to open the door… before I break it down."

Silence.

And then the sound of a window shutter opening. Crispin stepped back and rammed his shoulder into the door. It rattled on its hinges. He shoved again. A crack. Another hard shove, and it fell open. The window lay wide open and the cold air of the November night rolled into the room.

Crispin leaned over the sill and looked down. He heard no steps, no running, and saw no one. "Damn!"

Turning back to the room, he looked around in the dimness. Papers lay on the table. He picked through them. They were sermons in French and Latin. Clothing lay on a coffer—a long gown, an out-of-fashion foreign houppelande with patched elbows. At the hearth he spotted something and knelt. He picked up the stiff strands of black hair, merely the trimmings from what appeared to be a recent hair cutting. Dropping them, he turned toward Jack to comment when he noticed that the boy was not there. He stepped out onto the gallery and searched for him down below.

Other doors along the gallery opened slowly and cautiously, and faces peered at him from the cracks. He glared in their direction, a challenge to any of them. Widened eyes assessed him and quickly slammed their doors. Sounds of locks turning and chairs pushed against them trailed down the length of the gallery.

Crispin turned at the sound of Jack stumping back up the stairs, face damp with sweat.

"When I heard the window I run down, trying to catch him coming out," said Jack. "But the sarding innkeeper had locked his door good and I had a devil of a time just getting out of it. And by the time I came around to the window, the man was gone. Have you learned anything from the room?"

"Just some clothes, some sermons. Clippings from a haircut. But the clippings were of black hair. Does not our preacher have auburn hair?"

"Aye, sir. Perhaps he *does* have a confederate."

"That's what I was thinking." He glanced at the window again. "Not a confrontational sort of man, is he?"

"A stranger knocks on his door in the mid of night and threatens to cleave the door in? I'd be out the window, too."

"You have a point. Will he be back, I wonder?"

"His things are here."

"But maybe not tonight."

Jack stepped through the room and closed the shutters, shivering from the chill wind passing through. "Should I keep watch, sir?"

"If you would. Perhaps downstairs by the fire."

"Yes, Master."

They passed the innkeeper on the stair. "Master Tucker will remain the night." Crispin reached into his pouch, his hand closing on the golden nail before his fingers moved nimbly and grabbed a coin instead. "For your trouble and for his night's lodgings."

The man gestured with his thumb up the stairs. "What of yon patron? And my door?"

Crispin pulled out another coin. "For the door. And I believe your patron will be back. His things are here, at any rate. And if he does not return, you have that to sell, at least."

"Cold comfort." He wiped his nose with his sleeve. "Told you not to make a mess."

"I apologized for the door. That coin should make good on it."

He and Jack hurried down the stairs. Jack nestled himself by the fire, trying to stay in the shadows and still keep warm. Crispin nodded to him and to the innkeeper, still watching him from the stairs as he left.

Outside, he breathed deeply of the hard, cold air. He had failed in all ways this night. He had failed to protect the Stone—whether he believed it was real or not—and he had failed to capture the man who had abducted Perenelle Flamel. And something about this chase, this hunt for riddles, was troubling him. He did not think it was merely a ruse to keep Flamel away from his shop. He thought it was a very clever game that someone was playing. Someone who knew Flamel and who hated him.

How could Crispin ever find her? Was he doomed to follow those insane clues to their bitter conclusion? The abductor wanted them to chase all over London, to solve the clues, and to find her or... or what? If they stopped, what would he do? Maybe it was time to find out. They needed another message from the man. It might draw him out, but it might also force his hand. No, Crispin was certain that the man *wanted* to play this game, to prove how clever he was and also to wipe their noses in the fact that he was now in possession of the Philosopher's Stone. Would he know how to use it? He was at his so-called Great Work, that of divining the Stone, but what if he still did not know how to use it? He'd still need Flamel and his expertise. It was not over. Not yet.

Crispin stepped into the street and paused. Something wasn't right. A tingle at the back of his neck made him turn, but it was too late.

Shadows rose up and hands clapped over his arms and one over his mouth. He tried to fight them, to cry out, but ropes twisted around his wrists, binding them together. The glare of a torch in his face blinded him and he stumbled forward, unable to resist being dragged forth into the snow-wet street.

twenty-one

It wasn't long before he realized he was heading toward Newgate Market and then up the steps to the prison itself.

He was yanked around until he saw the sheriffs' serjeants in the firelight of their brazier.

"Why, look who's here, Wendell," said Tom. "It's Crispin Guest. The man with the impertinent mouth. Just so there won't be any backtalk…" He swung. Crispin's head snapped back and his mouth was suddenly flooded with the steely taste of blood. He spat it out on Tom's boot.

Tom glared, but the serjeants holding on to Crispin whipped him around. "There'll be plenty of time to settle this later," one guard said gruffly before pushing Crispin up the stairs.

Crispin stumbled and tried to save his chin from barking on the stone step by throwing his tied hands forward. He managed to barely avoid it before they grabbed his arm hard and yanked him upward.

One shoulder scraped along the wall as they ascended the spiral stair and he was marched past the empty alcove where the clerk usually sat and into the warm sheriffs' parlor… where they shoved him hard and he fell, knees first, onto the floor before the crackling hearth.

Both sheriffs stood on either side of the fireplace and looked down at him, each encased in their cloaks. The light shifted on their faces, but they wore unmistakable twin scowls.

"Guest, you are a nuisance and a traitor, and I wish to God I had nothing more to do with you," said Sheriff Venour.

Sheriff Fastolf lifted his booted foot and shoved Crispin in the shoulder, pushing his face to the floor despite Crispin's trying to prevent it with his bound hands. "What were you supposed to do, eh, Guest?" Fastolf ground out. "What did we tell you to do at the outset? You were supposed to find out who killed that apprentice! Nothing more, nothing less. And now it's poisoned cisterns and sneaking abroad at night where you clearly do not belong!"

"I oft go abroad at night, my lords. How else am I to track a murderer?" His mouth was still bloody and he spat again, this time away from the sheriff's boots.

"And you expect us to believe that?" He crouched down and looked Crispin in the face. "I want you off this task, Guest. I want you to forget it. Leave this for the coroner's jury to solve." He jabbed a finger into Crispin's face. "And I especially want you to stay away from the cisterns. It's none of your concern. You're meddling again. We want you to stop."

"But my lord, the coroner's jury will not be able to—"

Fastolf raised his head and nodded to the serjeant. A boot to Crispin's gut silenced his protest. He gasped and rolled to the floor, trying to breathe.

"What was that, Guest? Were you trying to infer that you know better than we do?" He put a hand to his ear. "I don't believe I heard you aright."

Crispin took in a shaky breath and pushed himself onto his knees. He licked his bloody lips and glowered up at the sheriff. "Why now, Lord Sheriff? For days I tracked this murderer. You told me to do so. And now you bring me here to tell me to stop my work? You know how my curiosity is piqued when I am told to back away."

The sheriff stole a glance at Venour, who had a wild look in his eye. It was he who nodded sharply to the serjeant this time. Crispin girded himself, and when the boot came again, he grabbed it with his bound hands and twisted as he shoved. The guard gave a cry and flew backward. Before he landed, the other serjeant grabbed Crispin by his hood and slammed his head into the fat table leg.

Crispin saw stars burst behind his lids and hunched forward, hanging his head below his shoulders. Dizzy, he blinked several times and shook his head. "That would be a 'no' to answering my query."

"Guest," said Venour, exasperated, "you must truly have a death wish. As the king's emissaries to keep the peace, I am *ordering* you to cease this investigation. His Majesty's courtiers keep a sharp eye on our doings and have expressed their displeasure at your meddling."

I noticed. But who expressed it… and for what, exactly? They looked frightened, the both of them. Was it someone the sheriffs were protecting? They emphasized that there were courtiers watching their doings. Did this go that high? Higher? They were the king's emissaries, after all. Certainly the scope of the riddles all over town would seem to suggest it, for how could one man have accomplished it all?

But then it begged the question Why? Why in the world would King Richard need the Philosopher's Stone? If he believed all that was said of it, he might certainly want the gold. But he was a very devout man, and alchemy smacked of sorcery. Would he pursue such a thing? And if it were he, why abduct Perenelle? Would it not be more expeditious to steal the alchemist himself and force him to explain whatever the Stone was supposed to do?

He licked his swollen lips again. No. He couldn't imagine it. Not Richard. But his ministers, on the other hand… They had meddled before. It was Suffolk who wanted the relic Crispin had encountered only last year, but Crispin had been unable to prove Suffolk's complicity. Crispin would like it to be him. He'd like to corner Suffolk in some alleyway and show him how precisely he had injured Crispin and those he cared about.

But what of the poisoning of the cistern? The sheriffs had reluctantly obliged in protecting the water sources for London, but they seemed disinclined to continue it. Were they being told to back away? And again, by whom? Capturing the Philosopher's Stone was one thing, but poisoning London's water supply was quite another. One had nothing to do with the other. Except that the sheriffs couldn't help but speak of the two in one breath, and that was troubling.

A madman, perhaps, would poison the water, but it seemed more likely it was a French plot that they so recently mocked.

Who at the English court would protect a French plot?

"He is silenced at last. Perhaps that last stroke addled his brain." Sheriff Venour bent over to look at Crispin. "Will you behave, Guest? Or will my serjeants need to further convince you?"

"No, my lords. I am thoroughly convinced. There is just one thing."

Venour straightened and threw his head back impatiently. *"Yes?"*

"What concerns you dearest? The dead apprentice… or the poisoned water?"

Venour took a step back and gave a rushed look of terror at his companion. "Get him out of here," he said to the guards. "And see that you finish the lesson before releasing him."

Even though his lodgings were just down the street, it took a long time for Crispin to reach them. With the dark, it was twice as hard to navigate even a few yards. And he had to stop periodically and lean against a wall. Dizzy. Headache. And… was that double vision? "Perfect," he muttered.

Tom and Wendell had been invited to join in tutoring Crispin into behaving. Crispin clutched his sore ribs as he slowly climbed his stairs. When the door moved open by his mere touch, he was glad it wasn't an unwelcome visitor. He didn't think he had the strength to fight off anyone.

Avelyn made a cry of distress upon seeing him and rushed across the room. She ducked a shoulder under his arm and helped him to the bed.

He eased down, relieved to be on his bed at last. She knelt at his feet to remove his boots. "I don't know why you are here—you should be with your master—but I can't say I am not glad of it."

She lifted his feet onto the mattress and then cradled him so he leaned back until his head rested on the pillow. He knew his face must look like raw meat—felt like it—and one of his eyelids had swollen shut.

He closed the other eye and just breathed, thankful that he still could. Ribs weren't broken. That was a mercy. He didn't know how he'd avoided it, but he had.

Lying on his bed, he simply breathed for a time, relishing the warmth from the hearth. He startled upward when an ice-cold cloth slid against his face. Avelyn's fingers on his arm soothed him back down. She carefully bathed his sore cheeks and chin, leaving the cold cloth on the most swollen parts: his nose, cheek, and eye. It felt good.

Fingers started unbuttoning his coat and he gently closed his hand over them. "Leave it. My ribs hurt from the pounding they took." But she persisted and he found himself sitting up enough for her to pull off his hood, cloak, and coat. Fingers slipped up under his shirt and probed, testing the tender flesh and pressing gently on the ribs. When she was satisfied, she tucked a blanket over him and went to the fire to jam a poker in to urge it higher. He did not immediately notice when she left.

He must have dozed, for when she returned she was pressing something to his lips. A cup. He opened his mouth obligingly and drank. It tasted of herbs and earthy tones and was not particularly pleasant. But it did not take long for his limbs to feel warm and weightless, and it took the edge off the pain in his face. "You are a miracle worker."

"Not so much a miracle," said the unexpected voice of Flamel. "Alchemy takes many forms." Crispin opened his good eye and looked at the man standing by his table. Avelyn remained next to him on the bed, holding the cup.

"I thank you both."

"Such a dangerous job you have, *Maître*. So much sacrifice."

"It must be done."

"Yes, I see that."

"I have a question for you, Master Flamel."

"Perhaps you should rest, *Maître*. You have suffered much."

"Just one question. How long have you been in England?"

"Some three months. We arrived on the evening tide in August. And no one knew we were coming. We told no one we were leaving and booked passage the day we left. No one knew."

"But—"

"Rest, *Maître* Crispin. Rest."

He closed his eyes and let the potion do its work.

He awoke to Jack arguing with Flamel. "And you didn't think to ask how he got this way?" Jack stomped back and forth over the floor. "Could have been robbers. Could have been this man we are looking for. It could have been... ah! God blind me with a poker! Those men following us!"

"Jack, has anyone ever told you how loud you are in the morning?"

The boy stopped his furious pacing and flung himself on Crispin's bed. "Master Crispin! How do you fare, sir?"

"Knocked about a bit. How do you think I fare, especially with you yelling at the top of your lungs?"

"I'm sorry, sir. I was just worried about you."

He rested a hand on Jack's and patted it. He was surprised to note that he could see with both eyes. He raised a hand to his face and felt that almost all the swelling was gone. A miracle indeed. "Master Flamel was kind enough to minister to me and stay with me all night."

Flamel bowed to him.

"And it was the sheriffs' men. Our dear sheriffs wanted to make certain that I got a message: I was meddling where I didn't belong. Curious. I did not know I had gotten that far in my investigation, but clearly they thought I had. What do you make of that, Jack?"

Tucker scratched his lightly fuzzed chin. "I dunno. When did they grab you?"

"Right outside the Cockerel's Tail Inn."

"That is curious, sir."

"Did our preacher return?"

"No. Which leads me to believe, sir, that he has other lodgings."

"Accomplices?"

"Perhaps. I had many such bolt-holes when I was about my business as a young lad. Places to hide when on the run. He might have them, too."

Crispin lay back, resting his head on his bent arm. "Why should a preacher need such hiding places?"

"He is a very bad preacher?" offered Flamel.

"By all accounts he is a very good preacher. But I suppose the feeling is relative."

"Master," said Jack, leaning forward, "there is a great ruckus up Cornhill Street. People are rioting."

"What? Why?"

"The cistern. They demanded to know why it was closed. They blame the king and his ministers. The sheriffs' men at the other cisterns are having a time of it, so I hear. I went myself to the Standard and there is fighting there as well."

Crispin sat up. "Do you suppose there are more poisonings?"

"I don't know, Master. But at the Tun, I did notice this sign near it." He ran to the coffer, grabbed a wax slate, and brought it over. He sketched the sign and showed it to Crispin.

Flamel grabbed the slate from his hand and gasped. "*Maître,* this is the sign for arsenic."

"God's blood!" hissed Crispin. "The bastard was actually taunting us! Jack, did you see this at any of the other cisterns?"

"No, sir. I looked, but I found nothing."

Crispin lay back. His aching ribs were making themselves known again. "I do not know if that is a mercy or not."

"And something else, sir." He leaned in much closer to Crispin when he said, "I saw Lord Henry there, in the background. He was taking note of it all. And then he saw me and left hurriedly."

"Damn! Curse it all!" He threw himself forward and sat up, clutching his belly. Jack was poised, ready to catch him if he fell over, but even through the stabbing aches, he reassured the boy with a quick nod. "The sheriffs were not pleased with me. At first I thought it was for being out after curfew, and then for taking so long over investigating this murder of Thomas Cornhill—which they had admonished me to do in the first place. But then they were also angry that I was 'meddling,' so they said, in this matter of poison in the cistern. I got the impression that they were being censured for acquiescing to my demands to protect the water supply."

Jack gasped. "*They* were censured? The sheriffs have something to do with poisoning the cisterns?"

"I don't know. But they wanted me to stay out of it. I had begun to think that it might have been a French plot." Flamel stiffened at that, but Crispin ignored it and pressed on. "But instead, I rather think they are protecting someone. Someone in high places."

"Lord Henry?"

"No. They are after him, remember? It seems outlandish on the surface, and yet—"

"We have encountered the like before," Jack finished. "The earl of Suffolk," he muttered. "Aye, but how to discover it?" His face drained of all color. "Will… will we have to go to court, Master?"

"That seems unlikely. And you know how welcomed I would be there." With a grunt of pain, he rose to his feet and stood unsteadily. "At any rate, we must talk to this preacher, despite what the sheriffs desire. He has something to do with one of these events. At least he knows more than we do."

Jack offered Crispin a steadying hand. "Wine, sir? I've warmed some."

"Yes. I will take it."

"What are you saying, *Maître* Crispin?" said Flamel, giving him an arm to lean on as Jack hastened to fetch the wine. He helped Crispin to a seat by the fire.

"As strange as it seems, Master Flamel, there may very well be royal connections to not only the poisoning of the water, but to you *and* to your wife's disappearance."

"What? How? How can they possibly be connected?"

"This preacher. It can't be a coincidence that he knew of the dead apprentice. He spoke of a man hung by his heel like a traitor, and he also spoke of the signs carved all over London as signs of the Devil. And finally, he accused me of being an alchemist… although now that I think about it, I am not so certain he did."

"But he did call you that, sir," said Jack, handing Crispin a steaming bowl of wine. "I heard him."

Crispin drank and licked his lips, sighing as the hot liquid warmed his throat and chest. "The 'alchemist's lair,' is what he said. He knew. He knew that an alchemist lived there. How did he know if Master Flamel's being here was a secret?"

Jack fell silent, thinking.

"Master Flamel," said Crispin, "where might one obtain arsenic? An apothecary?"

"Of course. But one might also obtain it from an alchemist. But such men who sell these poisons... well. Alchemists of any caliber do not sell poisons to men they do not know."

"Perhaps he did know the man. I should query the local alchemists. I do know of at least one such man." He looked at Jack, whose mouth firmed to a stern line.

"Aye, Master. Let us ask this Bartholomew of Oxford."

Jack kept a keen eye on Crispin as they moved through the streets of London. He was grateful for the boy's concern, but his constant anxious looks frayed Crispin's nerves to the edge.

At last they found the sign of Mercury and slogged through the dung-soaked mud to the door. The shop was empty as usual, but they heard the telltale rustling of the man in the back room. When he stuck his carbuncled nose past the curtain, only his face emerged, and he kept the curtain around him like a shield.

"Master Guest," he said cautiously. "What is it you want— Oh! What happened to you, man?"

Though the swelling was down, he had no doubt that his face was a rainbow of purple and yellow bruises.

"A run-in with several disagreeable fellows."

"Perhaps you bedeviled them, too. Why have you returned?"

"You're the only other alchemist I know, Master Bartholomew. I wonder if you can tell me something."

The man gave a harried sigh. "Master Guest, you seem to think that men should feel compelled to cooperate with you. That they are at their leisure with nothing else to do. All this without charge. *I* do not. I must *sell* my goods in order to keep a roof over my head. And so it does not follow that I may give to anyone—whoever they may be—*free* information. My material is hard earned over many years of toiling. And my time is equally valuable. Surely you can appreciate that."

Crispin looked around the strange room. His nose flared at the unpleasant smells. "You want payment, then."

"Not so crude a transaction as that. Perhaps in exchange for my useful information you could make a purchase." Crispin grimaced, but the alchemist brightened at his own thought. "How about this?" He ducked away behind the curtain for a moment and then returned. He held aloft a small gauze bag tied with a leather thong as a necklace. "A fragrant sachet." He pressed it to his nose and inhaled. "Ah. Lovely. Surely a pleasant smell about your person could be most enticing."

"I don't need to be enticing," he growled.

"It will help soothe the pain you must surely feel. By my Lady, Master Guest, I do not know how, with a face like that, you can walk about at all."

Crispin snatched it from the man's hand. "How much?"

"Two pence."

"*Two* pence? That's robbery!"

The man shrugged and smiled, revealing one sharp, grayed tooth.

Swearing under his breath, Crispin dug his hand into his scrip, produced the coins, and slapped them into the man's hand. "Now will you answer my questions?"

"Put it on, sir. I would see my handiwork for what it was meant for."

After glaring at the man for several heartbeats, he pulled the necklace over his head and let it rest on his chest for only a moment before, annoyed by the scent, he stuffed it through the collar of his shirt. "Happy?"

"Most happy. That is my first sale of the day. And now. You wish to ask a question."

"Yes." He leaned in, feeling the bag rustle against his coat. It sent a musky floral aroma up through the cloth. He was reluctant to admit that it was more pleasant than he'd originally thought. "Do you sell poisons, Master Bartholomew?"

The man blinked, taken aback. "Poisons? What a question. Why should I sell poisons?"

"The question was not why, but whether you did or not." He leaned farther, within grabbing distance should the man decide to bolt. "Did you?"

He narrowed his eyes. "I take the measure of the man, Master Guest. Not everyone is up to no good. The use of some poisons is quite legitimate. Many alchemists use them in their experiments in the Greater Circulations. If a man will pay, I will sell."

"Have you sold any lately?"

His downcast eyes looked at his fingers fiddling with the loose threads on his robe's sleeve. "I… might have."

"And what might this worthy look like?"

"Well, let me see. His hair was of auburn color, and he had a way about him."

Coldness touched Crispin's heart. For the first thought that came to mind was Henry of Lancaster.

"Was he young?"

"Oh, no. I should not say he was young. A man of about my age."

Relief flooded him. "I see. You would not by any chance know his name?"

"No. We did not exchange such pleasantries."

"Did you know him?"

"No, sir. I did not. He convinced me that he knew what to do with it and I sold him the quantity he desired."

"How much?"

"A goodly amount."

"Enough to do… alchemy?"

"I should say so. Why? What's he done?"

Instead of answering, Crispin sneered. "Would you recognize him again should I bring him here?"

"I… well, yes. I think so."

"Good. Then plan on seeing me again. Much thanks, Master Alchemist." He turned away, then swiveled his head back. "I won't be buying anything when I return. Understood?" He made a show of resting his hand on his dagger.

With an audible swallow, the man backed away toward his curtain. "U-understood, Master Guest."

With a swirl of his cloak, Crispin passed through the doorway and onto the street, with Jack on his heels. "The nerve of him, Master."

"Yes. But it might be worth it. His description. Who did it remind you of?"

Jack nodded. "Auburn hair. Well-spoken. If I had to hazard a guess, I would say… Robert Pickthorn?"

"Could be. I wonder if that was the reason Avelyn sent us here. She knew of this Pickthorn spending coin at this shop."

"I don't trust her, sir."

"What's the matter, Tucker? Does she seem too wily for a servant?"

"Aye! I mean, no! Some servants are just as wily as they need to be."

Crispin smiled and patted Jack's shoulder. "Never fear. I'm rather fond of wily servants myself."

Jack gusted a relieved laugh. "You do have your jests, don't you," he muttered. "Where shall we look for this preacher, Master Crispin?"

"We shall ask around. That's a lot of ground to cover, but we might get lucky. And Jack, if you encounter him, do not engage him in any violence."

"You take the fun out of everything, Master Crispin." He smiled with a lopsided grin.

"Go on. Meet me at the Boar's Tusk in about an hour's time. I have a feeling I'll be needing a drink about then."

Crispin watched Jack walk away before he headed out alone along the Shambles until it became Newgate Market. He turned south on Old Dean's Lane with the intention of checking outside the walls. This man might be preaching in London's outskirts, along Holborn or Shoe Lane. He passed out of the walled part of the city at Ludgate, glancing again at the sigils inscribed on the stone of the arch that had begun their hunt.

While he walked, he began thinking of Flamel and the troubling words he had used that reminded him of Abbot Nicholas. *You must forget what you think you know. Beware of what you find.* Why had he chosen those exact words? Abbot Nicholas had used them, he was certain of it. Almost precisely a year ago as he lay dying. He had been speaking of the many relics that crossed Crispin's path over and over again. But the Stone was not one of God's relics. And yet… its power was reputed to transcend the ether. Was this not the Almighty's territory? Was Man foolish to dabble in it, trespassing on Divine creation?

What did it mean? *Forget what you think you know.* What *did* he know? He knew, in this instance, that a man was killed and a threat was levied to another man's wife, all for a ransom. But then, it *hadn't* been all for a ransom, had it? They were dancing to the tune of one man, of which, so far, only he knew the rules. And Crispin thought that Henry might be involved, for a man in his position naturally played a game of cruel suspicions and backroom transactions. But *was* he involved?

Beware of what you find. That was a certainty. He did not want to find that Henry was too intimate with this game of abductions, murder, and threats. He did not want to find that he could be as cruel as his father, and yet he knew that this was most likely the case, given who he was.

What else was he to find? The wife? Alive, he hoped. But also the culprit. And once he knew who he was, would Crispin be glad that he found him?

He looked up at the street, watching men with wooden yokes fitted across their shoulders, balancing their wares from each end in bundles, making their way toward London proper. Crispin walked around them and their burdens, while several dogs yipped at one another, prancing and following at the heels of the men on their way back through the gated arch.

Crispin pricked his ears, listening for that telltale voice that rose easily above the crowd. But all he heard was the noise of wagons rattling over the street, of masters admonishing their apprentices, of women laughing, and of brooms sweeping.

He scouted the streets of Farringdon and stopped a man or two to ask if they had seen the preacher. All shook their heads, staring at his bruised face. He moved up to West Smithfield and saw much the same. At midday, he bought some cheese and a roasted egg from a goat girl resting beside her charges along the road. He ate as he crossed the stark, snow-whitened fields near St. Giles church, leaving fragments of eggshell behind him. Eventually, he made his way back through the walls at Cripplegate. No sign of the preacher, and when he asked of a woman tending geese, she had not seen the man either.

Crispin stood at the crossroads of Coleman and Lothbury and made a scoffing sound. This was insane. London was too big a city for two people to find one man.

And just as he decided that perhaps it was time to give up and go to the Boar's Tusk, he heard a sound in the distance. A sound of many people. He hurried in that direction down Lothbury and came upon a crowd of people yelling at one of the king's guards. A solitary soldier with a kettle helm and mail under his surcote, he was standing before a cistern and looking as if he would rather be anywhere else.

"For the last time," said the guard with a roll of his eyes. He clenched his chapped hands over his spear shaft. "I'm not preventing you from getting your water. I'm merely *guarding* it. For your own sarding protection."

"Guarding the water?" said a strident voice above the melee of shouting wives and fist-waving men. "Guarding God's most precious gift to Man? And what does it need guarding from?"

Crispin strained up on his toes to see above the crowd, for that was the familiar voice he had been looking for. He pushed his way forward, ignoring the disgruntled grimaces that turned to look at him, and found his man, standing not too far from the flummoxed guard.

"Water from God's Heaven is the purest, and will renew and rejuvenate. Why did He choose water to baptize, to cleanse, if it were not safe for us?"

The crowd began to quiet and listen to the preacher. Crispin finally got a good look at him. With coarse reddish hair, he stood tall, though he had a slight paunch to his middle. His clothes were not as fine as even a merchant's, but neither were they patched or particularly worn. He surveyed the crowd with a confident air, sweeping his arm to encompass the cistern and the weary guard before it.

"'But he that drinketh of the water that I shall give him, shall not thirst without end; but the water that I shall give him, shall be made in him a well of water, springing up into everlasting life.' So says Holy Scripture. Who blocks this well from you? A sinner! Sent forth from sinners!"

The guard turned a squint on him. "Oi!" he cried, shaking a fist at him. "Who's a sarding sinner?"

"'What great troubles, many and evil, thou hast sent me! and then turned, thou hast granted me life, and hast brought me up again from the watery depths of the earth and hast brought me up again from the grave.' Good people of London. You are being deceived. This man claims to be guarding your cistern, but he is following orders from above, from those who would despoil this city from its rightful governor. For it is not the king that prevents you from the water, but the work of these so-called commissioners who have invaded the city, lords who would usurp God's anointed."

"That's enough of that!" shouted the guard, and with spear pointed toward Pickthorn, he advanced.

The preacher raised his chin at the man, seemingly unafraid. And soon Crispin saw why. Men in the crowd had surged forward to protect him, and he gave the guard a smile to show that he had the upper hand. But it wasn't until he swept the crowd with his proud gaze that it fell on Crispin, and the recognition in his eyes had a most profound effect on him.

He bounded off the makeshift platform of barrels and shoved into the crowd, beating a hasty retreat away from Crispin.

Crispin dove headlong into the surging people, not afraid to elbow hard anyone who got in his way. Once he was free of the heaving throng, he hit the mud running.

Pickthorn was well ahead of him. The man looked over his shoulder once with wild eyes, then lowered his head to pick up speed.

No, you don't, thought Crispin, feet hammering hard on the cobblestones and slipping when he hit a patch of snow or frozen mud.

Pickthorn rounded a corner, and when Crispin approached the same turn, he could see that the man was trapped by a flock of muddy sheep. The beasts bleated around him. By the mud and wet spots on the man's clothes, Crispin could tell that he must have fallen and was trying desperately to make his way through.

Crispin pounced, tackling the man to the frozen ground. Sheep bounded out of the way, and the drover, a boy of only eleven or so, shook his fist and swore at them like a whoremonger.

Crispin ignored him and struggled, subduing the preacher. "Stop! Stop your struggling." He hauled the man to his feet and untangled his wet cloak from Pickthorn's, whipping it behind him. He pushed the man against a wall and pressed him there.

"Let me go, you ruffian."

"If I let you go, will you talk to me?"

"It depends on what you have to say." Crispin mangled the man's coat in a tight grip and twisted until Pickthorn choked. "Yes, I yield! God have mercy!"

With a sneer, Crispin released him, stepping back to give the man room. "Why did you run from me?"

"You can be a frightening man. Witness for yourself what you have done to me." He wiped down the mud from his coat and valiantly tried to right his twisted cloak.

"My apologies," said Crispin without meaning it. "But I have been seeking you for some time." As the man straightened his clothes, Crispin spied a crystal phial hanging around his neck on a knotted red thread. It appeared to be empty. He grabbed for it and held it up. "What is this?"

The man snatched it back and clutched it in his hand. "What business is it of yours?"

"Perhaps nothing. Perhaps much. Tell me, what were you doing harassing that poor guard? He was merely performing his appointed task and guarding the cistern from mischief."

"Mischief indeed!" the man scoffed indignantly. "That guard was set there by those commissioners appointed by Parliament, that which is led by Lancaster's son." He said the last with such vehemence that Crispin pulled back. "It is sedition, is what it is," he went on. "Nothing more, nothing less. The Devil has whispered in the ears of these noble men and seduced them with lies and their own greed for power. The water doesn't need guarding. It needs renewing with God's gentle grace to allow the people to be reborn with the Water of Life."

Crispin wanted dearly to smack the man but held himself back. "That water has been killing people. Someone has poisoned it."

"What? Absurd. You, sir, fall into the same trap of believing what these commissioners say rather than the good king. Nothing whatsoever has happened to the water of this city—"

"I tell you the water was poisoned. At the Tun. It was infused with arsenic. Many young and innocent died from it. The guards are there to prevent it from happening to the other cisterns."

The man paused, eyes flicking over Crispin's face in disbelief. "No! That is foolish talk."

"I tell you I saw it! I saw the proof of it with my own eyes."

Pickthorn froze. He looked down at the phial in his hand, looked up once at Crispin, then down at the phial again and shook his head.

Crispin opened his mouth to ask but nearly bit his lip when Pickthorn shoved him back. Not expecting it, Crispin lost his balance and toppled backward, biting out a curse when he hit the ground hard.

By the time Crispin sat up, Pickthorn was gone, with only the sound of his escaping footsteps echoing in the alley.

twenty-two

rispin jumped to his feet and ran hard. He spied the man up ahead at the curve of the road. Pickthorn was older than Crispin, so Crispin had that advantage, at least. How far could the man go? Yet he had run quite a way and Crispin wasn't gaining on him.

Ahead, Crispin spotted a broom propped against a wall. As he ran by, he reached out and grabbed it. Cocking his arm back, he took aim and then heaved it forward. After spinning in the air, it slammed into the man's feet and over he went, skidding shoulder first along the muddy lane.

Crispin caught his breath as he stood over him. "Up you get," he grunted. He grabbed the man by his shoulders and shoved him into the nearest wall.

An old man with a basket of bread looked on as Crispin smacked the preacher in the face. "I don't like it when people run from me. Makes me angry."

Pickthorn touched his stinging cheek and ran his narrowed-eyed glare over Crispin's features. "You dare! I preach the good Lord's word and you dare to lay hands upon me!"

Crispin smacked him on the other cheek with the back of his hand. "You'll get more if you don't answer me."

"Hold! Stop! I… I don't know what you want."

"Yes, you do. This." He grasped the empty phial from the man's neck and held it up. "What was in here? What did you do?"

"I... I did not poison anyone."

Again, the flat of Crispin's hand struck up at his chin, knocking Pickthorn's head back against the wall. There were tears of pain in his eyes when he glared back at Crispin.

"I can show you the graves that tell me otherwise. What did you put in the water at the Tun?"

"Nothing harmful, I swear by almighty God!"

"For the last time, answer me, or I shall shove this down your throat. *What was in the phial?*"

"A... a harmless concoction of holy water and pulverized herbs. The man assured me that it would put the people in an amenable mood, to make them gentle as lambs so that they would be open and heed the word of the Lord."

"Holy water and herbs? Are you mad? It was *poison!*"

Pickthorn looked confused. "No. No, it couldn't have been. They *did* listen. They repented. The solution was working!"

"I tell you it was *killing* them. Had I not had the cistern closed, you would have killed more."

He blinked, eyes glistening with filling tears. "Jesus, mercy," he whispered. "What have I done?"

Crispin released him and stepped back. He watched the man's face collapse in despair. "Dead," he gasped. "Because of me?" He crossed himself and murmured his prayers into his tightly folded hands.

Crispin watched for a moment and sighed. "You were deceived. Now you must make it right."

"Yes, yes." He bent forward and wept into his prayerful hands. "Will I... will I hang for it?"

"That is for the law to decide. But I do not have in mind to turn you in to the law. Yet."

"What must I do?"

"Did you get this 'solution' from an alchemist?"

He looked up, face streaked with dirt and tears. "I did. I was preaching one day, and after I was done, he approached me, told me he could help me. I went to his shop and he gave me this phial and said to put it in the cistern and what it would do."

"Why did you believe him?"

"Because he seemed genuinely sincere. Told me that my words had changed his life and he was going to give up his sorcery."

"'Sorcery'? Is that what he said?"

"His words, I assure you, good Master. But now I see..." He straightened, a new determination lighting his eyes. "The Devil had taken hold of him. A damned man if ever there was one. Who but such a one who schemed with Satan could manufacture as diabolical a plot?"

"Indeed. And what of the sigils on the walls of London? What had you to do with those?"

"Why... nothing whatever. I saw them and knew they were the signs of the Demon."

"Do you know who I am?"

"You... you are the one that they speak of. You are the Tracker."

"Yes. And when you saw me some days ago, you said I was emerging from the alchemist's lair. How did you know that that was an alchemist's shop?"

"I was told it. By that other foul sorcerer." He frowned. "Oh, the Deceiver is clever and uses honeyed words, but they are all lies. I thought he had turned a new leaf. I thought he had repented and was declaring war on the others of his ilk. He told me about this other alchemist and that's why I chose that corner to do my preaching, to catch him. I thought at first it was you, but later I learned who you were."

"There is one thing more. You have a crusade against these commissioners appointed by Parliament. Against... against Lord Derby, it would seem, in particular. Why?"

"I am a law-abiding man, Master Guest. My king is my sovereign, not his Parliament. And these councillors would seem to want to take his crown, to make him nothing but a figurehead. No. No man who loves God can abide it."

"I see. You realize that these appointed men are only trying to make certain that the king conforms to his vows made before God? That the taxes collected were to be for the good running and defense of the kingdom, not for the use of his favorites?"

Pickthorn turned his reddened eyes to Crispin, peering steadily. "That, Master, is treasonous talk. And I hear that you were once a man who stepped into the cesspool of treason yourself. Is that why you support these usurpers?"

Crispin stepped back, chastened. "I assure you…" His voice was unsteady and he cursed it. "My loyalties are with the crown. I will not make that mistake again." He heaved an angry breath and stared at the ground, toeing the mud with his boot. "And now what to do with you."

Pickthorn sagged against the wall. The red marks Crispin had made to his cheeks were fading in the cold air. "I will turn myself in to the sheriffs, of course. I… I have sinned against my fellow man—" His voice choked off with a whimper.

"Not of your own devising. I tell you what you must do instead, Master Pickthorn. You must lay low, forget your preaching for a time."

He raised his face. "But—"

"I tell you, you must lay low! I will smooth this over with the sheriffs. It is this alchemist to blame. I will take care of him. Go back to the Cockerel's Tail Inn."

He took Crispin's hand and laid his cheek upon it. "Bless you, Master Guest. I shall pray for your kind soul, and for your deep repentance. And I shall further pray to soften your hardened heart so that you may truly see. For I fear you are blinded by your past loyalties. You must see the evil that Lancaster and his son are spilling into the heart of London, just as surely as if they poisoned the waters themselves."

Crispin snatched his hand away. "Pray if you must for my soul, but leave the rest. Now begone. I will do what I can."

"Thank you, Master Guest. May the Lord make His face to shine upon you and give you peace."

"Yes, yes," he grumbled, watching Pickthorn out of the corner of his eye as the preacher scurried away. Something about the man unsettled him, and it wasn't merely his politics. He shook it off. He had other work to do. "Bartholomew of Oxford," he sneered. He looked up, assessing the gray sun disappearing behind the heavy drapery of cloud. "You're next."

It was drizzling by the time Crispin neared the alchemist's street. The drifts of dirty snow along the lane were melting away.

Crispin had worked himself up into full indignation. The man had looked him in the eye and lied. Lied for days. Told him fantasies of the Stone and how devoted he was to his craft. "Witchcraft, more like," he muttered. What was his game? Was he in league with this abductor, this killer?

The drizzle became a steady rain, and though his leather hood protected most of his head, his face was spattered with droplets and his lashes were sticky and damp. He pulled his dagger and was stomping toward the shop when someone grabbed his dagger arm.

He spun, yanking his arm away from those grasping fingers. Turning, he readied to strike at his attacker—and stumbled to a stop instead.

He lowered the blade and made a growl of exasperation. "You damned woman!" He sheathed the blade and took Avelyn by her shoulders. "I nearly killed you."

She ignored his warning and took his hand, dragging him away.

"Wait," he said, digging in his heels. "What is it? What's wrong?"

She tried to sign it to him, but he closed his hands over her wildly gesticulating fingers. "I can't understand you." He glanced once at the shop with the sign of Mercury over the door and relented to Avelyn's endless tugging.

They hurried over the rainy streets to Flamel's shop. Avelyn reached the porch and waited for Crispin. When he arrived, she shoved him through.

"Master Flamel? What is it? I was in the middle of—"

Flamel turned to him, his face pale as bone. Crispin moved his gaze from his face to what was in his hand. Another scrap of parchment... and a lock of hair.

twenty-three

er hands were nearly free. She could feel the rope loosening. But then a light shone from under the door. He had returned. And now she heard his furious stomping about the room, heard glass retorts and metal instruments clatter behind the wall. With the sound of fuel snapping and a poker pushing around coals, she knew he was busy at that fire, at his athanor, concocting his ridiculous work. Fear still coiled in her belly, but it was tempered now by anger and indignation. How could he? How could he do this to her?

She wrapped up the loosened end of rope in her hands and waited.

Her door slammed open, hitting the wall behind it, and he stood in the doorway, a dark silhouette against the flickering light from the hearth in the outer room. His hands opened and closed, fingers curled angrily.

She allowed a brief spike of envy for the warmth she saw flooding the outer room, a warmth she was not allowed unless she "won" it with one of his senseless games.

"You have a champion," he said.

She turned away, feigning disinterest. She knew this irked him the most, that she did not hang on his every word. She had given him her full attention at first but soon learned it played into his deepest desires. And now he had the Stone. He had showed it to her last night, bragged about how he would soon use it. But by his words she suspected he hadn't the faintest idea *how* to use it.

"*Madame,* did you hear? A most renowned man in London. I have just learned of him and his feats. Have *you* heard of him? He is called the Tracker. And he is tracking *us.*" He laughed. "It's delightful. And most invigorating. It makes the game that much more entertaining, don't you agree?"

She said nothing, relishing the aggravation surely building with her silence.

He went on, heedless of her stillness, or so it seemed. "Tracker." He laughed. "His name is Crispin Guest. He's a private sheriff, tracking for hire. These English." He shook his head affectionately. "I've asked about him. Seems most of the London citizenry have heard of him. He was a traitor, but his life was spared by none other than Lancaster himself. Is that not amusing, *mon amour*? Is that not ironic? He finds lost things, lost people. Do you think he will be clever enough to find you?"

"You're a fool. And I don't care what you think. Will you release me? My bones ache from being in this position for so long."

"Dear, dear. Shall we toss for it?"

"No more games! For the love of the Holy Virgin! Do a kindness for kindness' sake. Can you not do that, at least? For the sake of our pasts."

But as soon as she said it, she knew it was a mistake. His strangely jovial demeanor hardened. "For the sake of our pasts?" he whispered. "For that sake, I would keep you tied up *forever, Madame*!"

"I did not mean—"

"For all eternity!" He moved with such speed, such agility, it was hard to fathom that he was nearly the same age as Nicholas. He got down on one knee beside her so that his face could be close to her ear. She pulled at her restraints to get as far away from him as possible. "I have the Stone now." His voice was harsh at her ear. His spittle pelted her hair, now disarrayed and falling from her careful coiffure. "I can do what I have planned. These other things are merely an amusing distraction. The cauldron is bubbling, my love. The retorts are full of the compounds I need."

"It is a shame, then, that you do not know what you are doing."

"I *do* know!" he hissed. His breath at her ear suddenly felt dirtier than her body felt from days without cleaning herself or changing her underclothes. "I know it," he said more calmly. She remembered that about him, that he could change his outward calm on a wisp of the breeze, though now the change seemed more abrupt, more like a twitch that one could not control. "And what I don't know, I will make Nicholas tell me," he went on. "For I think he will be here soon. With the help of his Tracker."

Her arm jerked, and though she willed him not to look, he did, and saw the loosened rope. He laughed. "Oh, *ma chère*. How clever you are." He strode to the other side of her chair and pulled on the rope. "I must make this especially tight, then, so that you will not escape."

She cried out as the rope dug into her already chafed skin.

"Nice and tight," he said, securing the last knot.

Her heart sank and the fear she had held at bay crept over her again. Escape was growing further away from her. And now she feared for Nicholas, too. Was he planning on trapping Nicholas? Would he kill him as he killed their apprentice? She would stall him, then. Tell him a partial truth. But she would have to tread carefully. He was wild now. Wilder than he had ever been.

"I could help you. In exchange for a little freedom. And proper food and water. I can help you."

"Help me? Would you now. We will make the Elixir together, then?"

"Yes. But you must release me. Let me walk about. My legs ache."

"Hmm. An interesting proposition. I shall think on it."

She lowered her head, looking away so that he would not see her eyes, for through her fear she also felt elation. He might be tricked. It might work. And Nicholas had gotten the help of a man who found things, found people. A champion! Would he find her in time?

twenty-four

he game is not over. What are you waiting for?

Crispin read the words on the scrap of parchment again. He glanced at the lock of hair, red gold, streaked with gray, that Flamel would not release, and turned at last to Avelyn.

"Avelyn, do you know where the Boar's Tusk is? A tavern on Gutter Lane?"

She nodded.

"Go with all haste and bring back Jack Tucker. Don't take no for an answer."

She leapt up and darted out the door.

When the door slammed shut, he took Flamel by the arm and sat him on a chair by the fire. "Master Flamel, *is* this a lock of hair from your wife?"

He nodded, eyes never leaving the strands tied with a blue ribbon of cloth.

Crispin lowered the parchment. "He has the Stone. But it isn't merely about that, is it?"

The alchemist shook his head again. "He… he must want my help in order to use it. It is a most complicated process. And so I must… I must…" His chin hit his chest and he shivered.

"Master Flamel, he did not speak of your helping him. He spoke of a game."

Flamel shot to his feet, hand now curled around the lock. "But he is dead! It is impossible!"

"Hadn't you better tell me everything, sir, no matter how *impossible* it might seem?"

Wild-eyed, he glared at Crispin. "Very well. My… my wife was married before me. But her husband died and left her a wealthy widow. But that didn't matter to me. I was in love."

He shuffled to the fire and leaned an arm over the hearth. The flames' light danced over his long face, creasing the lines in deep shadow. "She was not as enamored of me, however. I was younger than her, rash. She had a suitor in France in those days. He was somewhat relentless in his pursuit. But… well… she eventually spurned him in favor of me. I am afraid he took a long time to get over it. But this was many years ago. He married someone else. Had children. Then there was a fire… he was killed along with his son."

"The man's name?"

"Piers Malemeyns. A brilliant alchemist himself. But he could never achieve even close to the Philosopher's Stone. He was always too impatient. Too greedy. He could not understand that the *journey* is the achievement, not the end result."

"I fear he is not dead and that he is behind more than this abduction, Master Flamel. I think he is the man who hired others to poison the cistern."

"But why? It makes no sense. If he wanted Perenelle, if he wanted the Stone, all he need do is deal with me."

Crispin nodded. "Yes. That is a problem of logic."

"But no! *Maître*, it cannot be. He is dead. I am certain of it."

"But I am not so certain." He looked at the parchment again, holding it up to the light to be sure there were no other hidden messages. "I feel this is a good sign rather than a bad omen. There is still something he wishes to negotiate. Or to gloat. Either way, I feel that Madam Flamel is still alive." He deliberately left out *and unharmed*, for of that, he was no longer certain.

He read the parchment again.

The game is not over. What are you waiting for?

"He's watching us. He's watching us find the clues. He knows we have not pursued the last one and he wants us to continue."

"It is a trap, then!"

"Perhaps. In that case, Jack and I will pursue this alone."

The door flung open and both men whirled. Jack Tucker stood in the doorway, with Avelyn clutching his shirt as if she had dragged him the whole way. He smacked her hands away and glared at her. "I'm here, you sarding woman! Let go of me. Master Crispin?" He eyed his master. "I thought you would meet me at the Boar's Tusk."

"More has come to light, Jack. I want you to stay here with Master Flamel. At no time are you to leave him. We received another message." He shoved the parchment into the boy's hand and then cocked his head at the lock of hair in Flamel's fist. Jack read and looked again at the lock of hair. "God blind me," he whispered.

"And that's not all. I did encounter our Robert Pickthorn, but he was a dupe, thought he was only helping the people of London and putting a draught in the water that would make them pliable. The true villain is the alchemist Bartholomew of Oxford. Master Flamel?"

"Yes?"

"Do you know this alchemist?"

"No. I never heard of him. But I do not know the alchemists of London. I kept my presence here a secret… or so I thought."

"It's that apprentice," said Jack. All eyes turned to him and he lowered his head sheepishly. "Thomas Cornhill. May he rest in peace. But he must have told others. Proud of the new job he got. His family, too. If anyone asked and he said that he was apprenticing with the French alchemist Nicholas Flamel, well… Someone must have overheard."

Flamel nodded and lowered his head to his hands. "Foolishness. I should have sworn him to secrecy. I did not know. How could I have known?"

"Jack, stay here. Help them to clean up this disorder. I must deal with this other alchemist."

"Right, Master Crispin. I won't leave his side until you yourself tell me to."

"Good lad."

Crispin glanced once at the pensive face of Avelyn before rushing out the door.

Back he went to the sign of Mercury and tried the door. Locked, of course. He was too angry to try to pick it. Brute force seemed to be what he wanted most, and he drew back and slammed his shoulder into the wood. He heard a crack but little more. He tried it again and again, little feeling the sore ache to his shoulder and arm with the blows.

"Here! What do you think you are doing?"

Crispin turned, and a man of middle years with mousy brown hair shook a pilgrim's staff at him. Behind him was a boy a few years younger than Tucker, gripping the lead of a mule bearing the burden of parcels and luggage packed high on its back.

He stepped forward and looked Crispin up and down. "I'll call the law on you. What do you think you are doing?"

"Pardon me, good sir," said Crispin with a hasty bow. "But I beg you to stay out of it. This is none of your affair."

He drew back to slam the door again when the staff landed hard on his shoulder. Crispin whipped toward the man, his hand on his sheathed dagger. "If you value your life," Crispin growled, "you will not do that again!"

"Go for the sheriffs," said the man to his young servant. The boy, mouth agape and eyes like mazers, dropped the lead, ready to run.

"Hold!" Crispin grabbed the boy's arm, and the lad shrank from him, dropping to the ground with a shriek. Crispin let him go. "I'm not going to hurt you... or your master." He gestured toward the door. "My grievance is with the alchemist within, Bartholomew of Oxford, and him alone."

The man blustered, "Well then. What do you want?"

"Are you mad or deaf? I have business with the man who owns this shop."

"And that would be me," said the man.

Crispin dropped his face in his hand. "No, good sir. Not with the owner of the building, but the man who runs this shop."

"Yes!" he said more sternly. "*I* am Bartholomew of Oxford, you demented churl!"

"No, you're not. I—" He stared at the man, at the boy, at the mule packed high with luggage, and then at the man again. "You... are the alchemist whose shop this is? But I have been dealing with the alchemist here for the last few days."

"What? Impossible. I have been out of town for a month. I have been traveling, and buying ingredients. This shop has lain empty."

Crispin lowered his head. "I apologize, Master Bartholomew, but I regret to say that it has *not* lain empty."

It was the alchemist's turn to lay his face in his hands. The boy ran to fetch ale from the nearest alehouse, and Crispin lit candles and sat the man down in his shop by the hearth, explaining as much of it as he dared, leaving out about Flamel and the Stone. But he did speak of the arsenic and the poisonings. As he spoke, he moved about the shop surreptitiously, seeing if any clues as to the man's identity and whereabouts were indicated. He parted the curtain and found only a small bed and personal items.

The athanor was still warm. The ashes had been hastily stirred and extinguished. Eating bowls were left dirty and unattended. Pots and kettles were disturbed and lay crusted with whatever the impostor had devised.

Crispin had described the man, but the true Bartholomew of Oxford did not recognize him.

"The gall of the man," said the alchemist. "What utter gall to use my good name so."

Crispin pulled at the collar of his coat. He felt a bit warm and his stomach churned. No doubt because he had eaten very little today. "Might I inquire if you have ever heard the name Nicholas Flamel?"

"Nicholas *Flamel*? What alchemist has not heard of him? He is famed far and wide for his reported creation of the Philosopher's Stone. What has Flamel to do with this business?"

"Perhaps nothing," he said, rubbing his stomach. He thought it best to keep his client's identity safe… but he had to know if he had been duped in the matter of Flamel's fame as well. Clearly not. "But his name came up," he offered.

"This is abominable. My clientele! Oh, I dearly hope he has not soured those who have kept their trust in me. We must call in the sheriff!"

"Forgive me, Master Bartholomew, but there is very little the sheriffs can and will do. But I assure you that *I* will do my best. There is a greater deception being perpetrated. A very dangerous one." Crispin glanced toward the cracked door. "I apologize for any damage I have done to your door, Master." He reached for his scrip, but the man stayed him with a wave of his hand.

"No, Master Guest. I quite understand. I only hope that you will find this culprit. Should we fear his return?"

"No, Master, I do not think he will return here. He has done most of what he set out to do. Now it is up to me to do the rest."

And as far as Crispin could reckon, that meant that the hunt all over London for those clues must continue and the "game" had to go on.

Fatigued and with an aching belly, he returned to Flamel's shop. When he entered, Jack sprang to his feet and met him at the door. "You weren't gone very long, Master."

"No. A great many deceptions are overtaking us. The alchemist whom we thought was Bartholomew of Oxford was instead an impostor. I fear he may very well have been the abductor." His eyes flicked to Avelyn, who must have read his lips, for she suddenly paled. "Why did you lead me to that particular place, Avelyn?"

Flamel twisted round to look at her. Her sorrowful eyes were locked on Crispin's, and without looking at Flamel, she signed to him.

The alchemist scrubbed his eyes. "She says he was the first other alchemist she could find. She prays that you—that *we*—forgive her, for putting us in the madman's path." He gave her an avuncular smile. "You foolish girl. Of course I do. What would I do without you?"

She fell into his arms, and he held her as a father holds a child. But when she lifted her face, there were no tears there. Slowly, she pulled free of him and walked toward Crispin. She looked up at him, trying to gauge his expression.

"I, too, forgive you. How can I do any less when your master— who has known you far longer—has done the same?" She reached up and kissed his cheek.

A wave of nausea made him dizzy, and he held her hand to steady himself. He dismissed her look of concern. "I have not eaten much today. Perhaps a little wine and bread before we rejoin the hunt."

She hurried to comply and ran into Jack, trying to do the very same thing. They argued over who poured the wine and had a tug-of-war on a loaf of bread.

By the time they both placed the spilled beaker of wine and torn hunk of bread in front of him, his roiling belly couldn't stomach the idea of eating or drinking. He sipped the wine anyway and decided to forgo the bread.

"I'm not as hungry as I thought. Jack, let us go."

He moved toward the door, but not before he noticed Jack make a face at the girl.

"Tucker! Must you?"

"She started it!" At Crispin's glower, the boy looked only slightly chastened. Jack stood at his side on the threshold as they surveyed the street. Jack buttoned his cloak. "Do you know what is going on, sir?"

"No. But I have my suspicions. Let us follow the latest clue."

"What did it say again?"

He took out the parchment from his scrip. "'Eyes bold, skin cold, silver-armored, breath hold. Multiplying, fortifying, never thirsting, shore shying.'"

Jack thought for a moment. "Sounds like a dead man. A dead knight. But what does 'multiplying' and 'fortifying' have to do with it?"

"Think, Jack. What was multiplied while at the same time fortifying?"

"Multiplying, eh?" His face opened in surprise. "Loaves and... fishes! A fish has wide eyes, cold skin, and 'armor.' Clever, that."

"Correct. My supposition is Old Fish Street. Shall we?"

Fish Street was like any other lane in London, crammed with houses and shops shouldering one another and creating a narrow canyon, dimming the street with lonesome shadows and smoke. Citizens passed them by on their way to do business. Chatelaines inspected the silvery bodies of fish laid out on folding displays; cockles in baskets; live eels in tubs of water. Wives haggled with the fishmongers, and cats roamed for fallen scraps. The mud of Fish Street sparkled from discarded scales and smelled like fish guts and the stench of death.

Crispin and Jack spread out, searching for the next clue. Crispin hoped this would all soon be at an end. The fourth day of Perenelle's abduction was coming to a close and there was no sign of her yet.

He spotted a scratched-out sigil on a post and ran for it. He ignored the stares of the shopkeeper and pulled a parchment from a tiny niche.

Well done, Crispin Guest. But not correct. Keep looking.

He froze. Looking over his shoulder, Crispin felt a chill. It had been personal for Flamel from the very beginning. The abduction of his wife, the killing of his apprentice, and all for the Philosopher's Stone. But now, the man knew Crispin was involved. Said so by name. This was far more troubling.

Of course, that knave at the alchemist's shop knew Crispin now, whatever the bastard's true name was. Likely it was the same man who stole Perenelle. The same man leaving these clues. But if he was leaving them using Crispin's name, then he wasn't far ahead of them.

He crushed the parchment in his hand before he let it fall to the mud.

Jack came tearing around the corner. "Master! Master Crispin! I found it! I found it!"

He skidded to a stop before Crispin and saw the crumpled parchment hit the muddy path. "What's that?"

"The wrong direction. But this time, Jack, he mentioned me by name."

"What?" He dived for the parchment and unfurled it. His eyes scanned the smudged words and he let it fall again. "Blind me. He's watching us. Too closely."

"So it would seem. What have you found?"

"Oh. Er... back there. Another one of them symbols. It's on a high eave. Passed by it the first time."

"Then lead the way."

Jack fell silent as he walked beside Crispin. This whole episode was getting under his skin. He didn't like his enemies getting the upper hand. And spying on him was certainly not acceptable.

"Master, might Master Flamel be right? Could this all be a trap?"

Crispin locked eyes with the anxious boy. "I know it is a trap."

Jack lurched to a halt and grabbed Crispin's arm. "Then, sir! Why are you walking blindly into it?"

"First, I am not walking blindly. And second, we gain nothing by sitting on our arses. We must let him think that we are walking into it unmindful. There is little choice, at any rate, if we want to recover Madam Flamel."

"Is she still alive, do you think?"

"Yes. He sent us a lock of her hair to prove it."

"Do you think it is that man that Flamel thinks is dead— Perenelle's old suitor?"

"He said he died in a fire along with his son. But someone else could have been mistaken for him. One charred body looks much like another. Though why he should wait so long for his revenge is more to the question."

"Motivation and opportunity, that's what you are always telling me," said Jack, moving forward again. Crispin followed beside him. "Motivation? Well, Flamel said she spurned him in favor of Flamel. But from what I gather, that was a long time ago."

"Only a heartbeat to the mad."

"That's true enough. And opportunity? That's a tougher one, isn't it? If they all knew one another in France, why'd they come here to do it?"

"And how does he know all of London's landmarks? Perhaps I made a hasty assumption."

"It's the only one we've got. The only one that makes any sense."

They came at last to a halt. "It's here, Master." A grand structure, or at least it had been. Some sort of ancient hall in disrepair. It did not look as if it had been used in the last fifty years. The shutters were boarded up and a bird's nest sat on the porch by the door, the skeletal remains of a bird still residing there.

"It's just here, Master Crispin," said Jack. He had climbed the stair and up onto one of the pillars upholding the pediment. He stretched the long length of him to nearly touch the sigil.

"Can you reach it, Jack? Can you see if there is a pocket for the clue?"

"Aye, sir. I think I can." Like a squirrel, the boy shimmied up the pillar, grabbed hold of the overhanging pediment, and swung himself up to the rickety roof.

"Be careful," Crispin murmured, and then chastised himself for the old woman he was becoming.

Jack leaned over the side of the roof and, nearly upside down, reached underneath and plucked the parchment from its hiding place. He looked up with a wide grin and waved it about. But then he jerked forward and slipped off.

Crispin gasped, helpless to do anything as the boy plummeted over the side, heading for the stony road below.

Arse over heels, Jack somersaulted and at the last moment threw a hand out and barely caught the edge of the eave. Ink-stained fingers gripped the icy tiles. He hung by one hand, legs swinging carelessly, until he let go and landed on his feet in a crouch before he straightened and heaved a satisfied breath. "Nearly broke me neck," he said almost proudly, before shuffling down the stairs and handing Crispin the parchment.

"Nearly," muttered Crispin. "See that you don't. I'm too old to train a new apprentice."

Jack sidled up to him and Crispin unfolded the parchment.

You are a clever man, Crispin Guest. You have reached your goal.

"Our goal?" echoed Jack. "What? Here?"

Crispin climbed the steps and tried the door. Barred. He leaned over toward a shuttered window and peeked through the cracks. An empty space, with dried leaves on the checkered floor and dust on every surface. The walls were punctuated with niches that seemed to have once held something, like statues, but what statues remained stood on the floor in no particular semblance of order. The candles that were in the sconces had long ago burned down to nubs, and all that remained were cascades of wax hanging from them.

He could see no doors, nothing leading to any other room. It was only a barren hall.

He trotted down the stairs and studied the foundation. There did not look to be enough of it to offer a cellar or mews below. Whatever he had meant by this clue, this was not where Perenelle Flamel was being kept.

"It don't look inhabited, sir."

"It *doesn't* look inhabited," he corrected. "And it isn't."

"Then he's lying."

"No, that is not part of the game. That wouldn't be playing fair, Jack, and so far he has not lied to us."

"How can you defend him? He's killed, and stolen that woman!"

"I am not defending him, Jack. I am merely trying to understand him. He has set the parameters of this game and he means to keep to them. He does not like it that we step out of line, and tells us when we are wrong. And now that he is mentioning me by name, he obviously enjoys the novelty of adding me to the game. You see, Jack, to defeat your enemy you must learn how he thinks. The game is fair. It is up to us to figure out the rules."

"How? If this is our 'goal,' then where is Madam Flamel?"

Crispin handed him the parchment. "Read it again."

"'You are a clever man, Crispin Guest,'" he read aloud. "'You have reached your goal.' I don't understand, sir."

"What is *my* goal, Jack?"

"Finding Madam Flamel."

"Is it? Not according to him. By his reckoning, I must have another goal."

"Finding... *him*?"

He smiled. "And so. This building must mean something to him that I can use to find him."

"He *is* mad. It's nothing but an abandoned building. There are many such in London."

"But he led me to not just any abandoned building, but to this particular one. What is it, I wonder?"

"Guildhall of some kind."

"What do your reasoning skills say about the building, Jack?"

Jack dug his teeth into his bottom lip, thinking. "Well, sir, it's abandoned. It's a guildhall. And… and… Blind me. I see, Master Crispin. All guilds are proud of who they are and what they represent, and proudly display their ornaments or arms. But this one…"

"This one doesn't. Not one thing to indicate who the guild members are or of their vocation. And what does that suggest to you?"

"I… I don't know, sir. That they didn't want nobody knowing which guild it was?"

"Ah!"

He climbed down the steps, with Jack following. Something caught his attention off to the left. Had that shadow moved? His hand found his dagger.

"What sort of guild would that be, Master?"

"A very good question, Jack. Walk with me."

Jack scrambled to fall in step beside him. "I can't think, sir, of what guild wouldn't be proud to be—"

"Jack," Crispin said quietly out of the side of his mouth, "we are being followed by our shadows again. I don't know about you, but I weary of it."

Jack straightened, all business. "How many, sir?"

"Two, this time. One on each side of the road. Perfect. You take the one on the left and I'll take the right. On the count of three." He raised his chin, looking straight ahead. "One… two… three!"

They turned. The cloaked man tried to throw himself against the wall of a fishmonger's stall. Crispin dove for him and wrestled him to the ground, punching him once in the face. His fist skidded off the man's cheek and hit his nose but did not break it. It gushed with blood, and while the man was distracted by it, Crispin hauled him to his feet.

Jack was dragging his own bruised captive toward Crispin, where they threw them both up against the wall. Jack drew his knife and looked more than ready to use it.

Crispin folded his arms over his chest. "This ends here. Why have you and your ilk been following me?"

"We mean no harm, Master Guest," said the one with the bloody nose.

"Oh? Is that so? Then why have you been tailing me for days? I have seen you, and two more of your peers. You need not lie."

"No, Master. There is no need to lie. We were merely keeping watch of you. And now you've come... here." He cocked his head toward the building they had just left.

"Here? And just what is 'here'?"

The bloodied man looked toward his bruised companion. The other nodded, seeming to give permission, while keeping a wary eye on Jack and his knife.

"Very well, Master Guest. I shall answer. We, and others like us, have used this guildhall for generations. But it has fallen into disrepair for some time."

"And this guild? What is your company?"

The man touched his chest and bowed. "We are of the noble and secret society of London alchemists."

twenty-five

rispin snorted at the man with the blood on his face. "Lovely. Secret society. Damned secrets." He grabbed the man by his coat again and shoved him hard into the wall. The sound of it made even Crispin wince. His face was smooth and pale. It was hard to tell just how old he and his companion were. "Where is she? Where is he keeping her?"

The man tried to look toward his companion again when Crispin slapped his face, leaving a red mark on the pale cheek. "Don't look at him when I'm talking to you. Answer me!"

"I... I know not who you are talking about."

"Don't you? And what about him?" He thumbed in the direction of the other man, whom Jack had surrounded with his long, wiry limbs. "Does he know? I don't care if you both take a beating for it. One of you will tell me. One of you *might* still have *teeth* with which to tell me."

The man in front of Crispin held his hands before his face and cringed down, shoulders hunching up to his ears. "Wait! I'm speaking the truth! Please! Blessed Saint Luke preserve me!"

"How do I know you are speaking the truth? You and your ilk have been following me for days. Don't lie, I saw you. Why were you following me if not working for that foul villain?"

"We don't know who you mean," said the other man, trying to jerk away from Jack's sudden grip on his arm. "As soon as we learned that Nicholas Flamel was here in London, many were chosen to guard him, to follow all who came and went to his shop. We mean you no harm. Nor him. We… we greatly admire his work and wish to allow him the grace in which to do it."

"Out of the goodness of your hearts, no doubt."

The man before Crispin lowered his head. "Well, we hoped that he might share some of his secrets with us. However unlikely that was. We thought he might be grateful enough…"

"Good Christians, all. God save Flamel from his saviors." He released the cowering man and stepped back, loath to continue touching him. "Prove it. Prove to me that you are not lying."

The man wiped his palm up over his nostrils, trying to stanch the trickle of blood. His hands were now red with it. "But how? How may we prove our sincerity?"

"Tell me, then. How did you discover Flamel was here?"

"His apprentice." He crossed himself. "Bless his wretched soul. Someone overheard him talking. And *I* heard them say it, and… well. We approached him, told him who we were. I told him that to boast of the name Nicholas Flamel was not only dangerous but disingenuous. I questioned him, only wishing to know if his master was *the* Nicholas Flamel. But he grew suspicious of our interest. Clearly his master did not entrust him with… certain knowledge. After a time he would talk no more with us. It was soon thereafter that it was agreed that we should watch Master Flamel's comings and goings."

"Did you see anything of his apprentice's abduction?"

"No, alas. We saw him leave the shop with the alchemist's wife. But we were not concerned with them. Only Master Flamel."

"How convenient." Crispin rested his hand on his dagger hilt. "What of these other alchemists of your guild? I would meet them."

The man made a strained sound, halfway between a laugh and a cough. "Perhaps you forgot that we are a *secret* guild, Master Guest."

"Oh, well. Quite understandable." He gave Jack a false smile. Jack did not return it. "Then you would not mind should I decide to announce this secret society on the streets of London?"

"W-what?"

"This secret society," he said, raising his voice.

The two alchemists shushed him. "Master Guest!" the other cried.

"I'm simply bursting with the need to share what I have learned.

A *secret* society," he rattled on, raising and lowering his voice. "Fascinating, don't you agree? The citizens of London would also be fascinated, as would be her sheriffs and aldermen. And the bishop of London, too, I should imagine. I understand how well thought of are alchemists."

"Master Guest, please. That is very ungracious of you." He snorted a bubble of blood back up his nose. "We have told you all we can."

"I don't think so." He put his hand on the wall beside the man's head and leaned in. The man shied back, turning his face away and blinking rapidly. Crispin noticed he was young. He hadn't expected that. He didn't think of alchemists as particularly young, though why he didn't was his own ignorance. Flamel was young once, as was the real Bartholomew of Oxford. Young and successful. As had been this other, this knave who kept them playing this cruel game all over the city.

"Acquainted with a Piers Malemeyns?" asked Crispin, close to the man's ear. He watched his face for any sign of recognition at the name. There was none.

"No," he said, voice quivering. "I tell you we know nothing of this other mischief."

"But you have been following me all over town. Do you have any idea what we have been doing?"

He swallowed, his Adam's apple bobbing on his thin, beard-stubbled neck. "You have been following the alchemical symbols etched on the walls of the city. We... we wondered about them. We tried to scratch them out when we found them. We thought that someone was trying to expose us. We had no idea that there were messages hidden near them."

"We saw you extract the parchments," said the other, eyes glued to Jack's stern glare. "And so we, too, investigated. When we saw that they were little more than riddles and taunts, we left them alone."

"Are you certain of that?" Crispin gritted his teeth. It wasn't good news at all that they might have tampered with the messages.

"I swear by my Lady, Master Guest. We read them, and knowing that you would come upon them, we replaced them as we found them."

Crispin toyed with his dagger hilt, raising it slightly from its sheath. The metal gleamed in the dim light. "I'm having difficulty believing you."

"It is the truth, Master Guest," pleaded the man he had cornered.

"Prove it, then. Get me into that guildhall."

The man sucked in a breath. He wiped his nose futilely one last time, smearing blood on his face, before he nodded. "Peter has the key."

Crispin looked to the other one. "Are you Peter?"

"Me? Oh, no! Not I. I am Damian Fallowell." He nodded in an abbreviated bow. "And this... er... this—" He gestured to his companion cringing under Crispin's menacing posture. "This is Cosmas Blusard. We are not the keeper of the keys."

"Then you had best take me to him."

"But we can't do that!" cried Cosmas.

Crispin turned calmly to him. His dagger was in his hand. "Why not?"

The alchemist stared cross-eyed at the dagger in front of his face and slumped down the wall, knees nearly buckling. He licked his blood-smeared lips. "A good question. I truly don't see why not."

"Cosmas!"

"You don't have a dagger in *your* face, Damian!"

"Oh, very well! We shall be thrown out of the guild for this. And after all the trouble we went through. We'll take you to Peter."

Crispin couldn't help but feel he was getting in deeper than he liked. It was a simple matter for Jack or himself to easily break into the guildhall, but there was obviously more to all of this than he was aware of.

"Lead on," he said, sheathing his dagger.

The two alchemists took Crispin and Jack down several alleys off of Old Fish. They came to a dead end at a crumbling wall in a narrow close. Crispin drew his dagger and Jack did likewise. "What is this?" Crispin demanded.

Cosmas blinked at him stupidly. Mouth open, face smeared with blood, he was the picture of perplexity. "It is the way in," he said, indicating some distant point in the darkness.

Crispin stepped between the men and grabbed Cosmas's arm. Jack followed suit and curled his fingers around Damian's arm above the elbow, digging so deep that the man winced. "Then we'll go in together," said Crispin.

Cosmas stumbled as he tugged Crispin with him. The crumbling wall reminded Crispin of Lenny's hideaway. Thinking of the thief caused a hollow in his belly. Or was it only part of his earlier nausea that was rearing up again? He felt sweat ripple over him and he swallowed an excess of saliva that had flooded his mouth. Was it guilt he felt at banishing the thief from his presence? The man wasn't worth the trouble, this he knew. But still. Crispin felt he had let the man down, hadn't cultivated him enough. Though not every thief could turn out to be a Jack Tucker.

He looked over his shoulder at his apprentice. Face chiseled into a stoic expression, Jack steered his charge forward, his dagger clutched in his other hand.

This illness that had overtaken his belly was making Crispin unsteady, but he tried to mask it by pushing the alchemist forward. The crumbling wall was only a façade, hiding the true entrance to a dark parlor.

Cosmas tried to pull away, but Crispin yanked him back.

"Master Guest, I must… light a candle."

Crispin released the man and covertly clutched his stomach. "Very well. Make haste."

He followed the alchemist with his gaze as he stumbled about the room, finding a tinderbox. A spark lit all the points of their faces before flame touched candlewick.

Cosmas held up the lit candle on its silver sconce. The light shone dully on lackluster blond locks that hung to his shoulders. "He is in the next room. I'll get him."

"No," said Crispin, adjusting the grip on his dagger. "*I'll* get him."

He strode to the door. He didn't bother knocking. He lifted the latch and pushed through.

He beheld a room full of the instruments that were becoming familiar to Crispin, with bubbling cauldrons and foul smells. A man sat at a tall writing table, bent over parchments and books. A quill was poised in his ink-stained fingers. A candle on the desk lit him and his work in a pool of golden light. Perhaps he had not noticed in his industry that the hearth had nearly gone to glowing coals and the room was cold. He did not look up as he said, "Yes?"

"Men to see you, Peter," said Cosmas. "I tried, but I couldn't prevent them. It's… it's Crispin Guest and his apprentice."

At that, the man raised his face. He squinted into the darkness, peering at them. He pushed away from the table and hopped off his high stool. "Crispin Guest, you say?" He spied the dagger and the grip Jack still had of the other man. "Yes, I see." He smiled. His dark hair hung straight down over his ears. He wore a skullcap on the back of his head like a tonsure. His face was long and pale, clean-shaven and sallow. He looked to be a man who seldom left his dark room.

Alchemists, Crispin snorted inwardly. He looked around the room, assessing. Yes, the same smells as Flamel's shop, the same clutter, similar beakers and retorts. Cobwebs in the corners and an unused broom leaning against a far wall under a shuttered window.

"He wishes to enter the guildhall," Damian said in a loud whisper.

"Does he? And why is that?"

Crispin sheathed his dagger with one brisk slide. "Because I was led there. Do you know by whom?"

Peter raised his dark brows. "I presume you mean the one who has been leading you about London on a merry chase. No, I don't know who this puppet master is. And I don't care to know. I do not approve of his methods."

"You seem to know quite a lot."

"Like you, Master Guest, I observe."

"You didn't happen to observe the man who abducted Perenelle Flamel, did you? Or who killed the apprentice Thomas Cornhill?"

He gestured toward Damian. "Is that necessary?"

Jack was still holding the man's arm with one hand and his dagger with another. "Is it?" Jack asked Peter, mimicking Crispin's tone.

"Perhaps not," Crispin told him. "You may give the man some relief, Master Tucker. And sheathe your dagger. I'll tell you if I think you need to withdraw it again."

Jack quickly complied, showing all and sundry who he believed was in charge.

Crispin smoothed his expression. "And now... Master Peter, is it? I would appreciate your cooperation in this. My first priority is to find Madam Flamel alive and unharmed."

"And you believe our guildhall is the means to that end?"

"I don't know what I believe. I only know I was led there. And your peers, here, have told me that your hall is no longer in use."

"I don't believe they would have said that precisely, Master Guest. I think that rather, they must have intimated that it has fallen into disrepair. That doesn't mean we haven't used it." He looked down at the ring of keys hanging from his belt. "Now then. I take it you are in a hurry?"

"Yes."

"Then let us go now."

They returned quickly to the guildhall as the bells struck Vespers. The blue shadows of twilight lay like ribbons along the street. Most of the snow had been melted by recent rain, but the clouds were heavy again, and the gray surrounding them was more drizzle than mist, which began to fly about in lazy loops like midges in the summer. It was becoming snow again, and each tiny flake winged over Crispin's head. But their dizzy dance only exacerbated his nausea. He licked his dry lips and tried to ignore it, thinking of anything but how miserable his belly felt.

Peter lifted his keys. *Saint Peter,* Crispin thought, *with the keys to the kingdom.*

He unlocked the door and pushed it open. It was warped and scraped along the tiled portico inside, pushing dried leaves with it into a musty pile. The place felt as cold as a tomb and was just as stark. Empty of everything but its checkered tile floor and statues of saints scattered here and there. Crispin walked into the center of the room, uncaring whether these alchemists wanted him to or not. His gaze rose to the vaulted ceiling and its cobwebbed stone. Lancet windows were sealed with cracked glass. Still others were covered with wooden shutters keeping them dark and safe, like closed eyelids.

Crispin turned his head, not looking back entirely over his shoulder. "You say you and your guild have used this place to meet?"

"I said that the place has not been entirely abandoned."

He pivoted to look at Peter straight on. "Do you play games with me, sir?"

"Me? Not at all."

Crispin studied him. He was short, wiry, young. "Then what is your meaning?"

"What I mean to say, Master Guest, is that though we meet infrequently, we have been known to meet here. And other places."

"And where might those other places be?"

"Well, that, I cannot say. Alchemists must be cautious, as surely you can understand."

"But I am looking for an alchemist, a man who has perpetrated murder, abduction, and perhaps a host of other crimes. Would you shield him?"

"To protect my brethren, I might."

Cosmos and Damian looked nervous on either side of him, but they did not naysay their apparent leader.

Crispin snorted and pointedly turned away. He made a slow circle about the space, feeling along the walls for secret entrances. All the while, the thrum in his belly made him feel wretched and disconnected.

Jack, though wary of their companions, noticed. He came up alongside Crispin. "Are you well, Master?" he said quietly.

"I feel a little poorly. Maybe it's time to go home. I see nothing here."

"Shall I… shall I give it my own inspection first, sir?"

Sensible. He nodded, rubbing his stomach, and watched as the boy made his own perusal. He looked in areas under windows and near pillars that Crispin hadn't thought of, making him wonder yet again about the extent of the lad's past criminal experience.

From across the room, Jack looked back at Crispin and shrugged. There was nothing to be gleaned here. Nothing while Crispin was distracted by the pains in his stomach.

"Let us go, Master," Jack said reluctantly, joining him again.

Crispin turned to the alchemists, standing in the doorway. "I thank you for your hospitality. And I beg that you follow us no more."

"As you wish," said Peter, stepping aside for him.

Crispin escaped down the stairs, looking back once they had gotten to the corner of the street.

Peter still stood at the top of the stairs, listening intently as his companions spoke softly to him.

It was a relief to get home at last. And a comfort to see the fire stoked and Avelyn beside it. But the food she had brought made his stomach turn and he flung open the window to breathe the fresh air of a dark London.

"Take the food away. I cannot abide it."

But he'd said it out the window, and Avelyn had been unable to read it on his lips. He heard the sounds of Jack intercepting her and her bowl of whatever she had cooked.

"He don't want it," said the boy, too loudly. "Can't you see he's poorly?"

Crispin leaned on the sill, certain he was going to sick up out the window, when he heard Avelyn return the bowl to the pot on the fire. Her light steps came up behind him and soon there was a touch on his arm.

"No," he whimpered. "Let me be."

She would not leave him alone—*damn the woman!*—and turned him instead. Her concern furrowed her brow and she led him and then helped him to the bed, allowing him to lean heavily on her arm.

"*I'll* care for him," said Jack. His voice was more than a little petulant. "He's my responsibility, not yours."

But as usual, Avelyn ignored that which she chose. She stuffed the pillow under his head and began unbuttoning his cotehardie. It was a relief, for he had begun to sweat again.

Jack was suddenly leaning over him, too. "Here? What are you doing?"

She elbowed him out of the way, and Crispin heard the boy's breath *whoosh* and then a cough. "Sarding woman!"

Crispin closed his eyes, willing the room to stop spinning. It had all the earmarks of a night of binge drinking without the former benefits. "Avelyn, he's only trying to help, as are you." He licked dry lips.

He opened his eyes when he heard her gasp.

She was holding the little bundle of herbs sold to him by Bartholomew of Oxford. Only it *hadn't* been him, but an impostor. She clutched it in her hand and stared at it, before raising her eyes to Crispin's. Without hesitation she yanked it from his neck, snapping the knot in the leather thong.

Crispin jerked up to a sitting position and rubbed the back of his neck. "Ow! What the devil? It's only a sachet."

She shook her finger at him and her face darkened. She clutched it in her hand, turned, and heaved it into the fire. The hearth flared in bright colors of greens and blues. Crispin stared at it as the smoke curled up to the ceiling. He was about to shout at her, but just as suddenly as the fire had flared, so did the discomfort slip away from him. He no longer had an ache in his belly, nor did the room turn and roll as it had done. He felt better. And hungry.

"God's blood. What the hell was in that?"

She made a sign with her fingers he did not know, but he did not need to interpret to know instinctively what she meant.

"Poison."

Jack stood before the fire, mouth hanging ajar. "God blind me! That devil of an alchemist tried to poison you!"

Crispin chuckled from pure relief. "And I even paid him for the privilege. The whoreson."

Tucker knelt at his feet. "Master, are you well now?"

"Yes. Yes, by God! I feel much better. I could use a dollop of food now. And some wine." Jack scrambled, even pushed Avelyn aside, to serve it himself. Crispin shook his head at the boy but turned to Avelyn and made the sign for "thank you" at her. She smiled.

Crispin rose and moved to the table, but he glanced back at the fire and devised just how he was going to get his hands around the neck of that knave.

As night fell around them, Crispin cast a glance at their distinctly domestic scene: Avelyn kneeling by the fire, absently pushing the coals around and sending an occasional sparking ember spitting up the chimney; Jack sitting opposite Crispin at the table, his chin on his crossed arms, eyes scouring the chessboard as the pieces slowly made their way across the squares.

For the last two hours, Crispin had taught his apprentice the intricacies of the game, and he was pleased and swollen with pride that Jack was such a quick study. Even so, most of the captured white pieces sat on Crispin's side of the board, while his own black pieces began crowding round the white king.

Jack sighed. "If I move there, your bishop will get me."

Crispin nodded.

"And if I move there, the castle will. So in… one, two, three moves, you'll win anyway."

"Can you see no way out of it?"

He shook his head and rubbed his nose. "No, sir. I'm defeated. Again."

"Quite right."

The boy tilted his king over. "I like this game," he said, sitting up. "I might even win it someday." He grinned.

"I daresay you will." Crispin set about putting the pieces carefully back into their box.

Jack stretched, bones cracking. "I can see why you like chess. It's a bit like what we do out in the city, isn't it? Trying to stay one step ahead of the enemy."

"Exactly. Games of strategy have always intrigued me." He placed the last piece in its velvet-lined niche and closed the lid. "I'm very pleased you have taken to it so readily."

Jack raised his chin with a wide grin. "Aye. Well, I've a good teacher, don't I?" He rose and yawned. "I'm for bed, then. Unless there is aught else you need, sir."

"No, nothing." He glanced at Avelyn by the fire.

Jack thumbed in her direction. "What of her?" he whispered. "Is she staying? I thought you told her to stay with Master Flamel."

"She does what she pleases. There's little I can do about it." Which was strictly untrue, and Jack well knew it. Crispin saw the tilt of the boy's brow and the smirk that didn't quite bloom on his face as he worked to suppress it.

"Well, good night, sir." Jack retreated to his pile of straw, where he kicked off his shoes, unbuttoned his cotehardie, and laid it carefully aside. Then he slipped onto the straw, pulling his heavy blanket over himself, and curled, settling.

Crispin sat in his chair and watched Avelyn for a while, her slow stirring of the coals soothing and restful. It occurred to him how good it was having a woman about the place, even though Jack kept his lodgings clean and stocked with food and wine. Still, the feminine silhouette before his hearth was a gentle reminder of his childhood and of the safety and warmth it elicited in his heart. But then, like a bucket of cold water, his chest deadened with the idea that Perenelle Flamel was not at *her* hearth. The fourth day of her abduction had set, and the uncomfortable sensation of time slipping away was making him wonder if he would fail, if she would never return.

He rose and lightly touched Avelyn's shoulder. Without alarm, as if she'd sensed him beforehand, she turned her face toward his and offered a warm smile. He couldn't help but offer one in return. "Avelyn," he said quietly so as not to awaken Jack, who was already snoring softly in the corner, "shouldn't you be by your master's side this night? He must be lonely and in fear."

She made a drinking motion, and by that he understood her to mean that Flamel had found a way to console himself.

"You're staying, then?"

Her smile grew and she rose, looking up at him under heavy lids.

"You know you shouldn't be here." His hands slid over her shoulders and slowly drew her in. She was warm against him. Her little hands stretched around his back, arms enclosing. "I shouldn't have let you stay. You have a way of bewitching me. I am not so certain you are not a witch."

She licked her lips, mouth parted in a wicked smile. He cupped her chin and leaned down, kissing her for a moment before drawing back. "Sweet to the taste," he murmured. "And moist, like a pomegranate. I think you *are* a witch."

She shook her head and slipped her arms free of him, only to twine them about his neck, trying to pull his face down again. But he gently took her wrists and lowered them. He wanted to lose himself in her, in her kisses, in the sweet warmth of her body, but his mind was a whirlwind of thoughts. His smile lagged. "I'm thinking too much of where Perenelle Flamel is tonight."

She sobered, too, and caressed his cheek in sympathy.

"I wish you could speak, could share your thoughts and insights." He sat again in his chair and scooted it closer to the fire. He watched the mesmerizing flames for a time as Avelyn knelt beside him, petting his thigh until she laid her head upon it. He lifted his hand and caressed her bright hair in slow, even strokes. "I fear for her," he whispered. "I have never felt so helpless. I almost poisoned myself, I've been perplexed by these clues, and taunted by a madman. I can't remember feeling so… so useless before."

Her fingers ran gently up and down his calf. He looked down at her and tapped her shoulder. "I must go. And so should you, back to your master tonight."

She shook her head and looked pointedly at the bed and then up at him again.

He sighed softly. "Well, do as you will. I might be late."

She didn't look back as he rose and donned his cloak.

He glanced at her once more before he left. She was kneeling at the fire again, tending to each glowing coal.

Down the quiet streets of London he crept. Crispin followed the sinewy shadow of a cat down Friday Street, thinking it wise of the lone animal to keep to the walls under the shadow of the eaves.

The cat looked over its shoulder at him once before, with a flick of its tail, it disappeared through a hole in a wattle fence.

Only the rustle of vermin in the dead underbrush at the side of the road and a distant soft hoot of an owl in a tree kept him company. He welcomed the silence. It was familiar, like a comfortable shoe. But it gave him time to think of the knave he was pursuing, to anger at the audacity of his trying to murder Crispin with poison. Cowardly. For only a coward would steal women from the streets and hide behind games instead of facing a man eye to eye. His hand went instinctively to his dagger, where he rubbed the palm of his hand over the well-worn pommel.

He slipped down Old Fish Street and made his way again to the alchemists' guildhall. The building still stood silent and dark, a turtle that had left its shell behind.

But as his eyes took in the dim street and adjusted to the layered darkness, he noticed a shadow figure silhouetted against the stone and plaster, looking up at the same building. Stepping back out of the faint light from distant cressets, Crispin hugged the wall and watched. The man—for he could see it was a man—ascended the stairs of the silent guildhall, stopped on the porch, and tried the door. When that yielded him nothing, he turned to the closest window and peered inside.

He did not notice a second stealthy figure creep around the corner and come up behind him. Crispin saw a flash of a dagger, and the first man turned in time to halt the descending knife.

Crispin darted out into the street. The man with the dagger looked in his direction, slammed his fist into the face of his victim, and took off. The victim fell, tumbling down the steps.

Crispin paused. Should he go after the assailant? Tend to the victim?

The man on the ground groaned, and it was decided. Crispin knelt at the man's side, listening with regret as the other's steps receded into the distance.

He touched a shoulder as the man rolled in the mud. "Fear not. He's gone. I'm not going to hurt you. Are you well? Can you stand?"

"C-Crispin?"

The incredulous voice came from the shrouding hood. Crispin pushed it back and looked into the bruised face of Henry Bolingbroke.

twenty-six

enry!" He helped the young man to a sitting position. Henry rubbed his forehead where a goose-egg bump was forming.

"God's blood and bones!" he swore. "Dammit, that hurts like a sonofabitch. Help me up."

"Are you certain—"

"Help me up, damn you!"

Crispin took hold of his arm and lifted. Henry suddenly bent double and retched, spitting the bile into the mud.

"I told you so," said Crispin, unable to resist.

"Just let me stand here a while till the world stops spinning.... Ah, better."

He turned to Crispin and pushed his hood back fully. Crispin did likewise. "Crispin, thank God you were here. But... *why* are you here?"

"I should ask the same thing, my lord."

Henry looked at him, blinked, and shivered. "Your lodgings are near here, are they not? Do you have any of that Lancaster wine left? I could use some."

"Er... certainly, my lord."

With an arm slipped through his, Crispin allowed Henry to lean against him as they made their way to the Shambles.

Crispin speculated wildly as they moved in silence. For someone supposed to be in hiding, Henry was certainly turning up quite a bit.

They rounded the corner of the Shambles and hurried along the silent avenue to the sign of the tinker. Crispin helped him up the stairs, though Henry's strides were surer now. When Crispin opened the door, Avelyn stood by the fire, the poker in her hand.

Jack sleepily raised his head from the pile of straw. His eyes widened when he beheld Crispin and Henry at the door, and he popped up out of his bed, straw flying all around him.

"Master Crispin! My Lord Derby! What… what is going on?"

Crispin helped Henry to the chair and stood above him. Jack shrugged quickly into his cotehardie and hissed at Crispin's elbow, "I thought you were going to bed!"

"Change of plans," he whispered back. "Bring us wine, Jack."

Buttoning his coat, Jack hurried to comply. Henry was looking at Avelyn admiringly. "Who is this, Crispin?"

Crispin felt his cheeks suddenly warming. "Erm… she's… she's…"

"Another servant, my lord," Jack said quickly, placing a full wine bowl before Henry and offering the second to Crispin.

Henry eyed the fading red on Crispin's cheeks and gave him a leering smile. He took up the bowl and, thirstily, drank it down. He set aside the now empty bowl and wiped his mouth with his hand. Crispin sipped his, studying Henry over the bowl's rim.

"And so," Crispin said after a moment, "may I ask what you were doing there?"

His eyes settled on Crispin's. The playfulness was gone and so was the teasing smile. "I was playing the fool, apparently. Stupid." He touched the lump on his forehead again and winced.

Jack was instantly at his side. "Can I get you a cold cloth for that, my lord?"

"No, boy. But much thanks for the thought."

"Jack, my Lord of Derby, here, was about to tell me why he was skulking around the alchemists' guildhall."

Jack gasped at the same time Henry perked up. "*Alchemists'* guildhall, eh? Strange."

"Perhaps not. Tell me."

He wheezed out a long sigh and drummed his fingers on the table. "I… I received a missive. Anonymous. It told me to be there."

Crispin gritted his teeth, biting down on what he wanted to say. "And are you in the habit of following blindly what anonymous missives tell you to do?"

"You sounded just like my father in that instance."

"Henry! This is no laughing matter."

"Who's laughing?"

"Answer the question!"

"I have a hell of a headache now. Don't yell at me. People are always yelling at me. My uncle, my advisers, my *father*..."

"Perhaps it is time to *listen* to them."

Henry slammed his hand to the table. "You're not my father!"

"Neither are you!"

They glared at each other for a long moment before Henry relented first, dropping his head on his hand. "I know," he said quietly. "But I'm trying."

Crispin scraped his knuckles uncomfortably along the table's rough surface before he sat on the stool opposite the young lord. "You are under much duress, I know. But there are factions after you. I would have thought you would lie low. What made you follow this missive's instructions? It was clearly an ambush."

"Because I had gotten two like it before."

At this rate, his teeth would be ground to stubs. "Explain," he said tightly.

"One I received when I arrived in London a few months ago. It was innocuous enough. Told me where I could find some information I needed, and I did find it. When I got the second, I recognized the hand. It told me to go to St. Paul's. And that's when I encountered you."

"At the foot of the statue? It told you to go there specifically?"

"Yes. And that I would reap a reward. More information, that is. Was there really a ransom there?"

"Yes."

"Good God. For whom?"

"A woman, who is still missing. And I, too, was similarly led to that guildhall."

"Someone is playing both of us for a fool."

"No. It is more insidious than that. This time, it was to trap you in

227

an ambush. I shudder to think what might have happened had I not decided to return tonight."

"Wait. You mean you had already been summoned there earlier?"

"Yes. Our missive writer could not have known I would return and discover you."

"Interesting. Were you attacked, too?"

Crispin sipped at his wine. "No. It was under… other circumstances that I arrived there."

"You don't have to tell me," said Henry, eyes narrowing.

"But you *do* have to tell *me*. What was so important that you would risk your safety to investigate in such a foolhardy way?"

Henry puffed up and frowned. Crispin swore that he would smack Henry himself if the man spouted some half-arsed quip or tried to lord it over him.

But Henry deflated quickly, looking contrite. "Crispin, you know why I am in London, do you not? The missive told me of further corruption in King Richard's court. Fuel that I need to press our advantage over my cousin."

Anger bubbled up in Crispin's breast. "And so you thought you'd just go alone into uncertain danger. Did you even know the nature of this evidence?"

"No, but I had to investigate it. Don't you see?"

"No, I don't see! Henry, you have vast responsibilities. You can't just go yourself into these situations. You must use your head. You should have sent a servant at the very least—"

"*You* would have gone."

"That's different."

"How? How is it different? Because I am not a man like you?"

"Because you are more important than I am, you fool!" He shook his head. "Henry, Henry. I am not a lord any longer. I am not one of the king's barons. I am… nothing."

"Not to me."

It stopped Crispin's tirade cold. He lowered his face. He didn't know what to say to that and so chose to ignore it. "Nevertheless, you mustn't indulge your fancies, my lord. You must not. Your work is important. If you wish to rein in Richard, then you had best keep hold of those reins yourself. Let others put themselves in danger. Stand back and observe. It's… it's what your father would have done."

Irritation smoldered in Henry's eyes and his lips pressed tight, but he said nothing. Instead, he threw himself to the back of the chair, arms folded petulantly over his chest, and brooded.

"You were lucky to escape with only a bump on the head," Crispin went on. "It could have gone much worse. Anything could have been behind those messages. This, the missing woman, the poisonings of the cisterns. Anything."

"Hold. Poisoning of what cisterns?"

Crispin proceeded to tell him of the deaths and what he'd discovered, and how the sheriffs had reluctantly agreed to guard them.

Henry leaned forward. "Was that why there were riots at the Tun today?"

"It was to save lives."

"Are you certain of that? That it was poisoned?"

"Yes. And further, I think it has to do with the missing wife of the alchemist."

"Alchemist, eh? More than just a coincidence I was sent to that particular guildhall?"

"It's not a coincidence at all. It is all tied together somehow."

"But why me? What have I to do with an alchemist?"

Crispin toyed with his bowl. "There is a lay preacher who does not like what you and your lords are doing. He says as much in his sermons. While you are seeking to discredit the king, might someone else be plotting to discredit you?"

"An alchemist? A preacher? An unlikely conspiracy."

"I'm not convinced it's so unlikely. It's taken some planning to get to this point. It would take money and influence."

"Influence. Crispin, you don't mean to say that you think someone at court had aught to do with these unrelated events?"

"I'm beginning to think so."

"Who is feeding you this tripe? It can't be true."

"I have seen the like before, believe me. And either killing you or discrediting you, the result would be the same. You would be out of the way and your assembly of lords would be in disarray."

"Richard?" he whispered. "You don't think—"

"I don't know what to think!" cried Crispin, running his fingers through his hair.

Henry was on his feet. "They tried to kill me! I don't take kindly to that."

Crispin straightened. "No. Neither would I." He stared at the table, at the whorls of wood grain, the patterns of spilled wine, and the dribble of pooled wax dripping from the candle dish. "Who at court would have a particular crusade against you?"

Henry stood woodenly, staring vacantly into the fire. "I don't accuse Richard. I can't believe that of him. We are kin, after all."

Crispin kept his thoughts on the subject to himself. History was littered with bodies dispatched by the victim's own relatives. "What of his advisers?"

Henry's lip curled in a snarl. "Yes, I can well believe that of them. But which one?"

Leaning forward, Crispin pressed his hands to the table. "You said before that you wanted to help me, Henry. Do you? The woman I seek is still missing, may be in terrible straits. I must still find her."

Henry's eyes glinted from the candle flame between them. "I do. What would you have of me, Crispin?"

"See what you can discover about Richard's advisers. About anything that might hint at this lay preacher, about the Tun. You cannot go to court yourself, but surely your men can keep their ears peeled, ask discreet questions. I would know of anything they might discover."

"Yes. I would know the swines who put my life at stake. Is there anything else?"

"Yes, Henry. For my sanity's sake, lay low."

Henry chuckled and bowed. "Very well, Master Guest."

Crispin glanced at both Henry and Jack in turn. "Both are troublesome and neither wish to mind me when I clearly know what I am talking about."

Henry laughed again and even slapped Jack on the shoulders. "Young Jack, I think he's talking about us. Did you know, Jack, that Crispin here raised *me*, too? Taught me to be a knight. Or at least how to comport myself as such. He left when I was still quite young." His voice softened when he said to Jack, "In many ways, I envy you."

"*Me,* sir?"

"Yes. He's tutoring you, isn't he?"

"Yes, sir." He flicked a glance at Crispin's reddening face. "He taught me to read and write. Taught me history, and arms, and languages. And Aristotle—"

"That damned Aristotle!" Henry shook his head, but he was still smiling wistfully.

"Oh, he's most wise, sir, is Aristotle. He wrote sage words on life and such. Like 'All persons ought to endeavor to follow what is right, and not what is established.' That's a hard thought, isn't it? But that's what Master Crispin always does, don't you, sir?" he said to Crispin. "My master lives by them words… *those* words, sir. And I would, too."

Henry's eyes twinkled. "I see. Well, young Jack, you listen well to your tutor. I've no doubt it will make of you a better man."

Jack raised his chin proudly. "He already has, sir."

Crispin cleared his throat. "Hadn't you better be on your way, my lord?"

"I'm going, I'm going," he said, grabbing the door latch. "God keep you both." He leaned into Crispin and asked, "I suppose you know what you're doing."

He smiled. "Never."

The door closed after Henry's chuckles, and once his steps no longer thudded down the stairwell, all fell to silence again.

And then Avelyn stirred the coals once more.

"Can't she stop doing that?" Jack held his arms over his chest and swung away, standing at the back window and looking out over the rooftops of St. Martin's Lane.

He watched the boy for a time before turning to Avelyn and touching her shoulder. "Put the poker down. Perhaps it is best if you go."

She shook her head again, but Crispin insisted. "We have much to plot this night. I won't have time for you."

She huffed and sneered in Jack's direction. Her fingers had their say, showing her displeasure. He could only imagine what they said.

"Beastly woman," he muttered, and steered her toward the door. She resisted, but he pushed. Hard. She stumbled and righted herself. When she turned toward him, he expected a scolding, but she only grinned slyly. The implication made him blush. "I repeat. You are a witch."

She made a silent chuckle and then a gesture to come closer. He complied, already regretting sending her away. When he was directly before her, she grabbed his coat and dragged him down for a kiss. It was wet and warm and full of promise. And he nearly forgot he was sending her away when his hand found her hip and squeezed the plump flesh there.

She stepped back out of his embrace and raised her chin. She winked and turned quickly, slipping out the door.

He closed it slowly behind her and leaned on it, bringing his breathing back under control.

"You didn't have to do that, Master," came the soft voice behind him.

He adjusted his braies and straightened his coat before turning to face Jack. "I did. She is… distracting." He stared at the fire for a moment before he went to the table and opened the box with the chess pieces. "Fancy another game?"

"Aye. Might as well." He sat on the stool and shuffled it to the table.

Crispin laid out the board and waited for Jack to begin. They moved pieces, Jack taking more time to examine his options, sometimes speaking them aloud so Crispin could instruct.

Crispin moved a piece and settled his chin on his hand. "Once it is daylight, Jack, I want you to go to Flamel's shop and guard him."

"Why can I not go with you, sir?" he asked, moving his rook. "I'd rather help you gather more clues."

"You sure you want to do that?"

Jack looked up with shock etching his face. "Help you with clues?"

Crispin nodded to the board. "No. That."

"Oh, blind me." He scoured the board once more and finally nodded.

"Very well." Crispin captured the rook with his knight.

"Dammit. I missed that."

"You're a little distracted." He settled his elbows on the table and closed his hands together. "I trust you. That is why I want you to guard them. Someone must."

"But you're the one going into danger alone. Why can I not protect *you?*"

"Because it might be a trap and I want at least one of us to keep the alchemist safe. He might do something foolish."

"How long must I wait for you, then?"

"I reckon I will be gone for a good part of the day. Check."

"Check what, sir?"

"Your king is in check."

"Oh." His eyes scanned the board. Most of Jack's pieces had been taken. The lad's mind was clearly not on the game.

While Jack studied the board, Crispin yawned and only casually glanced at the array of pieces. He was tired. He should go to bed. And he would do so once the game was done. He was sorry he had made Avelyn leave. She would have kept him warm. He shivered slightly and wrapped his arms around himself.

When he glanced down at the board again, his sleepy eyes snapped open. "God's blood!" He nearly upended the table jerking to his feet.

"What? What is it?"

He pushed back the wayward locks of his hair. "I missed it. I completely missed it."

"What did you miss? Did I win?"

"Get your cloak."

"What? *Now?*"

Crispin was already at the door and pulled down his mantle from its peg. "Get your cloak!"

twenty-seven

Jack scrambled up and seized his cloak as Crispin threw open the door and carefully stepped out onto the icy landing. The cold hit him hard, and he paused to pull up his hood. Down he went, hand easing over the railing and ready to grab it if he slipped.

He made it to the slushy snow at the bottom. The light snow had continued from early evening, blanketing the street in lacy white. It reflected the sparse light from a wayward crescent moon that dodged clouds slipping over its face. It was enough light to see, at any rate, and Crispin quickened along the lane, partly to keep warm and partly because he wanted to hurry.

He turned up Old Fish and headed for the alchemists' guildhall for the third time this night and found himself waiting for Jack to catch up to him.

"What are we doing here again?" Jack whispered.

"Let's get in," said Crispin, climbing the stairs. "Keep watch. I don't want to be coshed like Lord Henry."

Jack stayed at the bottom of the stairs while Crispin drew his dagger. After examining the door with cold fingers, he slid the blade between door and jamb and managed to force the bolt. The door creaked open.

"Come along, Jack," he hissed.

Jack's muffled steps crossed the landing and Crispin told him to bolt the door again. Kicking dead leaves, he walked across the littered floor. "Does it look the same, Jack? Has it changed since we encountered it earlier today?"

"I... I suppose. I think it's the same."

"Are you certain? We must be certain, or we've thrown away the most valuable clue."

He looked around helplessly. "Yes, I... but I don't know what I'm looking for."

"Don't you?" Crispin strode to the nearest pillar with its intricate carvings on its plinth and capital. He set his foot on the ledge of the plinth and hoisted himself up. There was enough pitting and cracks in the column's cylinder to stick his foot in and pull himself higher. Holding on to the stone foliate of the capital, Crispin turned, looking down.

The room was dark. Slivers of light cast stripes on the tiled floor from the shuttered windows, just enough for Crispin to see. "God's blood," he whispered.

Hopping down, he gestured toward the pillar. "You go," he said to Jack.

Jack gave him a doubtful expression. It was full of his assertion that Crispin had finally gone mad, but as always, Jack shook his head and shuffled to comply. His foot lodged on the plinth and limber legs wrapped around the column as he shimmied upward. Fingers wrapped themselves over the carved foliations as Crispin had done. Nearly hanging free like an ape, he swiveled and looked down. "I'm looking," he confirmed.

"But what do you see?"

"A floor. Some statues."

Crispin punched his fist into his hip. "What sort of floor?"

"Checkered."

"And?"

"And... I don't know what you want me to see, Master."

"Keep looking."

He heard some grumbling and a few oaths before Jack switched hands and swung the other way. "I'm still looking," he said.

"And still not seeing. When I think of the hours I spent tutoring you on the finer points of observation..."

"Wait!" He saw it dawn on the boy's face. It was unmistakable in the widening of his eyes and the sudden slackness of his jaw. "God blind me with a poker! It's a chessboard!"

"See here," said Crispin, pointing to the floor at the base of one of the statues. "See the marks on the tiles where it was deliberately dragged to this spot?"

"Aye, Master. So now. What does it mean?"

"Well, let's look at it."

One statue was of a female saint. "Let's call this a queen," said Crispin, running his hand over the cold stone. Just to the left of the "queen" stood a figure, which leaned against a rocky brace, but on closer examination, the rocky outcropping appeared to be a castle tower. "And this a rook." Another figure stood nearby, and in his hand he held a harp.

Across the room stood another figure. Carved from marble, the figure seemed to be emerging from another castle-looking structure. Beside it a few squares down was another figure of a saint wearing robes and a miter. "A bishop." Crispin eyed them all. "Jack, from your vantage, whose move is it?"

"I can't be sure, sir. But I'd say the queen was about to be captured by the rook. The... erm... pawn—if that fellow with the harp could be called so—is not in a position to help her."

"Yes. But I see no king on this board."

"There, sir." Jack pointed. Crispin followed the track of his finger and came upon a wreath of ivy on a black square, hidden by a swath of dried leaves.

"A crown?"

"So it would seem, sir."

"Hmm. What does this tell us?"

"I was hoping you could tell me."

"You may come down."

Jack didn't bother climbing. He leapt away from the pillar like a squirrel leaping from a tree and landed on his feet. He joined Crispin and stood beside him. "I suppose the queen is meant to represent Perenelle Flamel?"

"Possibly. A castle will capture her... or she is near a castle. But there are two on the board. Two castles."

"Two castles," Jack murmured. "Two kingdoms? France and England? No." He snapped his fingers. "Two castles... The Tower, sir, and Westminster Palace!"

"Correct. But which one is which?"

The "queen" was soon to be overtaken by the castle figure to her right. Crispin walked over to it and circled it, and then the "pawn." No help there. He walked over to the other "castle," looked it over, and then rested his hand on the "bishop." "This rook has a bishop," he said. "What does that suggest?"

Squinting his entire face, including eyes shut tight, Tucker thought hard. "Bishop. Bishop and a castle." His eyes snapped open. "The abbey, sir? Westminster?"

"Indeed. So the other must be the Tower of London."

"She's near the Tower, then! I told you! Let's go!" He spun on his heel to race away, but Crispin grabbed the point of his hood.

"Not so hasty, Tucker. We don't know *where* by the Tower."

Jack slumped. "Oh. Right."

Crispin walked back to the "queen" and patted the head of the "pawn." "What of this fellow?"

"The pawn. You?"

"If that were the case, then I would think that our knave's sense of wit would have to have made him a knight instead. But it is true I do feel like a pawn in this. No. He is a squire of sorts. Some saint or other personage. And he is carrying a harp."

"He's a minstrel. Should we look for a minstrel? No, no. That's foolish. A harp is a symbol for the Irish. Could he be an Irishman, this knave?"

"You're thinking *too* hard, Jack. And at any rate, if I am right, he is a Frenchman. I was supposing Harp Lane. It is near the Tower."

"Blind me! It is!" He ran his hand over his jaw. "What will we find there, Master? Will Madam Flamel just... be there for the taking?"

"I very much doubt that. I suspect more tricks, more games."

"When should we go?"

"Tomorrow. And not you. Me. I've already told you. You have another job to do."

"But I won't need to guard Master Flamel if you find Madam Perenelle."

"There's more to this than one madman, Jack. Far more. Lord Derby has been dragged into it, and that means a conspiracy. Richard needs to know that his closest men are arranging some mischief to one of the heirs to the throne."

Jack gasped. "But... but Lord Henry is not the heir. That's some other noble. The earl of March... isn't it?"

"Let me see if I can explain this. Roger Mortimer, earl of March, is descended in the female line from Edward III's second son, whilst Henry is descended from the third son. Do you see? His grace John the duke of Lancaster is the *third* son of King Edward, not the first, as was Edward of Woodstock, Richard's father, or the second son, Lionel of Antwerp. *Lionel* would have been second in line. Therefore, because Lionel's only child, Philippa, married into the Mortimer family and bore Roger, Richard's cousin, it is Roger earl of March who is the presumptive heir. And if *he* has no sons, then it *may* still fall to Henry."

Jack blinked. "Blind me. It's complicated, isn't it?"

"Very. But most important."

Jack sucked on his fingers. "Lord Derby. So he could be the heir. He could be the next *king*. Blind me! He's been in our lodgings!"

"Yes. A few times now."

"Christ! The heir to the throne." Jack fell silent, thoughtful. He raised his eyes under his long fringe. "Master, Lord Derby. He isn't... that is... *he* isn't trying to... to..."

"No." The boy was sometimes too perceptive. "I... I am quite certain of that." Though he wasn't certain at all. "He is sincere in his desire to see that Richard is put on the right path. Many of the noble houses would like to see Richard put aside these favorites of his. He has no choice. He must."

"Or?"

"Or... well. I shouldn't like to think of the consequences. It shall certainly devolve into war."

"War? Here?"

"Yes. At our very door. London will not be spared. Lord Henry's army already awaits outside the city."

Jack crossed himself. "I pray it shall not come to that."

"As do I." *But I think it inevitable.* He would not say it aloud. He feared that the dread he saw in Jack's eyes was contagious. He cast about the room one last time, hoping for further inspiration but finding nothing more. "I think we should go home and to bed. We've been up late enough."

"Aye, Master. We both have a busy day ahead of us."

They crept out, checking the empty street first before doing the best they could to lock the door behind them. With snow-dampened steps, they returned to the Shambles.

With the dawn of the day, both Crispin and Jack were silent as they prepared themselves. As usual, Jack heated water for Crispin's shave, warmed the wine, and toasted some heels of bread for both of them before smearing them with slices of pungent cheese. Then they ate in silence.

By some mutual signal, they both rose at the same time. Jack banked the coals in the fire and helped Crispin on with his cloak before he shrugged on his own. Together, they trudged down the steps.

They both traveled up Fleet, found Flamel's shop, and knocked on the door. Avelyn greeted Crispin and curtseyed as he pushed inside. Jack followed.

"*Maître!* Is there any hope? On this the Lord's day, have you come to tell me to prepare for the worst?"

"Of course not. But it is time for answers, Master Flamel. I fear you have still not confided in me."

Flamel's deadened eyes looked him over, and without a word, he retreated to his athanor. He stood over the bubbling vessels, the steaming retorts, and silently took up an iron pincher. With the instrument, he carefully removed each vessel from the fire and set them on the stone of the high hearth, off the heat.

With a heavy sigh, he laid the pincher beside the hot kettles and shuffled to the table. The lines of his face seemed scored deeper since the first day Crispin had met him. He sat at the table and motioned for Avelyn to approach. She attended him less like a servant and more like a dutiful daughter.

The alchemist sighed. "Piers was more than a colleague to me, as you have already guessed, *Maître*. He was more like a brother." Flamel opened his hand, and what Crispin at first took for a rosary was instead a gold button. He turned it in his fingers absently, just as one might finger the beads of a paternoster. "He came from England," he went on, "but was born of French parents. He lived here many years, in London, in fact. But as a young man, he traveled to France and it was there that we met. He knew his alchemy and we bonded instantly. We worked together for many years. We even began together on the Great Work some twenty years ago. He was a genius with compounds. He understood their character, their formulations. He was the perfect master of cupellation, that is, separating base metals from precious metals. In other words, *Maître,* he had the touch! So few truly do. These alchemists in London." He shook his head and frowned. "They play their games, they make their potions, but they have no true understanding, no true *feel* for it. Do you catch my meaning? They are mere apprentices. Piers was a master. But…"

Flamel looked down at the button in his hand, worn smooth by his stained fingers, and slowly stuffed it back in his scrip. "Piers was envious of any talent greater than his own. For such a man, his pride sometimes overtakes his better judgment. Alas, I was the master of him. I could do such alchemy that he could only dream of, and look on with craving. I soon surpassed him, and this he could not stand, though he tried to hide his feelings from me. Alchemy is a secret thing, *Maître,* as I have intimated before. And only shared between master and apprentice. But we—Piers and I—worked as one. Yet I could not make him understand the finer points of the Great Work. He could not open himself to it. His mind was only a narrow channel and would not branch out to embrace that which he could not easily grasp." His eyes flicked upward toward the slowly rotating brass planets, suspended in the air. "Alchemy demands such thinking, I am afraid."

"I already surmised he was a master alchemist."

"Yes, but it went much further even than that. You see, when I met Perenelle, she was still married. But I fell in love with her. It was a chaste love, *Maître,* for we would not cross the boundaries of the marriage vow. But Piers fell in love with her, too. If there was something I coveted, he would covet it as well, much like competing brothers. And yet, he desired to do me one better. He wooed her, but she refused him. And then when her husband suddenly died, he pressed that much more. But now I was also free to woo her." A faint smile passed his lips as he recalled it.

"Master Flamel, is it possible that this Piers... murdered Perenelle's husband?"

He looked up at Crispin, eyes heavy with sorrow. "It never once crossed my mind before. But now..." He lowered his face and crossed himself. With his face lowered and in shadow, he continued his tale. "We used to play many games and wagers to decide this and that, Piers and I, as young men do. Our competitions and puzzles often became fierce. But it was always only in fun. Yet this time, he challenged me to a game of chess to decide who should woo the fair Perenelle and who should step aside. I won that game, *Maître* Guest, and never was I so happy to have been a champion."

"How did he take that news?"

"He was furious, naturally. But he did stand aside as I won her hand and married her. He remained friends with us. I thought he had put it behind him, for he had found a woman of his own and married her. They had a son. Perenelle and I, alas. We could never have children. It is perhaps why I indulge our Avelyn here as I do." He chucked her chin and she smiled at him. "But when the child was three, his wife was taken ill from a fever and died. He moved to estates in Limoges. Not long after that, English troops marched into France. Limoges was sacked, burned. He and his son burned to death. It was a great tragedy. I mourned their passing for years. It was over."

He passed a hand over his face and stared at the candles on the table.

"Were you a witness to this, Master Flamel?"

"No. I was not living in Limoges at the time. Perenelle and I had moved to Paris by then. But there were many witnesses. Many who saw him in the flaming house, running from window to window. And I saw nothing of him more. He was dead. Dead. Or so I thought."

"This man who has captured Madam Flamel likes to play games.

And he is an alchemist. He knows his poisons," Crispin said ruefully. "Is it possible he survived after all?"

"I suppose. It must be!" Desperation glittered his eyes. "And he will have his revenge."

"What sort of revenge does he desire, Master Flamel? Do you think he means to keep Perenelle?"

"This is my greatest fear," he said quietly. "But he wanted the Stone, too. This, he could never achieve on his own. But what he did not realize is that Perenelle was instrumental in helping me achieve it. Her mind is keen, more than any other woman I have ever met. I had notes from my *grand-père*. It was said that he had made the Stone once before he died. But his notes… They were a jumble, the rambling of an old man. It was Perenelle who made sense of all the dross. Without her, I could not have made the Philosopher's Stone. We were on the verge of creating the Elixir of Life. But without her I cannot."

"Is that what he means to do, sir? Is that why he wants her, besides sticking a dagger into your heart?"

He laughed, a dry, unpleasant sound. "Yes, he means to stick a dagger in my heart. He *has* done it! But I think he does intend to make the Elixir and keep Perenelle… forever."

Crispin shuffled on his seat. "When you say… forever…"

"I mean *forever*! Once they achieve the Elixir, they will both be immortal. She will never be free of him." He dropped his face into his hands, but he did not weep. Crispin feared he was beyond weeping now. "Our only hope is that she keeps silent, does not let slip how much she knows of how to make the Stone and the Elixir. If she tells him—or, God help her, is *compelled* to tell him—then all is lost. What can we do?"

"Tell me one thing more, Master Flamel. Who was the leader of this English army who killed Piers's son?"

He lifted his face. "Do you not know? It was the late Prince Edward and his brother John, the duke of Lancaster."

He heard Jack's startled gasp from over his shoulder.

Crispin *had* known. After all, he had been there at Limoges as well, fighting at the duke's side, some seventeen years ago. And now it all made sense. "He is alive, Master Flamel, and he is seeking revenge not just on you, but on Lord Derby. He is Lancaster's son. At first he tried to discredit him, but just last night, Lord Henry was attacked. Had I not been there, he would certainly have been killed."

Flamel slammed the table with his hand. The candles wobbled, spitting wax onto the table. "It must stop! We must rescue Perenelle and stop him, *Maître*."

"We will stop him. Jack, here, will stay with you, keep watch. But before I leave, would you know of anyone from court who would sponsor such an operation? For I am convinced that Piers came to England at the urging of another. And with the true purpose of poisoning London's water supply."

"The poisoned cistern," he murmured. "But King Richard's court? No, I am sorry. I am unfamiliar with those of the English court."

Crispin nodded. "It doesn't matter. I received another clue last night. He's given me the last clue, the last place I might find him. But he has many tricks. I need to know how to get past his defenses. He played a game of chess with me, but I do not yet know who the winner will be."

"There are no defenses. But if he has made the Elixir and has drunk it, then you may try to kill him but you will not be successful."

"I do not believe it. Only God can give us everlasting life."

He stared at Crispin steadily now. "Believe what you like, *Maître* Guest. I only know what I know. But you must forget what you think *you* know."

Crispin stopped. His heart pounded. Those words again! Though it was true. Whether Nicholas de Litlyngton told him or Nicholas Flamel, he had to forget what he thought he knew.

twenty-eight

rispin strode down Harp Lane, taking in both sides of the street with sweeps of his gaze. He did not know what he was looking for, but he assumed he'd know it when he saw it.

Above the rooftops, he could just see the tall battlements of the Tower of London. Surrounded by a moat, it was the most secure place in all of the city, save Westminster Palace itself.

Eyes scanning the street, he saw the usual shops and houses. Nothing that could help him in his quest. Had he been duped again? Was this a false lead? No, the man played fair, and playing was what he did best. Flamel might use his means of sorcery to stop the man, but Crispin had only his own senses, and they were not helping him.

"Where is the bastard?" he muttered. He had to come out sometime, didn't he? But where was Crispin to look for him? He ran the chessboard at the guildhall over in his mind. All pointed to Harp Lane, and as diligently as he looked, he knew he would not find any alchemical symbols to help him this time.

Leaning against a wall and folding his arms under his cloak, he settled in to wait.

Hours passed. The ringing of the bells told him so, as did the many passersby with their carts and donkeys, traveling to and from their parish churches. It was Sunday, the Lord's day, and cause to celebrate, for the citizens of Christendom were not burdened with work on this day. None but Crispin.

He looked up to the gray sky above the rooftops, watched his own cloud of breath escape heavenward, and settled his gaze on the lane again, shadowed under his hood.

He was surprised to spy Robert Pickthorn striding down the lane, a sack over his shoulder. The man's gait was sure but careful, and he checked from side to side and over his shoulder. What business did he have here? Especially after Crispin had told the man to lay low. Was it a coincidence his coming to this particular street? Crispin had the urge to follow him, but there was little reason to do so. The man had been a dupe of this scheme and was of interest only because Crispin was bored.

He let it go, though he watched him make progress north toward the curve of the road until he disappeared in the crowd.

So much for that. Crispin wondered if he should move on to another section of road, but at the thoroughfare seemed as good a spot as any. He had a good view of most of the lane, yet it was frustrating not knowing just what he was looking for.

Another hour passed. He rolled his shoulder and stomped his feet to get the feeling back in them. If he stayed much longer, he'd become an icicle. The clouds above were heavy with snow, he could feel it, and the air was dense with waiting. A dog wandered nearby and Crispin had been so still that it never even looked his way as it sniffed along and lifted its leg to a post.

Coming from the opposite direction, with his head covered by a hood, was Pickthorn again. His coarse hair protruded from under his hood. Someone stopped him to talk and he listened patiently, though Crispin sensed the tenseness in his shoulders and restless hands.

Then he turned his head and smiled.

Crispin jerked up. His hand fell to his dagger.

God's blood! So that was what had unsettled Crispin. That smile. He'd seen that smile before. That one gray tooth in just the same place. Oh yes. He'd seen it twice now. He'd seen it on Pickthorn, but he'd also seen it under the bulbous nose of the impostor Bartholomew of Oxford. The alchemist wasn't an accomplice. *He was the same person!*

Pickthorn continued on, without seeing Crispin. Crispin let him get several yards ahead and then peeled away from the wall and followed.

The man went nowhere in particular. He stopped at a grocer and picked through the bruised apples. He ran his hands into a sack of dried peas. Leaving that behind, he wandered farther and examined pelts from a fur merchant.

What was he doing? Crispin wondered. Simply shopping? Or did he know he was being followed and had decided to lead Crispin on a useless route to throw him off the scent?

Crispin had been patient thus far. He could continue to be so.

Pickthorn left the furrier and continued on his aimless path. Now Crispin was certain the man knew he was being followed. Or perhaps *hoped*. Crispin stayed back as far as he reasonably could. He wanted the man to doubt it, to make an uncalculated move. But he seemed steady in his determination to travel carelessly and purposelessly.

At last he ducked into a tavern.

Crispin waited as long as he dared. How could he go in without the man noticing him? He couldn't, that was plain.

A boy carrying a sack over his shoulder scampered in front of Crispin, and Crispin stuck out a hand and grabbed the boy's shoulder. The child looked up with wary eyes.

"Boy, how would you like to make a quick halfpenny?"

Wide-eyed, the boy set his sack at his feet. "Aye, sir. What would you have me do?"

"I want you to go into that tavern and look for a man with red hair. He is wearing a dark gown, to his ankles. Tell me where he is sitting."

The boy scratched his head. He could not be more than ten or eleven. "That's all?"

"That's all. Make haste now."

He shouldered his burden again and went to the door, pushing it open. Crispin stepped away from the open doorway and into the shadows. He waited, keeping his eye on the door and on the men leaving the tavern. Soon the boy returned and set his sack on the ground before him.

"I'm sorry, sir. But there was no one there with red hair. Can I still have the coin?"

Crispin frowned. "Are you certain?"

"Yes, my lord. I saw no one like that."

Crispin narrowed his eyes in thought. Absently, he reached into his scrip for the coin purse. He took out a coin and handed it to the boy, who stared at the bounty in his dirty palm.

"By my Lady!" he gasped, and closed his hand. "Thank you, my lord!"

"Be on your way," he said, and scoured the street once more.

The boy scurried on, kicking up clods of mud as he ran. *Back door,* Crispin thought. *Must be.* Unless…

He backtracked, following the circuitous path that Pickthorn had led him on. When he arrived at the place Crispin had originally kept his vigil for the first few hours, he spotted a man in a long, dark gown. It looked the same. He was heading back the way Pickthorn had come. Crispin followed far behind, and it wasn't until the man turned once to skirt a wide cart that Crispin saw his face. No dark beard. No red hair. Extremely short brown hair, above his ears.

He didn't have Bartholomew's nose, for that was a disguise. Or his dark beard and hair, for that, too, was a deception. Nor did he have Pickthorn's lank red hair, coarse, more like that of a horse's tail. But it was the same man, all three of them. And he wondered now if he was finally seeing Piers Malemeyns with his true visage, however fleeting.

The man moved up the lane. Crispin followed.

Keeping his distance and hiding behind several men haggling over the price of a brace of coneys, Crispin watched Piers—for he was certain, this time, it was he—descend a short flight of steps to unlock a door set in the foundation of a plain-looking shop.

The windows were shuttered, and anemic smoke spilled from the chimney over the broken slate roof. Either he had forgotten to bank his fire or someone, a confederate, was inside.

Or even his victim.

The front door was out. Too defended, he was certain. He made his way round to the back courtyard. The house stood alone on its corner, perhaps too far away to hear the cries of a helpless woman. The back courtyard was small, with only enough room for a privy. He stepped over the wattle fence and slid behind the foul-smelling pit. Listening for any movement, he was satisfied when he heard none. He used the rickety fence to get a leg up and climbed to the privy's roof. From there, he leapt to an upper windowsill of the house, hanging for a moment before he could swing his leg up. He crouched on the narrow ledge, holding on to the projections from the window frame. He peered in through the cracks of the shutter. A room, empty, except for crates and sticks of furniture piled one atop the other. Storage, he supposed.

He released one hand, steadied himself, and pulled his dagger. With one quick jerk of his hand, the latch lifted and the window fell open. He sheathed the dagger and rolled over the sill, landing as lightly as he could.

Silence.

He slipped his dagger from its sheath again and fitted the hilt comfortably in his hand. He took in the dark room and confirmed it was used for storage and nothing more. He crept along the walls like a cat, mindful of creaking planks.

Just as he made it to the door, an unholy noise exploded below. Wood splintering, shouts, tumbling across the floors.

Crispin yanked open the door and peered down over the gallery.

Two men were struggling below with Crispin's quarry. He glanced quickly around, but there was nothing to help him, nothing to hurl down at the men beneath to stop their battle. And who were these men now fighting Piers?

He girded himself and leapt up onto the railing, measuring the scene and tallying his choices. No help for it. He'd have to join the fight.

He fixed his aim toward the center of the melee and dove over the side.

twenty-nine

The men looked up just as Crispin landed on their chests. They all tumbled backward, scattered and disoriented. He took advantage of it to grab Piers by his throat and hauled him to his feet. His dagger was at the man's cheek.

"The games are over," Crispin growled.

Piers glared at him, his bruised face long and open. And then his blood-cracked lips curved into a smile. That gray tooth gave him away again. "You are a clever man, Crispin Guest," he got out before the others clambered to their feet.

They were swathed in dark cloaks and dark hoods. Their shadowed faces were not ones Crispin recognized, but they did not run as he'd expected. Instead, they dove forward, drawing their swords.

Crispin glared back at Piers. "It appears they want you dead. As dead as *I* want you."

"So popular," he grunted, before freeing himself from Crispin's grasp with one jerk of his shoulders. He ducked Crispin's swinging arm and head-butted one approaching assailant.

They hollered and the one fell into the other, but both recovered quickly, brandishing their blades. Catching a glance at Piers, Crispin saw that he did not seem as much concerned as excited. He, too, had a dagger in hand. He cocked his head at Crispin.

"Fight together, then fight one another?"

There was no other option. One man went for Piers and the other for Crispin.

Crispin blocked the sword blade with his dagger hilt and tried to shove it away, but the man forced his dagger hand down. Crispin twisted, releasing their locked blades with one swift arc of his arm. The sword *whooshed* toward him. He ducked, smiting the man's back with his fist. The man grunted and lurched forward, off balance. Crispin took advantage and kicked at the back of the man's knee. A crunch and he howled, going down. Crispin flipped the dagger in his hand and used the hilt in his fist to deal a punishing uppercut to the man's jaw. A fan of blood swept across the floor as he dropped.

Rubbing his fist, Crispin swiveled toward the other two clinched in mortal combat.

Piers landed a blow to the man's belly, knocking him backward right into Crispin. They both struggled to keep their feet. When they righted, retreating footsteps told Crispin that Piers had bolted. The door swinging freely made it a certainty.

Crispin went after him, but someone yanking on his hood wrenched him to a halt. He turned. The assassin gripped his hood and tugged it down, exposing Crispin's neck. The sword swung down to behead him.

With all his might, Crispin rolled to the side, pulling the man with him. The man let go of the hood and Crispin twisted away, rolling on the floor away from the assailant, but the man pursued. His sword clanged down against the floor near Crispin's head, once, twice.

Still on the floor, Crispin grabbed a chair with his legs and shoved it at the man, right into his belly. The man staggered back and with gritted teeth chopped down with the blade again. The chair splintered.

Crispin jumped to his feet and rushed him, closing him in a bear hug. His dagger plunged deep into the assailant's neck before slashing it outward.

Blood shot forth, spurting with each heartbeat. The man fell back, gurgling on his own blood. The metallic smell of it filled the air. He slipped in the gore and writhed and rattled on the floor. Crispin stepped back out of the way and watched dispassionately as the man's eyes rolled back, his thrashing ceased, and the blood pooled.

He wiped his blade and his hands on the man's cloak and turned his eyes on the other, still unconscious on the floor beside him. Crispin didn't know how long he had. Piers was gone. But what of Perenelle?

"Madam Flamel! Are you here?"

A muffled cry sounded from the room beyond the archway. He stepped over the dead man and tried the door. Locked. With the flat of his foot, he kicked hard at the feeble lock and it caved in as the door slammed open.

The room was dark and cold. A figure seated on a chair moaned and moved its head from side to side, blowing out a cloud of breath. Crispin approached and saw a woman, hair disheveled, face weary and dirty, and mouth stretched taut with a gag. He grabbed the gag first and stripped it away from her. She spit on the floor, away from him.

"Madam Flamel?"

She nodded, tears glistening in her eyes. "And you must be Crispin Guest," she said in a dry voice. He was surprised she knew of him. Her mouth was cracked and chapped. She laid her head back and licked her lips as Crispin worked his dagger through her bindings.

He tried to lift her, but she resisted, shaking her head. "Please. I thirst."

He hurried back into the outer room and found an untouched flagon of wine. He sniffed it, making sure it was what he thought it was, and then found a goblet on the floor. He returned, pouring it for her.

Her trembling hands came up to hold it, but he could see she had no strength. He cradled her head and fed the goblet to her lips. She drank greedily, slurping it. It dribbled down her chin to her dirty gown.

She breathed when the empty cup was taken away. "I am weak. I haven't used my legs in days. They are feeble. Please help me up."

He took her by the shoulders and lifted her, and she cried out. Had she been tied to the chair all this time, for five days?

"I've got you," he said. "But we must leave. It isn't safe."

"Have you killed him?"

"No."

She said nothing to that. He helped her cross the threshold of the room. Her gown was soiled and she stank of urine. His anger boiled and he wished he *had* killed him, killed him slowly.

They headed toward the door when she stopped him. "The Stone. You must find it."

"We haven't time."

"He mustn't keep it. He mustn't make the Elixir."

"It won't do him any good when I kill him."

"You don't understand. He won't be able to *be* killed."

"I don't believe in that nonsense. I must get you out of here."

But when he tried to pull her through the front door, her clawed hands held on to the jamb. "I won't leave without the Stone!"

"God's blood, woman! Bah! Very well." He propped her against the door and she leaned down and kneaded her legs through her soiled gown.

Crispin looked about the room. In their fight, tables had overturned and chairs had been smashed. The detritus of broken crockery and instruments were everywhere. "Malemeyns might have kept it on his person," he said to her as he looked. "He might not have—"

"No, he couldn't. He had to… had to keep it in a crucible in order to make the Elixir. If he knew even that much, it will be here."

"If he knew that much?"

She looked down at the bodies on the floor, one that would move no more, covered in his own blood, and the other that still breathed shallowly, though through a gurgle of red. His jaw might be broken or dislocated. He might die anyway. Crispin didn't mourn it.

"Piers was skilled in the alchemical sciences," she went on, unmoved by the plight of the bodies lying at her feet. "But he could not master the Stone. And if one could not master that, then he could not master the Elixir. But it has been a long time. He had time to learn. And if he had notions to bring Nicholas here to help him, he hadn't realized that it was me instead, all along."

He said nothing as he searched.

Slowly, using the jamb, she straightened, wincing. "Do you think women are only for softness and bearing children? We have many other skills. And mine was in alchemy. It's what drew Nicholas to me and, I am afraid, Piers. Can we stop him?"

"We will. This I vow to you. But first we must flee this place."

"Not without the Stone."

"Women are also considerably more stubborn," he muttered. Yet he admired her. For she had truly suffered much in the past week, and even as safety was nigh, she would not turn her course. He envied Flamel.

With his dagger, he carefully turned over broken beakers, their contents hissing and bubbling on the wooden floor. What at first he thought was a shard of glass, he recognized as the Stone Flamel had shown him before. Crouching, he pushed it with his blade out of the mess and tipped it into the stained tablecloth lying on the floor. He wiped it off and straightened. Returning to her, he handed her the crystallized Stone.

"You knew what it looked like," she said, her voice, even as scratchy as it was, filled with awe. She clasped it tight in her hand. "Nicholas showed you."

"Yes. I made him show me once we discerned what Malemeyns wanted." He unbuttoned his cloak, took it off, and threw it over her quivering shoulders.

"He wanted more than that," she said, leaning into him as he led her out the door. "He told me the terrible things he was doing, *Maître*. He was brought over from France in order to poison the cisterns, and make it look as if it were a French plot, turning against his own people."

"I see."

"But more. He was also to discredit the duke of Lancaster in the process. When he discovered the duke was in Spain, he turned his attention to his son."

"So I also suspected."

"Did you? Nicholas was wise to find you. But what this English lord who hired him did not know was Piers's great hatred for Lancaster. For killing his son. He wanted to do his own justice and kill Lancaster's son in return. But when he found Nicholas here…"

"He hatched many plots indeed. But tell me. Did he tell you which English lord hired him?"

"Oxford was the name he used. I do not know if it is a name or a place."

"Oxford?" Not Suffolk. "It is both," he said absently. So. Robert de Vere was playing his hand. And was he not recently appointed the justice of Chester, in direct control of Henry's lands? Did Richard know about all this? He'd like to know the answer to that.

They moved through the streets. Crispin kept the pace slow for Perenelle's sake. He kept looking back over his shoulder, but no one pursued them.

"The many plots seemed to have collapsed," he said. "For one, those men were sent to dispatch Malemeyns. Perhaps Oxford's patronage had expired."

"Assassins," she said. "But they did not get him."

"I'm afraid I arrived at an inopportune moment."

They shouldered past a man burdened with bundled sticks over his back. "A pity you could not have been delayed a few moments more."

"I fear if I had, they might have gotten to you."

"Me? How could I be a threat?"

"You were a witness. You knew it was Oxford. And even if you did not, they could not take that chance. They would certainly have killed you."

She snorted. "I had the protection of the Holy Virgin. She kept me safe and I am alive and unhurt."

"So you are."

"And she sent you. I am most grateful. I will light many candles for you, *Maître*."

He felt his cheeks warming, even in the cold and without his cloak. He said nothing.

"Piers discovered that Nicholas and I were here. And he changed his strategies. You see, when his house burned and took the life of his son, it also destroyed his work. He claims he was close to creating the Stone. But that, I doubt."

"Yet it seems as if Master Flamel is famed for creating the Stone, at least among alchemists. How did Malemeyns dare steal it and call it his own invention?"

"He is mad. Mad with vengeance and envy. And hatred. It was an accident, but long ago, Nicholas was responsible for his wife's death. He mixed a potion to heal her, but she reacted very badly to it. She died, painfully. I am certain that was part of the reason he stole me and treated me so abominably."

"A man will have his revenge," he said, thinking now that he'd like to take his own revenge on Piers. "He seemed also to take on many guises. Another alchemist, a preacher. He sounded like a Londoner to me."

"He was from London as a child and often returned. Though once he was married he traveled less often. He made a name for himself in England, but that was not what he wanted. He wanted to be the prima alchemist of France, to have the king bestow honors on him as he had upon Nicholas. He felt in his heart he was a Frenchman, and to use the English in this plot was his greatest jest."

"Do you have a clue as to where he is now?"

"No. He told me much, but he was also careful. I got the impression he had many hiding places within the city."

"So he did, even to using the house of a man away on travels and pretending to be him."

"So clever. So unafraid. So without scruples." She bundled the cloak tightly about her. "A man like that can feel he can do anything, that he is entitled to do so. A man like that is the most dangerous of all."

They said no more and moved up Fleet at last to the shop. Even as she leaned upon him, he felt her urge him forward. Crispin knocked on the door and he spied Jack for only a moment before Avelyn threw him aside. Perenelle seemed to lose the control she had carefully kept. *"Ma chère! Je suis si contente de vous voir!"*

Avelyn cried out and took her elbow, and Flamel was instantly at her side, enclosing her in his arms. The two of them rocked together, soft sobs escaping both of them.

"It was Piers," she murmured, and he drew back, staring at her. "But your gallant *Maître* Guest saved me… and this." She opened her hand to reveal the Stone.

"Ah!" he cried, folding his hand over hers, and the both of them clutched each other again, as well as the Stone. *"Maître, Maître!"* He looked with a tear-streaked face up at Crispin over the top of his wife's head. "How… how can I ever thank you? What shall ever be enough?"

"It isn't over, Master Flamel. He escaped me and I fear he may still do harm."

"But you will find him. I know you will. And Thomas can now rest in peace. Come, Avelyn," he said, signaling the girl. Avelyn was looking adoringly at Crispin when Flamel finally caught her attention. "Take your mistress and bathe and clothe her. See that she is comfortable."

Avelyn nodded and took Perenelle's hand, kissing it before she led the drooping woman away. Perenelle stopped, straightened, and removed Crispin's cloak from her shoulders. She handed it to him and he took it, crushing it to his chest. "May our Lady bless you, *Maître*. May she bless all who hold you dear."

He bowed low as she was led away. Jack looked on with stoic admiration. Flamel's hands on Crispin's sleeve brought him back to his attention. "You did it! You did it! You are a miracle."

Crispin moved away from the man's embrace to spin his cloak over his shoulders and step closer to the fire. He didn't feel much like a miracle. He felt like a failure. He hadn't captured Piers yet, let him escape. Though he supposed he *was* busy at the time.

But that also meant that Henry was still in danger.

Jack nudged Crispin's elbow, offering ale, and sat beside Crispin, sipping his own. Crispin related to him how Piers was not only Bartholomew, but Robert Pickthorn.

"No! That cannot be," he said with a snarl. "How could he have deceived us so!"

"He is a master at it. At disguise and guile. Perhaps he even uses his sorcery to do it. A false nose, wigs, false beards."

"But all them people. How did he ever get away with it?"

"I've told you before, Jack. People see only what you force them to see. We saw him only in an alchemist's shop as Bartholomew, and when we saw him as Pickthorn, he was fiery and bombastic, just as we expected to see. Change the voice a bit and add an accent, a stooped shoulder, and none will be the wiser. I've done it myself."

"You never!"

"I have."

Jack let out a breath. "He's laughing at us."

"Let him. He won't be laughing when my dagger goes through him."

"So what now? He's still after Lord Derby."

"Yes. That worries me. Henry is wise enough now not to follow any more anonymous missives, but what if Malemeyns puts *my* name to it?"

Jack shot to his feet. "God's blood, sir! He can't do that!"

He stared at Jack anew and tried mightily not to smile at his apprentice's use of Crispin's favorite oath. "No, he certainly cannot be allowed to. But I don't know where Henry lodges."

"And just how is it the Tracker finds that out?"

"Right." He got up and headed for the door. Abruptly, he stopped. "Jack, I want you to stay here."

Jack slumped. "What! Again?"

"They need guarding, Jack. I fear that Malemeyns may try to return. And remember, he can disguise himself."

Jack looked disappointed for only a moment before he pushed his shoulders back. "Aye, Master Crispin. I'll stay. I'll do my best. I'll make you proud."

"You already do."

thirty

Of course Derby had estates in London. Lancaster castles they had aplenty, spread all over England and outside London's precincts, but they had houses in London. The Savoy had been under slow reconstruction after the riots of Wat Tyler back in the fifth year of Richard's reign, but he knew Henry wouldn't be there. He wouldn't be at any of them. If there was an encampment outside the city, that's where he'd be.

With his hood up against the cold as well as for secrecy, Crispin hurried through the late afternoon streets. He was deeply disturbed by the fact of Oxford's treachery. What had he hoped to gain by eliminating Henry? Did Oxford fear more than the commissioners' impositions? Did he think Henry threatened the crown itself? Of course Oxford would do anything to defend Richard, for Richard kept him in riches, heaping upon him honors and titles. Duke of Ireland, justice of Chester, marquess of Dublin. Rumor had it that Oxford had even put aside his wife in order to marry one of the queen's ladies. He thought he could commit any atrocity he wished, any foul exploit, and remain immune. Poison the cisterns and blame it on the French, as a distraction, no doubt. A distraction! Killing innocent lives just for that. Yes, there was great call indeed for Henry's commissioners.

But worse. Crispin was no longer in any position to challenge him, to stop him. He had to rely on Henry to do that. Was the boy strong enough? Was his cadre of lords powerful enough to stop Richard and his men from these misdeeds? He hoped so, and he prayed that Lancaster would soon return from his mission in Spain. He could not come home soon enough!

After a time, Crispin passed through Bishopsgate and took the lonely road toward Spitalfields. He heard the sound of troops before he reached it over a rise. Men-at-arms strode the fields and tended to horses. Colorful pavilion tents crowded together like a market day. Banners with the arms of Henry's lords whipped in the wind and Crispin headed toward the one with the arms of Lancaster, feeling distinctly vulnerable as heads turned toward him. The question now was, would he be admitted?

He strode up to the entrance of the encampment and to an assembly of men-at-arms. He bowed gravely. "Masters," he said, "I would speak with his grace, Henry of Derby."

No one spoke, and for a moment, Crispin wondered if anyone would. After all, who would come to such a camp without a horse, without a retinue?

One wary guard ventured forward, clutching the shaft of his poleaxe. "Who comes to see his grace?"

"Crispin Guest. With a matter of some urgency."

By the men's expressions, Crispin could well see that they recognized his name. The men-at-arms exchanged a silent consultation before the first man licked his lips and gave a curt jerk to his head for Crispin to follow.

Crispin was only slightly surprised but did not stand by musing over it. He hurried across the muddied field behind the man-at-arms and traipsed between the tents, where they met another guard.

The man gestured back toward Crispin. "Crispin Guest to see Lord Henry."

The new guard, wearing the Lancaster colors, openly assessed Crispin.

"Please," said Crispin. "You know who I am. You know I would never betray him."

The guard studied him for a long time before he said in a gruff voice, "I will announce you." He turned and walked away, leaving Crispin to stand on the chill plain with the single guard behind him.

It wasn't long until another man in livery arrived. He, too, looked Crispin over. "I am Hugh Waterton, Earl Derby's chamberlain. What makes you think that Lord Henry will see you?"

"He will."

Again, Crispin stood under scrutiny. Waterton glanced out over the encampment, where his gaze finally landed on the man-at-arms standing by. He gave him a dismissing nod and turned to Crispin. "Come with me."

Crispin followed him through the aisles between more tents and finally to a large pavilion, whose sides rippled with the wind. Waterton pushed aside the tent flap and held it open for Crispin.

Crispin bowed to the man, held the flap for himself, and ducked through. The flap fell back in place behind him.

The floor was covered in carpets. A large oak table with folding chairs encircling it sat in the middle of the tent, but there was still room enough for a large bed, coffers, and several cots. Candles burned from sconces beside an altar at the far end, where a man knelt at a prie dieu. He was enrobed in a long cloak that draped over his feet. A sword hilt poked out and lay across the carpeted floor.

After a long moment, he turned.

Henry.

He rose quickly, smoothly, and strode across the tent. A frown furrowed his brows. "Why did you come here?"

"Forgive me, my lord. But I had to warn you. I did not want to send a message that might go astray."

"Well, then?"

"There are assassins who seek you."

He barked a laugh. "This is not news."

"Their origin is. It's Oxford. He is sending them."

"What?" His hand went to his sword hilt.

"It does not please me to relate this to you, my lord. But Oxford is behind all the schemes of late in London. The poisoning, the missives you received, and the men sent to kill you."

"How... how does he *dare?*"

"He is loyal to Richard."

"Does Richard know?"

"I... don't know. But I doubt it. I think Oxford is doing this on his own for his own interests as well as the king's."

Henry's hand closed into a fist as he stared at the floor. His shoulders rose and fell in a quick succession of breaths. "Who else knows that you know?"

Crispin shrugged. "No one but you and me."

"My men have told me that Oxford and Suffolk are preparing to leave court. They might be gone already."

"Why, Henry? What is happening?"

He lifted his head. "I have a message to deliver to his Majesty. Today. An appeal of treason on his advisers."

"Don't go, Henry. Send others to do it."

"How can I not go? Especially when one of the names is Oxford. You see, Crispin, I already know what a swine he is."

"I beg you, Henry, don't go."

"Because of what it will look like?"

"It will look like you are making a move on the throne."

Henry paced away from Crispin. His long cloak feathered along the carpeted floor after him.

"I don't... want to know whether it's true or not," said Crispin. Henry looked over his shoulder at him, brows raised. "I don't."

"It's not," he answered quickly.

Crispin breathed again. He licked his lips. "Don't go to court. He'll arrest you."

"Whom should I send, eh? If not myself?"

"Send your uncle, at least. As a show of good faith to Richard."

"Who else?"

He shook his head. "I do not know who your commissioners are. Not all of them, anyway."

"Richard Fitzalan, Thomas Mowbray, Thomas Beauchamp. Should I send them all and not go myself?"

"Send Arundel and Warwick, then, along with your uncle. A small delegation. Not too intimidating."

"But I think rather that they *should* be intimidating."

"The message is intimidating enough, don't you think? Richard will not take it well."

A small smile formed on his face. "Would it interest you to know that my uncle Gloucester made all the very same arguments? I suppose I should take that advice, then, if the both of you are in agreement."

261

"Gloucester and I have agreed on so few things. Perhaps this is the time to listen."

He nodded. "Very well. I'll send the message. And I'll stay here. For now."

"What will Suffolk and Oxford do?"

"God knows. I know what *I* would do."

"And what's that?" But Crispin already knew the answer.

"Bring back an army," said Henry.

rispin took his thoughts with him back to Fleet Street. Before he reached it, however, he heard a noise and looked up. Above the rooftops were not the dark, dense clouds full of rain, but great billowing, choking clouds of smoke from a fire. Like many others on the street, he started running. A fire in the city could easily spread from street to street in the tightly packed parishes. Any able-bodied man was required to help.

His fear doubled when he saw the roof of Flamel's shop engulfed. Sooty men were passing buckets of water to one another and tossing their contents on the blaze flickering through the doorway.

Crispin ran up to a man who seemed to be in charge. "The people?" he asked. "Did the people get out?"

"I don't know. I came upon it when the fire appeared to start. I called out but heard no one within."

The smoke and fire in the doorway parted for only a moment, and Crispin leapt through.

"Wait! Damn fool."

Inside, the place was like the pits of Hell. Fire leapt from every surface. Heat surged all around him. He put his cloak up over his mouth and nose, but his eyes stung from the smoke. He squinted through the tears and cast about. "Is anyone here?"

He kept low, below the rolling smoke, searching in all the corners. When he could find no sign of anyone, he grabbed the ladder to the loft. He was coughing now and closed his eyes as he climbed each rung, saving his eyes the pain from the heat. Once he gained the top, he looked around. "Flamel! Jack!"

Flames licked at him from the railing and the now rickety floorboards. In the smoke, the brass planets continued their slow progress, oblivious to the carnage around them.

Crispin looked up. In the rafters he caught sight of a square that looked like the sky, and when he coughed enough, and blinked enough, he saw that it *was* the sky. A trapdoor to the roof yawning wide open.

He stumbled his way toward it, trying to breathe only through his damp cloak, and stood under the door. No ladder. The remnants of it were burning nearby. They must have made their escape that way.

He looked back the way he had come.

The flames covered the railing now, engulfing the ladder to the loft. That way was barred. And the fire was gaining on the floorboards. Already some of the floor had given way and gaping holes with spitting flames were all around him. The roof was his only exit, but how to reach it?

Everything was aflame. Even the bed was smoldering… but not yet engulfed. He grabbed it and pulled it away from the wall. It was heavy. It dragged across the floor with a great groan. All at once, part of the floor gave way, and one corner of the bed sank into the fiery hole. Crispin grabbed hold of one post and heaved. It swiveled on its one axis in the breached floor and one post was suddenly poised under the trapdoor. That would have to do.

Crispin climbed atop the bed and jammed his foot on the carvings on the post, hoisting himself as high as he could go. It wasn't quite enough. "Dammit." He looked down. The room was red and gold, with more heat than he'd ever encountered before. It was not a good way to die, he decided, and turned back up toward the square of sky, trying to breathe any air filtering down.

He'd have to jump for it.

Just as he positioned himself to climb again, the bed lurched.

The hole in the loft widened and the bed tilted into it. The mattress caught fire and began to smoke furiously in black billows.

Quickly, he jumped away just as the bed, in a loud bellow of creaking timbers, crashed through the floor, sending up a great belch of dark smoke and shooting flames.

Trapped.

The planets *whooshed* slowly by and Crispin saw it was his only hope. The railing was barely intact. He waited till the sun on its outer arm swung closest toward him before jumping onto the rail. He sprang forward and grabbed hold of one of the sun's rays, wrapping an arm around it. The contraption groaned and wobbled under his weight but continued to move slowly toward the trapdoor. He knew he had only the one chance left. If he missed it...

The brass sun finally creaked directly beneath the trapdoor. Crispin prayed and leapt.

His fingers caught the edge of the opening and he dangled over the fire crackling and spitting upward from two floors below him.

With a grunt, he slid an arm up and over onto the roof, gripped tight, and swung his leg up, catching it on the opening's edge. Gritting his teeth and bellowing with the rest of his strength, he used his leg muscles to pull himself up the rest of the way until he was able to grab hold of the roof itself. His arms did the rest of the work and he slid across the broken tiles to fresh air.

Once his feet were free of the fiery room, he lay on the tiles and breathed.

Where were they, the Flamels and Jack and Avelyn? Were they safe?

He gained his feet. The tiles were hot under his boots. The roof wouldn't last long.

When he looked up, he spied figures being hauled into an attic window on another rooftop across the lane. A woman was being handed down, assisted by a soot-covered blond-haired girl. Avelyn, helping her mistress. And there was Flamel, with Jack last.

"Jack!" He waved his arm.

Jack looked up and saw him. "Master!" he called across the rooftops. "Come on!"

Crispin moved, but out from behind a chimney, a figure in a long black gown emerged.

"You can't help but get in my way, can you, Guest?"

"Malemeyns." He drew his dagger. "I was hoping I'd have my chance at you. You started this fire."

"Of course I did. My son died in a fire. Why not Nicholas?"

"He wasn't responsible for that."

"No, Lancaster was accountable for it. But Nicholas killed my wife, stole my Perenelle. He ruined my life and I'll ruin his."

"It's over. You won't be committing any more murders."

"It is justice. What would you know of that? Oh, I know your tale. I weep for it," he said sarcastically. "But it was different for me. All was lost, never to be recovered."

"And so, too, was my life lost."

"But now you thrive, is that it? I should do the same? You *are* clever, I will give you that. But you have no one to blame but yourself. I have Nicholas. And Lancaster. And I'll have my revenge."

Crispin heard the joists give way beneath him and he leapt aside. Flames shot up from the rafters.

Piers smiled. His teeth gleamed from a sooty face... all but his one gray tooth. He, too, had a dagger in his hand. "Who will triumph, I wonder?" He cocked his head toward where Flamel had escaped. "He can try to hide from me, but I'll never stop harrying him. I *will* prevail. Perenelle will be mine one day. For I have already made the Elixir. I have time. All eternity, in fact."

"I think you're lying. Perenelle told me you didn't know what you were doing."

He ticked his head. "Poor deluded Perenelle. She chose so unwisely."

"But she didn't choose. You lost her. In a game of chess. Isn't that right? You like to play games."

He frowned. "So I did. The next game won't be as easy to lose. Nicholas never would have found her without your help. And you won't be there the next time."

"Oh? I was rather thinking that this was your last game."

"A game?" His face brightened. "Shall we play one? One last time?"

"I'm through with your damn games."

"Oh, no! Games are always appropriate. What can we play up here?"

"How about catch the dagger?" Crispin lunged with his blade... but Piers stepped aside. Almost skidding off the roof, Crispin windmilled his arms and righted himself at the last moment. It was a long way down.

"But I already told you, Guest. I have taken the Elixir. I cannot *be* killed. I know the potion worked. I prepared it myself with the use of the Stone. You will always see me just as I am now. Vigorous. Invincible. For now I shall never age."

He stomped down hard. The roof cracked, buckled... and suddenly gave way under Crispin.

A fireball leapt up, barely missing him, and Crispin fell through the roof. He barked his chin on the way down, but it bounced him enough that his arms reached out and gripped the edge of the broken tiles.

Piers approached and crouched down to face him. "Looks like you lose."

Arms trembling, Crispin slammed a fist on the tile nearest Malemeyns's foot. It crumbled and the man slipped. He lost his footing and toppled, rolling to the edge of the roof.

Crispin used that distraction to haul himself up, and none too soon. He could feel the fire licking at his boots. When he looked down, the leather was singed and smoking.

By then, Piers had regained his footing. He was wagging a finger at Crispin. "You must have nine lives, Crispin Guest."

"I must," he agreed.

"It's a pity. Such a keen mind and a nimble body."

"Why did you lead me to Old Fish Street? I never would have found you had you not left clues."

"It's the game, Master Guest. Have you never played games?"

"Isn't the object of the game to win?"

"Of course it is. But the object of the game is also to play. And while I knew that ultimately Nicholas would lose, it doesn't diminish the sport of the game itself." He shook his head and tsked. "I would have thought a man such as yourself would know that."

"It's important to have the advantage."

"Yes, isn't it? And I have that."

"Do you?"

"You're trying to stall. How amusing. Let's play." He jabbed forward with his dagger and Crispin leapt back. They circled each other. Crispin knew the man was older than him, but he didn't seem to be tiring. It couldn't have to do with that Elixir, could it? No! He refused to believe it. Piers was propelled by madness, nothing more than that.

Crispin made a lunge, but Piers stepped nimbly out of the way. Smoke surrounded them and both their faces were covered in soot, but Piers was smiling, his teeth bright.

He made a feint at Crispin and then swept his blade down the other way. It caught Crispin's shoulder. A stripe of blood appeared beneath the tear in Crispin's coat and then a sharp pain bloomed. He ignored it.

Piers smiled in triumph and took a swing with his blade at Crispin's head. Crispin leapt out of the way but lost his footing on the slanted tiles. He was falling backward and reached out wildly, grabbing hold of Malemeyns's cloak as he fell. He yanked the man with him, and they tumbled one over the other toward the roof's edge, stopping short of the precipice.

Each tried to stab the other, and each fended the blades aside with their free hands clutching each other's wrists. Piers gritted his teeth, smiling a rictus at Crispin. Crispin clutched the man's dagger arm for all he was worth, forcing it back, trying with only one hand to slam it down against the tiles. Slowly, inch by inch, he managed to force it down until he gave the man's arm a twist.

The dagger fell from his grip and hurtled over the side to the ground below.

Piers cried out in anger and used both hands to grab Crispin's dagger arm.

Crispin rolled them both uphill, back to the fiery hole now licking its flames upward through the tiles amid black curls of smoke.

Malemeyns pushed, knocking Crispin back. Piers was suddenly free and he skittered across the rooftop back toward the chimney. He crouched and grabbed loosened tiles, hurling them one after the other at Crispin's head. Crispin ducked and dodged them, feeling them crack painfully across the forearm he held up for protection.

The missiles stopped, but Piers was suddenly standing above him, and though Crispin tried to scramble to his feet, he kept slipping on the slick tiles. Swinging a flaming faggot of wood broken off from one of the rafters, Piers approached.

"I'm done with you, Crispin Guest. Quite done."

He swung at Crispin's head, but Crispin managed to duck. He jumped up and jerked backward away from the flaming wood. Malemeyns swung again, gritting his teeth.

Crispin fell to one knee, dodging it by leaning to the side. He twisted and shoved his knife upward... right into Malemeyns's gut. He jerked the blade higher, relishing the tearing of more flesh, doing as much damage as he could before withdrawing the knife.

Shocked, Piers looked down at the blood spilling from the wound. A portion of his entrails dangled free. "But..."

Panting, Crispin watched as the man's skin paled and his blood gushed. Piers doubled over. "Forever doesn't seem to be as long as it used to be," said Crispin.

With surprise still etching his features, Piers fell forward into the hole in the roof, just as a burst of flame erupted and swallowed him up.

thirty-one

Days shifted into weeks. Perenelle recovered from her ordeal, and they found new lodgings in which to complete their work. Avelyn visited Crispin many more times, spending long nights there, but when he awoke in the morning, she was always gone.

By the end of November, Avelyn brought a message from Flamel, telling Crispin that they were sailing for France.

He met them at Queenhithe wharf. They would take a skiff to the sea, where they would pick up a ship to sail the channel.

Their luggage was there, being loaded by wherrymen. Crispin bowed to Perenelle. "I suppose I am surprised you stayed this long."

"I wanted my wife fully recovered. And yet, being so late in the year, we may be waiting at Dover for some time anyway."

Crispin turned to Avelyn. She was looking at him fondly. "I am sorry to see you go," he said to her.

She smiled and signed to him.

He laughed and stilled her hands, holding them in his. "I have not yet mastered your language. Now I never shall." He touched her face, trailing his fingers along her jaw until he took her chin and tilted it upward. He leaned over and pressed a soft kiss to her pliant lips. "I will miss you," he whispered, and then he signed her name, making her smile.

"We shall not see you again, *Maître* Guest," said the alchemist, moving between them. "How should we ever thank you enough? There is not enough gold in all the world. But here is a small token." He offered a pouch, but Crispin did not take it.

"You already paid me, sir."

"But you have earned more than that. Take it. It will be a cold winter in London, I fear."

The news was still not good, and Crispin bowed to the wisdom of it. At least he and Jack would stay warm. Reluctantly, he cupped it in his palm. He was relieved that it felt like coins.

"Must you go? Must… Avelyn go?" He admitted, at least to himself, that he'd grown fond of her.

But Flamel, looking cheerful at last, shook his head and touched her long braid lovingly. "Oh, we couldn't possibly leave her behind. She's been with my family for years… and years." He leaned toward Crispin and whispered, "You see, she was once my nursemaid." He smiled and nodded before he turned to climb onto the boat, steadying it for Perenelle. He held her hand and would not let go until she was settled.

Crispin laughed. "You jest with me, sir. She's far younger than you."

Flamel cocked his head and smiled at Crispin. His eyes glittered mischievously. "Is she?"

Avelyn leapt onto the boat and turned to Crispin, giving him a wink.

The boat skimmed away from the dock, and they all waved back at him.

"Master," said Jack at his elbow, "can that be true? Master Flamel did say that his grandfather had created a Philosopher's Stone. Could she be—"

"Nonsense, Jack. Of course not." Avelyn kept looking at him with a sly smile. "Let's go home." But even as they drew away, he turned back one last time to gaze at the young woman. She stood upon the deck at the railing, old eyes looking distantly ahead.

December arrived, and anxious over the tidings at court, Crispin drank too much at the Boar's Tusk and listened, along with every other citizen in London, about Richard and his advisers and Henry of Lancaster's commissioners. But it was never detailed enough, never full of the information he wanted to know. He wanted news of the commissioners. He wanted news of Henry.

But he did hear, along with everyone else, about the appeals of treason levied at the king's closest advisers. Crispin had reluctantly sent Jack to loiter near the palace to get any news he could. The boy soon found himself a popular visitor to the Boar's Tusk.

Jack sat by the fire, a beaker of ale in his hand. Crispin and Gilbert Langton, the alehouse owner, sat close to him as he sipped. "Just as you predicted, sir," Jack said quietly, eyes darting here and there about the tavern. "I heard tell that Suffolk fled the country. And not only that, but the Archbishop Neville disguised himself and escaped back to his diocese at York."

Crispin snorted. "They tested the wind and saw it was an ill one."

"Aye, Master. A very ill one indeed. There was another. One of the king's knights who was chief justice. I forgot his name—"

"Sir Robert Tresilian," Crispin offered.

"Aye, that's the one. Well, he went into hiding in Westminster. And the former lord mayor is said to remain in London."

"That fool Brembre," muttered Crispin. "He surely must believe no harm will come to him, and that London would be loyal to him."

"You do not think that is so?" said Gilbert, pouring more wine into Crispin's beaker.

"Surely you must sense it, Gilbert. The feeling in London is one of anger and betrayal. I fear they will not stand with Brembre. He is for the gallows for certain."

Gilbert winced. Crispin knew he did not like such free talk. Even Crispin scanned the room immediately around them, but men seemed to be concerned in their own tight circles, probably discussing the same issues.

He turned to Jack. "What of Oxford?"

"Just as you feared, sir. Oxford retreated to his lands and is mustering an army."

By mid-December, the word had spread throughout London that

Oxford would march on the city. The citizens hunkered down. The bitter cold kept most from the streets, but it was also the wait for a siege that made the lanes empty. Henry's forces left the fields around London and set out for Oxfordshire while London cowered, waiting for news.

Crispin sat for hours by his window, staring through the crack in his shutter until Jack roused him with a touch to his shoulder to admonish him to eat his weak pottage.

At last, when the news came that Lord Henry had stopped Oxford's army at Radcot Bridge, a collective sigh of relief came from the city. But Crispin knew it was far from over.

The commissioners' armies returned to camp outside of London, making certain that all of the court knew they were there. The panicked city was in turmoil once more. Food was hoarded. Goods were scarce. Advent was a subdued affair.

Crispin watched by his window and was one of the first to hear the man riding down the Shambles. "The king retreated to the Tower!" he cried, his voice harsh with desperation.

Crispin pushed open the shutter and leaned down. "What's that, man? What are you saying?"

He yanked on his reins and the horse turned, shaking its head. He looked up at Crispin. His face was sooty and his cloak was torn.

"The king and his retinue, sir. They've gone to the Tower and barricaded themselves within."

Crispin's fingers curled tightly around the edge of the shutter. "Why? What's happened?"

"I don't know, sir. But every able-bodied man must prepare himself. If I were you, I'd head to your parish church for prayer." He kicked the horse's flanks and hurried the beast toward Newgate, sending clods of muddy snow behind him.

Crispin pulled back inside, away from the harsh cold, and closed the shutters. He looked at Jack. "It's begun."

For days Crispin and Jack waited for news, for any kind of hint at what was happening. Occasionally someone would ride through the streets and call out a snippet here and there. But there was never enough. Nothing to pin any hope to.

Finally, they couldn't stand it any longer. Crispin and Jack had burned the last of Henry's wood anyway, and with cloaks wrapped tightly around them, they trudged over the frozen streets to the Boar's Tusk.

Crispin settled in by the fire, with Jack on his right and an anxious Gilbert on his left. Men gathered in clusters, talking among themselves, peering over their shoulders. For the first time in Crispin's life, he was on the outside along with every other citizen of London. He knew nothing of what was transpiring. He was not at the right hand of the duke or the old king, ready to take to the battlefield with them. He hated it. He hated not knowing.

The door slammed opened and everyone jumped. A page tore through the entrance with a wild face and fretful eyes. "He's done it!" he cried. "He's done it!"

Crispin, along with every man there, rose to his feet. His heart pounded in his chest.

Someone shoved a beaker of ale into the lad's hand and he gulped it down in one. He wiped his mouth with his sleeve and was suddenly swept up by the crowd and settled by the fire.

"What happened, boy?" someone asked.

His eyes searched the room, and when his audience had quieted, he took a deep breath. "The king. He's come out of the Tower. They're escorting him back to Westminster."

"As... as the king?" Crispin finally asked. Every man in the place quieted, waiting to hear.

"Aye," said the boy. And everyone breathed a sigh—Crispin, too, and was surprised at himself for it. "Henry of Lancaster—that is, Lord Derby—he and his lords went to the king to plead with him to return to good governance. But King Richard wasn't pleased with them. They showed him letters from the earl of Oxford written to the French king, appealing to *him* to help Richard against his own people."

The men growled at that.

The page held up his hand. "Aye, I know. Lord Henry's lords were angered by that and it was said that the king was chastened by this news. They rebuked him. Said he was deceitful and dishonest."

A man from the crowd leaned in toward the page. "They said that to him? To the king?"

"Aye, they did. I saw Lord Henry myself. His eyes were angry, but his voice was steady. He was on a white horse and his cloak was made of ermine. He looked like a king himself, did Lord Henry. He warned the king to correct his mistakes and that he was to rule better or else. He warned him that he had an heir of full age."

The room gasped, and men turned toward one another, murmuring.

"What did the king say to that?" asked an old man by the page's elbow.

Gilbert poured more ale into the lad's cup and he drank again, throat rolling. When he set the cup down on his thigh, he leaned toward the crowd again. "He agreed to submit to their demands. He said he agreed to be guided by their wholesome advice."

The page stopped talking and looked at all their faces. Some men murmured while others fell silent. No one knew what to think.

Until, almost as one, they all turned to Crispin.

He didn't notice at first until Jack elbowed him. Scouring their anxious expressions, Crispin merely raised a brow at them. "I do not have the ear of the court," he said quietly.

"But they say you speak to Henry of Lancaster," said the old man beside the page. "And that he speaks to you. What can you tell us, Master Crispin?"

"I honestly don't know. These tidings are as new to me as they are to you."

Some clearly did not believe him, and before it turned to arguments and fights, Jack wisely took Crispin by the arm and pulled him out of the tavern.

They both said nothing as they returned to the Shambles.

They stayed in for the rest of the day, and at nightfall, they huddled beside the small fire, drinking the last of the warmed wine. Their feet, wrapped in extra stockings, were nearly tucked into the coals.

A rap on the door well after Compline made them look at each other. Jack hesitated. "Can't be a client this late."

"It might be. But I'll get it. You... be ready."

Jack unsheathed his dagger and stood behind the door. Crispin thought of unsheathing his own but decided against it.

When he opened it, he was glad he hadn't.

Henry, looking tired and worn, hung in the doorway.

"God's blood, Henry. What are you doing here?"

He staggered in and stood before the fire. In his hand he held a long wrapped bundle. "Have you heard?"

"Yes. Is… is the king truly back at Westminster?"

Henry nodded wearily. "Yes. And because I know you will ask it, he is still the king."

Crispin nodded. Jack closed the door and came upon Henry on his other flank. Henry turned to Jack and smiled a little. "Young Jack. I'm glad to see you are safe here with your master."

"What happened, Henry?" Crispin was nearly thrumming with impatience. "There is so little news."

"Yes, I forgot you would not have heard much. Richard's hens are scattered and will meet the noose should they return. And my cousin has promised to do as he ought. There was a moment when my uncle and I… argued. But I had only just received a letter from my lord father." Henry smiled and sat, laying the bundle across his thighs. "He cautioned me in no uncertain terms to resist taking the crown. Oh, but it was hard, Crispin. It was nearly there for the taking."

"You did the right thing, Henry," he said solemnly.

"Did I? Well. It's done, at any rate." He sighed before holding out the bundle with one hand. "Here. Take it."

When Crispin closed his hand over it, he knew immediately what it was. "What—?"

The wrappings fell away, revealing a sword in a plain leather scabbard, wrapped with a belt.

"What's this?"

"The spoils of war," said Henry. "With a few additions."

"Why are you—"

Henry looked at Jack. "You have a fool for a master, young Jack. He has forgotten what a sword is."

"I haven't forgotten." He pushed it back into Henry's hands. "You very well know I am not allowed to own one. The king does not wish it and I have no right of property."

"Right of property, he says."

Crispin spread out his arm, showing the humble room. "Does this look like twenty pounds' worth of property to you? I own none of it and it isn't worth a privy."

He shoved the sword back into Crispin's hands. "I told you, it's the spoils of war. With additions. Withdraw it."

Crispin stared at it. At the unadorned leather sheath and the plain roundel pommel.

"You do remember how to withdraw a sword, don't you?" teased Henry.

With a growl, Crispin pulled it partway from the sheath. The blade was shiny, but it was not new. And there were words newly engraved on the blade, words in Latin. He pulled it farther.

"Read it aloud," Henry urged.

"'*A donum a Henricus Lancastriae ad Crispinus Guest—habet Ius.*'"

Jack was at his elbow and translated aloud. "'A gift from Henry Lancaster to Crispin Guest—He has the Right'... Oh, Master!"

Crispin couldn't breathe. He stared at the words till he couldn't see them anymore.

"You served our household well, Crispin. You saved my life. You saved the crown, if it comes to that. Who has the greater right to wield a sword? And now, with those words, you have proof of that right. I wish I could grant you your knighthood again, Crispin, but as my royal cousin will never allow it, this is the best I can do. Here, young squire. You'd best learn now how to buckle on a knight's sword."

Crispin didn't move. Henry tried to show Jack, but the boy's hands trembled so badly that Henry had to do it himself.

Henry put his hand on Crispin's shoulder once the sword hung at his left side. "Feels good, doesn't it?"

Crispin still could not speak. Henry smiled. "I still have much to do this night. This is far from over. But I'm certain, Crispin, I will see you again." He turned toward the door and stopped before it. He nodded toward the sword hanging now from Crispin's hip. "Very soon—too soon—you might need that. God be with you."

And with a cold gust of night wind and a few flurries of snow, he was gone.

Afterword

So what about Nicholas Flamel? He didn't belong just to the world of Harry Potter. He was a real fourteenth-century fellow. But was he a famous alchemist? It depends on whom you ask and when you ask them. He was a writer and manuscript seller in fourteenth-century Paris, but because of his interest in and study of the Philosopher's Stone, he was thought by many to be an accomplished alchemist, though much of that speculation came long after he died, mostly through writings about him and alchemy from the seventeenth century. His house in Paris still stands and is the oldest stone house in the city. He and his wife, Perenelle, were known in their day as gracious benefactors, donating their wealth to hospitals, churches, and the poor. They seemed to live a long and happy life in France.

Did they live an *unusually* long time?

Flamel was about eighty-eight when he died and Perenelle about ninety-two. Not bad for the Middle Ages. So, Philosopher's Stone? Hmm.

The imposition of Piers, Avelyn, and Flamel's trip to England was my little fiction.

But that's not all that was happening in this book. The end of 1387 in England was quite a turbulent time. It really got started a year before, when Richard was backed into a corner. As you may remember from *Blood Lance*, Crispin's previous book, Parliament wanted to oust Michael de la Pole, the earl of Suffolk and one of Richard's closest friends, but Richard wasn't having it. In fact, it was Richard's strategy that if he traveled around the country and just never opened Parliament, his troubles might fade away. But the lords and commons reminded him that he was obliged to open Parliament at least twice a year so that "errors of government might be made right"—and, oh, by the way, the people had a right to know how their taxes were being spent. They further reminded Richard that any king who refused to take his lords' advice could be deposed, just like his great-granddaddy Edward II. Reluctantly, Richard returned to London, and when Parliament opened, they impeached Suffolk, since they couldn't very well impeach Richard. Further, a council was appointed to watch over all the expenses of court, and they radically cut Richard's household funds. That hurt.

By 1387, Richard was not even running the country, hadn't any money, and felt pretty closed in because this council was *always* there, looking over his shoulder! Who was king around here? To get away from prying eyes, he did a lot of traveling between Windsor, Westminster, and his hunting lodge in the Thames Valley. And while he was out and about, he tried to muster support among the sheriffs and judges in the shires.

Richard's favorite cronies were all pretty well disliked by the lords and even the people by this time. Suffolk was the former chancellor and spent the tax coffers of the kingdom on too many personal items for Richard and his pals. When he was impeached, he was driven from office essentially for dereliction of duty, but he stuck around. But by the end of 1387, he had to flee to France, was sentenced to die in absentia, and had his title stripped from him. He never returned to England.

Sir Robert Tresilian, another household friend and adviser, had been appointed Chief Justice of the King's Bench by Richard, and he was the one who urged all those judges that Richard mustered around the country to say that the commissioners didn't have the right to impeach Suffolk. He was executed for treason the following year.

Yet another adviser, Sir Nicholas Brembre, former Lord Mayor of London, had often loaned money to the king and thought himself so beloved by the people of London that he was untouchable. He was also executed for treason the following year.

Alexander Neville, the archbishop of York, was in Richard's pocket. He was supposed to serve a life sentence at Rochester Castle, but the pope took pity on him, and with papal help, Neville managed to slip from Henry's fingers and ended up as a parish priest in Flanders, where he spent the rest of his life.

And Robert de Vere, the earl of Oxford, was possibly the most odious of them all. Not of royal blood, he was nevertheless heaped with honors, titles, and lands, even above those of the king's uncle Thomas of Woodstock, the duke of Gloucester. Oxford was made marquess of Dublin and duke of Ireland, and he was given the castle and town of Colchester, the castles of Queensborough in Kent and Oakham, and the sheriffdom of Rutland. He also put aside his wife—the granddaughter of Edward III—for one of the queen's ladies-in-waiting. He was sentenced to death in absentia after he fled the country following his failed march on London, and his lands and titles were forfeit to the crown. He died in a hunting accident in 1392, also in Flanders, and three years later, an aggrieved Richard had his embalmed body brought back to England for reburial. He really was a favorite of Richard's.

When this book opens at the end of 1387, clouds of dissent are building. But the truly sad part is, Richard never really learns his lesson. And as for Henry Bolingbroke, this is just a practice run. At one point in December 1387, when Richard holed himself up in the Tower, Henry and his uncle Gloucester argued about possibly taking the crown, only they argued as to which one of *them* it would be. Gloucester wanted it for himself, because he was a fourth son and he never got anything! It seemed like a good time to go for it because his brother John, the duke of Lancaster—warrior, statesman, and all-around rich guy—was conveniently out of the country.

Henry, naturally, thought that he himself should get the crown. After all, it was his army that went to all the trouble to head off Oxford at Radcot Bridge.

In the end, they decided against it, mostly because of a timely letter from Lancaster warning them to stop it or else.

Sadly, boys in armor can't ever play nice, and it will all come to a head again in 1399. But that's for a future book.

In the meantime, Crispin and friends will return in another adventure, this time concerning something King Richard desperately needs to find, in *The Silence of Stones*.

Glossary

BEZANT: A medieval gold coin.

CHAPERON HOOD/HAT: A hood that comes down and covers the shoulders in a short cape. When this was bunched together and wound onto the head, it became a hat, and later it was designed exclusively as a hat.

COXCOMB: The comb on the head of a rooster, or shaped like it.

DAGGED: An edge cut with decorative scallops.

DISSEISE(MENT): To dispossess a person of his estates and title.

MASLIN: Bread made from wheat and rye.

MAZER: Outer wooden part of a bowl used for drinking.

PILIER CANTONNÉ: A compound pier or pillar used in Gothic architecture.

PSALTER: A prayer book.

SCRIP: A small bag, wallet, or satchel.

Acknowledgments

As always, none of this happens without the careful work and mentoring from my agent, Joshua Bilmes, my editor, Keith Kahla, the proofreading and fact-checking team at St. Martin's Press, my Vicious Circle, Ana Brazil and Bobbie Gosnell, and my husband—my first reader—Craig. But I would also like to acknowledge the loyal following of my mystery Readers who go out of their way to get my books, to come to my events, to send me notes and e-mails, who support me by reading my blogs, sign up for my newsletter, show up on Facebook, Twitter, and Goodreads, and who just generally send out their love and encouragement from afar. To all of you, a very heartfelt Thank You!

Further mysteries in the Crispin Guest *series are available in eBook and print editions from* Severn House

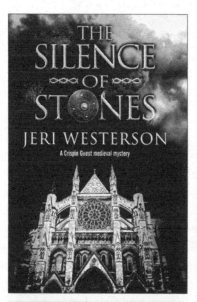

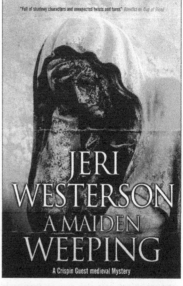

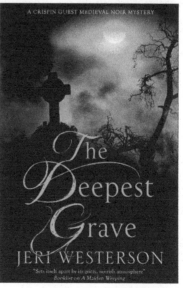

FOR NEWS ABOUT JABBERWOCKY BOOKS AND AUTHORS

Sign up for our newsletter*: http://eepurl.com/b84tDz
visit our website: awfulagent.com/ebooks
or follow us on twitter: @awfulagent

THANKS FOR READING!